VOYAGE *of* SLAVES

BRIAN JACQUES

VOYAGE of SLAVES

A Tale from the
CASTAWAYS *of the*
FLYING DUTCHMAN

Illustrated by DAVID ELLIOT

PHILOMEL BOOKS

To Nan Melia,
always a pal!

PHILOMEL BOOKS
A division of Penguin Young Readers Group
Published by The Penguin Group
Penguin Group (USA) Inc., 375 Hudson Street, New York, NY 10014, U.S.A.
Penguin Group (Canada), 90 Eglinton Avenue East, Suite 700, Toronto, Ontario,
Canada M4P 2Y3 (a division of Pearson Penguin Canada Inc.)
Penguin Books Ltd, 80 Strand, London WC2R 0RL, England.
Penguin Ireland, 25 St. Stephen's Green, Dublin 2, Ireland (a division of Penguin
Books Ltd.)
Penguin Group (Australia), 250 Camberwell Road, Camberwell, Victoria 3124,
Australia (a division of Pearson Australia Group Pty Ltd).
Penguin Books India Pvt Ltd, 11 Community Centre, Panchsheel Park, New Delhi—
110 017, India.
Penguin Group (NZ), Cnr Airborne and Rosedale Roads, Albany, Auckland, New
Zealand (a division of Pearson New Zealand Ltd).
Penguin Books (South Africa) (Pty) Ltd, 24 Sturdee Avenue, Rosebank,
Johannesburg 2196, South Africa.
Penguin Books Ltd, Registered Offices: 80 Strand, London WC2R 0RL, England.

Published simultaneously in Canada.   Printed in the United States of America.
Design by Semadar Megged.   Text set in 11-point Dutch766.
Library of Congress Cataloging-in-Publication Data available upon request.
L.C. Number: 2006043298.
ISBN 0-399-24549-9
1 3 5 7 9 10 8 6 4 2
First Impression

VOYAGE
of SLAVES

MUGGIA
VENICE
POREC
LOSINJ

ADRIATIC
SEA

TYRRHENIAN
SEA

MEL

CATANIA
SIRACUSA
CAPE PASSERO

SICILIAN CHANNEL

MALTA

VALLETTA
HARBOUR

MISURATA

Book One

LORD
of the
BARBARY
COAST

THE LEGEND OF THE *FLYING DUTCHMAN* IS known to all men who follow the seafaring trade. Captain Vanderdecken and his ghostly crew, bound by heaven's curse to sail the world's vast oceans and seas for eternity! The curse was delivered by the angel of the Lord, who descended from the firmament to the very deck of the doomed vessel. Vanderdecken and his evil crew were bound, both living and dead, to an endless voyage. Only two were to escape the *Flying Dutchman*—a mute, ragged orphan boy, Ben, and his faithful dog, Ned. They were the only two aboard who were pure of heart, innocent of all wickedness.

The angel had them both washed overboard in a storm off Cape Horn—castaways of the *Flying Dutchman!* Barely alive, they came ashore at Tierra del Fuego, the tip of South America. Unfortunately, they, too, were casualties of the angel's curse, destined to live endlessly, without growing older by a single day. However, heaven, being merciful, decreed that Ben was granted the power of speech in any language. Additionally he could communicate with the dog by process of thought.

Thus began a friendship that would last through many centuries. Their destiny was to wander the world, all its lands, seas, and oceans, never stopping in one place to watch mankind growing older before their eyes. Ever on the move before anybody could detect that the boy and his dog stayed eternally young. Haunted constantly by the spectre of Vanderdecken, seeking to bring them back amid the ghastly crew of that hellship, the *Flying Dutchman,* and having to travel constantly at the angel's command.

Ben and Ned shared many thrilling adventures on their travels. From the tip of Cape Horn, up to Cartagena and the

Caribbean Sea. Shipping with French buccaneers, pursued by Spanish pirates and an English privateer, in a sea chase across the vast Atlantic. Wrecked and cast ashore, straight into another drama, across France, and into the Pyrenees, pitted this time against evil kidnappers. Their adventure culminated in the Bay of Biscay.

From there, Ben and Ned, castaways once more in a small open boat, ventured into Mediterranean waters. Waifs of fate, they coasted the shores, living on their wits, always awaiting the decree of heaven, that they should drift into yet more dangers and perils—with the spectre of the *Dutchman* ever looming over them.

CIRCA 1703. THE MEDITERRANEAN SEA.
SOMEWHERE BETWEEN ALEXANDRIA
AND THE ISLAND OF CYPRUS.

FROM CLOUDLESS, AZURE VAULTS,
the great golden eye of the sun
shone down on the sea below. Its
pitiless glare took in
the boat, a small,
weather-beaten craft.
With no zephyr of breeze to
stir it, a tattered gamboge sail hung uselessly over
the prone figures of the boy and his dog, lying side by side.
The big black Labrador's tongue lolled out, its flanks rising
and falling as it panted against the relentless noontide heat.
The boy raised his head, brushing thick, tow-coloured hair
from his vision. With an effort, he hauled himself up, his
strange blue-grey eyes scanning the horizon. Running a
swollen tongue across his cracked lips, he groaned. Nowhere in
any direction was there a hint of land, only endless expanses of
limpid turquoise-and-aquamarine sea. He lay back down,
shielding his eyes as he sought the oblivion of sleep.

Totally becalmed, the little vessel floated in the doldrums, moving neither back nor forth on the shimmering surface. There was no respite from the searing heat; the sun's blazing orb presided over all in flaming splendour.

As languid day tapered slowly into evening, the sky bled crimson with the sun's death into the western horizon. Darkness fell over the tired waters, bringing in its wake the realm of nightmare. Both imprisoned by their dreams, Ben and Ned—the boy and his dog—whimpered and shivered uncontrollably, trapped in the memories of blood-chilling times, almost a century ago. They were aboard that heaven-cursed ship, the *Flying Dutchman.* Ploughing the storm-ravaged oceans at the world's end, off the coast of Tierra del Fuego, southernmost tip of the vast Americas. Sounds of roaring seas thundering upon rock and reef assailed their minds. Ice hung thick from the shattered masts and torn sails. Dead men danced aloft, their bodies swaying as they dangled amid the tangled rigging. Like a thunderbolt, a fearsome visage confronted them. Vanderdecken, the mad captain of the doomed vessel! Hellfire blazed from his bloodshot eyes, salt crusted his frozen beard and wild locks. Baring frostbitten lips, he exposed yellowed, tombstone-like teeth, bellowing at Ben and Ned.

"Ye will sail with me into eternity! Forever, across the mighty wastes of seas and oceans! Never will ye know rest, peace, or happiness with me and my fated crew! I am Vanderdecken, chased by the Hounds of Hell! Driven endlessly by the Almighty God, whom I cursed in my wrath! Condemned by His angel's command!"

His heavy hand slapped Ben's face, again and again. The boy woke to find not an apparition, but a man, striking his cheeks. Ben understood his words, he was shouting in Arabic.

"This one is alive, see! Cast that black beast into the sea, Mahmud. Shaitan* himself dwells in such creatures!"

As weak as he was, Ben strove upward, hitting out at the fellow and shouting, "Leave the dog alone, he is mine!"

However, he got no further. Wielding an oar, the one called Mahmud hit Ben from behind, laying him out senseless. Ned was flung, snapping and biting, into the sea. The two men left Ben lying in the small boat. Scrambling back aboard their own larger craft, they tied the little vessel in tow and rowed off into the night, shouting insults at the dog floundering in their wake.

"Drown, ye beast of ill fortune! See, Nassar, that thing almost bit off my thumb!"

Nassar spat in the direction of Ned. "May the sharks feed from its accursed body! Look at my chest, I'm scratched almost to the bone!"

The black Labrador trod water, frantically sending out mental communications to the boy. "Ben! Have they hurt you, are you injured, Ben?"

Unfortunately, Ben was lost in the black pit of unconsciousness, unable to answer his faithful friend.

Both boats were soon lost in the Mediterranean darkness, but Ned swam stubbornly on, still trying to reach his master.

"Ben! Ben! Answer me, are you alright?"

*Shaitan (Satan).

TWO DAYS LATER. TOKRA, A SETTLEMENT OFF
THE COAST OF LIBYA, NOT FAR FROM BENGHAZI.

BEN GAGGED AND CHOKED AS HE TRIED TO GULP
down water from the gourd that Nassar was holding to his
mouth. The man judged that his captive had drunk enough. He
 struck at the boy's hands with a cane, loosening
them from the gourd. Without a word, he shoul-
dered the water carrier and hurried out of the
mean hovel, securing the door from outside. It
was a stable, or a pen for animals of some kind.
Ben was shackled by his left ankle to an iron ring in the wall. He
crawled as far as the short chain would allow, not quite reaching the door, but able to see through a rift between the
wooden slats.

Outside was a fat woman clad in
dark robes, cooking fish over a fire.
Ben's stomach grumbled as
he sniffed the odour

of food. Nassar set the gourd down and sat beside the woman as Mahmud came to join them. Mahmud stirred a pot of maize meal porridge which was resting close to the flames, enquiring of Nassar, "Did you give the infidel something to eat?"

His companion snorted. "I gave him enough water to keep life in him. Let Bomba feed him once he is off our hands."

The woman turned the sizzling fish on its spit, nodding. "Aye, there is barely enough for us to eat."

Nassar kicked her half-heartedly. "Keep your mouth out of this and attend to our meal!" Taking a shallow earthen bowl, he slopped maize meal into it. "Here, take this to him, Mahmud. He must live. Bomba is not permitted to buy dead flesh."

Ben shuffled back from the door as Mahmud entered. He placed the bowl alongside the boy, uttering a single word. "Eat!"

Ben dipped his fingers in, scooping the mush into his mouth. He looked up at Mahmud. "You are going to sell me. To whom?"

Mahmud brushed a fly from his eyebrow. "Where did you learn to speak our tongue?"

The towheaded boy shrugged. "I don't remember. You have no right to sell another human being."

Mahmud walked away, turning in the doorway. "One more word from you, spawn of a chattering parrot, and I will cast you back into the sea as I did your dog!"

Mention of Ned cast Ben back into unhappy despair. Hungry though he was, he kicked the food aside and sat there with tears welling in his eyes. All the mental messages he had sent out to his dog since regaining consciousness were to no avail. Ned had not answered.

Ben began to call upon the only other being he knew, the

angel who had guided all his and his faithful hound's wanderings. He strove in thought to reach his guardian. "Please hear me, O Messenger of the Lord, Ned is my only friend in this world. Let me know, where is he, does my dog still live?" The boy lay back amid the straw-strewn sand and fell into a weary slumber.

Gradually a soft, golden light filtered through his mind, followed by a gentle voice from afar. "Do not shed tears for the creature who lives, ye will meet again. Save thy tears for the fall of the Dark Angel!"

The dream faded, and Ben slept on, not knowing or caring who the Dark Angel could be. Without Ned at his side, the boy felt a huge, leaden weight of loneliness within him. Ned was everything to Ben, friend, confidant, comforter and constant companion. No mere human being could take the place of his faithful Labrador. They had been together through many years, and countless adventures, across oceans, seas and continents. Surviving perils and enduring hard times, sharing the happiness and laughter of good and peaceful days, twin hearts, bonded by mutual respect and affection.

The hot dawn light of another dusty day seeped through the door slats. Ben was wakened by the braying of mules and the creak of cart wheels. Mahmud and Nassar unbarred the door. Unlocking the boy's leg shackle, they hustled him out into the sunlight. Not far from the woman's cooking fire stood a big wagon, with four mules harnessed to it. The conveyance was like a solid wooden shack on wheels.

From a door at the rear of the wagon a man emerged. He was a tall, well-built fellow, but running to fat; a broad, leather belt supported his loose, baggy pantaloons. He also wore a short, sleeveless bolero jacket, and a close-fitting skullcap. In one hand he carried a supple quirt, made of cane and bound with plaited strips of leather. Nassar and Mahmud approached him respectfully. He stared at Ben, addressing the pair without looking at them.

"So, is this little bag of bones all you have for me?"

Mahmud was the spokesman of the two. He clasped his hands and bowed his head slightly. "The boy is a blue-eyed infidel, valuable merchandise, Bomba, my friend. He would bring a good price on the block at Tripoli!"

Bomba's substantial stomach quivered as he gave a snort. "Hah! This worthless camel's offal, have you no others to show me but him, you sons of the misbegotten?"

However, Mahmud could see that Bomba was interested in the boy, otherwise he would not be scrutinising him so keenly. He replied in an offended manner.

"Bomba my friend, why do you insult us thus? Here, look!" Still holding the chain and leg manacle, he swung it at Ben's ankles. The boy jumped smartly, avoiding the chain. Mahmud spread his arms, as though justified.

"See, my friend, he is swift and healthy. Take a look at him for yourself!"

Bomba seized Ben's arm in a powerful grip, pushing the captive's chin upward with his quirt. "Let me see your teeth, infidel brat!"

Ben tried to pull away from the slave trader, but the big man growled warningly, "Be still, little sand flea, or I will snap your arm like a twig. Show your teeth!"

Drawing back his lips, Ben snarled out, unafraid, "You have no right to take a free man into slavery!"

Bomba exerted more force on his victim's arm, laughing. "He speaks our language, boldly, too? Listen to Bomba, O mouse of misfortune. The life of an obedient slave can be good, but the life of an insolent one is always painful and short. Mahmud, I will take this one!" Bomba took a purse from his belt and shook out a number of thin gold coins into Mahmud's outstretched palm.

The Arab looked witheringly at the woefully small pile. "You insult me, my friend. I have thrown more than this into the bowl of a beggar who sits in Benghazi marketplace!"

Bomba scoffed. "Then be a little more careful with thy charity to beggars. That is my price, take it or leave it!"

Nassar piped up indignantly. "But the infidel boy will fetch ten, nay, twenty times that amount on the block in Tripoli!"

Bomba tapped the Arab's chest with his quirt. "But this one is not going to the block. Al Misurata is taking him, and others, as cargo aboard the *Sea Djinn.*"

Mahmud made a signed gesture with his index and little finger, to ward off evil. His voice was hushed with awe. "Al Misurata!"

Bomba nodded. "Aye, the very same. If you have any complaints about the price I paid you, then ye are free to take the matter up with him."

Mahmud backed off, bowing as he went. "We have no complaints. It is always a pleasure doing business with thee, my friend."

The big man narrowed his eyes contemptuously. "Snake of the dunes, ye are no friend of mine!"

Lifting Ben by one arm, he flung him inside the wagon and locked the door. Climbing up onto the driving seat, he nodded at the old man holding the reins. "Get me away from this fleabound doorway to Eblis!"*

As the wagon trundled off, the woman tending the fire remarked, almost to herself, "So, it was Al Misurata's coin that bought the boy."

Mahmud kicked her away from the fire. "Silence, O brainless one, forget ye ever heard that name!"

*Eblis (hell).

ON THE SHORES OF SEBKHAT TAWORGA,
SOUTHEAST OF THE TOWN OF MISURATA.

HERR OTTO KASSEL ROSE DRIPPING FROM THE SEA.
Wiggling the water from one ear with a fingertip, the huge man
strode ashore. Whenever he got the opportunity, Otto was fond
of an early morning dip. One hour's swim in the
dawn Mediterranean waters was a real pleasure to
the giant German strongman. Since his midteens,
Otto had been a professional exhibitor of his
prodigious strength; it was an occupation which
had taken him to many lands. Brushing beads of salt water from
his huge shaven head, he commenced some daily exer-
cises. Flexing massive muscles, he bent, jerked,
stretched and arched. Otto took great care of his
magnificent physique, he was scrupulous about
hygiene, and rigorous in training.

Donning a robe, he sat on a duneside.
From his pocket, he brought forth a polished silver snuff box. In it was a small
comb and scissors, plus some special wax
pomade for his moustache. Using the

inner side of the lid as a mirror he combed his upper lip growth meticulously, snipping off any stray hairs. He anointed the moustache with pomade, twirling both ends until they stood out like two miniature spikes. The big fellow smiled with satisfaction. Now he was ready to face the day.

Then he saw the dog.

It was a good-sized beast, lying flat on one side in the sand, apparently dead. Otto studied it from where he sat, some ten yards away. The strongman was kind and compassionate to animals. Poor creature, what had brought it to this? It was rake thin, and heavily coated from head to tail in sand, which had dried to a crust under the searing heat. A few gulls landed and began circling the pitiful carcass. One hopped boldly forward and pecked at the dog's flank. To Otto's amazement, the dog tried to raise its head and issued a faint growl. The strongman leaped up and ran forward waving his arms, chasing the predatory birds away.

Crouching beside the dog, Otto reached out a ham-like hand, patting it gently. Thick matted sand fell away; at first he had supposed the dog was light brown, but beneath the sand the dog's coat was black, it was a black Labrador. Otto had once owned a large black dog, when he was a boy back in Germany. He had called it Bundi. He used the name now as he stroked the dog.

"Hello, Bundi, where did you came from, boy?"

The dog whined feebly, lids flickering as it tried to open its eyes. Otto licked the corner of his robe, screwing it into a twirl. With this he probed gently, rooting away the coagulated debris of sand and moisture from the dog's eyelids. He spoke reassuringly as he worked. "Trust me now, Bundi, I'll get you back to the cart and fix you up properly. I'm not going to hurt you, boy, be still while I carry you."

• • •

The Travelling Rizzoli Troupe were preparing breakfast in the shade of their cart. It was garishly painted in bright green, blue, red and gold, with a canvas awning depicting bulbous-limbed people performing impossible feats of bodily contortions. They numbered nine in all, including Otto; a python called Mwaga; and Poppea, the old, white mare who pulled the cart.

Signore Augusto Rizzoli was the owner and leader of the troupe. A small, tubby travelling showman, he possessed numerous talents, which included a shrewd business brain and a resounding tenor voice. His wife, Rosa, known to all simply as Mamma, was general handywoman, seamstress, cook and confidante, ever ready to help or assist the others. Signore Rizzoli's two brothers were the clowns. Their names were Beppino and Vincenzo, but they also answered to their stage names, Buffo and Mummo. They were two happy-go-lucky fellows, pleased to let their elder brother deal with everyday troupe business, whilst they laughed and joked their way through life.

The final two, La Lindi and Serafina, were native Africans from Mozambique. Both had totally unpronounceable names, so Mamma Rizzoli had chosen new titles for them. Signore Rizzoli had spotted them entertaining in the bazaar of a small Tanganyikan place called Lindi. Recognizing talent, he had hired them on the spot. They agreed readily. Life for two black ladies playing the markets and bazaars of the African coast, with nobody to protect them against slavers, was risky. Better to travel in company, with a safe place in the wagon, and no worries about providing food for themselves. Mamma Rizzoli christened the older lady La Lindi, after the place where they had met. The younger one, who was in her midteens, was a strikingly beautiful girl, tall, slim and gracious, with large, almond-shaped eyes which radiated tranquility. Mamma called her Serafina because she liked the name so much.

Serafina and La Lindi were not related. They had fallen together by chance whilst crossing the border into Tanganyika, fleeing Mozambique slavers. La Lindi was a dancer who could fascinate onlookers as she danced with Mwaga, her python. Serafina sang and played a variety of musical instruments for the dances.

All in all, the Travelling Rizzoli Troupe was a motley collection, four Italians, a German and two Africans.

Augusto Rizzoli was busy brewing some aromatic Turkish coffee for breakfast. Mamma was tending to her breadmaking, and Mummo, who enjoyed cooking, was stirring a concoction of peppers, tomatoes and eggs. Buffo was readying Poppea's nosebag when he spied the strongman arriving, carrying the limp form of the dog. He called out jokingly, "Otto, you caught a dogfish, is it still alive?"

The troupe gathered around as Otto laid the black Labrador on the wagon step. La Lindi inspected it, she checked the sand-coated tongue, slobbering loosely out of the creature's mouth, then lifted one of the eyelids to view the dully glazed eyeball. Holding her face close to its muzzle, she sniffed, then shook her head.

"He will be dead before the setting of the sun, I think."

Otto protested. "But you could be wrong, Fräulein.* Bundi is alive still, and where there is life there is hope!"

*Fräulein (lady).

Mamma patted the big man's shoulder sympathetically. "You must trust La Lindi's judgement, Herr Kassel, she knows about animals."

Serafina stroked the dog's head tenderly, obviously saddened by La Lindi's pronouncement. "He's a good dog, I feel it, we can't let him die. Signore Rizzoli, let me and Otto care for him, we'll get him better. Please?"

Augusto Rizzoli had the final word in any troupe decisions. However, he could not resist Serafina's plea. "Do what you can for the poor beast, *bella ragazza.** Even if he does die, he will do it in comfort among friends. He looks as if he has suffered greatly."

Otto dipped a ladle into the water cask which hung on the wagon's side.

"You get some fresh water into him, little one, I'll clean him up. Mummo, beat one of those eggs up, but don't cook it. Maybe Bundi will like some."

Ned (for it was he) vaguely saw a pretty black girl pouring water into his mouth. It was the coolest, sweetest water he had ever tasted. He gulped at it with what little strength he could muster, licking at the girl's hand as he did. Without warning he heaved, vomiting an alarming amount of water back. The strongman nodded approvingly.

"Good boy, Bundi, get all that seawater out of your gut! Leave him a moment, Serafina, let him recover a little before you give him more. What do you think now, Fräulein Lindi?"

The enigmatic dancer raised her eyebrows. "I think your dog is a stubborn beast, he hangs onto life with a strong grip.

Bella ragazza (beautiful girl).

You could be right, Otto, there is hope. But he will need much care."

Ned did not hear this last remark. He had lapsed into a semiconscious sleep, his mind was blank. He could remember nothing, not his former life, or Ben, nothing. However, a spectre was haunting his troubled dreams, coming at him through a sudden nightmare of icy, storm-tossed seas. It was Vanderdecken, beckoning from the storm-battered deck of the *Flying Dutchman.* Triumph shone from the captain's ghastly blood-rimmed eyes. He roared at Ned above the shrieking gale. "Now you are mine, dog, come to me. Where is your master?"

Serafina was washing and combing the matted dirt from the dog's coat. She patted him reassuringly as he shivered and moaned. "Poor Bundi, are you having bad dreams? There now, be calm, you are with friends. Hush now, hush!"

Gradually the shivers and moans subsided as Ned slid back into the deep well of dreamless sleep.

ONE WEEK LATER. A HOUSE ON THE NORTHERN
POINT OF THE GULF OF SIRTE. JUST
OUTSIDE OF THE TOWN OF MISURATA.

BEN, AND THE OTHER THREE WHOM
Bomba had picked up on his journey,
blinked against the midmorning sun as
 they emerged from the wagon.
All four were shackled together by
their ankles. There was an Egyptian
boy, about two years older than Ben, whose
name was Omar. The other two were about the
same age as Ben: a Cretan girl called Lucia, and a boy who
claimed to be Sardinian, his name was Sandro. The wagon
had pulled into a courtyard, with high walls and a barred gate.
This was guarded by rough-looking men, four of them, wearing burnooses and armed with long jezzails* and scimitars.
Throughout the journey, Bomba had fed them with maize
porridge and water. They had quickly learned to be obedient
and silent, scarcely daring to speak with one another.

*Jezzail (the eastern flintlock rifle).

Now the four captives gazed around the area, a veritable oasis of water and greenery in the wasteland of Libyan desert outside. Date palms and fig trees, interspersed with gnarled olive trees, bordered the flowered walks and well-groomed lawns. Tiny ornamental bridges crossed a moat filled with clear, placid water. Upon the moated island stood a large, well-appointed house, three floors high, with broad, open windows and a flat, low-walled roof patrolled by more guards.

Bomba slapped his riding quirt against a palm to gain their attention. "Listen now, you little bazaar rats. I am going into the big house yonder, but I'll be back." He tossed the manacle key to one of the guards. "See they are cleaned up for my return, make them presentable to your master!"

The guard spoke little. After loosing their shackles, he pointed to the moat. "You boys, over there, get in and wash yourselves." He called over the bridge, "Jasmina, see to this girl!" A stern-faced woman, clad in black robes, emerged from a side door of the house. She beckoned at the girl, Lucia, with a stick she carried, shouting orders in Arabic at her. The girl looked at her blankly until Ben spoke to her in her own language.

"She is telling you to come around the other side of the house, out of sight from the men and us boys. You are to wash yourself in the water."

Lucia bowed slightly to Ben, thanking him, then went to follow the woman.

The water was glorious, still and cool. Ben flung himself in. Pulling off his meagre clothing, he scrubbed at his dust-caked skin with handfuls of sand from the bottom of the moat, which was no more than three feet deep. Omar and Sandro followed his example.

• • •

The top floor of the house was open to soft breezes flowing in from the nearby Mediterranean Sea. The large room was opulently furnished. Pattern mosaic tiles decorated the walls, silk hangings rippled in the breeze. The floor was strewn with many precious rugs, some of which had come from far Cathay.* Slender columns of roseate marble supported the frescoed ceiling. Small decorative palmettos and flowering plants were much in evidence, with parrots and cockatoos wandering about amidst them. At the centre of the room, perfumed rosewater tinkled pleasantly into the scooped-out base of an alabaster fountain, where ringed doves perched on the basin's edge. Next to this was a sumptuous divan of ivory, ebony, and patterned damask satin, which had once graced the saloon of a sultan's ship. Now its new owner sat on it in solitary splendour. This was Al Misurata, the most feared pirate on the Barbary Coast.

Al Misurata was only a name he had taken from that region he had called home for three decades. Nobody knew his proper name, or where he had come from. In reality he was the son of a Moroccan servant girl and a Turkish janissary.** He had embarked on a career of piracy in his youth. From there he had plundered and murdered his way to infamy.

Al Misurata was a man in his fifty-third year. Tall, lean and cruelly handsome, his dark, hooded eyes and curved nose gave him the visage of a hungry desert hawk. Dressed all in purple

*Cathay (China).
**Janissary (a soldier of a sultan's guard).

silks, and carrying a sword made from the finest Toledo steel, he was a captain of captains, a figure to obey without question or argument.

He heard Bomba enter the room, but did not concern himself with turning to greet him. Sipping lemon sherbet from a thin crystal goblet, the pirate sat admiring his supple burgundy boots of best Cordovan leather. He waited until the slave driver addressed him.

"Lord, I have brought thee four fine specimens. A girl from the Isle of Crete, sweet-natured and pretty. Also three boys— an Egyptian, another from Sardinia and a blue-eyed Frank, light-skinned with fair hair. They are all sound in wind and limb, healthy and fit . . ."

Al Misurata silenced Bomba with a single glance. "I will judge them myself. No doubt you stole them all?"

The slave driver spread his arms, smiling and shaking his head. "Alas, no, lord, all were bought with thy gold."

Al Misurata put aside his goblet, extending a hand. Bomba dug the chamois purse from his wide belt and placed it on the pirate's palm. Al Misurata tossed it up and down a few times, gauging its weight.

"If they are as good as you say, you did well."

Bomba made an overelaborate bow, touching his fingers to his lips and forehead. "I live but to serve thee, Master!"

The pirate threw him the purse. "Keep it!"

Bomba's eyes shone greedily. "No man is more munificent than the great Al Misurata, Lord of the Barbary Coast . . ."

The pirate cut him short. "Go now, bring them here in the cool of the evening. I will see them then!"

• • •

It was mid-noon. Ben sat with the other two boys and the girl in the shade of the wall, under the watchful eye of the guard. They were all clean, even their clothing, which had dried out quickly in the fierce heat. The stern woman came out of the big house, with another younger one in tow. Between them they carried a basket of fruit—dates, figs, oranges, pomegranates and a big yellow melon, which had been cut into slices. They placed the basket at their feet.

"Eat now, and try to stay clean!"

Ben chose a slice of melon, nodding gratefully to her. "Thank you. What do they call this place, who owns it?"

The older woman rapped Ben's back with her stick. "I said eat, not talk. One more word from you, boy, and you will feel how I can really use this rod!" She stared at the strange, fair-haired lad for a moment, then turned and strode back to the house.

Evening arrived, tempering the heat by drifting sea breezes over the land. Ben and the other three captives were herded into the upper room by Bomba. They stood bewildered, trying to take in the splendour surrounding them. Al Misurata watched them from his divan. Standing behind him, the stern-faced Jasmina leaned forward. Whispering in his ear, she pointed at Ben. The pirate nodded toward the boy, and Bomba shoved him forward. Al Misurata spoke in French to Ben. "Tell me, infidel, do you have rich parents?"

Ben replied in fluent French. "I have nobody but myself,

my parents are long dead. Sir, it is a crime against my god and yours to buy and sell human beings. Slavery is a wicked thing."

Al Misurata had a smattering of many languages. He replied to the boy's accusation in English. "I serve no god. My sword and my wits provide me with gold, that is all Al Misurata, Lord of the Barbary Coast, needs. How is it that you can speak in other tongues, O Defender of the Righteous?"

Ben answered the ironic question in English. "I have always had a good ear for languages. I pick up things here and there, it's not hard."

Al Misurata pointed to the other three slaves. "Ask them if they have wealthy families who would want to ransom them."

Ben translated the enquiry to Lucia, Omar and Sandro. One by one they shook their heads in silence.

The pirate switched back into Arabic. "So, they are all worthless beggars. What do you suggest I do with them, boy?"

Ben was not afraid of the Barbary pirate. He replied promptly, "Why do you ask me? You have captured us, and you are going to sell us into slavery, to obtain the gold which you worship. But someone once said to me that in the end, gold can only buy you an expensive coffin and a great marble tomb."

Bomba leaped forward, raising his quirt to strike the boy down for his insolence. However, Al Misurata stopped him in his tracks with a single glance. "Take these others and lock them away for the night. The infidel boy stays here with me. Go!"

The slave driver bowed and ushered his charges away.

Al Misurata stroked his forked beard, studying Ben intently. "What is your name, and how old are you?"

The boy's strange blue-grey eyes stared solemnly back at

his captor. "I am called Ben, nothing else. As for my age, I'm not really certain."

The Barbary pirate's eyes narrowed. "I think you are about fourteen years of age, but about two hundred in the head, eh?"

Ben shrugged. "I suppose so, but my head isn't much over a hundred, certainly not two."

Al Misurata smiled thinly, indicating a round table nearby. It was piled high with food for his evening meal. "You are a remarkable boy, not like the usual peasant clods Bomba brings here. Do you want food? Take some, it is very good. Come on, I never yet met a young one who was not hungry. Jasmina, give him a plate."

The hard-faced Libyan woman scowled. "I would as soon give him a back marked with stripes for his insolent tongue!"

Al Misurata raised his hand imperiously. "Silence, woman, you forget yourself! I am the master and you are the slave. Take yourself out of my sight!"

Clasping her hands, Jasmina bowed low. She glided wordlessly away. Ben hesitated for a moment, then hurried to the table. Taking two circles of flat, unleavened bread, he made a hefty sandwich with slices of warm, roasted lamb and cooked yellow peppers. Biting into it, the boy chewed ravenously—the food tasted magnificent.

The pirate nodded approvingly. "When a man is wealthy, only the best is good enough. Look at this room, is it not splendid?"

Ben's mouth was crammed, but he nodded agreement.

Filling one of the fine crystal goblets with a lemon sherbet cordial, Al Misurata passed it to him. "I could use a boy like you, bright and intelligent. You could serve me in this house, be my eyes and ears, tell me who are my friends and who are my enemies. It would be a life of luxury, you would want for nothing."

Ben cleared his mouth before answering. "Except freedom."

The pirate's mood changed like lightning at this remark. Rising angrily, he strode to the long, open windowspace, taking in the lands outside with a sweeping gesture. "Fool, what do you know about freedom? Hah, beggars in soukhs and bazaars, shaking their bowls! Men breaking their backs at hard labour! Women scavenging the fields and the shores! For what? Just to feed themselves and their ragged brats! Toiling like animals from dawn 'til dusk as they pray for their gods to help them! You call that freedom? Only gold can truly buy the power to give any man freedom. That is the real truth, is it not? Answer me, infidel!"

Ben knew he would further enrage the man by arguing, yet he carried on, defending his right to reply. "The truth is that those poor folk cannot sleep safe at night, knowing men like you might come and sell them into slavery. Yet look at the freedom you have bought by trading in human beings. You want me to serve you by spying upon those in your own home. I pity you, with neither god nor real friend to turn to. Gold will never buy you that."

The enraged pirate struck Ben across the face, the crystal goblet shattered on the floor. Food scattered into the fountain, parrots squawked and doves fluttered wildly to the ceiling as Al Misurata shouted.

"Guards, get this infidel out of here! Chain him in the cellars without food or drink!"

Two burly sentries rushed in; seizing Ben roughly, they dragged him from the room. The pirate followed them to the door, venting his spleen on the boy.

"Ungrateful worm, now you will know what it is like to be a slave! I have killed men with my bare hands for saying less than you did to me! That's what I get for offering you the hand of friendship, eh? Before I am done you will be begging on your bended knees to serve me without question!"

The cellar door swung open, and Ben was hurled inside. He clattered down a flight of stone steps into complete blackness. The guards barred the door, one of them calling down to him, "Little jackass, we'll see if you still feel so bold in a week or so. If you make a sound in there we'll send Bomba to silence you with his quirt!"

Ben heard their retreating footsteps. Then there was only silence, and inky darkness. A large insect scuttled over his hand. He crawled forward until he felt the wall. Sitting with his back against the rough limestone, he buried his face in both hands and wept uncontrollably. "Ned, where are you? Answer me, Ned, answer me!"

CONTRARY TO LA LINDI'S PREDICTION, NED DID LIVE
to see the sunset, though he slept deeply for most of the day.
He came awake in the dark, still sprawled upon the wagon step.

Not far from him, the troupe sat around the fire,
eating their supper. Savoury aromas from a cauldron over the flames fanned hunger pangs within
the black Labrador. He had no recollection of
when he had last eaten, nor of anything else in his
life before he had been washed up on the Libyan shores. Driven by hunger, Ned tried to stand. His legs buckled under him,
and he fell flat on the sand.

Mummo was stirring the contents of the cauldron when he
saw the dog fall from the wagon step. "Look, Otto, your dogfish
has come to life!"

Serafina grabbed a rug and ran to Ned's side, spreading it.
"Otto, lift him onto this, it will keep the sand from his coat.
Poor Bundi, your legs aren't working properly yet, but you're
nice and clean, all soft and silky."

The big German lifted Ned easily onto the rug. He began
massaging his dog's ears fondly. Ned grunted with pleasure.
The strongman murmured soothingly, "*Ja, mein Heer,** Bundi,

Ja, mein Heer (yes, sir).

you will soon be well again, won't you, old fellow? Watch his eyes, Serafina, I think he's trying to thank us for saving his life!"

Bringing her face close, the girl peered into Ned's eyes. "Oh, I'm sure he is, just look at those wonderful eyes, Otto."

If Ned could have spoken, he would have returned the compliment a hundredfold. The girl Serafina was the most beautiful human being he had ever encountered. Reflecting the fireglow, her skin shone like polished black marble, her teeth were white as fresh milk; as for her eyes, Ned judged that any comparison with his was out of the question. The girl's eyes were almost almond-shaped, and they were very large. Twin dark, starlit orbs, in settings the hue of old ivory. He was captivated by the warm, husky sound of her voice.

"Poor Bundi, you must be hungry."

"Hungry?" Ned thought. "I could eat my own tail, un-cooked!"

The strongman passed Serafina a bowl. "Try him with this, *Mädchen,** it's a raw egg beaten in goat's milk. I put a pinch of salt in, it should do him good."

Serafina held the bowl to Ned's mouth, restraining him slightly to prevent him gulping it. The Labrador took it all, licking the bowl and the girl's fingers thoroughly. She patted his head. "Good boy, Bundi, we'll try you with something more solid tomorrow."

Ned gave her fingers an extra lick. "Thank you, pretty miss, I'll look forward to it!"

Supper being over, and the fire burning to embers, the

Mädchen (maiden).

troupe prepared for rest. Mamma Rizzoli and La Lindi went inside the tented wagon, telling Serafina not to sit up too late with the dog. Buffo, Mummo, and Otto lay under the cart, wrapped in long Arab robes. Signore Rizzoli attended to Poppea, covering the mare with a blanket, tying her running line to a cart wheel, and leaving her a pail of fresh water nearby. "Rest now, my noble lady, we move on tomorrow."

Donning a long Italian army officer's greatcoat with caped shoulders, the showman went to sit beside Serafina. "You need your sleep, *piccina,** so does your Bundi by the look of him. We'll be travelling tomorrow."

The girl rubbed her eyes. "I'm going into the wagon soon. Look, Signore, Bundi is nodding off, too. See how sad his eyes are? He looks completely lost. I wonder whose dog he is, and how he came to be here with us." Serafina gave Ned a final pat, then went into the wagon.

Through drooping eyelids Ned stared up at the Mediterranean night sky. It was moonless, but pierced by twinkling pinpoints of countless stars. A comet blazed its path across the dark vaults, the brief, flaming brilliance almost instantly gone amid the uncharted heavens. The black Labrador's eyes closed. Soon he was lost in the clouded seas of forgetfulness, with no knowledge of his past, his master, or any of the events which had brought him to this far shore.

Sounds of distant seabirds greeted the dawn as waves broke endlessly over the Libyan coast. Ned wakened to view the

Piccina (child).

broad, freckled back of Herr Otto Kassel, going off for his morning swim and exercise. Thirst was the uppermost thought in the dog's mind—he needed water. Feeling much better than he had on the previous day, Ned rose shakily. Once he found he could stay upright, he ventured carefully over to the pail of water near the horse. Poppea was still asleep, so he drank his fill gratefully. Feeling greatly refreshed, he decided to make himself helpful to his benefactors, and set off at a sedate pace along the shore to seek out firewood.

Mamma Rizzoli was the first of the ladies up and about. She bustled out of the wagon and went to stir up the fire embers. The good lady was surprised to see a small heap of driftwood lying beside the remains of last night's fire. Then she spied the dog. Ned was coming up from the tideline, head held to one side as he tugged along the broken shaft of a large oar he had found. Mamma watched him bring it right to her. She smiled broadly, hugging the dog's neck.

"Good Bundi! Good boy! What a clever dog you are!"

She roused the troupe as she banged on the side of the wagon, calling to Serafina, *"Bella mia,* see what your dog is doing, bringing wood for the fire. What a fine fellow he is!"

Buffo stopped Ned going off for more. He shook the dog's paw heartily. *"Grazie, amico.*** Here, let me cook you a good breakfast, truly you are a dog among dogs!"

Ned suddenly felt better than he had for quite awhile. He went from one to another, wagging his tail furiously as they

Bella mia (my beauty).
**Grazie, amico* (thank you, friend).

patted and complimented him. Otto arrived back and was told of the black Labrador's cleverness. The strongman picked Ned up, as though he weighed nothing, and hugged him. Tears flowed openly from the big German's eyes, for he was an extremely sentimental man.

"I knew he would get well. This is a great dog we have, Serafina. Bundi the Great!"

Ned sat between Serafina and Otto, eating toasted bread and an omelette, which Buffo had cooked specially for him. The atmosphere was jovial and carefree, with Signore Rizzoli dropping broad hints.

"Serafina, do you think you could teach him some tricks? Maybe you could do an act together. What do you think, Signore Bundi, we'll feed you well and give you a nice place to sleep. Well, what do you think, my friend?"

To everyone's surprise and delight, Ned held out his paw. Buffo shook it heartily.

"See, I think Bundi wishes to join us. Be careful, Augusto, this good fellow will be doing your job soon!"

Signore Rizzoli raised his eyebrows comically. "Listen, brother, if it comes to a contest, the dog will have replaced you before nightfall!"

Mamma stroked the black Labrador. "Oh, you're a clever dog, but I don't think you could sing or play as sweetly as my husband. Show him, *caro*."*

Signore Rizzoli fetched a mandolin from the cart. He tuned

Caro (dear).

it briefly, and soon his fine tenor voice was ringing out as he
sang and played an old travellers' melody.

> "See now this land, 'tis nought like my home,
> not as green as the fields I knew,
> where the sky was a softer blue.
> Tired now and slow, down the dusty road I roam,
> growing older with every day,
> trudging on in my weary way,
> far from the country I love. O play mandolino play oh!

> "Say now my horse, ah trusty old friend,
> do you miss the cool winding streams?
> Quiet spots where we dreamed our dreams,
> pulling our cart, down a track which has no end,
> wand'rers caught on the wheel of fate,
> swept along with the wind too late.
> far from the country I love. O play mandolino play oh!"

Ned threw back his head, howling along with the last notes
of the tinkling mandolin. Serafina giggled.

"What a lovely harmony our Bundi sings, eh, Signore?"

Augusto Rizzoli clutched the mandolin to his chest.
"Maybe he does, *bella mia,* but keep him away from this in-
strument. It belonged to my pappa, and Signore Bundi might
scratch it if he tried to play it!"

Otto caught the sight of riders coming along the shore toward them. There were a dozen men, heavily armed, and
mounted on camels. The strongman sidled over to the wagon,

feeling for an old blunderbuss which was mounted on brackets beneath the steps.

Keeping his eyes on the riders, Signore Rizzoli cautioned the big German, "Stay away from that weapon, Herr Kassel, we are heavily outnumbered. Don't run to the wagon, ladies, they have already seen you. Please remain calm, everybody."

Mummo began backing Poppea into the wagon shafts, casting a dubious eye over the mounted men. "I don't like it. What if they are slavers, or robbers?"

La Lindi extinguished the fire by kicking sand over it. "Let's just hope for the best, maybe they'll leave us alone."

The camels lolloped, splay-footed, up to the troupe and halted. The leader, a tall, hooded man, tapped his mount's front legs with a quirt. The camel knelt, allowing him to dismount. Throwing back the hood of his burnoose, the leader pointed the quirt at Otto.

"Are you in charge here, big man?"

Smiling and bowing, Signore Rizzoli stepped forward. "Signore, I am Augusto Rizzoli, these are my troupe of entertainers. We are merely passing through here."

The man swept his quirt in a wide arc. "All these lands belong to my master, Al Misurata. You are trespassing without his permission!"

The showman spread his arms apologetically. "*Commendatore,** pray forgive us, we meant no harm or insult to your master."

The man rapped the quirt against his pantaloons, staring at each of the troupe in turn. "Hmm, travelling entertainers, eh?

Commendatore (commander).

Well, let's hope you put on a good show. I am Bomba Shakal, my master is a lover of diversions and entertainment. We will see if you can amuse him. Pack your belongings and follow me!"

Signore Rizzoli masked his reaction to Bomba's overbearing manner. Still smiling, he nodded to his companions. "Do as he bids, we will entertain his master."

Ned sat on the back steps of the wagon with Otto and the two clowns. Inside the wagon behind them, Mamma, La Lindi and Serafina leaned on the sill of the open half-door. Signore Rizzoli sat in the driver's seat, holding Poppea's reins, while Bomba rode at the horse's side, making sure the wagon was on course.

Buffo stared at the outriders surrounding their flanks and rear. "Well, my friends, it seems we've been given an invitation which we can't turn down, eh?"

Mummo shrugged. "Bomba wouldn't look kindly on refusals. I wager he'd kill us at the blink of an eye."

Mamma nodded grimly. "Let's hope his master is a more reasonable man."

Buffo grinned foolishly, waving at the outriders and shouting in Italian, "Is Al Misurata a jolly old buffer, you clod-faced sons of she-goats?"

The riders' dark eyes stared back at him over the black cloths they wore to shield their faces against blowing sand.

Buffo continued calling to them. "Nice to know you don't speak good Italian. Hah, you probably just grunt, like sows around a trough!"

Leaning over, Mamma cuffed his ears lightly. "Don't push them, who knows what languages they can speak. Anyhow, they haven't harmed us so far."

Otto ground his teeth audibly. "Ach, I feel so helpless, sitting here like a chicken that is being brought back from the market!"

Even though the strongman could not hear him, Ned agreed. "We're all chickens, mate, surrounded by hawks!"

FOR MORE THAN TWO DAYS, BEN HAD BEEN LOCKED IN the cellar, though he had lost all count of time in the total darkness. Sleep was out of the question—rustling, scrabbling,  scratching and other odd noises warned him about the presence of other living things moving round in the blackness. Insects, scorpions, rats, maybe even a snake, he could not tell. Whenever he sensed anything coming near he would fling handfuls of sand and snarl like a wild animal to keep the unknown creatures at bay. His eyes were sore from rubbing to keep them open, his lips were cracked and his tongue dry and swollen from thirst. He had given up trying to contact Ned mentally.

All his prayerful pleas to the angel seemed to be of no avail; he was completely alone. Feeling constantly dizzy and disoriented, he crouched against the wall, wondering. What had compelled him to argue with Al Misurata? This was something he could not explain, though maybe it was because he rebelled against the feeling that he was being treated as no more than an animal. A dumb chattel, something to be bought and sold offhandedly. However, the time he had spent being punished for his words had completely subdued him. He felt beaten and defeated by hunger, thirst and worst of all, loneliness.

Ben grunted with surprise as the lock grated and the small door swung open. Sunlight caught him in a golden shaft, temporarily blinding him. Men entered the cellar, two guards crouching low. He was grasped beneath the armpits; unable to resist, the boy slumped limply, his feet scraping the floor as he was hauled roughly out into the daylight. Groaning, Ben shielded his eyes against the sun's midday glare. He looked down and saw a pair of handsomely tooled Cordovan boots. The boy's eyes travelled slowly upward, until he was staring into the pitiless gaze of Al Misurata. The Barbary pirate placed his boot heel against Ben's chest, shoving him flat into the dust. The slaver's voice challenged him ironically.

"So, my little bleating goat, do you feel like lecturing me further on the subject of my wealth and your views on it?"

Ben could only gaze up dumbly at his interrogator.

The boot heel pressed harder on the boy's chest. "Answer me, do you?"

Ben shook his head. The pirate smiled thinly.

"Don't spare my feelings, just say if you wish to continue the argument. Then I can send you back to the cellar." He saw the look of fear on the boy's tear-grimed face. "Well? I'm waiting."

Ben shook his head a second time. It seemed to satisfy his captor, who turned to the guards.

"Let him bathe, give him something clean to wear. Have Jasmina feed him. She can instruct him to wait upon me at the evening meal."

The guards walked Ben to the moat and pushed him in. They stood watching impassively as he washed and drank at the same time. After awhile, Jasmina appeared. The stern-faced woman dropped a loose white gown on the bank of the shallow moat. Leaning forward, she wagged her stick threateningly at Ben.

"Finish splashing about, now, put that on and come to the kitchen. Any more insolence from you, boy, and I will wear this stick to a splinter on your back. Understood?"

Ben nodded, but she had turned away and gone inside the house. One of the guards chuckled.

"Be a good little frog, or Jasmina will take the hide off you. She knows how to use that cane."

Ben completed his bath in silence.

Jasmina was seated at the kitchen table. She indicated two bowls, one filled with water, the other with food. "Eat, drink and listen to what I tell you, infidel."

The food was plain, but good. A sort of warm semolina, with scraps of boiled goatmeat in it. Ben used his fingers as a scoop, alternating with gulps of cold, fresh water as he listened to his instructor.

"This evening you will serve the master. Kneel on one knee beside his divan. Do not look about, keep your eyes lowered, as a good servant should. Do not speak, but watch the master's left hand. If he rubs his fingers together, bring him a bowl of scented water and a hand towel. If he holds his goblet out, you must fill it quickly. I will be watching to see if you spill any drink. If he points to any food, fruit or meat, bring the dish to him. Hold it close so he may choose from it. When he waves his hand then you must remove it immediately. Do you understand?"

For the first time in days, Ben ventured to speak. "I understand, madame." He winced as she rapped the cane sharply against his arm.

"What did I tell you? Either nod or shake your head. Slaves only speak at the command of their superiors. Now, do you understand, boy?"

This time Ben nodded his head once. Jasmina touched his chin with the end of her cane. "You will learn."

For the remainder of the afternoon she allotted various tasks to Ben: fetching, carrying, cleaning dishes and sweeping the stone floor, then sprinkling water around to keep down the dust. If she caught her pupil looking up, even briefly, Jasmina rapped the tabletop with her cane. "Eyes down, slave!" Ben would drop his eyes swiftly. He wished he had never let her, and all the others, know of his skill in speaking different languages. Then he would have avoided their attentions, and merely been left with the other prisoners. He permitted himself a quick, humourous thought: Slaves, especially servants, must become experts on flooring. After all, they spent most of their time just staring at what was beneath their feet.

It was late afternoon when Ben heard the main gates opening. He detected the sound of animals, men's voices and the creaking of a wagon. He had thought Jasmina was taking a nap, but she was watching him like a snake with a bird.

"The little pig has big ears, eh? What goes on outside this kitchen does not concern an infidel slave. Clean under this table, it's covered with dust and crumbs. Move!"

Ben scrambled beneath the table and began brushing. Finding himself facing the open doorway, he risked a fleeting glance. Beyond the little moat bridge, but obscured by a date palm trunk, he glimpsed the hooped canvas top of a wagon. It was covered in crude artwork, with the name Rizzoli emblazoned in prominent letters. Then the wagon rolled out of view. Jasmina's cane tapped the sole of his bare foot, so he lowered his gaze promptly. Returning to his task, Ben wondered what a Rizzoli could possibly be. The stern taskmistress interrupted his thoughts abruptly.

"Lie down now where you are, take some rest. You'll be no good falling asleep this evening." Jasmina's chair scraped back as she rose from the table.

Ben lay on his side, watching as she spread a dark blue cloth over the table. Its tasselled fringes reached down to the floor, cutting off everything within sight. Ben was not unduly bothered. He was very tired. Closing his eyes, he fell into a slumber, still thinking about the name. Rizzoli? Again, the strange boy's inherent humour crept out of his thoughts. A man maybe? The Great Rizzoli, master of magic and mystery? He drifted into sleep with a smile on his lips. An animal maybe? See the only Rizzoli in captivity! The smile faded. Poor Rizzoli. Like him, it, too, was a captive.

Al Misurata looked out from the windows on the second floor of his big house. Beside him stood another man. This one was slightly older than the pirate, and more simply garbed. By his manner and bearing he was obviously a man used to seafaring. Ghigno the Corsair was first mate of Al Misurata's ship, *Sea Djinn*. He was Sicilian, and the name Ghigno*—Italian for *sneer*—was an apt title for him. He had received a dreadful wound in a stiletto fight many years ago; from cheekbone to jaw a deep, ragged cut had severed the lower facial muscles. When it healed, he was left with a permanent sneer on his face. Ghigno was Al Misurata's second in command, often deputising as captain of the *Sea Djinn*. The two men had known each other since their wild young days. They stood sipping wine, watching as the cavalcade, with the wagon at its centre, entered through the main gates.

Ghigno shook his head in mock bewilderment. "What has Bomba brought you now, *amico*?"

Al Misurata caught Bomba's eye and beckoned him to come up. "I'm not quite sure, Ghigno, but we'll soon find out. That Bomba, he'd sell his own mother if she were still alive."

Bomba shed his cloak as he came into the room, accepting a goblet of wine from Ghigno. He pointed his quirt at the troupe emerging from the cart. "Well, Master, what do you think?"

The pirate stroked his beard thoughtfully. "What am I supposed to think? Who are they, where did you find them and why have you brought them here?"

Bomba bowed, touching chest, lips and forehead. "For your amusement, Lord, what else? They are travelling entertainers whose path I crossed along the shoreline. Tonight they will perform for you."

*Ghigno (pronounced Jeenyoh).

Al Misurata assessed the troupe in the compound below. "They came of their own free will, I take it?"

Bomba smiled expansively. "Well, of course they did, merely to entertain the great Al Misurata. They require no payment, merely some food and lodging for the night."

Ghigno interrupted. "How many are they?"

Bomba counted on his fingers. "Four men, three women, a horse, a dog and a snake."

Al Misurata smiled mirthlessly. "What need have I of a horse, a dog and a snake?"

Bomba warmed eagerly to his explanation. "The animals count for nothing, Lord, but look at the people. Did you ever see such a fine, strong specimen as that big shaven-headed fellow? Also there are two clowns, and the small round one, their leader, is a fine singer. The woman is his wife, she is of no account. Look at those two females, though—the older one is a snake dancer, probably a contortionist, too."

Al Misurata was gazing steadfastly at Serafina. "The girl, who is she?"

From his fingertips, Bomba blew a kiss into the air. "Ah, that one, a princess of Africa, is she not? Limbs as graceful as a gazelle, teeth like milk pearls, and look at those eyes, twin oases in the desert night. Such a vision, Lord, does she need to do anything but stand and look as she does? Perfection!"

The pirate's eyes were still keenly glued to Serafina. "For once, Bomba, I agree with you. What do you think, Ghigno?"

The sneer on the Corsair's face deepened, indicating that he was smiling. He uttered a single word. "Dreskar!"

Al Misurata held up his goblet. "My clever Ghigno, a perfect choice. Dreskar, of course!"

Bomba looked dubious. "But Dreskar is very far away, master."

The pirate patted Bomba's paunchy stomach. "Your brains are all in there. Leave the thinking to me, there is an answer to any problem if I put my mind to it. But first we will let our new arrivals entertain us this evening. I trust you will join me for a meal and some harmless diversion, my friends?"

The three men clinked goblets as they laughed aloud.

Ben knelt to one side of the divan, his eyes riveted on Al Misurata's left hand. Bomba, Ghigno and several other guests sat upon a thick Persian rug, reclining on bolsters and cushions. Four servants tended to their needs, but Ben's task was to wait solely upon the master of the house.

A sumptuous banquet of food had been laid out, including a whole roast lamb, salads, an array of seafoods and bowls of fresh fruit, plus a selection of desserts and confections. Jasmina moved among the guests, pouring wines and cordials. Her watchful eyes were constantly checking on Ben, but so far the infidel boy had acquitted himself well.

Ben ministered promptly to Al Misurata's needs, which were fairly modest. He was fond of a pale golden wine, but did not eat much, only some fruit, a lamb chop, and a little dessert, though he was very fastidious about washing his hands frequently.

The guests talked among themselves, ignoring the servers. However, they fell deferentially silent whenever Al Misurata spoke. He was indeed lord of all he surveyed, constantly consulting and questioning his guests, all of whom were stewards and overseers of his extensive lands and properties. When the food was cleared away, Al Misurata clapped his hands at the guard next to the door. "Let the entertainment commence!"

Clad in a baggy peach-and-brown silk suit, Signore Rizzoli strode in. Strumming on his mandolin, he bowed to the company, and announced in a singsong voice, "Signores, it is my pleasure and honour to present to you, for your diversion, the esteemed Troupe Rizzoli!"

Serafina entered, carrying a long, narrow Kongo drum. Every eye was on the startlingly beautiful black girl as she knelt and began beating a roll on the drum with her palms.

Signore Rizzoli called out, "Herr Otto Kassel, the Teutonic Samson!"

Draped in a leopard-skin costume, Otto paraded in, followed by the two clowns, Buffo and Mummo, who between them were rolling the strongman's huge barbell. This was a long steel bar with a big cast-iron ball on either end. Otto stood to one side, watching in amusement as the two clowns tripped and fell over the mighty weight. They immediately leaped up, their painted faces trying to look strong and dignified. Buffo waved Otto out of his way. Pointing to himself, then indicating the barbell, he pantomimed that he, Buffo, was going to lift it. Mummo expressed scorn. He felt Buffo's arm muscles, then shook with silent laughter. Placing his thumb in his mouth, Mummo began blowing hard. His biceps began to swell. Buffo did likewise, and his arm muscle began to swell also. Both clowns continued puffing until each had a enormously swollen muscle ballooning at their tight stretched sleeves.

Together they strained at the barbell, trying to lift it. The mighty weight never budged a fraction. Buffo and Mummo straightened up painfully, pulling droll faces and rubbing at their backs. Otto prodded at both clowns' inflated muscles as Serafina struck the drum hard. *Bang!* The false muscles exploded simultaneously, causing the clowns to collapse in a comical faint. They lay draped over the steel bar as everybody, even Al Misurata, laughed.

Then Otto crouched over the bar, gripping it tight. With a sudden roar he lifted the entire thing, barbell and clowns, swinging it high over his head and holding it there. Buffo and Mummo hung like two pieces of washing on a line. The onlookers applauded Otto's fine feat of strength.

The clowns went into their routine, causing much merriment with their antics. Otto did more of his strongman act, which included pulverizing a coconut with a single blow of his fist, and bending a metal spear in his teeth. He concluded by lifting the Kongo drum on the outstretched palms of his hands, with Serafina sitting on it. The strongman and the clowns made their bows and departed.

Signore Rizzoli then began picking a poignant melody on his mandolin, whilst Serafina accompanied it with a slow, muffled drumbeat. A rapt silence fell over the audience as she sang an old love song. Her voice sounded young, but very appealing, with a sweet, husky quality. Even Jasmina was distracted by the singing, relaxing her vigil over Ben. The tow-haired boy was enchanted by Serafina. His eyes and ears were filled with the sight and sound of the slender, beautiful black girl as she sang her sad song.

> "Oh love is a mystery nobody knows,
> who sees the dew making tears on a rose.
> Through night's dark veil see a maiden forlorn,
> ever seeking a key to the gates of the dawn.

As she waits for her love from the sea.
Away in the east comes the sunrise anew,
gently painting the skies gold and blue.
Waves whisper secrets of old to the shore,
telling of ships that will sail there no more.
As she waits for her love from the sea.
Under the bridge of a rainbow so fair,
he comes bringing spices and ribbons for her.
A ring set with pearls to adorn her young hand,
and words sweet as honey, but worthless as sand.
Then she knows he'll return to the sea."

A brief silence ensued as the last tremulous notes floated on the warm, tropical evening, then there was appreciative applause, interspersed with cries for an encore. Al Misurata leaned down and whispered something in Ghigno's ear; both men nodded and smiled.

Unfortunately, Ben had not been able to hear what it was about—he was diverted by the dramatic entrance of La Lindi. Tinkling two tiny cymbals attached to her thumbs and index fingers, she glided in. Draped across her shoulders and both arms was an enormous snake. This was Mwaga, her green-gold python, a fearsome-looking reptile. The pair were almost as one, each as sinuous and graceful as the other. La Lindi undulated among the guests, with Mwaga swaying and coiling about her.

Serafina provided a soft, rapid drumbeat, the cadence of her voice rising and falling in an eerie, wordless chant. One or two of the braver guests reached out to stroke the snake. Each time they did, La Lindi would make a clicking noise with her tongue, and Mwaga would hiss fiercely, coiling as if to strike. This soon made the bolder spirits withdraw their hands swiftly.

That evening, Al Misurata and his guests were thoroughly entertained by the Travelling Rizzoli Troupe. When the performance was ended they all came on to take a bow: Otto, Buffo, Mummo, La Lindi, Serafina and Mwaga. They waved and smiled, then began to make their exit.

However, as a new finale to the act, Serafina had thought of a novel idea. La Lindi held the python as if its weight was becoming too much for her. Otto tried to pick Mwaga up, but at La Lindi's signal, it hissed and bunched up for a strike. The strongman took a step back, calling out, "Where is the basket for this monster?"

That was Mamma Rizzoli's cue. She opened the door, allowing the basket carrier to enter. Wearing a tiny conical hat on his head and sporting a ruffle about his neck, Ned trotted in, holding the big wickerwork basket in his jaws.

The roar of Ben's voice shocked everybody with its intensity. "Ned! My Ned, you're alive!"

IT WAS AS IF LIGHTNING HAD RIPPED the dark curtain from the dog's mind—everything came back to him in a brilliant flash. Dropping the basket he rushed in the  boy's direction, barking aloud as his senses shouted out, "Ben! Ben!"

Jasmina was standing in the black Labrador's path. Quickly assuming that it might attack her master, she swung her cane, whipping it across Ned's back. Raising the cane again, she yelled, "Guards, get this evil spirit out of here!"

Ben was rushing to stop her when he was knocked aside by Al Misurata. Bounding forward, he snatched the cane from his housekeeper's grasp and struck her with it.

Jasmina fell to her knees. Ashen with shock, she stared up at him. "Master, I thought the beast was going to savage you!"

The pirate's eyes flashed angrily as he brandished the cane over her, his voice thick with scorn. "And did you think that I, Al Misurata, needed a woman to protect me against a dog?"

The unfortunate woman touched her forehead to the pirate's feet. "Master, I am sorry, I did not think. . . ."

He flung the cane at her head. "Am I to be shamed in front of my guests by a stupid servant? Begone from my sight, fool!"

The unpredictable Al Misurata turned to Ben, who was hugging Ned tightly. "I thought this dog belonged to the entertainers, but evidently you seem to think he is yours?"

The boy's eyes glared defiantly at his captor. "He is mine, he was always mine!"

Al Misurata returned to his divan. "We will see. Guards, hold the creature until I command you to release him. Keep him to one side."

Two guards looped a belt around the Labrador's neck and held him midway between Ben and the Rizzoli Troupe. Ned sat placidly between the guards, sending a mental message to Ben. "Don't worry about me, mate, I'll do the right thing. You just stay calm."

Ben's reply flashed through his mind. "I've no need to worry Ned, you're back and you're alive."

Al Misurata questioned Ben. "If the dog is yours, how did you lose him?"

The boy answered promptly. "The two men who took me from my boat threw him into the sea. I thought he had been drowned."

The pirate turned to the Rizzoli Troupe. "How did you come by the dog?"

Otto stepped forward. "I found him on the tideline one morning, he was almost dead. Serafina and myself nursed him back to life. Bundi is a good dog, very sensible."

Al Misurata signalled the two guards. "Let the dog loose, now we will see who it goes to. You may call him."

Serafina crouched, clapping her hands gently and calling, "Bundi, here boy, good dog, come on, Bundi!"

Ned trotted over to her, wagged his tail and licked her hand.

Ben shot him a concerned thought. "What do you think you're doing, mate?"

The Labrador returned his query. "Merely saying thank you to those who saved my life. She's much prettier than you, Ben, have you noticed?"

Otto patted the dog's head fondly. "Good boy, Bundi!"

Ned looked at Ben and flinched. "Poor Otto, he means well, but I'm almost flattened whenever he pats me. He's got hands like mallets!"

Ben smiled inwardly. Ned had not lost his sense of humour. "When you're finished thanking those good people, perhaps you might come over here and prove you're mine. If it's not too much trouble, of course?"

Ned gave Serafina's hand a final lick. "Coming, O impatient one. How about calling me by my real name? I wasn't very fond of being called Bundi. Silly name, made me feel like some sort of stuffed toy!"

Al Misurata looked quizzically at Ben. "See, the dog has gone to the girl, but you say he belongs to you. Why do you not call him?"

For answer, Ben uttered the dog's name quietly. "Ned."

The black Labrador padded over dutifully, commenting, "Huh, your dog, their dog, his dog, her dog. Nobody's consulted *me* in all this—who was it that said every creature belongs to itself alone? Must've been me, I suppose."

Ben chuckled as he patted Ned's sleek side. "Don't get your feathers ruffled, I'm just trying to prove that we belong together. Now I'm going to ask you to do a few things to establish the fact."

Ned replied huffily, "Oh, I'm back to being the performing Bundi again, is that it?"

Ben reflected, "Well, you seemed to be enjoying it a moment ago. Actually, you look rather cute in your little hat and neck ruffle. How about returning them to those nice folk?" He commanded Ned aloud, "Give the hat and collar back to the pretty girl, please."

Ned managed to remove the little conical hat by rubbing his head against the ground. Scratching with his back paw, he relieved himself of the ruffled collar.

Carrying them over to Serafina, he laid them at her feet, then returned to Ben's side. She glanced at Ben, her slow, beautiful smile melting his heart.

"He is not our Bundi, my friend, he is your Ned."

The way in which the young black girl called Ben her friend, and the charmingly husky tone of her voice, tied the boy's tongue in a knot. He barely managed to stammer out, "Thank you for taking care of Ned, you're very kind." He was aware of Ned's doggy chuckle.

"Hoho, told you Serafina was prettier than you, mate!"

Ben savoured the name. Serafina, it was so . . . so . . .

He cut off his thoughts when he became aware of Ned; the dog was actually smirking at him.

Al Misurata interrupted any further reveries. "So, the dog really is yours, boy!" He raised his eyebrows as the dog placed his paw in Ben's hand, as if to confirm his statement. "Remarkable, I'd swear the thing understands what I'm saying."

Ben hastened to deny any such thing. "Oh no, sir, Ned is just glad to be back with me."

The pirate addressed Signore Rizzoli. "A talented animal, he would be an asset to your show. How would you like to have him, as a gift from me?"

The showman protested, "No, no, *Commendatore,* I could

not bear to take the dog from this young fellow now they are re-united. Thank you, but it would be too sad to see them parted."

Al Misurata never said or did anything needlessly. He was famed among his peers as a devious, and dangerous, man. He smiled disarmingly at the showman, choosing his words care-fully. "Well said, my friend. I can plainly see you are a man of true character. Tell me, to whence do you travel from here?"

Signore Rizzoli shrugged expressively. "Wherever the winds of chance steer us—markets, villages, town squares. Anywhere that we may gain a few coins, some food or a night's lodging. Entertainment is our business."

The pirate nodded understandingly, pausing to sip his wine. "I see you are Italian, signore, where in Italy are you from?"

Mamma Rizzoli answered for her husband. "We are from Vicenza, a lovely little place in the fields and meadows below the mountains. My Augusto and I were childhood sweethearts there many years ago."

Al Misurata signalled a servant to furnish the troupe with drinks. He seemed sympathetic and attentive to them. "Those places of early years stay in our memories forever. Would you not like to visit your home in Vicenza again?"

Signore Rizzoli smiled regretfully. "Alas, it is a wonder-ful dream, but impossible. We have a little money, far too lit-tle, I'm afraid. Also we have no means of crossing the wide seas."

Al Misurata rose from his divan, pacing about thoughtfully. "A great pity, my friend. However, all is not hopeless. Listen now, I have a proposition for you. Your performance tonight was very amusing, a rare diversion from my cares as a businessman. I enjoyed the show thoroughly. A week from now I set sail in my great ship to Slovenija.* I have business there, at a place called Piran, close to the Italian border. I have traded there many times before. I could transport you and your troupe there. But as I say, I am a businessman, and everything has its price. To earn your passage you must put yourselves at my disposal, staging a show and entertaining me and my friends every evening, until the day of our departure. Does my plan sound agreeable to you, signore?"

Augusto Rizzoli spoke in hushed tones. "You have a ship big enough to accommodate us all, horse and cart, too? *Mamma mia!*"

Ghigno the Corsair topped up the showman's goblet. He seemed amused at Signore Rizzoli's surprise. "The mighty Al Misurata owns the greatest ship in this hemisphere. We do much trade in horses, with Albanians, Greeks, Slavs and Italians. The *Sea Djinn* sails the coasts of all their lands. It would not trouble my master to give passage to you and your whole show."

The showman's eyes were moist as he clasped his wife's hand.

"Ah, to return to the green pastures of our homeland again, just think of it, *cara mia!*"**

With tears in her eyes, Mamma turned to Al Misurata. "Such kindness, signore, but why do you do this for us?"

The pirate smiled, shrugging expressively. "I like to help good people when I can, it is no big thing. But the choice is

---

*Slovenija (Slovenia).
**Cara mia* (my dear).

yours, either go on your way tomorrow, or accept my offer. Though I must warn you, there is dangerous country 'twixt here and the Straits of Gibraltar if you are travelling west. It would sadden me to hear you had fallen into the hands of robbers or brigands."

Mamma was about to speak again when her husband interrupted. 'You are right, signore, we accept your most generous offer!"

Whilst the conversation had been going back and forth, Ben and Ned sat close to one another, mentally conversing. Ben transmitted a warning to his friend.

"It's a trap, I'm sure of it. Al Misurata is a slave trader!"

Ned groaned inwardly. "Oh no, just when I thought things were beginning to go smoothly for a change. Though I must say, I didn't like the looks of that fellow, what's his name, Al Miserable, from the moment I clapped eyes on him. So, what do we do now, mate?"

Ben kept his eyes on the pirate's left hand, as he had been instructed. "I don't know yet, Ned, but we've got to help your friends—and ourselves, somehow." He checked his thoughts as Al Misurata spoke.

"So be it then, you will put on a performance for me and my friends each night until we are ready to sail. In return I will transport you over the sea to Italy, or as close to the Italian border as I am going. Bomba, see that the signore and his people have ample accommodation." He beckoned to Ben. "Bring your dog and come with me."

Ben mused as they followed the pirate, "I wonder what he wants us for?"

Ned growled quietly. "Who knows? But never mind, mate, as long as we're together again."

• • •

The gardens and walks of the downstairs courtyard were extensive, redolent with the scent of blossoms and fruit. Fountains tinkled in the warm night air, and a soothing breeze barely stirred the feathery palms. Al Misurata leaned against a low, sculptured wall as he stared long and hard at the strange fair-skinned boy and his dog.

"Go on, speak your thoughts, infidel. Don't be afraid, I won't punish you."

Ben immediately accused his captor. "I think those people will never see their homeland. You are leading them into some sort of trap!"

Al Misurata moved like a striking cobra. There was a swift hiss of steel, and Ben felt the pirate's swordblade against the side of his neck.

Ned bared his teeth savagely. He stood stiff-legged and snarling, ready to defend his friend.

Ben cautioned him mentally, "Stay where you are, Ned, this is a very dangerous man!"

Al Misurata spoke softly, but in a challenging tone. "Are you calling me a liar, infidel?"

Ben could not help swallowing hard, but he stood his ground. "You said it. I am only doing as you told me, speaking my mind."

Al Misurata withdrew the sword. Placing its tip upon the wall, he rested his chin on the gold-chased hilt. Never once did his piercing glance leave the boy. "You are a puzzle to me. You seem so young, yet something tells me your eyes have seen the sights of several lifetimes. Also, I think that you and the dog speak to one another. How is that? Tell me about yourself."

Ned cautioned his friend, "Watch what you say, mate!"

Ben studied the wall, avoiding the pirate's keen gaze. "There's nothing much to tell. I think I must have been the son of ship's officer. The dog and I were the only survivors when the vessel was wrecked in the Gulf of Gascony. I don't remember anything very clearly, so I must have been very young. Ned has always been with me, we've travelled the coasts together for a long time. I'm afraid that's all I can tell you."

Al Misurata sheathed his blade, smiling thinly. "Now who is the liar, eh, boy?"

Ben remained silent, taking in Ned's mental comment: "We're not fooling that one, he's got brains!"

Surprisingly, the pirate patted Ben's back. "No matter, boy, I started out just like you. Though I can tell you've never been a slave before. I know you're the same as me in one respect— you'd never bend your knee to any man willingly. Tell me, how would you like to go to Italy with that band of players?"

This came as a shock to Ben. He did not know what to think about his unpredictable captor. "You mean you're really taking them to Italy?"

The pirate nodded. "Of course I am, they are of no great significance to me. I am merely letting them pay for their trip by entertaining me for a few days. Life isn't all gold and slaves to me; sometimes I am not a bad fellow to know. Well, would you like to join them, Ben?"

Completely taken off-guard by the friendly use of his name and the man's open manner, Ben nodded eagerly. "That would be wonderful, sir, thank you. Thank you!"

Al Misurata made a dismissive gesture. "It's a fine night, Ben. You may sleep out here with your dog, Ned, that's his name, isn't it? I'll speak to Signore Rizzoli about you tomorrow.

Good night." He strode off, back into the big house, leaving the pair alone together.

Ben sat down with Ned, beside the wall. "Well, what do you make of that?"

The black Labrador scratched his ear with a back paw. "I've no idea, mate. Maybe we both misjudged old Al Miserable, who knows? But I intend to make it my business to find out more. Us dogs have our ways, you know."

Ben leaned back, scratching his dog's ear gently. "I should be used to your ways by now, my faithful hound."

Ned held still, so that Ben could scratch more easily. "Less of the hound, you cheeky pup. Ooh, that feels good, scratch a bit lower. Aaaahhh, right there! I missed you."

Ben tweaked Ned's ear playfully. "Only because nobody can scratch your ear like I do."

Ned stretched out blissfully, closing his eyes. "Correct, mate, keep going. A bit lower, no, to the left. Just there. Don't stop, slave!"

Ben watched the guards through half-closed eyes. They patrolled the walls constantly. "Aye, that's me, a slave, bought and sold. But not for long if we're to believe the great Lord Al Misurata."

Ned opened one eye. "Hmph, that's a big if!"

DAWN CREPT STEALTHILY OVER THE DESERT COAST, pale gold and shell pink, interspersed with banks of dove-grey mist over the sea. Serafina rose early, leaving Mamma and La Lindi still sleeping in the women's guest chamber. She padded silently out into the newborn day. It was her turn to tend Poppea, the troupe's wagon horse.

Even before she opened the stable door, the mare whickered eagerly, aware of her presence nearby. Serafina led her out into the paved yard, murmuring to her, "Good morning to you, old lady, did you think I'd forgotten your breakfast?" She filled a nosebag with bran and chaff. Poppea waited patiently, head bent, as Serafina strapped it in place. "This is good provender, you're lucky to be at the home of a horse trader. Better than being out on the road, eh?"

Whilst Poppea chomped and scrunched her way noisily through breakfast, the girl brushed away at her dusty white flanks and withers, still chatting. "Just think, you've got a week's rest, no more pulling the cart and sleeping in the open. You'll live like a grand lady alongside all this merchant's expensive horses. I do hope you mind your manners."

Poppea turned her head, watching with huge, liquid eyes as the girl braided her mane.

"When you've eaten that I'll take you for a nice drink of water from the moat. How would you like that?" She started slightly as a voice answered.

"No need for that, miss, there's a trough behind the stables."

Serafina found herself looking into the clouded blue-grey eyes of the boy she had seen the previous evening. They stood staring at each other in silence for a moment, then the spell was broken as Ned romped up and began frisking around the girl. She knelt, ruffling and patting him happily.

"Good morning, Bundi . . . er, I mean, Ned. Well, you're in a cheerful mood today. Is it because you've found your master again?"

The boy flicked his unruly, tow-coloured hair off his eyebrows. "I'm not his master, really, I'm his friend. My name's Ben."

The girl rose and began unbuckling the nosebag from the mare's head. "I'm Serafina, and this our wagon horse, Poppea. Will you show me where the trough is, Ben?"

Ben took the mare's halter. "With pleasure."

Ned interrupted mentally. "My my, aren't we the perfect gentleman. She must be swept off her feet by such good manners."

Ben tugged the Labrador's tail. "Better than being almost knocked flat by a gallumping beast like you, most undignified Bundi!"

Ned growled. "If you want to see something really undignified, just trying calling me that silly name again. We'll see how dignified you look with that pretty girl watching me tear the seat out of your britches, my boy!"

They sat in silence by the trough, watching Poppea drink her fill. Ben could think of nothing to say to this beautiful black vision which had entered his life. Serafina! She was so serene and graceful. Every move she made had a leisurely rhythm. Her hands were slim and long, extremely deft. He watched as she braided the mare's tail, trying to think of something to say to her. It was Serafina who finally spoke.

"Where do you come from, Ben?"

He heard himself laugh foolishly. "Sometimes I wish I knew." Ben was mentally berating himself for the silly reply when Ned's warning cut across his thoughts.

"Be very careful what you tell her, mate!"

At the same time, Serafina spoke again. "How long have you been at this place?"

Completely confused, Ben replied aloud to Ned's caution. "Don't worry, I know what to say."

The girl smiled quizzically at him. "You don't have to say anything you don't want to, Ben. I'm sorry if I seemed to be prying, it wasn't my intention."

Ben's cheeks went red with embarrassment. Impulsively he took her hand, blurting out, "Serafina, no, it's me who should be apologising. I got mixed up, it was something that Ned . . ." His voice trailed off miserably as he released her hand.

Her soft dark eyes sought his. "We don't have anything to be sorry about, Ben, you can talk to me as a friend."

Ben looked down at the trough, where he could see her shimmering reflection in the water as he strove to marshal his thoughts. "I'd like more than anything to be your friend. But there are certain things I can't explain right now. Maybe some-day. . . ."

Serafina looked up as Otto came around the corner of the stable. The big German strongman grinned cheerfully.

"Come now, *mein Schatzi,** they have given us lots of food for breakfast. You must be hungry, *ja*?"

Serafina took Poppea's halter. "Thank you, Otto, I am. Ben, would you and Ned like to join us? I'm sure there'll be plenty for everyone."

Ben took the halter from her, his heart singing with joy. "We'd love to, wouldn't we, Ned? Thank you!"

The black Labrador trotted along between Poppea and Otto, sharing his thoughts with Ben. "I'm famished! Oh, thanks for including me, mate, but watch what you say, and don't go tripping up over your tongue." He winced under Otto's heavy pats. "You should be glad you're human, Ben. I'm being patted into the ground by my big friend here. Oof! Oh dear, he means well, I suppose."

Jasmina and some servants had delivered lots of food to the performers: fresh fruit, bread, goat cheese, eggs, small cakes filled with sultanas, strong Turkish coffee and the sweetened fruit juices known as sherbet. Ben immediately felt at ease as Serafina introduced him to the friendly group. Being no stranger to the troupe, Ned was welcomed with open arms; he gambolled about, being petted and fed by everyone.

Ben remarked laughingly to Serafina as they watched the black Labrador, "That fellow makes himself right at home!"

Mein Schatzi (my treasure).

Ned gave Ben a doggy grin as La Lindi coaxed him with cheese. "Hoho! This is the life, matey, I could really get used to being part of this jolly gang!"

Ben accepted a piled-up plate from Mamma, thanking her as he mentally replied to his dog, "Aye, so could I. Though I'd best keep quiet about what Al Misurata said to us last night. We'll just play along and see how things develop through the day."

Buffo began feeding Ned some cake. He nodded to Ben. "You've got a good dog here, a real clever fellow. I bet you could work up a good act with him."

Serafina's expressive eyes shone. "What a great idea. I think he's intelligent enough to learn lots of tricks!"

Ben stifled a giggle as he heard Ned replying, "Well, I'll teach him what I can, but boys can be very difficult sometimes, especially my Ben."

Serafina was entranced by the scheme. "Well, what do you think, Ben, could you and Ned get something together? I'd help you, if you wish."

The boy tried to stay noncommittal, though it was difficult to refuse any offer from the charming black girl. "It's a nice idea, let me think about it, Serafina."

Mamma Rizzoli interrupted the conversation. "Serafina, and you, Buffo, leave the young man alone, stop trying to put ideas into his head. The master of this place may have totally different plans for Ben and his dog. Then where would all your fine schemes be, eh?"

Augusto Rizzoli agreed with his wife. "Yes indeed, friends, we would appear presumptuous if we were to make plans for one of Al Misurata's servants. We must not abuse his hospitality."

Mummo pulled a mock sad face. "A great pity, really, young

fellow, you and your dog would have made splendid clowns. I was thinking what good names you could have had. Benno and Neddo!"

Otto gestured toward the big house. "Forget that now, the one they call Bomba is coming over here. I wonder what he wants?"

Without any formalities, Bomba indicated Signore Rizzoli abruptly. "Come with me, my master would speak with you!"

Mamma looked concerned. "I wonder what he wants with you?"

The showman reassured her. "Don't worry, *cara mia,* it's probably nothing. I'll be back soon."

Bomba took hold of Signore Rizzoli's arm. "Come along, my master doesn't like to be kept waiting!"

Otto reached out and caught the big man's arm above the elbow, squeezing his biceps in a grip of steel. Bomba winced, releasing his hold on Signore Rizzoli. The German strongman wagged a huge finger at him. "Mind your manners, *mein Herr,* especially with my friends!"

Augusto Rizzoli intervened. "Let go, Herr Kassel, I will go with him. Lead on, please!"

Otto watched both men walking across to the house. "I don't think I like that Bomba fellow."

Ben sent a thought to Ned. "I don't like him either, he's a slaver. But I think he'll tread carefully around Otto from now on."

The dog replied, "Aye, heaven help him if he ever tries anything with our Otto!"

The rest of breakfast passed in silence. Ben and Serafina helped Mamma to tidy up, whilst the others went off to rehearse their show behind the stables.

The morning was half gone before Signore Rizzoli re-turned. He called his wife into the wagon, where they held a conference. Ben and Ned were with Serafina, watching La Lindi going through her dance with the python. She had allowed him to stroke it, though she advised that Ned be kept away.

The dog snorted. "Huh, wild horses couldn't drag me near that monster, just the smell of that big snake makes me feel ill."

Mamma emerged from the wagon and called the boy. "Ben, my husband would like a word with you."

Ben entered the covered wagon, with Ned at his heels. Augusto Rizzoli offered him a seat.

"Listen to what I have to say, young man, and think carefully. How would you feel about joining my troupe and travelling with us to Italy? You and your good dog there?"

A surge of elation shot through Ben. He had an idea what the showman's meeting with Al Misurata had been about, but he feigned ignorance. "Signore, it would be wonderful, I'm sure Ned and I would enjoy greatly to be part of your show. But why do you ask?"

Augusto Rizzoli leaned forward, speaking confidentially. "I think Al Misurata knows you will never make a good servant. He wants me to take both you and the dog off his hands."

Ben heard Ned commenting mentally, "I know you don't like telling lies by silence, mate, but you'd best not tell this good man what you know until we're certain of what's going on."

Signore Rizzoli continued his explanation. "Al Misurata told me he was a horse trader, and not a slaver. But his associate, the one called Bomba, is a slave driver. Is it true that Bomba sold you to him?"

Ben nodded. "There were four of us, signore, three boys and a girl, we were all sold to Al Misurata by Bomba. I don't know what happened to the others. But if he is a horse trader, as he says, then why does he purchase slaves?"

Augusto Rizzoli shrugged. "He says he sells them on, to kindly masters, good folk who will treat them well. If he did not, they could fall into the hands of evil masters who would ill-treat them. Personally, I think he is a man of good intentions, though I do not like his friends, that Bomba, and the scar-face, Ghigno."

Ben saw the small purse in the showman's hand. "So he is selling me to you, is that it?"

Signore Rizzoli clasped the boy's hand. "I am no slave dealer, Ben, I am paying him to gain your freedom. You are under no obligation to me—once I pass the gold over your fate is your own. I only ask you to join us out of friendship."

A tear sprang unbidden to Ben's eye. "Thank you, signore, from the bottom of my heart. I would be honoured to join you and your troupers. But have you got enough gold to meet the price?"

The showman rose. "I have very little, my wife keeps the funds. But Al Misurata assured me that whatever I had would be sufficient. Perhaps we misjudge him. No matter, once we reach Italy we can always earn more. Though usually it is in the form of food or lodging. I never went into this business to get rich, but we get by somehow, and that is enough, eh, Ben?"

The boy wiped his eyes roughly on his sleeve. "If it's enough for you, it's more than plenty for me, signore. What happens now?"

Augusto Rizzoli weighed the paltry purse in one hand. "Now I go to seal the agreement. Come on, my boy, this is no time for tears, this is a lucky day for both of us. My wife was just saying that you may be the best thing that ever happened to our troupe. So now you'll have to really think of getting up an act with your Ned, eh?"

Ben watched the good-hearted Signore walking back to the house. He patted Ned. "Go with him, mate, see what you can find out!"

Tail wagging, the black Labrador trotted off. "Leave it to me, I'll be better than a fly on the wall!"

Signore Rizzoli looked down at the dog walking by his side. "So, you are to be my guard dog. Good fellow, come on!"

BOMBA GESTURED THE SHOWMAN INTO THE PALATIAL
upstairs room. He put out his foot to bar the dog entry, but Ned
bounded over it, baring his teeth and showing his contempt of
 the slave driver with a low snarl. The big man
backed away as Ned ambled in behind Signore
Rizzoli. Al Misurata was seated on his divan,
while the scar-faced Corsair, Ghigno, stood behind him. Augusto Rizzoli bowed formally to the
pirate, who patted the cushioned divan.

"Sit here, my friend, and let
us talk business."

Ned lay on the floor be-
tween the two men.

Al Misurata smiled briefly.
"So, you have brought a companion?"

Augusto stroked the dog's head. "He followed me."

Ned lounged casually, his tail wagging lazily, tongue hanging out, just like any dog would. Except that he was watching,
and taking in every word that was spoken.

Signore Rizzoli held out the little purse. "I brought the
gold you asked for. It is not a lot, we are after all only entertainers."

Ghigno took the purse and turned out its meagre contents

on a small coffee table nearby. Al Misurata sorted through it with a fingertip. The coins were mainly gold, with a few silver ones thrown in—they were all very old and thin. The pirate raised his eyebrows. "Truly this is a pitiful sum. If you were not my friend I would feel insulted by such an offering."

Signore Rizzoli replied, his voice a humble murmur, "It is all we have, *Commendatore.*"

Ghigno insinuated slyly, "Don't you have any other valuables, a ring or two, maybe a necklace?"

Al Misurata frowned at the Corsair reproachfully. "Ghigno! You can see our friend is an honest man. If that is all the wealth he possesses, how could I doubt his word?"

He patted Augusto's hand reassuringly, then went on to stroke Ned's ears as he continued. "Signore Rizzoli, I accept this money in exchange for the boy, because I know you will treat him kindly. As I told you, I am a simple horse trader, it is not in my nature to buy or sell human beings. This sum you offer me is not even a quarter of what I paid to save the boy from being sold on the block in some slave market. But, like you, I am a soft-hearted fellow, and I can afford to take a slight loss now and then. It is all in a good cause. Take the lad, and take with you my good wishes for a happy visit to your homeland."

Augusto Rizzoli stood, extending his hand to Al Misurata. "May the good Vicenza, patron saint of my town, bless you, Signore Misurata!"

The pirate returned his handshake solemnly. "Go now, and tell that young man your good news."

Signor Rizzoli hurried from the room. But Ned stayed. The black Labrador closed his eyes, allowing Al Misurata to stroke his head. However, he was fully alerted.

There was silence in the room as the sound of the showman's footsteps receded down the stairs. Ghigno swept the money back into the worn, leather purse. He handed it to the pirate, imitating Signore Rizzoli's voice as he did. "It is all we have, *Commendatore.*" Both men suddenly burst out into coarse laughter. Al Misurata grabbed the purse from Ghigno, who shook his head in amazement.

"Is there nothing you wouldn't do for gold? You should have heard yourself. 'I am a soft-hearted fellow, I can afford to take a slight loss now and then.' Hahaha, you almost had me weeping!"

The pirate spread his arms expressively. "What would you have me do, Ghigno? Sell them on to Count Dreskar, who would immediately search them for any gold they were hiding? This way I get two lots for the boy, the pittance from that Italian jackass and the proper price from Dreskar. Gold is gold, no matter where it comes from!"

The Corsair wiped tears of merriment from his eyes. His manner became businesslike. "So, what's the plan?"

All this time Ned had not stirred, though he dearly wished he could sink his teeth into the hand that was stroking him. He continued to listen as the pirate outlined his scheme.

"What we must do is keep them completely in the dark regarding their fate. If they knew they were being sold into slavery, it would make them troublesome on the voyage. We'll keep everything friendly, and treat them with respect. They must not suspect anything. When we dock at the port of Piran, I will tell them that to avoid the authorities, and any trouble about not having papers for the two African women, they must stay in their wagon. Bomba!"

The big slave driver hurried forward. "Master?"

Al Misurata gave him his instructions. "Once they are in-side the wagon you will lock them in. Harness the horse and drive the wagon to the outskirts of Piran, then wait in the old woods by the stream for me."

Bomba nodded. "I know the place, master."

The pirate turned to Ghigno. "You will come with me. I will be meeting Count Dreskar in the town, at the Crown of Slovenija hotel."

Ghigno tapped the jagged scar on his face. "I'll have the crew with me, we'll stay in the background in case of trouble. Right?"

Al Misurata stroked his beard. "Right, my friend, and when our business is done . . ."

The Corsair chuckled. "We'll kidnap a few of the good townsfolk of Piran, take them on board and sail for home!"

This time Bomba joined in the laughter. Al Misurata poured drinks, and they toasted the coming enterprise.

"To trade, and to the gold to be made on both sides of the sea. A successful voyage!"

As Bomba took a pace back, Ned saw his chance to get out. He yelped aloud, as though the Corsair had trod on his paw.

Bomba drew his dagger. "Whining cur, get from under my feet!"

Al Misurata chided the big slave driver. "Bomba, don't be cruel to poor, dumb animals, put that knife away and open the door for our friend Bundi, or is it Ned?"

Bomba opened the door and Ned trotted down the stairs, thinking to himself, "I wish Otto had given his childhood pet a better name. Bundi? Ugh, it makes me sound like an old, fat donkey!"

When Ned arrived back at the wagon outside the guest accommodation, he found himself in the middle of a very welcoming troupe. They all patted and stroked him as he wagged his tail furiously, enquiring of Ben, "This is all very nice, but what's all the fuss about?"

The boy sent him a mental reply. "They're welcoming us as part of the troupe, mate. We're going to become performers, the great Neddo and Benno. But you haven't reported back yet, did you hear anything of value over at the house?"

The dog avoided Otto's ham-like hand playfully. "I certainly did, and none of it's good news. These nice people wouldn't be celebrating if they'd heard what I've just listened in to."

Ben took Ned's chin in one hand. He dipped a scrap of rag in some warm water and began cleaning the corners of the Labrador's eyes, communicating impatiently, "Well, are you going to sit there hinting all day, or are you going to tell me what they said?"

Ned launched into his mental account of what was planned for the Rizzoli Troupe, finishing with his assessment of Al Misurata. "You wouldn't believe the way old Miserable changed the minute Signore Rizzoli left the room. He's a very evil man, sly and greedy, he'll do anything for gold."

The news came as no surprise to Ben. He stared into his friend's eyes. "I knew it. Though for awhile I thought there might have been some good in that man. Now I'm certain that Al Misurata is a cold, treacherous snake. His only god is gold, he is ruled by his greed."

Ned placed a paw on Ben's arm. "But what are we going to do—how can you tell our friends what we know? You can't very well announce that I told you I'd overheard a conversation. Who'd believe us, mate?"

Ben sighed. "You're right, but it's still up to us to do something about the problem. I think it's best that Signore Rizzoli and the others know nothing about it for the moment. It would only create a lot of trouble and worry for them. We must really put our minds to reaching a solution. Let's discuss this tonight, when everybody's asleep."

They joined the rest of the troupe, who were sitting about on the wagon steps. Mamma looked curiously at the pair. "Well, have you finished your talk?"

This took Ben by surprise. "Talk, Mamma, what talk?"

She smiled shrewdly. "I was watching you both, you can't fool me. Oh, your lips weren't moving, there was no sound. It was the way you were staring at each other. You were making a contact somehow, I'm sure of it."

Serafina saved Ben further embarrassment. "I know what you mean, Mamma. I stare into Poppea's eyes a lot, and she looks back at me. We don't have to say anything, it's just a feeling of friendship. Some animals have the most gentle eyes—Poppea does, and Ned, too."

Buffo interrupted. "Oh, I know that. I stared into the eyes of La Lindi's serpent once, they were fascinating."

Mummo shuddered. "Ugh, that awful python, what happened?"

Buffo grinned. "It hypnotised me and tried to swallow me whole!"

Mamma cuffed him playfully. "A pity it never did, you great fool!"

Signore Rizzoli began tuning his mandolin busily. "Come on, you lot, let's work out this evening's show."

Passing a huge hand over his shaven head, Otto flicked perspiration from it. "Ach, it is too hot to think in this heat of Libya, can we not just sit and rest awhile?"

La Lindi stretched out lazily. "A good idea, Herr Kassel. Serafina, sing us a pretty song, you know, the one which goes, lala, lala, laaa . . ."

Augusto picked up the melody on his mandolin. "You mean this one? It's a sad song, but nice. Sing it for us, *bella ragazza.*"

The beautiful black girl waited for him to finish the introduction, then sang slowly in her hauntingly husky voice. It was a song of forlorn love.

> "A long time ago, a lifetime away,
> I knew one who loved me,
> could it be the same today?
> Why does my heart still yearn,
> the way it used to do,
> old songs make teardrops fall,
> when I remember you.
> Lala lala lalala laaaaaaaah.

> "If I saw you now, my poor heart would say,
> stay with me forever,
> never ever go away.
> Fools say that love is blind,
> I know that isn't true,
> your face would tell me so,
> if I could look at you.
> Lala lala lalala laaaaaaaalah!"

The echoes of Serafina's voice hung on the still, warm air. A feeling Ben had never known came over him; it was like an actual ache in his chest as he gazed longingly at the girl. Suddenly, Ned's calls were echoing through his bittersweet thoughts.

"Ben, Ben! Wipe it from your mind, it's impossible! You know we will have to move on someday without her. Remember the angel's command! You would have to watch Serafina growing older. What would happen if she saw the years passing, and you hadn't aged by a day, what then?"

Ben continued looking at the girl. However, he heard his dog's impassioned plea, and cast his eyes down, blinking. "The angel's command, eh, Ned, the words that change my blessing into a curse!"

The faithful dog felt his friend's single tear dampen his outstretched paw.

Augusto Rizzoli broke the spell. Putting aside his mandolin, he rose energetically. "Friends, we cannot sit here idle all day. Ben, have you been thinking about an act for you and your fine dog? That is, if you wish to take part in our show?"

The boy strove to shake off his feeling of sorrow and appear both eager and happy. "I'll help with any work that needs doing, signore, but I haven't really thought about performing."

Mamma shook a finger at her husband. "Augusto, leave the boy alone, maybe he doesn't want to be a trouper like us."

Ned's indignant thoughts cut across Ben's mind. "Huh, does nobody care about my wishes? I don't know about you, but I rather fancy being an entertainer. The applause, the admiration, the fame. . . ."

Ben replied to his friend's thoughts. "I wouldn't take up singing if I were you, mate, you've got a dreadful voice."

The Labrador sniffed disdainfully. "Hah, speak for your-

self, m'boy, your voice sounds like the creaking of a rusty gate.
Wait, I've got an idea!"

Ben became aware of Serafina encouraging him. "I think
you and Ned could work up a great act, Ben. Come on, give it
a try, please!"

Ben glanced at the troupe's expectant faces. "Well, alright,
leave us to practice a bit first. Ned and I will try out a few ideas
behind the stables."

From the window of the upstairs room, Al Misurata and his
two associates had been watching the group on the wagon
steps. Ghigno nodded toward Serafina.

"That pretty girl is worth her weight in gold. She has a
voice that would put the birds of paradise to shame."

The pirate nodded agreement. "As long as Count Dreskar
meets my price. Then he can lock that beautiful songbird in a
gilded cage where she will sing only for him. We must treat her
with extra-special care."

Bomba snorted. "Slaves are all alike, master, give them cos-
seting and wrap them in silk if you want trouble. Special treatment makes slaves insolent and moody." The big man knew he
had spoken unthinkingly when Al Misurata's withering glance
fell on him.

"Your mother bore your father a fool, jackass! The girl does
not yet know she is to be a slave. If she knew she was going to
be sold off, she would grow troublesome and sullen. I have
seen it happen before. Once Dreskar has paid for her, it is his
own affair how he treats her. But I get the top price for slaves
by selling my goods in perfect condition. Then there can be no

dispute about their quality. We will keep her, and all of them, blissfully ignorant."

Ghigno chuckled, looking pointedly at Bomba. "Just like him, eh?"

The pirate shook his head. "Blissful ignorance is a condition even sensible people can feel. But Bomba is stupid, he was born a fool. Right?"

The big man shuffled uncomfortably, muttering, "It is as you say, master."

It was mid-noon. La Lindi sat watching the stables as she anointed her python's scales with a mixture of sweet oil and warm water. "How long is that boy going to take?"

Mummo spotted Ben and Ned emerging from the rear of the stables. "Here they come now!"

The pair paced up with majestic slowness. Ben bowed to the company, and announced in a theatrical tone, "Eminent people, exalted guests, pray give attention to Benno, Master of Mystery, and the Magnificent Neddo!"

The good-natured group applauded encouragingly.

Ben appealed to them. "Would some kind person like to step forward and blindfold me?"

Folding her silken neckscarf several times, Mamma obliged, binding it firmly across Ben's eyes.

Mummo held up his hand, calling out, "How many fingers am I holding up, O Mysterious Benno?"

Ben smiled. "Fifteen, my good fellow, and I noticed your hands never once left your wrists while you did it." The audience chuckled as Ben waved his arms for silence. "Silence, please, my assistant and I do this at great risk to our health.

And now, the Magnificent Neddo is going to visit you in turn. Give him any little piece of your property, a trinket, a keepsake, a priceless jewel. Anything . . . and I will attempt, whilst blindfolded, to identify it. Magnificent Neddo, you may proceed!"

Ben heard Otto whispering. "Hoho, this I must see, *ja*?"

Then he heard Serafina's soft tones. "Please, Otto, silence, give Ben a chance!"

Ned went immediately to Otto. The German strongman placed in the dog's jaws an object. The dog communicated what it was to Ben as he trotted back and dropped it on the ground behind the boy.

Ben placed his index finger in the centre of his forehead. He appeared to be concentrating as he spoke. "The spirits of air and water tell the Mysterious Benno that a bent iron nail lies on the ground behind me!"

Applause, coupled with puzzled whispers, greeted Ben's announcement. Ned went to each of the troupe in turn, placing the objects he collected behind Ben, who identified them all accurately.

A spool of cotton from Mamma.

A small, blue button from Buffo.

La Lindi's earring.

Augusto Rizzoli's pocketknife.

A woven cord bracelet from Serafina.

And, finally, a cheap metal ring from Mummo.

They clapped and cheered heartily, until Ben removed the blindfold and called for silence once more. "Your attention, my friends. The Magnificent Neddo will now return your property correctly. Observe!"

He picked up the cotton spool, declaiming dramatically, "O Magnificent Neddo, to whom does this thing belong?"

A flash of the black Labrador's humour came to Ben. "I think I may have a thread of an idea!"

Picking up the spool, Ned delivered it to Mamma. There were gasps of astonishment as he restored each item to its owner at Ben's command. Amid rapturous cheers, Ned held up a paw in salute, and Ben bowed, touching his fingertips to heart, lips and forehead in the Eastern manner.

Signore Rizzoli was elated, but very perplexed. "Benno, truly you are mysterious, and Neddo is surely a dog among dogs. Anybody would swear you were both highly skilled magicians. I hope you will perform your marvellous act in our show this evening. But how do you both do it?"

Ben was aware that questions would be asked. He had spent most of the time behind the stables working out an answer with Ned. Now he winked broadly at the showman. "Oh, it's an old trick really, and quite simple. But if I were to tell you how I did it, the mystery would be gone. The magic becomes just a trick once the secret has been told to everybody."

La Lindi made an eloquent gesture with her expressive hands. "He speaks truly, Signore, you especially should know that good performers do not willingly give away their secrets. Benno is Mysterious, and Neddo is really Magnificent. Why not leave it at that, and preserve the illusion?"

Buffo offered an explanation. "It's not Benno who's the brains, it's Neddo. Let me have a word with him." Wagging a stern finger at the dog, the clown put forth the question. "How did you do those tricks, Signore Neddo? Confess!"

Standing on his hind legs, Ned put his forepaws on Buffo's chest and barked. "Woof! Woof! Woof! Gurrrr!"

The clown pulled a wry face at Augusto Rizzoli. "There, now you know!"

The tubby little showman laughed. "What did he say?"

Buffo grinned. "Neddo told you to mind your own business!"

Ben sent a thought to his dog. "Did you, really?"

Ned replied, "Aye, I did, though we'll have to watch that Buffo. I didn't know he could translate doggy language!"

FOR THE ENTERTAINMENT THAT evening, Al Misurata had invited several more of his dubious associates from the

 coastal areas. The pirate was enjoying his temporary position as entrepreneur and host—it was good for business to talk with others whilst providing leisurely diversion. The Rizzoli Troupe had changed their act, putting more variety into it for this, their second performance. The guests lounged about on silken cushions and bolsters, their every need catered to as they were served food and drink.

Then the performance started. Augusto Rizzoli entered. Strumming his mandolin, he bid the guests welcome, acknowledging their host, Al Misurata. Buffo and Mummo opened, tumbling and somersaulting.

The clowns did a clever routine, juggling with Indian clubs. One of the clubs was not made of hardwood like the others, but was fashioned from cork and balsa wood. This caused much hilarity when it kept hitting them on their heads whenever they missed catching it, with practised skill. Both clowns caused consternation when they hurled what appeared to be pails of water at the audience, followed by laughter when the water turned out to be paper confetti.

Next, Serafina heralded La Lindi with a rolling beat of her Kongo drum. The snake charmer had on a costume of gold and green sequins, with her arms and legs painted to match. She wore a tight headmask with dark slash markings around the eyes. The whole thing created a reptilian effect as she went into her dance, undulating and writhing like a snake. Sweeping the python, Mwaga, from its basket, La Lindi whirled sinuously about amidst the seated guests. They were slightly apprehensive, but fascinated by the gyrations of the snake lady and her live python. Sometimes it was hard to distinguish one from the other, they were so closely entwined.

After that, Otto entered, bowing and flexing his impressive muscles. The German strongman excelled himself. He balanced a great cart wheel on his chin, whilst expanding his chest and snapping a metal chain which had been tied around him. Everybody gasped as he bent a dagger by placing the top of the hilt against his biceps, and the blade tip on his forearm. Bending the arm slowly, he turned the dagger into a U shape, leaving only a deep dent where its tip had rested.

After several more feats, Otto coaxed three fat merchants from their cushions and sat them together on a bench. Crouching beneath the bench, he set his broad shoulders against it, then stood upright. Bearing the weight of the three fat men, he paced a dozen steps, with not the trace of a tremble to his sturdy legs.

Serafina watched from the doorway as the strongman concluded his act amid applause and cries of admiration for his Herculean strength. Turning, she gave Ben and Ned their cue. "You're on now, good luck!"

Ben was garbed in baggy black trousers held up by a broad green sash, a sleeveless, embroidered bolero jacket and a light purple cloak, which Serafina had loaned him. The rest was from the company wicker basket, including a white turban decorated with a spray of green feathers. Ned wore his frilly neck ruffle and the small, conical clown hat.

With her fingers crossed, Serafina watched from the doorway as Signore Rizzoli announced them.

"Honoured guests, the Rizzoli Troupe has the pleasure to present, for your entertainment, a piece of real magic! Please welcome the Mysterious Benno, and his assistant, the Magnificent Neddo!"

The pair strode on confidently and went straight into their act. Ben already had a silken scarf ready. When he made a request for an audience member to blindfold him, Bomba swaggered out, winking broadly to his companion Ghigno. The big man bound the scarf cruelly tight around the boy's eyes. Giving the knot a final twist, he smirked.

"If you can see anything through that, infidel, then surely you are mysterious!"

Ignoring the constricting blindfold, Ben explained in theatrical phrases what he was about to do. At his command, Ned trotted out into the audience and began collecting their offerings, whilst Ben kept up an amusing commentary with the guests.

At the doorway, Otto stood behind Serafina; he was impressed with the boy's easy manner. "He has the tongue of silver, I could never find the courage to speak with an audience like that. Your Ben is a very good speaker, *ja!*"

Serafina was slightly taken aback. "My Ben?"

The strongman nodded his huge, shaven head. "*Ja,* your Ben. I am thinking you like him a lot, *Fräulein.*"

The girl tried to appear noncommittal. "Well, of course I like Ben. We all do. You, too, Otto?"

The big German smiled. "Hoho, yes, we all like him, but not the same way as you do, *kleines Mädchen.*"* He tweaked Serafina's ear lightly. "I think you would give your heart to that boy!"

To hide her confusion, she looked away from Otto, concentrating her attention on the performance. Serafina's eyes picked up an odd movement between Ghigno and Bomba, which she pointed out quickly. "Otto, see that man with the scar? He was whispering to the one called Bomba, then he slipped something to him. Do you think they are planning on upsetting Ben and Ned's act?"

Otto shrugged. "There is nothing we can do about it right now, just watch and hope for the best."

The Corsair had indeed passed something to Bomba—it was a shark's tooth on a thong, a talisman often worn by seafarers in that area. Bomba gave the tooth to Ned, who deposited it on the ground behind Ben, informing him mentally, "It's a fish's tooth on a neckthong, shark, I think. I saw the one with the wounded face pass it to Bomba. I think they're cooking something up, mate, be careful!"

Ben identified the object aloud. "Ah, this sounds a bit fishy to me, a tooth on a leather strand. It's a sharktooth necklet!"

Whilst the audience was applauding, Ned went to Ghigno, who gave him a gold coin for Ben to identify. As it clinked on the ground behind him, he pronounced, "Ah, I smell gold, there is a wealthy man among us. It is a coin, a Spanish gold doubloon!"

Kleines Mädchen (little maiden).

Amid the gasps of awe and the hand clapping, Ned told Ben, "Bomba didn't give me anything of his own, that scar-faced rascal slipped him the sharktooth."

Ben nodded. "Well spotted, mate, you know what to do!"

When Ned had gathered in all of the offerings—which included a string of amber worry beads from Al Misurata himself—Ben removed the blindfold.

Serafina watched worriedly as Ben picked up the gold coin. "Oh, I do hope nothing goes wrong, Otto!"

The strongman reassured her. "Do not fret, pretty girl. Your Ben is not stupid, *ja,* and neither is Ned. He is smart, just like my Bundi was."

Ben gave the doubloon to Ned, declaiming loudly, "Seek out this rich man, and give him back the gold that is his, O Magnificent Neddo!"

The black Labrador went straight to Ghigno and dropped the coin on his foot. The audience cheered heartily.

Now Ben picked up the shark's tooth and gave it to his dog. "O Magnificent One, return this to its rightful owner!"

Ned loped back to Ghigno and dropped the tooth on his other foot. Bomba sneered triumphantly.

"Stupid cur, it was I who gave you that!" He bent to pick up the tooth, but Ned bared his teeth, snarling at the big slave trader. Guests moved away from the two men and the vicious-looking dog.

Al Misurata rose from his divan. Spreading his arms, he stared enquiringly at Ben. "What is the matter with your dog, why did he not give the sharktooth back to Bomba?"

Ben pointed at Ghigno. "Because the tooth belongs to him. He slipped it to Bomba so that my performance would be ruined."

Al Misurata strode over to the Corsair and the slave trader. He picked up the tooth and the gold coin, glaring from one to the other. Then he tossed the sharktooth necklet to Ghigno. "I have seen you wearing this about your neck. Speak the truth, it belongs to you, does it not?"

Shamefaced, Ghigno avoided the pirate's irate gaze. "It is mine, we meant it merely as a joke."

Al Misurata had always trusted and liked Ghigno; they had been together many years. He shook his head disapprovingly. "You disappoint me, my friend. What pleasure would this foolish act have gained you? Was it to demonstrate that I was putting on a poor entertainment for my guests?"

Aware that every eye was upon him, Ghigno bowed his head, realising that what he had done was to offer insult to the mighty Al Misurata. He went down on one knee. "Lord, you are right, it was a foolish thing, and I did it unthinkingly. I beg you to accept my humble apology."

Al Misurata was silent a moment. Then he gestured for Ghigno to rise. "We will speak no more of this, your apology is accepted, my friend." He placed the gold doubloon in Ned's mouth and patted him. "Good dog, take this to your master, he has earned it!"

Bomba thought the incident was over. He was smiling foolishly when the unpredictable pirate turned to vent his wrath on him.

"Wipe that grin from your stupid face, idiot! Jasmina, take this mindless oaf down to the stables and see that he cleans them out properly. Stand over him, and use your cane unsparingly. Get him out of my sight!"

Ben caught one hate-laden glance from Bomba as Jasmina prodded him from the room with her cane.

An awkward hush had fallen over the guests. Then Al Misurata returned to his divan. Smiling, he clapped his hands at the servants. "More wine and food for everybody. Let the entertainment continue, eat, drink and enjoy the evening, friends!"

Signore Rizzoli picked out a tinkling melody on his mandolin as the pirate's associates continued their feasting. However, they fell silent again when their attention was taken by Serafina's entrance.

The girl glided smoothly in, clad in a gown of shimmering gold and white. Her hair was encircled with a garland of small flowers, and her luminous eyes surveyed the room over a veil of transparent silk hemmed with tiny silver coins. Otto set her long Kongo drum by the fountain, where she perched on the stone rim. Serafina caressed the drumhead with deft movements of her slender fingers, interweaving a pattering beat to the mandolin music.

Ben's eyes were riveted on the beautiful vision whilst she sang her song. This was in the form of a riddle, which performers sang in bazaars to attract the attention of passersby.

"Hark to the question I ask you,
how does a seed grow to a tree,
what pays no heed to the seasons,
and treats beggars and kings equally?
Soft as the breeze o'er the desert,
travelling afar from the sea,
warm as the sand, that sifts through my hand,
wise man, will you heed my plea, O tell me?

"Something which moves on forever,
and cannot be hoarded away,

like the gold of some old miser's treasure,
in some deep hidden cavern to lay.
A daughter has more than her mother,
a father has less than his son,
yet everyone rues the day it is gone,
wise man, will you heed my plea, O tell me?"

Ben was standing close to the door when the answer dawned on him. Raising his hand, he was about to call out the answer to Serafina. Otto's large hand covered his mouth from behind suddenly. The big German whispered in his ear, "It is for the audience to answer, not the performers!"

Al Misurata raised his voice. "Time is the answer. Time!"

There was a rousing cheer, both for the singer and for the one who had solved the riddle. Serafina went across to the pirate. Plucking a flower from her head garland, she offered it to him. As Al Misurata reached out and took it, the girl kissed the back of his hand lightly. There was more applause.

Ned sent the boy a thought. "You should have got that, mate."

Ben shrugged. "I'm not bothered."

Ned nuzzled his hand gently. "You can't fool me, mate. Not bothered, my tail. Huh!"

The week passed rapidly for Ben and Ned. Each evening their act improved, getting more smooth and professional. They now included comic interludes, often assisted by Buffo and Mummo. It would have been a happy time for both boy and dog, had it not been marred by their knowledge of Al Misurata's intentions. Thus far they had not fathomed a solution to their coming misfortunes. They felt guilty about not revealing the truth to their friends. However, Ben reasoned that in this case, ignorance was bliss for the Rizzoli Troupe. His silence would save them stress and misery, also keeping them from thinking up rash schemes that might get them into deeper trouble.

The Barbary pirate kept up his cruel deception, showing kindness and consideration to his would-be victims.

Ben and Ned were revolted at the manner in which he could chat amicably with the Rizzolis about how much they were looking forward to being back in their childhood home. Apart from being in the same room as Al Misurata for the show each evening, Ben and Ned avoided him. It became obvious that he was concentrating his efforts on the troupe, when one night the other captives were secreted onto the slave wagon and shipped off furtively.

Ned learned, by listening in to the guards, that the girl and the three boys were bound for Tripoli, to be auctioned off at a private sale. Had they come from wealthy families, all four could have been ransomed to their kin. But they were only ordinary slaves, with no particular talent or outstanding features, sent to the selling block by the callous decision of their captor. Bomba did not accompany them. Ben and Ned watched him closely—he was constantly seen around the house and its spacious grounds. Having fallen into disfavour with his master, the big slave driver blamed Ben for his ill fortune. He would glare and mutter dire threats whenever he saw the infidel boy.

On the morning before they were due to sail for Slovenija, Ben and Ned accompanied Serafina as she exercised Poppea by walking her around the compound. Ever on the alert for trouble, the black Labrador sent out a warning to his master. "Careful, mate, here comes old bigmouth Bomba!"

Ben turned to see Bomba creeping up from behind.

The slave driver saluted Serafina with his riding crop. "Good day, my little songbird. Tell me, why do you befriend flea-ridden curs and infidel trash? Come, take a stroll with a real man. Here, I'll hold your horse for you!"

Ben steered Serafina away, murmuring to her, "Pay no attention to him, he's just a troublemaker."

The big man barred their path. He waved the leather-bound riding crop in Ben's face, allowing the tip to touch his chin. "I haven't forgotten you, little bazaar rat. Before you're much older I'm going to teach you some painful lessons!"

Ned sprang at him without warning, burying his teeth in the slave driver's baggy behind. Bomba shrieked in agonised shock. Wrenching himself around, he grabbed the dog's hind legs. However, Ned hung grimly on to his enemy's rear end. They both fell over heavily, with the dog kicking furiously to free his paws. Bomba let go of Ned, unsheathing an ornate curved dagger from his waistband. As Poppea began rearing and whinnying, Serafina went up with her, pulling on the reins in an attempt to calm the panicked mare. Ben avoided the flailing hooves, circling the choking dust cloud that enveloped the combatants as he sought an opening.

Seeing Bomba raise the dagger high, Ben jumped in, seizing the big man's arm with both hands. Ned was still snarling like an enraged wolf, digging his teeth into the foeman's buttock.

Seemingly from nowhere, Otto appeared in the midst of the fray. Ben felt like a small child as he was pulled off Bomba and tucked under the strongman's arm. In the same instant, the German stamped his foot down on Bomba's wrist, trapping both him and the dagger to the ground. Thrusting Ben to one side, Otto broke the hold of Ned's jaws, dragging him free of the screeching slave driver. Kicking the knife away, Otto took the bridle from Serafina. He held the mare still by main force, whispering softly to her, "Easy, *Fräulein* Poppea, I am here now!" The big German helped Ben to his feet. "Are you alright, is your dog hurt?"

Ben hugged Ned, running a hand over him as the dog chuckled mentally. "Stop that, it tickles!"

The boy was still shaking as he replied to his rescuer. "No harm done, we're fine, thank you, sir!"

Bomba had risen to his knees, his face creased with pain as he gingerly touched his bottom to assess the damage. The German strongman shot out a ham-like hand; gripping Bomba by the throat, he hauled him upright. Otto's voice was dangerously calm.

"I will talk with you now. Listen carefully, *Dummkopf,** keep away from my friends, far away, or I will kill you. *Verstanden,*** *mein Heer*?" As he talked, Otto tightened his grip, lifting Bomba until he was poised on tiptoe.

The slave driver's face was turning an unhealthy purple, and his eyes were beginning to bulge. He managed to gasp out, "Gyuurrrsssh!"

Serafina grasped her friend's outstretched arm, pleading, "Please don't kill him, Otto. Please!"

The strongman gave Bomba a mighty shove backward. He

*Dummkopf (stupid).
**Verstanden (understood).

hit the ground with a bump, raising another dustcloud. Turning away, Otto shook his huge, shaven head, smiling at the girl.

"*Nein, nein, Mädchen,* I would not kill him in front of one so gentle. Not this time, at least." Leaning over the defeated slave driver, Otto twisted his ear hard. "Say thank you to the pretty girl for saving your worthless life. Speak up, I can't hear you!"

With his head twisted to one side and tears coursing through his dust-coated face, the big man babbled out as Otto applied more pressure to his ear, "Thank you thank you thank you! Yeeeeaaaargh!"

The strongman released him. Retrieving the riding crop, he snapped it like a twig, tucking the broken halves in Bomba's waistband. "You may go now!"

Ben read Ned's thoughts as they watched the slave driver limping off, clutching his bottom. "Yukk! I think I'll wash my mouth out at the trough. Three cheers for our big Otto, eh mate?"

Ben patted dust from his dog's flank. "Aye, but it's thanks to you, too, mate. That villain was going to flog me, and he would have, but for you!"

Serafina wiped the dust from Ben's face with her silk scarf. "You were very brave. Bomba is such a big man!"

Ned's indignant thoughts intruded on Ben's mind. "Er, excuse me, but what about the faithful dog's part in all this? Go on, you tell her, mate!"

But Ben did not have to, the girl was already fussing over Ned. "You were so fierce and courageous, good boy, Ned!"

The black Labrador licked her hand cheerfully. "Ah, that's better. Us heroic dogs deserve our due, y'know!"

Calling to him, Serafina led Poppea off to the trough at the rear of the stables. "Come on, boy, I think you should wash your mouth out!"

Wagging his tail, Ned bounded after her. "Hah, she's a mind reader, too. I think we should ask her to join our act, Ben. The Magnificent Neddo, the Mysterious Benno, and the Sensational Serafina. Sounds rather good, eh?"

MIDMORNING OF THE FOL-
lowing day found the troupe
outside their guest quarters.
They were rehearsing some routines, when the
stern-faced Jasmina came with news from Al
Misurata for Augusto Rizzoli. "My master orders
me to inform you there will be no entertainment
today. You will be leaving here to board his ship.
Pack all your belongings, and be ready to travel this evening
after the noon heat dies down."

Ben was helping Serafina to groom Poppea. He scratched
the mare's muzzle. "Do you hear that, old girl? You're going to
become a sea horse shortly."

Mamma Rizzoli questioned Jasmina. "Where will we be
sailing from, how long will it take for us to get to the ship?"

The servant woman replied curtly. "The *Sea Djinn* is anchored at the pier near the town of Misurata. It is no great distance, you should arrive about dawn tomorrow."

Ben looked up from his work. "Will you be coming, too?"

Jasmina shook her head. "You never learn, do you, boy?
Still asking questions."

The boy's curious eyes shone disarmingly. "Sorry!"

She drew him to one side, her severe face softening for

awhile. Dropping her voice, she spoke to him confidentially. "My place is here, as a servant, I will not be going on the voyage. But Bomba will be sailing with you, boy. Watch your back, and sleep with one eye open—he will kill you and your dog if he gets the chance. I know Bomba, he is a dangerous man. He blames you for all his woes, and the master's loss of respect for him. Believe me, Bomba will not rest until he has had his revenge upon you. He carries grudges like a camel carries its hump." Jasmina avoided Ben's searching gaze as he replied.

"Thank you, marm, but why do you concern yourself about me? We'll probably never meet again once I leave here."

She lifted Ben's chin lightly with her cane. "Truly you are a mysterious one, so bright and clever. I feel that the fates have marked you for better things than death at the hands of a thick-brained idiot. Go with your God, young infidel, and may his shadow protect you!" The woman's face returned to its customary stern cast. "As for that dog, I do not like it, I have always feared dogs. As far as I am concerned, its fate is in the wind. But you remember my advice and tread carefully!" She turned, hurrying off back to the big house.

Ben stroked Ned absently as they watched her go indoors. The Labrador commented mentally, "What a shame, oh dearie me, so she doesn't like dogs, eh? Well, I'm not too fussy on hatchet-faced harridans who go about waving canes, so there!"

Ben tugged his dog's ear. "Still, it was good of her to warn me—she could have just tended to her own affairs."

Augusto Rizzoli beckoned Ben to sit beside him on the wagon step. He nodded knowingly. "So, it seems trouble is about to cross your path, Benno. These old ears are keener than they have a right to be. Didn't I hear the lady mention Bomba's name more than once?"

Ben sighed. "Yes, Signore, Bomba has become my enemy."

The showman began packing his mandolin carefully into its travelling case. "Ah, but I feel you are not telling me all. There is more, eh, Benno? Something tells me you are concerned about our little family . . ."

Ned placed a paw on Ben's foot. "Go easy, mate, don't tell him too much—think of what you say!"

Holding the mandolin case as the showman secured it, Ben made his decision. "Signore Rizzoli, Ned and I owe you a great deal, so I will try to be as frank as I can with you. The troupe will be in no danger until we dock at Piran, in Slovenija. Al Misurata is not what he seems, he is a pirate and a slave trader. But you must keep this knowledge to yourself, or it will cause hardship and misery to your wife and friends. I cannot tell you any more at the present, but I promise you that Ned and I will see that the Rizzoli Troupe reach Italy together. Show Al Misurata that you suspect nothing, act normally, but do not trust him or the one they call Ghigno. At the moment my life is in great danger. Ned and I need to escape Bomba—also, we must be free if we are to help you. So, if at some time I go missing, please do not think badly of me, but rest assured my dog and I will return to your aid."

Ned's thoughts interrupted Ben. "Oh, so we're going to escape. Thanks for telling me!"

Ben sent a silent plea to the dog. "Can we discuss this later, Ned, please?"

Augusto Rizzoli sat staring at Ben in silence for an uncomfortably long time. Then he took the boy's hand firmly. "Benno, where do you come from, who sent you to us? I understand little about all you have told me, but I see the wisdom of ages in your strange young eyes. Know that you have my trust. I could not bring myself to think badly of you, or this good dog. Do what you must, Benno, for yourself, and for all of us!"

The hot Libyan day gradually faded to eventide coolness. Through the open compound gates, the caravan made its way into the dunes and desert scrubland. Mounted on a superb black Arab stallion, Al Misurata cut a dashing sight. He was dressed in a blouse and pantaloons of crimson silk, covered by a high-collared black cloak, topped off with a turban of white cotton.

The pirate rode at the head of the cavalcade with an escort of four horsemen. Behind them came three wagons, the middle one of which was the Rizzoli cart. To the rear were more fine-looking horses, presumably to be used in trade. Either side of the procession was a score of camel riders. These wore hooded burnooses and had dust bandannas pulled up to their eyes. They were hard-looking men, armed with the long, orna-mented, flintlock rifles called jezzails.

Two more guards walked alongside Poppea, holding her hal-ter on either side. Ben and Ned enjoyed the welcome evening breeze as they sat on the back step of the wagon, exchanging thoughts. At first Ned had been slightly huffy about not being told of an escape attempt. He regained his composure, however, not being able to stay silent for any great length of time.

"Er, this plan of yours, tell me more about it. I'm with you of course, just say the word, mate!"

Ben glanced at the armed riders surrounding them. "We'll have to watch for a chance. Not now, but when the right op-portunity presents itself. I know you're with me, Ned, I wouldn't dream of making a move without you."

The black Labrador settled his chin on his friend's knee.

"Maybe just before we sail would be a good time. If we could slip away unnoticed, it'd be too late for old Al Miserable to turn the ship around and search for us."

Ben dismissed the idea. "That would leave the whole of the Mediterranean Sea between us and the troupe. How could we help them then?"

Ned's tongue lolled out to one side of his mouth. "Silly me, I never thought of that. So, go on, what's the plan, O Mysterious Benno?"

Ben still had no formulated idea. "I'm not sure, Ned, but if we do try an escape, it'll be at either Malta or Sicily, before we reach Slovenija."

The Labrador gave a startled *wuff.* "What's all this about Malta and Sicily, mate? First I've heard about us going to either place."

Ben explained. "I overheard two of the guards talking. One of them hadn't made the trip before, but the other was an old hand. He said the voyage is always made in two stages. Al Misurata goes ashore to meet with his agents while the ship takes on fresh supplies. Usually they put in to Valletta in Malta, but sometimes they visit Siracusa in Sicily. It all depends on how Al Misurata feels. Nobody knows until he tells the helmsman to alter course. Either place would be suitable for us to make the break, because I'll wager there's lots of ships go to Slovenija and Italy from Malta or Sicily."

Night fell over the desert. A three-quarter moon illuminated the dunes eerily, casting pale light and deep shadow on both sides of the caravan trail. Mamma opened the half-door of the wagon.

"Come on in, you two, get a bite to eat and some rest."

There was not much room inside, but it was a cosy, lantern-lit atmosphere. Ben and Ned sat between Serafina and Otto, sharing some flat bread and fruit. Buffo and Mummo began to sing. They had good voices, and could harmonise cleverly, without the aid of instrumental accompaniment. Both men were from Vicenza, like their brother Augusto and his wife. They sang a local ballad extolling the virtues of home.

> "Soft as the breath of angels,
> breezes drift o'er my land,
> grape-laden vines entwining,
> await the harvester's hand.
> Sweet as the kiss of sunlight,
> gently carressed by the rain,
> O vale of my home, Vicenza,
> when will I see thee again?

> "O *bella mamma mia,*
> I hear the bells ring clear,
> the chapel of Santa Vicenza,
> calls to her children dear.
> Echoes from snowy mountains,
> cross pastures of peaceful green,
> to the poor wand'ring exiles,
> my children, where have you been?"

The cart trundled on into the star-strewn desert night. One by one its occupants dropped into slumber, lulled by the gentle, jogging motion of its spell.

It was almost dawn when Bomba banged on the door of

the wagon, haranguing them. "Come on, out with the lot of you. We've got to get this cart loaded on board, move yourselves!"

Serafina hurried to the door. "Listen, can you hear the waves? Ben, Ned, let's go and see the big ship!"

The *Sea Djinn* was truly a massive and curious-looking vessel. Al Misurata and Ghigno had stripped the superstructure from a captured Spanish galleon, and rigged it to suit their purpose. From the stern, right through the midships, four large masts had each been fitted with a large triangular sail, like a yacht or a dhow. On the forecastle deck was another mast, rigged with a big, single, square sail, like a Viking ship. The huge vessel was moored alongside a long jetty, which ran out into the sea. *Sea Djinn* loomed large and sinister in the gloomy half-light which heralded day.

Ben stared up the tarred black timber sides and ornamental rails to the dark red sails. He was filled with an unreasoning dread, which he conveyed to Ned.

"This is a big ship sure enough, but I don't like it, I can't say what it is. The *Sea Djinn* has a feeling of evil about it. What do you think, mate?"

The black Labrador shuddered, then shook himself. "Aye, you're right, it's a bad ship!"

Serafina stared upward, wide-eyed, at the mighty vessel. "It's the biggest boat I've ever seen in my life!"

Ghigno appeared at the stern gallery. He smiled down at the girl, his scarred face contorting into a horrid leer. "It's a ship, pretty one, not a boat. I hope you'll enjoy your voyage on *Sea Djinn*. Now you'd best move off this jetty before they start loading cargo."

Poppea reared and whinnied when she was brought to the

jetty. Digging her hooves in, the mare refused to go any further. Ned sent a comment to Ben. "You see, even the horse can feel it's a bad ship!"

Otto soon solved the dilemma. Unfastening Poppea from the cart shafts, he blindfolded her with his waistcoat and passed her into the care of Serafina. Ben and the girl stroked the mare, whispering softly to reassure her. The big German strongman stood in the shafts, pulling the cart along the jetty to where the midship rail had been removed. Whilst the crew wheeled the cart on board, Serafina and Ben walked the blind-folded horse along the narrow jetty, leading her aboard behind the cart.

By mid-afternoon the vessel was fully laden. She set sail, outward bound on the rising tide. It was smooth going, with a fair wind at their stern. The Rizzoli troupe were in high spir-its, thoroughly enjoying the feeling of being afloat. Ben stayed on deck with Ned whilst the entertainers went to explore their cabins, which were in the forecastle. It was not long before Serafina came hurrying out on deck. She waved to them.

"Ben, Ned, come and see our cabins. They're rather small, but very comfortable. Come on, I'll show you!"

Ben got as far as the alleyway between the cabins, then peered into the semidarkness, drawing back as a feeling of dread overcame him. "Er, no, thank you. Ned and I prefer it out here on deck."

Serafina began harmlessly teasing him, pulling Ben into the alleyway. "What's the matter, are you afraid of the dark? Come on, Ned, stop hanging back!"

However, Ben was unaware of her voice. Suddenly his en-tire being was filled with visions of Vanderdecken, the captain of the *Flying Dutchman,* and his ghastly crew. They were lurking in the gloom of the passage, waiting for both him and Ned. Hands with clawlike nails, bitten black and puce by frostbite, scrabbled to grab them. Grimacing faces of the long dead hissed curses of hatred at the pair, who had, by the grace of the Lord's angel, escaped the eternal voyage of the damned aboard the hellship.

Ben and Ned stood petrified within the alleyway opening as Captain Vanderdecken, master of the *Flying Dutchman,* loomed large in front of them. His insane eyes glittered balefully, and he snarled at them through bloodless lips.

"I have been waiting for you, my children, always waiting, knowing you would return to the sea, where I can claim you as my own forever. Come to me!"

Serafina left off teasing her friends, suddenly frightened and concerned for them. They were both trembling as if in the grip of a severe fever. Ben's face was ashen, coated in icy sweat, while Ned was whining, cowering like some beaten cur. The girl shook them, calling out in alarm.

"Ben! Ned! What is it, are you ill?" She tugged them bodily out onto the sunlit deck.

The black Labrador gave a long, piteous moan, and the boy collapsed in a heap. Alerted by the dog's howl and the girl's shouts, the troupe came hurrying from their cabins.

Bomba watched the scene, listening to what went on as he leaned against the midship rails. One of the crew was with him, a small, furtive-looking villain called Abrit. They saw Otto pick Ben up and carry him to the fo'c'sle deck, where he seated him with his back to a locker. Mamma Rizzoli chafed the boy's cold hands and patted his cheeks, trying to restore their colour.

"By all the saints, what happened to him, *cara mia*?"

Serafina looked up from hugging Ned, obviously baffled. "I

don't know, Mamma, he was afraid to go into the passage between the cabins—Ned, too. They went all pale and shaky, so I pulled them back out onto the deck."

Signore Rizzoli ventured a diagnosis. "Maybe it is the *mal de mer,* the seasickness. There are some who suffer badly from it."

La Lindi indicated the dog. "And Ned, too? It is very odd, both of them overcome by seasickness at the same moment."

Mummo suggested helpfully, "Perhaps Ned was not seasick. I think he was distressed just because his master fell ill. Look, Ben is beginning to come round!"

Opening his eyes slowly, Ben stared at the anxious faces gathered around him. He caught the thoughts Ned was directing at him.

"They think you've been seasick, mate, so stick to that explanation. We don't want them knowing about the Dutchman!"

Serafina passed a clean, damp cloth over Ben's forehead. "You had me worried. How are you feeling now?"

The boy's strange, clouded eyes blinked gratefully at her. He sat up straight, wiping damp hair from his brow. "I think seasickness suddenly took hold of me, Serafina. It was either that or the heat and darkness of that alleyway, I'm not sure. I'll be alright now, don't worry. Ned and I will stay out on deck for the rest of the trip. Thanks for the help you gave us."

Bomba saw Otto glance his way; he averted his eyes, making it appear that he had no interest in what was going on upon the foredeck. The slave driver whispered to the small crewman alongside him, "How would you like to earn two gold pieces, my friend?"

Greed shone in Abrit's eyes. "Two gold pieces, eh, who d'you want me to kill?"

The big man continued staring out to sea. "Are you still good at throwing the knife?"

Abrit patted the handle of the long, hefty dagger which he carried in the back of his waistband. "I can throw this blade like no other, you have seen me do it many times before, Bomba. Who do you want dead?"

Bomba drew close to the assassin's ear, whispering, "The infidel boy, he will be sleeping out on deck from now on. A swift throw in the dark night watches, one slain brat slipping gently into the sea. Who would know? The boy was ill anyhow. What could be simpler to one of your skills, little man?"

Abrit glanced up at Ben, then looked away. "The dog, it never leaves his side. For three gold pieces I would rid you of them both."

Bomba frowned. "You are the son of a miserly she-wolf. Two gold coins is a fair price, even for both of them. What do you say, eh?"

Abrit shook his head, sticking to his price. "Three gold coins, or you do the job yourself. The dog cannot be left alive once the boy is slain. Three!"

Bomba spat over the side, knowing the small man had won. "Three it is, then, but I want the thing done properly!"

Abrit nodded. "When I kill them, they stay dead, believe me. Payment in advance, give me the gold now, friend."

Grumbling, Bomba slipped him three thin coins. "There, it is all I possess. You are a mean little man!"

Testing each coin with his teeth, the assassin chuckled. "Aye, and you will be a big, happy man tomorrow morning. The poor boy leaned overboard to be sick during the night. Alas, he fell into the sea, and his faithful hound went after him. So, the ship sails on, and they are both gone forever. Then you will be avenged for the loss of face and favour with our master, Al Misurata!"

Bomba hated his fall from grace being discussed. "Shut your mouth and go about your business, you spawn of sundried camel spit!"

Abrit smiled sweetly, though his eyes were hard as stone. "Sometimes I do not throw the knife. Often I just creep up and slip it twixt the ribs of big men who have insulted Abrit. Guard your tongue, friend Bomba!" He strode jauntily off, whistling between his teeth.

SOFT AS DARK VELVET, THE MEDITERRANEAN CAST ITS
warm enchantment over the waves. Each riplet reflected glim-
mers of golden light from myriad stars, and a segment of cres-
cent moon.

Ben and Ned were on the fo'c'sle head deck,
taking their ease on a few blankets, which
Mamma Rizzoli had provided for them. Ben lay
gazing up at the beautiful night sky, the *Sea
Djinn* swaying gently on the swell as he conversed with
his friend.

"We're safe out here on deck, mate,
but I won't be really happy until we're
well clear of this ship."

Ned settled his chin across the
boy's feet. "Aye, back on dry land,
far from the ghost of old Vanderdecken. Y'know, it's odd that we
haven't had any messages of warnings
from our angel for a long time now. At least I
haven't, have you?"

Ben let his eyes close. "Not that I can recall. I expect sooner
or later the angel will let us know when it's time for us to move

on. Though I hope it's not sooner. I like being with the troupe, they're a good bunch."

The black Labrador wrinkled his nose. "What you really mean is that you like being with Serafina. Oh, don't deny it, mate, she's a pretty fascinating girl. I like her a lot, too, y'know—not in the way you do, though. Still, I suppose you're entitled to a little joy in this eternal life of ours. Just as long as you don't fall too deeply in love and get badly hurt by it."

Ben reached down and ruffled his dog's ears. "Poor old Ned, what about you?"

The dog sighed gustily. "Oh, I suppose in some century or other I'll stumble across a pretty, young, golden Labrador, a soft, doe-eyed thing with a coat like honey. Right, that's enough of talk like that, m'boy. Let's get some sleep. It's been a long day, and we don't know what tomorrow holds in store for us. G'night, mate!"

Below them, underneath the forecastle steps which led up from amidships, Abrit lay hidden, waiting with the patience of an assassin. He ran his palm along the deadly blade, caressing its razor edge and sharp point, thinking of how he would spend his gold in the seaport taverns of Slovenija. The little man had killed many times before; he never gave a second thought to his victims, only the pleasures their blood money could provide.

Time passed slowly, as minutes crept into hours. In the men's cabin Otto was tending to his moustache with elaborate care. Having trimmed and combed it fastidiously, he produced his scented pomade, massaging it into the hairs and twirling the ends into tight points, which bristled out either side.

Mummo held his nose as he complained, "Whew! Do you have to use that stuff, Otto? It smells like a camel's breakfast left to rot in some cheap bazaar!"

Using his snuff box lid as a mirror, the big German inspected his moustache proudly. "Ach, you have no appreciation of the finer things, Mummo. This pomade is made from attar of violets and the wax from honeybees. It is very special and most expensive, *mein Freund.*"*

The clown wiped a palm across his damp brow. His normally ruddy complexion had taken on a sickly pallor. "I wish you'd put it away. *Mamma mia,* the odour is making me feel queasy!"

"As you wish." The strongman put his pomade back in its snuff box, and settled into a hammock. Then he began to rock back and forth. This gave Mummo even more cause for complaint.

"Can't you keep that thing still, Otto? What with the ship going up and down, and you swinging from side to side, and the smell of that moustache ointment clogging my nostrils, it's making me giddy!"

Buffo nudged Signore Rizzoli, chuckling. "Another case of the *mal de mer*, eh?"

Mummo denied the accusation indignantly. "I've never been seasick in my entire life!"

Buffo had a mischievous twinkle in his eye. "I never said you were seasick, brother. You'll be alright in the morning, won't he, Augusto?"

*Mein Freund (my friend).

Signore Rizzoli caught on to the joke. "Of course he will, after a good breakfast of tomatoes and peppers, mixed in with scrambled eggs. . . ."

He got no further. Mummo clapped a hand across his mouth, and gave a strangled belch. Leaping up, he made a bee-line for the cabin door.

"Mmmmff! Goin' for a turn around the deck. Mmmfff!"

He dashed out, leaving his brother winking at Otto.

"Never been seasick before, eh?"

Rocking back and forth in his hammock, the strongman nodded solemnly. "*Ja,* but there is always a first time, I am thinking."

Abrit judged the time just right; he had waited long enough, both boy and dog were sound asleep. He came from beneath the steps and mounted them carefully, silent as a moonshadow. The small assassin kept to the edges of the wooden stairs. He walked splay-legged, to avoid any creaks. It took him awhile to negotiate the twelve steps, but Abrit was in no hurry. The business of murder, he knew, required stealth and patience.

Standing at the edge of the forecastle deck, he concentrated on his targets. The infidel boy was lying on his side, presenting his back as a perfect target. The dog sprawled on its stomach, close to its master's feet. Abrit drew his long dagger, the one he used for throwing. He checked that he had the other knife, a small, double-edged blade, stowed at the front of his waist sash. This he would use to despatch the dog speedily.

Drawing back the heavy throwing knife, he raised his elbow to shoulder level. Holding the blade's blunt back edge firmly with his whole hand, he felt the perfect balance between arm and knife. The assassin judged the distance, centering on the nape of the sleeping boy's neck and tensing himself for the throw.

Clad only in his nightshirt, Mummo padded out onto the deck barefoot. He leaned back against the midship rail, breathing deeply to rid himself of the nausea he was feeling. The clown avoided looking at the sea—it shifted too much. He glanced about the deck, and could not help seeing the man. Like a huge spider he was creeping up the forecastle steps, obviously up to no good. Reaching the fo'c'sle deck, he drew a long dagger and began hefting it.

As a performer, Mummo had seen knife throwers before. Ben was up there, probably asleep. The clown's brain was racing. What to do? He could not reach the man in time to halt his throw. Then he saw the belaying pins. There were several of them slotted through holes around the foremost of the midship masts. Mummo sprang forward and grasped one. It was a polished length of teak, about the same size and weight as the Indian clubs which he and his brother used in their act. He tossed it in his hand; it was a good weight, and had the right taper to it.

The man still had his back to Mummo, unaware that he was being watched. Now his arm came back, he was making the throw. All feelings of seasickness had deserted Mummo. Twirling the belaying pin in one hand he uttered a low whistle and hurled the pin forcefully at the assassin. Abrit turned at the sound of Mummo's whistle.

Thwock!

The teak belaying pin struck him squarely between both

eyes. He fell sideways down the steps to the midship deck, where he lay still, his head twisted at a grotesque angle, his hand still clenching the knifeblade.

Roused by the noise, Ben and Ned ran to the top of the steps. Mummo was standing below, looking up at them and holding a finger to his lips for silence. Boy, dog and clown all stood stock-still for several seconds, expecting crewmen to come running. However, the incident had passed unnoticed, nobody aboard had stirred.

Ben and Ned descended the steps slowly and quietly. They found Mummo kneeling by the fallen Abrit. Tears were streaming down the face of the clown as he explained brokenly, "Holy Mother, have mercy on me, I have killed a man! I didn't mean to, I only wanted to stop him throwing the knife at you, Benno. Lord forgive me, I have ended the life of a man, I've killed him!"

Ben touched the big throwing knife with his foot; it fell from the assassin's hand. He picked it up and threw it overboard. "But you saved my life, friend."

Mummo stared at the body blankly. "Look, he's dead, and I ended his life. I've never killed anything before, not even a rabbit or a fish!"

Ben latched his arm around the clown's quaking shoulders and drew him upright, explaining gently to him, "Hush now, this is no time for sorrow or guilt. That man was going to murder me, but you did a brave thing, you saved my life. Would you rather that I was lying dead with that knife in me, or that he is lying here, dead by accident?"

Ned interjected a thought. "Tell him he saved my life, too, that villain has another knife, see. I bet that was meant for me. Good old Mummo, well done, sir, that's what I say!"

The clown straightened his shoulders, drawing a sleeve quickly across his eyes and nose. "*Sì!* You are right, my friend, this fellow was a murderer. If I hadn't stopped him you'd be dead now."

Ben patted Mummo's back. "Right! Now let's get rid of him before anybody comes. You take the feet, and I'll get his arms. Luckily he wasn't as big as Bomba."

Between them they lugged Abrit up to the rail and slid him over. He made only a slight splash.

Ned sent out a quick, urgent message. "Look out, someone's coming!"

Ben picked up the belaying pin. Winking at Mummo, he spoke aloud. "See, I told you this isn't the same as your Indian clubs!"

The clown glanced over Ben's shoulder at the approaching steersman, who was yawning and rubbing his eyes. He had obviously been napping on duty. Mummo returned Ben's wink.

"Look, these things are the same as my clubs, pass me two more and I'll show you how to juggle with them!"

The steersman pushed Mummo aside and snatched the belaying pin from Ben. He scowled at them sourly. "That's a piece of ship's equipment, not a toy. Get out of my sight, both of you, and take that flea-bitten cur, too. Huh, playing games in the middle of the night like two idiot children. Got no beds to go to, eh?"

Mumbling excuses they climbed the steps, up to the fo'c'sle deck. Mummo sat on the blankets with Ben and Ned. He was still shaking with shock, but manfully trying to bring himself under control. He patted Ned and smiled nervously at Ben.

"Do you think the steersman noticed anything, Benno?"

The boy gripped the clown's hand firmly, giving him reassurance. "No, no, if he'd seen us tossing the killer overboard he'd have raised the alarm straightaway. Put it all out of your mind, just remember that you were very brave back there."

Mummo nodded gratefully. "Thank you, my friend, you are both good fellows, you and Neddo. I'll stay up here with you tonight, we'll take turns to guard each other."

Ben agreed willingly. "Good idea. I'll take the first hour."

The clown stretched out next to Ned. "I wonder why he wanted to kill you, Benno?"

The boy shrugged. "That man had no reason, he was a complete stranger to me. But I think that somebody paid him to do the deed—pity we didn't have time to search his pockets."

Mummo closed his eyes and lay back. "That makes sense. Still, I'd like to know who it was."

Ben scratched his head. "Aye, so would I!" he lied.

Ned opened one eye as he transmitted a thought. "Huh, I'll bet my tail that his name began with a *B*!"

THE FOLLOWING MORNING BEN SAW BOMBA COME UP on deck. He watched surprise register on the slave driver's face as he saw his intended victim still alive. The big man looked for a moment as if he was going to kill Ben on the spot, personally. Bomba turned, going back into the stern accommodation.

Gradually the ship came alive, with crewmen going about their duties. The troupe joined Ben and Ned on the fo'c'sle deck.

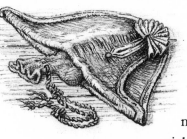

Otto began his daily exercise routine, remarking to Mummo, "So, you are no longer sick, Herr Mummo?"

The clown feigned astonishment. "What gave you the idea I was sick, Otto? I only came out on deck to escape the odour of your fiendish moustache lotion."

Signore Rizzoli raised an eyebrow. "Have you breakfasted yet?"

Ben came to Mummo's defence. "No, he hasn't, but he's ready for it, just like me and Ned, aren't you, Mummo? Come on, let's see what the cook is serving in the galley. The rest of you stay put, we'll get breakfast for you today."

Ned stayed with the troupe, placing his chin in Serafina's lap as Ben and Mummo hastened off.

"Aye, there's a good pair of fellows, go and fetch us beautiful ones some food. Step lively now, we're hungry!"

Ben's parting reply flashed through his mind. "Beautiful ones indeed, you great lolloping hound!"

The dog was about to reply when Serafina patted him.

"Come on, Ned, let's go and pay Poppea a visit!"

A fragrant aroma of roasting meat and spices emanated from the galley. Mummo joined the line of men in the alleyway waiting to be served. Ben chose to stay outside. He went to a canvas spread upon a hatch cover, where a steward was serving drinks and fruit. The boy selected a few oranges, a large melon and a pitcher of sherbet. Intentionally, Ben positioned himself behind Bomba and Ghigno, eavesdropping on their conversation. The Corsair was being rather curt with the slave driver.

"Why were you questioning my steersman about Abrit, eh?"

Bomba tried to keep his reply casual. "Oh, no reason, it's just that I haven't seen him around this morning."

Ghigno was not satisfied with this answer. "Abrit isn't your servant. The crew of this ship are under my command, not yours. So, what did you want with him?"

Bomba blustered under the scar-faced one's interrogation. "Er, er, Abrit owed me some money."

Ghigno treated him to a withering look. "What money, how much, tell me."

The big man looked at the sky, as though he were trying to recall the sum. "Er, it was three gold pieces, I think."

Ghigno obviously enjoyed goading Bomba, he continued sneeringly. "Three gold pieces you think? Hah, when was the last time you owned three gold pieces—in fact, when did you ever loan anything to anyone, son of a motherless thief? Go on about your business and leave my crew alone, or I'll lend you half the blade of my sword in your fat gut, you spawn of a camel tick!"

Catching Ben's smothered guffaw, Ghigno turned on him. "Have you nothing better to do than spy on men talking? Get out of my sight, infidel brother of a black dog!"

Ben joined Serafina and Ned on the forepeak, sitting out above the bow wave. The food was good, spiced roast lamb with rice and fruit. He watched the beautiful black girl as she ate and chatted.

"They don't let you roam about this ship as you like. Do you know, we were hemmed in, Ned and I, by four guards when we went to see Poppea. They wouldn't answer any questions or let us put a step out of place. It's as if they're hiding something from us."

Ben did not want to upset the girl by talking about Al Misurata's business. He tossed melon rind into the sea. "So, how is Poppea? Well, I hope?"

Serafina showed her flawless white teeth smilingly. "Oh, she's living the life of a queen, with lovely food, and four fine Arab horses for company!"

Ben ignored Ned's paw, which was prodding his back. "That's good, I'm glad she's happy."

Now the black Labrador's message entered his mind, accompanied by more paw prods. "Ship ahoy, mate, off the starboard bow, headed this way!"

Ben grasped a line and stood up on the bowsprit, his blue-grey eyes watching the approaching vessel as he exchanged thoughts with Ned. "She's a big ship, flying the Spanish flag, I think."

The Labrador jumped up beside him. "Dog's eyes are the best, let me take a look. Hah, I see officers standing on the bridge, and those sailors in the rigging, they're dressed in uniform issue. Y'know, if I'm right, that's a naval craft. What d'you think, mate?"

Ben felt hope surging through him. "Marvellous, Ned! It looks like she's going to lay alongside of us. At last! If I can get to the captain, or an officer, I'll expose Al Misurata as a slaver. This could be the saving of us and the troupe. Come on, let's go down to the midship deck!"

He turned to Serafina. "Excuse me, I have to attend to something!"

The pair hurried off, leaving behind them a slightly perplexed girl.

The *Santa Veronica del Mar* halted three shiplengths from the *Sea Djinn*. Like most Spanish men-o'-war, she was impressively large, bristling with cannon and ornate superstructure. Al Misurata appeared on the afterdeck, richly clad in flowing blue and emerald silks. Ben was surprised that the pirate showed no apprehension at being accosted by the Spanish navy. He gave no orders to run or fight. Highly unusual for one who plied his trade. Ned had his nose through the rails, watching the approaching ship.

"Look, they're lowering a boat, Ben, there's the captain and two officers getting into it. What's your plan, mate?"

The boy thrust out his jaw resolutely. "The first chance I get, I'm going to have a word with the captain, or one of those officers. Wait'll I tell them about what Misurata's up to, that should set the cat among the pigeons!"

The black Labrador wagged his tail furiously. "Hoho, I'll wager it will. I can't wait to see old Al Miserable, and Bomba, and that scar-faced rogue, led off in chains to a slaver's reward. I hope the authorities have a nice, damp, gloomy cell waiting for 'em!"

The jollyboat hove alongside, allowing the visitors to be assisted aboard the *Sea Djinn*. The captain stepped aboard, flanked by his aides.

Ben dashed forward, calling out urgently in Spanish, "*Capitano*, I must speak with you, señor!"

The captain, a tall, slender, grey-haired man with an elegant bearing, stared down his aquiline nose at the strange towhaired boy, then swept past on his way to the stern deck. Ben tried to follow, but he was tripped from behind by Ghigno. Ned leaped forward. He was in midair when a cruel kick from Bomba sent him through the rails, splashing into the sea.

Laughing, the Spanish sailors pulled the dog into the jollyboat. A burly bosun lifted Ned, heaving him back aboard the *Sea Djinn*.

"Not a good place to jump ship, you silly old seadog, out here days from land!"

Ben lay on the deck, clutching the soaking dog to him. The

opportunity had been lost. He felt foolish, surrounded by Bomba, Ghigno and several crewmen. Serafina pushed her way through to Ben. One of the crewmen tried to stop her, but she evaded him.

Ghigno warned her, "Get back to the fo'c'sle deck, girl!"

She ignored him and helped Ben up, whispering to him, "Ben, what's the matter, are you hurt?"

He rubbed his shin, where it had struck the coaming. "You shouldn't be here, get back to the troupe right now. Leave me alone, I can handle this. Now go!"

Stunned by his sharp rebuke, Serafina hurried off.

Al Misurata bowed to his visitor. "Capitano Mira, a pleasure to meet you again. Allow me to offer you some refreshment in my cabin."

Removing his high-sided hat and stowing it beneath one arm, the captain signalled his two officers to stop on deck. "Thank you kindly, señor, please lead on!"

Ned shook himself vigorously as he watched the two men go into the cabin. "Hah, there's something odd going on here, they know each other well. Maybe you'd have been better off holding your tongue, mate?"

Ben's clouded eyes watched the cabin door close. "Maybe so, Ned, we'll just have to wait and see."

It was not a long visit. Shortly thereafter, Al Misurata and Captain Mira emerged from the cabin. The Spaniard wiped his lips delicately with a lace kerchief, which he stowed into his brocaded sleeve. Still with his hat under one arm, he bowed briefly. "A delightful meeting, Señor Misurata, but alas I have duties at Cadiz which cannot be delayed further. Adios, my friend, and may success attend your voyage."

Al Misurata touched fingertips to his heart, lips and forehead, bowing in a dignified manner. "You grace my humble vessel with your presence, *Capitano*. My apologies for the boy, he is troubled in the brain. Good-bye, and may fair winds be ever at your back."

The two officers fell in behind their captain as he descended to the jollyboat amidships.

Bomba placed himself in front of Ben, blocking access to the Spaniard, but the captain gestured him aside. He spoke patronisingly to the boy, patting his cheek gently.

"You speak Spanish very well, for one who is weak in the head!"

Ben's heart sank as he saw the chamois bag and heard the gold clink. It was in the man's hat; the captain bent his head swiftly and donned it. Without another word, he stepped into the boat.

Ned gave himself a final shake, he was disgusted. "A bribe, eh, payment in gold for his silence. I thought so. That captain is as bad as Al Miserable!"

Al Misurata leaned over the stern gallery. He caught Ben's eye and shrugged mockingly. "Well, who did you expect him to listen to—the Lord of Misurata, or a feeble-minded infidel brat?"

When Ben made his way back to his friends on the fo'c'sle deck, he found his woes were increased. Serafina brushed past him and went to sit in her cabin. Formerly she had been very friendly and close to him. However, he guessed by her expression that she did not want to talk to him. He looked around at

the others, but they averted their eyes. All except La Lindi, who
gave forth a deep, bubbling laugh, and came over to sit by him.

"So, what have you done to upset our Serafina, eh?"

Ben stared at her blankly. "Me, upset Serafina, why should
I do such a thing?"

La Lindi shrugged. "I don't know, boy, but if you haven't
upset her, why is she avoiding you, and walking round with a
face that would bring bad weather?"

Mamma Rizzoli looked up from darning a shirt. "You must
have said something hurtful to her."

Ben spread his arms appealingly. "I'd never do that!"

Augusto Rizzoli smiled at Ben's wobegone face. "Poor
Benno, you have much to learn about the ladies." Tuning the
heads on his mandolin, he began singing.

> "O who knows the mind of a lady,
> alas I am nought but a man,
> and a lady's a beautiful puzzle,
> so please tell me now if you can,
> why when she says never it's maybe,
> though often her yes is a no,
> and her no is a yes, which could be more or less,
> so how's a poor fellow to know?
> Yes, who knows the mind of a woman,
> just give me a lifetime or so,
> and I'll find out why her lips say come,
> when her eyes are telling me go.
> She's the only one who can explain it,
> I care not what any man thinks,
> but if you wish to know, then you'll just have to go
> off to Egypt to question the Sphinx!"

Ben sighed ruefully. "Well, if I've got a lot to learn about ladies, that song wasn't much help, signore."

Always the clown, Buffo put on a tragic face, staggering about with one hand clasped to his heart, and the other held out trembling, as he sobbed in mock grief. "My mind will not rest! My lips will not let food pass them! Cast a single white rose upon my grave! I die for love! Ah, the sweet agony of it all, my friends, *addio*!"* He collapsed in a heap upon a coil of rope, but sprang up smartly when Mamma jabbed his bottom with her darning needle. She levelled a stern finger at her husband and the clown.

"Shame on you both for tormenting the boy, were you never young yourselves?"

For the rest of that day Ben sat alone in the bows, moping, whilst Serafina kept to her cabin. At one point, just before evening, he looked about, noticing that he had not seen Ned for hours.

Towards sunset, Otto came ambling along. He placed a hefty hand on Ben's shoulder. "Come and eat, my friend. Everything will turn out for the best, you'll see. It is not good for one so young to sit brooding over a maiden's frown."

Ben stared out at the last fiery remnants of the sun sinking below the horizon. "I'm alright, Otto, you go along. I may join you later." The desire for food had left Ben. Wrapping himself in a blanket, he lay down and slept.

Sometime during the night a cold, wet nose nuzzling his cheek aroused Ben. It was Ned. The boy sat up. "Oh, you're

Addio (good-bye).

back, thanks for your support and company to me, mate. Where've you been all day?"

The black Labrador gave him what passed for a lolloping grin. "Oh, just round and about, y'know, gathering information that could help you. Hah, you'd be surprised at what I've heard. I'm a pretty good listener!"

Ben yawned. "Go on then, surprise me."

Ned recounted his exploits. "Well, after you fell asleep, Serafina came out for supper. I sat with her on the fo'c'sle steps, just the two of us. After awhile she began talking to me, sort of telling me her troubles. Do you know why she was angry with you?"

Ben replied eagerly. "No, tell me!"

The dog explained. "After Ghigno tripped you this morning, she ran to help you, but you spoke sharply to her. I saw it myself, Ben, you were very short with the girl, though she was only trying to help you."

The boy shrugged. "Huh, was that all? I was trying to get her out of harm's way. Men like Ghigno and Bomba don't care who they kick out at, it wasn't safe for her to be there."

Ned shook his head. "But you never apologised later, that was what really hurt Serafina. She's never shouted at you. As far as I can see that girl has always tried to be your friend. She never expected you to act like that toward her."

Ben had been reliving the scene in his mind. Now the truth of it dawned on him. He ruffled Ned's ears warmly. "My good old mate! Thanks for telling me, I'll make it up to her first thing tomorrow."

The dog allowed himself to be patted before he continued. "Ah, but that isn't all. I heard another conversation this afternoon, while you were sitting up here wanting to be alone. It was between Ghigno and Bomba."

Ben felt suddenly apprehensive. "Go on, what did they say?"

The dog paused. "The news isn't good, mate. I was lying in the shade under the steps when those two blackguards came along. They leaned on the midship rails, talking together. So I listened in—they never even noticed me. Ghigno was saying that you were a danger to them, because you knew too much. He said, if that captain today had been a stranger, and listened to you, then they would all have their necks in a noose. Bomba agreed with him, but said that Al Misurata said you weren't to be harmed. The scar-faced one wasn't too pleased at that. He said that Misurata was putting them at risk through his greed for gold. Bomba's head was bobbing up and down like a pigeon pecking corn. He felt that you would get to someone who would take notice of your accusations, and what then? After all, it was a long journey to where they were bound, and who could stand guard over an infidel boy who was so clever and devious?"

Ben took hold of Ned's paw. "So what did they decide?"

The dog's answer came as no surprise to him. "By tomorrow night we should make Valleta harbour at Malta. Now I don't know the exact details, but that's where we're both going to be murdered and tossed into the sea. The sharks should take care of our bodies. All Ghigno has to do is to tell Al Misurata that we've escaped and gone ashore."

Ben looked grim. "Aye, that would work for them. Al Misurata could only stop for so long to have the island searched, then he'd have to leave. Very crafty, mate, nobody would ever be sure what really happened to us."

Ned placed his head in Ben's lap. "Poor old us, served up as shark stew just for being too knowledgeable. So, when do we jump ship?"

Ben answered promptly. "First chance we get as soon as we sight land. We'll have to take our chances quickly."

The dog raised his eyebrows. "Without a word to anyone, I suppose. It won't do your romance much good, mate, going off without so much as a fond farewell to that lovely girl."

Ben nodded. "She'll understand in time, I hope."

Next morning, Ben was up as dawn spread over the Mediterranean Sea. He saw Otto come out on deck and start his exercise routine. Then Serafina emerged from her cabin, calling to the strongman.

"When you've finished we'll go and get breakfast for the troupe."

Ben hastened to her side. "Leave Otto to his training. We'll go and fetch the food, you and I."

Ned sent the boy a thought. "That's the stuff, I'll stop here with Otto and allow you to make up."

They descended the steps in an awkward silence, then Ben turned and found his tongue running away with him. "Serafina, about yesterday, I'm sorry I spoke sharply to you but I wanted to get you away, to save you being hurt by Bomba and Ghigno. I didn't mind being knocked about a bit but I couldn't bear the thought of anybody trying to hurt you. But I had no time to explain gently, so I spoke harshly and I didn't get a chance to apologise later, you looked so cold and distant, you went into the cabin, and I couldn't follow you inside . . . and . . . and . . . I'm sorry!"

The girl covered her mouth, stifling the laughter that was bubbling out. Ben stared at her, nonplussed.

"What?"

"Oh, haha . . . oh, I'm sorry . . . Hahaha! Poor Ben, standing there gabbling away with your cheeks as red as tomatoes. How could I not forgive you, my friend? But can you forgive me? Flouncing off with my lip pouting, when all you were trying to do was to protect me. It was a silly thing for me to do."

Ben looked at the deck. "You could never do anything silly, Serafina. Are we still friends?"

She took his hand and squeezed it lightly. "Of course. Come on, let's get some breakfast for the starving players."

They walked hand in hand to the galley, though Ben could not feel the deck beneath his feet, and his heart was singing.

They set all the food on a piece of planking and carried it between them. Before they reached the steps Ghigno stepped out, barring the way. The awful scar made his face crease into a sardonic sneer as he stepped aside and did a flourishing bow.

"Good morning to you, pretty miss, and you, young sir!"

They passed by him in silence. At the top of the steps, Serafina turned to see Ghigno enter the galley.

"I wonder what made him do that?"

Ben shook his head. "Probably the sight of us made him feel unusually happy, what d'you think?"

Serafina reflected. "Hmm, perhaps it did, though I couldn't imagine the sight of him would make anybody unusually happy, not even his mother!"

Simultaneously the two young people took a fit of laughing.

Ned bounded around them, wagging his tail as he contacted Ben. "Well, thank goodness you two are happy again. Hurry up with that breakfast, please, there's a poor, starving dog aboard."

The infectious laughter had Buffo up cavorting about the deck. A wide grin split the clown's face as he danced around Ben and Serafina, strewing petals from an imaginary basket of flowers.

"The young lovers are joyfully reunited once again! I hear harps and violins, birds twittering and fish leaping gaily from the sea! No longer is my heart broken!" He tripped, and would have tumbled over the for'ard rail.

Luckily, Otto was nearby and hauled him back by the seat of his trousers. "Ach, your silly neck will be broken if you prance about like that much more. Sit still now, Herr Buffo!"

After breakfast Serafina went off to visit Poppea, whilst Ben and Ned sat on the fo'c'sle steps, discussing their escape. Ben watched Ghigno, Bomba and three crewmen, who were obviously meant to feature in their murderous plans.

"They're watching our every move, Ned, it's going to be hard for us to slip away unnoticed."

The black Labrador began grooming himself. "We'll just have to distract their attention when the time comes. Surely we can think of something."

Ben kept the men under observation as he replied. "That's a good idea, mate, create a diversion. But how?"

The dog raised a paw to scratch the back of his ear. "Patience, m'boy, let me think!"

Scarcely an hour later, a lookout with a spyglass cried out from the main topmast, "Land ahoy off the starboard peak!"

The two friends went up into the prow. Ben shaded his

eyes, peering ahead at the grey smudge on the horizon. He felt the *Sea Djinn* shift as the steersman took her bow on to the island of Malta.

"If we want to stay alive we'd better think of something fast, Ned!"

Book Two

A
DANGEROUS
FREEDOM

NINETY-THREE KILOMETRES SOUTH OF SICILY.
THE ISLAND OF MALTA.

A STIFF BREEZE WAFTED THE *SEA DJINN* INTO MALTESE
waters late that evening. The darkened waves, slightly choppy,
reflected waterfront tavern lights. Other ships showed stern

and bow lights as they lay at anchor or stood
moored to the quay in the harbour of Valletta. As
sometimes happens, the night temperature had
dropped, leaving the air rather chilled. The Rizzoli Troupe stopped in their cabins, but Ben and
Ned stayed up on the fo'c'sle deck. Serafina
brought them extra blankets. No sooner had she
delivered them and gone back inside, than
the boy and his dog went into action.
Ben knew they were being
watched by their enemies, so
he took extra care whilst rigging the diversion which he and
Ned had planned.

Standing with his back against the
foremast, Ben felt behind his back until

he touched the stout length of hempen rope which ran up the rear of the mast to a pulley right at the top. There the rope was secured to the long mainspar of the huge sail billowing out over the vessel's bow. The sail could be raised or lowered only by this line. Ben felt the curving iron cleats around which the remainder of it was wound. It would take fully seven or eight sailors to hoist or lower the big sail on this rope.

Whilst Ned kept watch at the top of the fo'c'sle steps, Ben began sawing at the tough cord with a sharp knife, which his dog had taken from the galley. Making as little movement as possible, the boy tried to appear as if he was merely leaning against the mast, though behind his back he was pushing the blade back and forth across the thick rope. Ned sent him an enquiry.

"How's it going back there, mate, having any trouble?"

Ben tried not to grimace as he exerted pressure on the blade. "The hard part is trying to keep my body still. But this rope's as tight as a fiddle string, so it's cutting through pretty well. Won't be long now. When I cough, get ready to move."

Gripping the knife hard, Ben continued sawing away, feeling the bushy fibres brushing against his wrists as the rope began to part. On the other side of the mast the big red sail towered over the fo'c'sle deck, straining against the breeze, as taut as a drumskin. Ben heard the rope creak drily. This was what he had been waiting for! Stowing the knife in the back of his belt, he coughed aloud, moving away from the mast.

Ned turned and barked defiantly at him, then bounded off down the steps. Ben ran to the top of the steps, calling angrily, "Stay, Ned, stay!"

The black Labrador nipped at a passing sailor and ran

down the lower deck barking. Ben came running down the steps after him, shouting commands.

"I said stay! Stop right there, Ned! D'you hear me?"

Gaining the steps to the stern deck, the dog raced up them and poked his head between the gallery rails, barking and snarling disobediently.

Crewmen left off their tasks, laughing at the infidel boy as he yelled at his dog.

"Come back here now! Bad dog, come here, Ned!"

The breeze halted for an instant, then it renewed; the sail slacked momentarily, then bellied forward. Under the sudden pressure, the rope's last strands parted, and the huge sail came toppling down. It came with such a flapping and rattling of rigging that it caught the attention of every man on deck. Cracking like a whiplash end, the severed rope flew upward. Jumping through the eye of the pulley block, it snaked out and down, following the confusion of sailcloth, spar and rigging. The entire thing crashed clumsily over the bowside and began sinking into the sea.

The steersman quickly lashed the wheel steady and ran for'ard, roaring, "Foresail down! Foresail down! All hands to the fo'c'sle deck!"

The *Sea Djinn* began yawing in an arc to port as crewmen leapt up the fo'c'sle steps to help rescue the big foresail. Ben and Ned crouched behind a capstan on the stern deck, watching the whole thing. They saw Ghigno and Al Misurata, both still holding glasses of wine, staggering out to stand not five paces from where they lay hidden. The pirate peered blearily toward the bows.

"What's going on up there?"

Ghigno groaned. "Looks like the foresail has broken loose!"

Al Misurata knocked the glass from the Corsair's hand. "Well, don't stand there, get up for'ard and see they fix it back right. And tell someone to drop the anchor, we don't want that sail trapped under our bows. Hurry!" He watched Ghigno dash off, then shuddered as the keen breeze pierced his silken garments. Draining the goblet, he flung it into the sea and stormed back inside to the warmth of his cabin.

Ned's paw nudged Ben. "Time to abandon ship—let's go swimming, mate!"

They hit the water with a splash which went unnoticed in the confusion at the vessel's other end. Ben felt himself plummeting downward into Stygian blackness with bubbles rushing by his ears. Then there was silence as he hung suspended, fathoms down in the sea's cold, dark realms. Scenes of the *Flying Dutchman,* wallowing in the icy ocean off Tierra del Fuego, flashed through his mind. Screaming men, frostbitten faces, tattered rigging and groaning timbers stricken by mountainous waves. Vanderdecken lashed to the wheel as he shook clenched fists at the storm-bruised skies, damning his crew, cursing the ship and bellowing oaths at heaven, at the very Lord who had made him.

Then Ned's urgent call cut through it all. "Ben, where are you, mate? Ben!"

Dragged back from his horrific memories, the boy struck upward for the surface, his legs and arms moving like pistons. He surfaced, gasping for air, to find himself facing the black Labrador, who was treading water alongside the rudder at the *Sea Djinn*'s stern. Grabbing on to a line hanging from some rope fenders, Ben allowed Ned to cling to his shoulders. They hung there, regaining breath and listening to the voices from on deck.

"Ahmed, hook that rope. Have you got it? Ali, Razul, help him. Now all together. Pull!"

It sounded like Ghigno giving the orders. Then they heard Bomba. "Look at the end of this rope—it's been cut!"

There was a brief silence, followed by Ghigno shouting. "Where's that brat and his hound? Where are they?"

This was followed by the sounds of running feet.

Ben sent Ned a thought. "I never allowed for this, they're searching for us. We'd better stay put under here, they'd spot us if we tried swimming out into the open."

Ned's reply registered in his mind. "It's cold here, but I'll stick it out with you, mate. We'll probably have to wait an hour or two, though."

Now they heard Bomba's voice again. "They're not in the cabins, I've searched!"

Serafina's plaintive call cut through Ben like a knife. "Ben, where are you? Ben! Ned! What have you done with them?"

Ghigno's irate snarl followed her plea. "Done? We haven't done anything, girl. See this mess, this whole sail, that broken spar and all that tangled rigging my crew are trying to salvage from the water? Well, they did this, I'm sure of it! I'll skin them alive when I catch them! Go on, get back to your cabins, all of you!"

Placing Serafina behind him, Otto faced the angry Corsair. "We will stay here on deck, to make sure nothing happens to the boy and his dog!"

Ghigno sneered at the strongman. "You'll do as I say, you big ox, unless you want to stop here and argue with musket balls. Guards!"

Al Misurata's men hurried for'ard, carrying their long rifles.

Signore Rizzoli cautioned his troupe, "Do as he says, friends, we cannot argue with armed men!"

Treading water beneath the stern, Ben and Ned heard the alleyway door slam as the guards locked the Rizzoli Troupe away.

Al Misurata joined Bomba and Ghigno. Once he had apprised himself of the situation, he began issuing orders. "Drop anchor here, out in the bay. If they're not aboard the ship, then they're in the water. They won't get far. Bomba, you see to salvaging the sail with the crew. Ghigno, spread my guards at the rails from stem to stern. We'll fire some rockets out over the bay—give my men orders to shoot them on sight, the boy knows too much to be left alive now. Keep the others in their cabins, don't allow them out. We'll rig the foresail up tomorrow and sail into port. I'll be in my cabin. Keep me informed."

Ned peered at Ben in the darkness. "Well, there's no going back now, mate, we've really done it this time. Whoo! Look at that!"

The boy backed water, pulling them both in close to the ship's hull as the rockets were discharged. Incandescent plumes of white fire burst over the waters, illuminating everything briefly. Then they sputtered and fell hissing into the bay. More rockets went up.

Two guards, leaning over the stern gallery, sighted their long musket barrels out, sweeping them back and forth. Ben heard one speaking.

"Do you think there'll be a reward for whoever hits them?"

His companion in arms muttered grimly, "I don't know, but I wager there'll be trouble if they aren't spotted and killed."

A voice broke in on them. It was Ghigno. "Stop gossiping and pay attention to your duties!"

One of the guards replied, "Aye, Captain, though it's not much use lookin' out to sea for the boy and the dog. If they were swimmin' for it, surely they'd be headed for land?"

Ghigno nodded. "You're right, but the master is giving the orders, we're not here to argue. They'll be running out of rockets soon, but he's told me you must stay at your posts."

The other guard spoke hopefully. "Will we be going in to land then?"

Ghigno sounded tired. "No, we're anchoring out here. Tomorrow I'll be taking her in, though not with all our sails. Bomba told me they only recovered half of the top spar, it broke in two when it fell. I'll have to wait until we're docked to have it fixed and rigged properly."

He wandered off, leaving the two guards at the stern. Soon the rockets ceased, and they put up their rifles. Sitting on the stern deck they eased their vigilance.

Ned's paw pressed against Ben's shoulder. "Stay here, mate, I've got an idea!" The dog began paddling silently away.

Ben called to him mentally. "Ned, where are you going? I'll come, too!"

His friend returned the thought. "No, Ben, stay put, a black dog in the sea at night is harder to spot than a boy and a black dog. I'm going to get that broken spar—it's our only chance. Trust me!"

Ben had no other choice; he knew what Ned said was true. He clung to the fender rope, his mind harking back to a century ago.*

* See *Castaways of the Flying Dutchman.*

A ship's timber had saved their life then, when they were swept overboard from the ill-fated *Flying Dutchman,* into the icy seas off Tierra del Fuego. Ned had dragged him, half-conscious, onto a spar which had fallen from the vessel. They had both drifted to shore, clinging to it. Good old Ned—Ben knew with a certainty that there had never been another dog like him, before or since.

The smooth end of the spar brushed against Ben's back as Ned's voice took his attention. "Ahoy, shipmate, one seadog coming in on your stern!"

The boy gripped onto the rope-tangled timber. "Well done, mate. It's a stout old piece of wood, sure enough. Are the guards still watching up there?"

The black Labrador scoffed. "Still watching? Listen, I've just paddled underneath their very noses and pushed this thing the length of the ship, and not one of 'em noticed. If you look up, you'll see the legs of those two above us, dangling through the gallery rails. Not a pretty sight, I'll grant you, but they're both snoring!"

Ben grinned. "Good, the angel's on our side tonight. What we'll do is, we'll swim out to sea a bit behind this spar, say six shiplengths away. Then we'll strike out in a curve toward the island. If anyone is still awake and watching, they'll be looking the other way. Right, I'm ready, are you?"

Keeping the spar between themselves and the *Sea Djinn,* they back-paddled away, toward the open sea. Ben was glad of the exercise—it took the numbness from his limbs. Ned gripped a rope between his teeth, doggy paddling away carefully, trying not to splash. He gave Ben the benefit of his opinion as to their progress.

"We're doing well, the tide's on the turn. Get a bit further out, then we'll run into land on the flood, it'll save a lot of paddling."

Ben flicked matted hair from his eyes. "Let's hope so, we don't want to be caught out in open water once it's daylight. What I wouldn't give to be on warm, dry land right now!"

The black Labrador mused, "Me, too, mate. Hmmm, I wonder if there's any sharks around here?"

Ben shot him a glare. "Thanks for that comforting thought!"

Al Misurata felt restless. Sleep was eluding him, so he left his cabin and went for a turn around the deck. Bomba lay snuggled beneath the stern steps. The irate pirate kicked him into wakefulness. "Fat slug, why aren't you out on watch?"

The big slaver driver protested. "But, Master, you told me to take care of the fallen sail. I've had it hauled back aboard, there's nothing can be done now until we're in port. Ghigno was supposed to be in charge of the watch."

He quailed under Al Misurata's look of cold command.

"Don't talk back to me, you bloated bazaar rat. You'll never live to be half the man Ghigno is. Now get looking for that boy and the dog. Move yourself!"

A vicious kick sent Bomba scurrying off. Aggrieved by the harsh treatment he had received, Bomba took up a tarred rope's end. He vented his ire upon any guards he caught sleeping on duty. The pair who were slumped against the stern rail were rudely awakened as he thwacked the knotted rope on their heads.

"Sons of she-camels, is this how you keep watch? Up, straighten up, and see to those jezzails. That boy could be splashing about under your noses for all you clods care!"

He strode off, leaving the two guards peering down their rifle barrels and grumbling resentfully.

"Huh, who does he think he is? Ghigno or the Master give us our orders, not that greasy slave driver!"

The other one agreed. "Aye, but we'd have got worse than a whack with a rope's end if Ghigno or Al Misurata would've caught us napping, so keep your eyes open. Anyhow, it's starting to get light now. Look! What's that over there?"

The first guard followed the direction in which his companion's finger was pointing. He lifted his musket, clicking back the flintlock as he took aim. "Let's see, shall we?"

Ben felt the impact as the lead ball drove deep into the spar, a fraction from his index finger. "Keep down, Ned, somebody's firing at us!"

A crack sounded out from the *Sea Djinn,* and another ball ploughed into the floating timber. The dog chanced a swift glance at the ship, then ducked his head.

"Surely they can't see us from there. Maybe they're just having a bit of target practice, to while away the time?"

A clamour broke out aboard the *Sea Djinn* as crewmen and guards came running to the stern, bent on discovering what the two shooters were firing at. Al Misurata and Ghigno hurried to the scene, elbowing bodies aside. The pirate confronted the two sheepish-looking guards.

"Did you see the boy and the dog, did you get them?"

One man bowed. "No, Lord, we were firing at that thing out there."

Ghigno peered into the gathering dawn. "What, you mean that? It doesn't look like a boy or a dog swimming round out there, does it?"

"No, Captain," they murmured in unison.

The Corsair stood, arms akimbo, viewing them scathingly. "Well, does it?"

They shook their heads as they repeated, "No, Captain."

Bomba, who had been watching from the sidelines, spoke out sarcastically. "That's because it's a piece of wood, half of the topmast spar which broke off when the sail fell."

Al Misurata stared Bomba into silence, before turning to both guards. "So, you shot a piece of driftwood, well done! Ghigno, teach these two idiots a lesson!"

The scar-faced Corsair grabbed the rope's end from Bomba and laid into the hapless pair. Not bothering to watch them being punished, Al Misurata turned to the steersman.

"Give the order to hoist anchor and sails, we'll ride in on the flood. Bomba, come here!"

The big man hurried forward apprehensively.

Al Misurata pointed to the floating spar, which was a fair distance off now, and headed smoothly toward the point, to the left side of Valletta harbour.

"Just refresh my memory—that is the spar which came from this ship, is it not?"

The slave driver nodded. "Aye, Lord."

The pirate leaned on the rail, his eyes never leaving the drifting length of timber. "Then why is it not floating alongside the ship? Why is it far away, out there?"

Bomba was stuck for an answer, so Al Misurata continued. "We can't overtake it right now, but you take my spyglass. Stop here and watch it. As soon as it touches land let me know. You can take four guards when we make port. Hurry to where the spar is, I'd like to know how it drifted off so far and got to the island faster than my ship. Was something pushing it along?"

Recognition spread across Bomba's face suddenly. "Lord, you mean . . ."

The pirate shook his head pityingly. "You'll only get a headache from trying to think, idiot! Just carry out my orders. Malta is a small island, they can't get far, you'll see."

LIKE A GLORIOUS BENEDICTION, THE MIDMORNING sun smiled down on the island of Malta and the sea surrounding it. The boy and his dog abandoned their broken spar and waded ashore through sunwarmed shallows. Ben threw himself down on the sand, watching Ned shaking himself furiously. It was not a very wide beach, mainly sand, gravel and boulders, with cliffs towering high in the background. A small crab scuttled to one side as Ned flopped down gratefully. Blocking its escape with a curved paw, the dog lectured it.

"Ah, land! Beautiful terra firma! You don't know how lucky you are, little shellback. Living here among the rocks and seaweed, with nice pools to play in, never having to go out on the high seas. I think I may just stay here with you and become a crabdog."

Ben interrupted Ned's canine reverie. "Well, that's all very cosy, mate, but I think we'd better get moving in case we've been spotted from the ship."

The black Labrador rose, grumbling. "'Tis a hard and weary life for the good and virtuous. Righto, we go to the left, away from the harbour area, I presume."

Ben chuckled. "You presume right, O wise one. Let's stick to the coastline awhile, and keep your eye out for food."

They strode off together, with the dog still ruminating. "Food, don't mention it. Can you hear my stomach gurgling? It's reminding me of breakfast this morning, or the absence of it!"

The *Sea Djinn* still had some short distance to sail before she made land. Al Misurata was dressing to go ashore when Bomba came running into the cabin, brandishing the still open telescope.

"I saw them, they got to shore about half a mile to the left of the harbour. It was them, the infidel and his cur!"

The pirate was adjusting a dark blue turban in the mirror. He spoke to the big slave driver's reflection without turning. "If you break my spyglass I will break your worthless neck. Which way did they go?"

Bomba folded the telescope gingerly, placing it on the table. "To the left, Master, away from the harbour. I came right away to tell you, as you ordered me to."

Al Misurata fixed a yellow topaz pin in the turban folds. "We'll be docking shortly. Ghigno will arrange the mast repairs. You take four guards with rifles and hunt them down. I will be taking to the clifftops on horseback, to make sure they don't cut inland. And Bomba, I want no mistakes this time—weight the bodies with stones and sink them in the sea. Understood?"

Bomba bowed his head dutifully. "Your wish is my command, I live only to serve you, Lord!"

La Lindi left the guards who had been posted at the alleyway entrance. She hurried into the cabin, where the Rizzoli Troupe sat waiting on what she had heard. The enigmatic black snake dancer murmured swiftly, "They got away, Ben and Ned escaped and made it to the shore. The guards said they used the broken sail spar to do it. So you see, Serafina, there was no need for all that weeping. Those shots we heard didn't hit them."

Wiping her eyes on the edge of her scarf, the beautiful young girl broke out crying afresh, though this time it was tears of joy and relief she shed.

"If Ben and Ned had died, I wouldn't have wanted to go on living!"

Mamma Rizzoli hugged her comfortingly. "There, there, *bella fanciulla,** didn't I tell you my prayers would work? I went five times round my beads, imploring the Blessed Mother to keep them safe!"

Otto paced the cabin restlessly, shaking his head. "I would like to be free of this ship also. Why are we being kept prisoners in this room? It is not right!"

Pappa Rizzoli decided the time had come to tell them as much as he knew. He beckoned the troupe close. "Listen carefully, my friends, I must keep my voice low to tell you this. Signora Lindi, go and talk to the guards outside the door, please, I will tell you later.

"Ben told me that Misurata is not an honourable man, he is not taking us to Italy out of the goodness of heart. Why he has taken us with him, only Ben knows. But the boy would not give me the true reason for fear that he upset us. Since we have been kept in here against our will, I have been doing some serious thinking. Ben told me he would try to escape so that he

*Bella fanciulla (beautiful young girl).

could help us. I'm not sure how he can accomplish this, but I think we are in serious trouble, my friends. If we get the chance to help ourselves, we should do so without hesitation. So keep your wits about you, everybody, but try to stay calm and don't do anything that may endanger us all."

It was Ned who first smelled the cooking. Rounding the bend of a small cove, he saw a fisherman and his son, a boy of about twelve years. They were sitting with their backs against a beached rowing boat, preparing their food by a small fire. The dog cautioned his friend, "Hide behind these rocks while I go on and take the lay of the land, mate. Humans don't pay much heed to stray dogs. I'll call you when I'm ready."

Concealing himself behind the rocks, Ben watched Ned lollop toward the fire—head down, tongue out and tail wagging idly, just like any friendly old hound. The boy tossed the dog a crust, but his father ignored it. Both father and son were only half-aware of Ned, as they were discussing something animatedly. Ben was out of range, so he could not hear the conversation. However, he waited patiently for awhile as Ned gathered all the information he needed. The dog sauntered off, back to Ben, where he disclosed the gist of the talk.

Ben nodded. "So, if we want to eat, it looks like we're into our act again, with a slight difference. Though we mustn't linger too long in case we're being followed."

Ned perked up. "Here goes then, mate, enter the Magnificent Neddo and the Mysterious Benno!"

The fisherman and his son were grilling freshly caught

sardines and some plump-looking scallops which they had caught early that morning. He looked up at the tow-headed boy with the strange eyes as Ben approached him with Ned in tow.

Ben flicked his forelock. "Good day to you, signore, and to your son. Those sardines and scallops look wonderful, did you catch them yourself?"

Splitting a cooked fish, the man sandwiched it between slices of thin-crusted bread which he had toasted. "What else can a poor man do but catch his own fish? I have no servants to cater to my whims. But how did you know this one was my son?" He indicated the boy.

Ben narrowed his eyes, the way he did when he wanted to look mysterious when performing. "I know many things, Francisco. . . ." He saw the boy's look of surprise and continued. "And you, too, Francisco, son of Francisco the fisherman."

The fisherman crossed himself and kissed his thumbnail. "Does the blood of the Knights Templar run in your veins? If so, then begone, we do not talk to wizards!"

Ben squatted by the fire, smiling as he patted Ned. "No, no, I am just one who means nobody any harm, though I have always had the gift of second sight. I can help you, and I would do so . . . if my dog and I were not so hungry. We are poor, but honest and truthful."

The man threw back his head and laughed. "Hahahaha! Poor, honest, truthful and hungry. So, you have the second sight. My grandmother, Lord rest her, had that, too. I was brought up with it."

He passed a jug of red wine, mixed with water, to Ben. Throwing the fish sandwich to Ned, he made another, adding scallops to it. From his pouch he produced a piece of goat's milk cheese and carved off two slices for them. "I never feared the second sight, it is a gift from the Lord. Go on then, young man, tell me what you know."

Ben was ravenous. He spoke between mouthfuls of the good food and swigs of wine. "What day is it today?"

The fisherman guffawed. "Sunday, of course, don't you know?"

Ben tossed a scallop to Ned and licked his fingers. "Oh, I know, I'm just reminding you to go quickly to the church and see the padre. This is what you must say to him. Tell him that the goatherd is too old to carry the cross in this evening's procession. That goatherd's name is Francisco, and yours is Francisco. Always the cross has been carried round the piazza* by one named Francisco. Now the goatherd is old and doddery— he could fall with the cross, and maybe damage it. But you are strong and upright, why, you can stand up straight in a storm at sea. Also, you will provide the fish for the church every Good Friday from now on, as will your son, Francisco, when he becomes a man. Remember, fish come from the sea, cheese comes from an animal. It is more fitting for the Lenten Fast. Besides, Francisco the goatherd is old, he has not many years left."

The fisherman gazed in awe at Ben, then he sprang up and began shaking the boy's hand furiously, grinning from ear to ear at his son. "My very words, what was I just telling you before our friend came along, Francisco? The very same thing! Come, my son, we must hurry and get to the church! Thank

*Piazza (the town square).

you, my friend, thank you a thousand times, surely you have the gift, you are blessed! But you must forgive me, we must go now, I have to talk with the padre!"

Ben stood hastily and bowed. "Of course, do what you have to, signore. Oh, may we borrow your boat for a few hours?"

The fisherman and his son were already haring toward the cliff path. He called back to Ben, "Take it with my thanks, but return it when you've done!"

Ben waved. "I will, and I'll clear the food up and put the fire out!"

Ned fanned a scallop with his tail, then wolfed it down. "Pretty good of us, I'd say, clearing away all this mess of food for the poor man. Let's get to work!"

Ben loaded the remainder of the meal into the little rowing boat. "I've got a better idea, let's eat when we're clear of the shore. Then nobody can sneak up on us."

The black Labrador scrabbled sand over the small fire with his paws. "Hah, I was watching their faces when you were talking. They looked like two fish gasping for air while you repeated the father's words to his son, not two ticks after he'd just spoken them. Poor old Francisco the goatherd. Still, I suppose it'll give his wobbly old legs a rest, eh!"

In the early noon, the sea was smooth as a mill pond under the hot sun. Ben shipped the oars when they were about a quarter of a mile from the land. They settled down to a leisurely lunch, enjoying the sense of freedom, though Ben kept gazing soulfully in the direction of Valletta harbour, which had vanished from view around the point. Ned lapped wine and water from a scallop shell, passing his friend a thought.

"Now don't start fretting, the pretty Serafina will be just fine for the moment. We'll rescue her and the others when the first opportunity presents itself, don't worry, mate!"

Ben looked out across the water. "I know, Ned, but I can't help missing her, and our other friends, too."

The black Labrador grunted. "You aren't the only one who's missing Serafina, you know. She's a much better stroker than you ever were, mate, real soft and gentle."

Bomba lumbered along the shore, breathing heavily as he tried to increase the pace. The long jezzail musket he carried felt heavy and awkward in his sweaty grasp. Behind him the four guards strode at a steady pace, refusing to hurry as he urged them on. "Come on, shift yourselves, they can't be far ahead!"

One of the guards lowered his black face scarf. "I'm taking no orders from a slave driver. Slow and sure gets the job done properly, I always say!"

Still pushing forward, Bomba snarled at the man, "I'm in charge of this party, you'll obey my orders or I'll report you to the master when we get back. Now mooo . . ." He slipped upon a matted heap of wet seaweed and fell heavily backward, his finger pressing on the trigger as he tried to hold on to the long rifle.

Craaaaackkk!

The gunshot sent seabirds wheeling skyward as it echoed off the cliffs and across the waters. The outspoken guard stood over Bomba. "Why don't you fire that thing again, just to make sure they know we're on their trail. Huh, slave drivers!"

• • •

At the sound of the shot, Ben and Ned instinctively threw themselves down flat in the bottom of the rowing boat. The dog sent out a thought. "What was that, was it aimed at us, I wonder?"

Ben started easing himself into a crouch, so he could look over the stern. "That was a gunshot for sure, but it couldn't have been meant for us, or we'd have heard the ball whistling by. Stay down, mate, I'll take a quick peek!" Ben's eyes darted hither and thither as he scanned the cliffs and shore. "No, I can't see anything. . . . Wait! Aha, it's Bomba and four guards, all carrying guns. They're just rounding the point. Now they've reached the place where we met the fisherman. There's a guard sifting through the ashes of the fire, he seems to be arguing with Bomba. Now there's some horsemen, they're leading their horses down the path from the cliff to the shore, five of them. It's Al Misurata with four of his guards!"

Ned's damp nose nudged Ben's foot. "Get down, mate, we'll just have to lay low out here and hope that we don't get spotted!"

Al Misurata remounted his horse. Holding out a hand, he gave Bomba a disgusted glance. "Give me that gun before you do any more harm with it. If the boy and dog are within a mile of us they'll have hidden themselves well by now. Get back to the ship. I'll wait until dark, then I'll send Ghigno out with an armed search party. He might be able to take them by surprise."

The horsemen swept off, back along the shore to the harbour, leaving Bomba and the four guards trudging behind.

This time it was Ned who ventured his head above the gunwales for a look.

"Luck's still with us, they've gone. I can just see Bomba rounding the point, they're going back to the ship. Well, what's our next move, do we go back ashore?"

Ben sat up and took the oars. "No, we're safer on the water. Let's carry on and see what lies beyond the next point. You watch our backs."

The dog sat up in the stern. "Sorry I can't help you much, Captain. Us dogs aren't much use at rowing, but we're good lookouts."

They passed two headlands, and two small coves, each much like the first they had visited. Then a large, wooded promontory sprawled out into the sea. Late noon sun beat down on Ben as he pulled wearily on the oars. "We'll round that big point and take a rest. My hands are beginning to get blistered."

The promontory, and a huge headland about two miles to the far side, formed a large natural bay, at the centre of which was moored a vessel. It was a long, lateen-rigged dhow, a beautiful craft, with four triangular white sails. Having been around the sea and ships for some years, Ben studied it admiringly.

"What a beauty, I'll wager there's nothing could catch that one with the wind behind her!"

Every line of the ship bespoke speed and elegance, from her sleek, black hull to her gracefully curved stern.

Ned viewed the whole thing more practically. "Who owns such a vessel, friends or foes, I wonder?"

Ben was still admiring the trim craft. He shrugged. "It looks like the owner is rich and powerful, I don't think he'd be bothered with a boy and dog in a little rowing boat. We'll go past her on the way to the shore over yonder."

Pulling out into the bay, Ben took a course which would give them a closer view of the sleek vessel. From within fifty yards of the ship, they could make out intricate gilding above the waterline from stem to stern. Ben could distinguish the name *White Ram* on her bows. At the head of the mainmast was a banner, bearing the silhouette of a charging white ram on a field of green.

They passed by the stern, with Ned commenting, "Doesn't look like there's any activity on deck—they must all be below taking a snooze, away from the noonday heat. No, wait, there's a lad standing on the rail, look!"

Ben saw the lad, a boy aged between ten and eleven. He had a shock of luxuriant brown curls and an impudently handsome face. Wearing a linen wrap about his waist, he balanced on the stern rail, not holding on to anything.

Ned commented, "Looks a bit young to be the captain, eh?"

The lad grinned from ear to ear, waving to them from his precarious perch.

Ben waved back, calling out, "Be careful you don't fall, this water's pretty deep!"

The lad gave him a cheeky grin, shouting confidently, "Don't worry about me, I've learned to swim, and I can dive, too. Watch!" Launching himself from the high stern, he went into an awkward dive.

Ben winced as the lad hit the water with a resounding slap. "Ouch, I'll bet that hurt, a perfect belly flop, eh mate!"

However, the boy surfaced, spitting out a jet of seawater, apparently unharmed. He began swimming, as though he had only learned a day or two ago, windmilling his arms and nodding his head to and fro.

Ned chuckled. "Ho ho, he actually can swim, after a fashion."

They watched him for awhile, then Ben shouted to him, "You'd best get back to your ship, the ebb tide is drawing you out—turn round, mate!"

A man appeared on the big vessel's deck. He was old, but tall and imposing, with a full, grey beard and long, silvery locks. His voice boomed out sternly at the lad in the water.

"Joshua, you've been told about going into the sea when there's nobody on deck to watch over you! Come back here!"

Ned suddenly sighted the deadly triangular fin cutting through the water toward the lad. He barked aloud, conveying an urgent message to Ben at the same time. "Shark! There's a shark in the water!"

Ben spotted it immediately in the clear Mediterranean bay. He could even see the predator's long, streamlined body beneath the surface—it was a monstrous size. Pulling madly on the oars, he began rowing toward the boy, trying to place the boat between the shark and its intended victim.

The old man roared aloud as crewmen came hurrying up on deck. "Shark! Swim for the boat, Joshua, hurry!"

But the old man and his crew were too far off to render any immediate help. Ned acted promptly, sending thoughts to Ben as he bounded over the side into the sea.

"I'll get the young 'un, you keep that shark away, mate!"

Ben shipped one oar, gripping the other with both hands. He slapped the water a few times, decoying the shark toward himself. The ugly snout broke the surface as it swam in close, snapping at the oar. Ben lashed out, holding the bladed end of the oar downward. A shock ran through his arms as he struck hard at the protruding dorsal fin, knocking the beast off course. Then he saw the staring round eye, and the fearsome rows of teeth as the shark went into a wallowing attack.

BEN ATTACKED THE SHARK LIKE A MAD THING, SMASH-
ing the oar down.

Smack! Slap! Crash! Splat!

 The sea frothed and billowed as he battered on, bellowing, "Come on, you filthy brute! Take that, and that!"

Ned latched onto the lad's waistcloth, striking out for the ship. The youngster was in a panic, kicking at the dog and swallowing seawater. Then a lifeboat crashed down from the *White Ram*. Four armed men leaped into it and began paddling furiously toward the pair in the water.

The old man raised his arms, roaring, "Save my grandson, help the boy into the boat!"

Willing hands hauled Ned and the lad into the lifeboat, then rowed on swiftly to aid Ben.

The shark had the oar in its mouth. Ben heard its teeth crunch wickedly into the paddle blade. He held on as it tugged and pulled, feeling as though his arms were being wrenched from their sockets with each fresh tug from the powerful seabeast. The thought that he had a tiger by the tail sped through his mind, fol-lowed suddenly by Ned's urgent commands.

"Let go of the oar, mate! Throw yourself flat, quick!"

Ben released the oar, flinging himself headlong into the bottom of the little boat as four flintlocks exploded. *Crack! Bang! Crack! Bang!*

Four musket balls thudded into the shark's body, then the rescue craft bumped against Ben's boat. Water was starting to bubble through the fishing boat's ribs when a strong pair of hands grabbed Ben and lifted him clear. Still kicking and yelling, he landed next to Ned and the lad.

The shark wallowed about in the sea, crimsoning the waters as blood gouted out of its wounds. Another volley of lead from the crewmen tore into it.

The man who had rescued Ben called out, "Cease fire! Back to the ship, look!"

Three more fins appeared out of nowhere. Homing in on the doomed monster, they began savaging it ferociously. In moments the water was an absolute melee of foam, blood and writhing bodies, as the sharks attacked each other indiscriminately.

The sturdy crewman winked at Ben, pointing to the ravaging fish. "Senseless savages, once there's blood in the water they'll rip anything to shreds, themselves included. Let them eat each other, and good riddance I say!"

The young lad had extraordinary powers of recovery. Once he had finished coughing and spitting out seawater, he began hugging and stroking Ned. He wrinkled his nose at Ben. "Told you I could swim, didn't I? This is a great dog you have. My name's Joshua, what's yours?"

Ben was completely disarmed by the lad's open manner. "I'm called Ben, his name is Ned."

They were helped aboard the ship, where the old man

awaited them on deck. Up close he was an impressive figure. His long, curling, silver hair was held back by a soft leather band across his brow, and he wore a simple red-and-black woven gown. His face was charismatic, brown as a walnut and deeply creased, with an aquiline nose, and calm, hazel-flecked eyes that seemed to contain all the knowledge of life and worldly wisdom. He bowed deeply to Ben and Ned.

"I owe you a debt beyond price—you saved the life of my grandson Joshua. I am Eli Bar Shimon of Ascalon, the leader of a family of warrior merchants. Name your reward, I will gladly give you anything it is in my power to give. Just name it, and it is yours!"

Ben returned the courteous bow of the old patriarch. "Sir, my name is Ben, my dog is called Ned. We need no rewards. Joshua is safe, I am glad we were of service to you."

Eli crouched to stroke Ned. His eyes twinkled. "This is a fine and wonderful animal. Benjamin, eh, a good Hebrew name!"

Ned nuzzled the old man's hand, sending Ben his opinion. "D'you know, mate, I've quite taken to this old fellow!"

With a pang of guilt, Ben suddenly remembered the fisherman's boat. He looked out to where the humble craft was settling low in the bay, still being buffeted by the frenzied sharks.

"Sir, our boat was loaned to us by a poor fisherman."

The old man nodded understandingly. "It would be a sad day if a poor fisherman were to lose his livelihood. Where does this man live, Benjamin, what is his name?"

Ben pointed to the clifftops, toward Valletta. "A small town up there, two bays back, sir. His name is Francisco. He has a son, about the same age as your Joshua, he, too, is called Francisco. He is a good man, and quite religious, the local padre knows him well."

Eli Bar Shimon spoke to the strong-looking crewman who had lifted Ben from the fishing boat. "Ezekiel, take the smaller lifeboat, the one with a mast and sail. Find this fisherman, Francisco." The patriarch took four heavy gold coins from his waist purse. "Give him the boat and this gold as compensation for his loss, and tender my apologies."

Ned communicated with Ben as he inspected the vessel in question. "Our old friend here is more than generous. That boat's worth ten of Francisco's rickety tub, and four gold pieces to boot? Hah, it surely was the fisherman's lucky day when he met us, mate!"

Ben agreed. "It's plain he loves his grandson more than anything. Joshua is a very fortunate lad."

Eli turned to Ben. "Will you accompany Ezekiel, to show him the way?"

Ned tapped Ben's ankle with his paw. "You can't go back ashore, they'll catch you for sure!"

Ben mentally replied to his dog, "I think I'd best tell Eli the truth, he'd probably appreciate it."

Ben looked the dignified old man straight in the eye. "Sir, forgive me, but it would be safer for me and Ned if we stayed aboard awhile. There are men on shore who are hunting for us. Enemies, who would do us harm."

The patriarch stared back into Ben's clouded blue-grey eyes. "I believe you, Benjamin, though it is strange for a boy and dog to have grown men as enemies. Ezekiel, arm yourself, and take a man with you. Be careful, and speak to nobody about our friends, except the fisherman."

The lad, Joshua, stood boldly forward. "I will go with him, Grandfather. Come, Ezekiel!"

Eli rebuked him severely. "You will stay aboard this ship, O disobedient one. Go to the galley, the cook will keep you busy for the rest of today, as penance for your willful behaviour!"

Joshua looked as though he were about to protest, his suntanned cheeks reddened. However, something in his grandfather's eyes warned him that argument would prove fruitless. He bowed to the old man and marched off, stiff-backed, to the galley.

Eli murmured to Ben, "Just like his father, a true son of the House of Shimon, a fearless warrior. He has many lessons to learn yet."

Ben smiled. "He is lucky to have you as a teacher, sir."

Eli took Ben's hand. "Come inside and enjoy our hospitality, Benjamin. Bring Ned with you. It is not wise to be seen out in the open by hawks, if you are a dove. I want to hear more about you and your fine dog."

Ned trailed inside behind Ben and Eli. "Fine dog? Will you kindly inform our friend that I am the Magnificent Neddo!"

Ben tugged his ear gently. "If you don't stop boasting, I'll tell him that your real name is Bundi."

Eli had a broad and spacious cabin at the stern of the *White Ram*. It contained a huge table and lots of chairs. There were cedar cupboards, shelves full of books and scrolled maps, and broad mullioned windows stretching in a long arc. It was more stateroom than cabin. Seated at the table with Eli, Ben watched as stewards cleared away charts and documents.

The cook and his helpers, one of whom was a red-faced Joshua, set out table linen, cutlery and dishes. They served a delicious chicken broth, followed by a dish of fresh fish with saffron rice and boiled chickpeas. There was orange juice, coffee or wine to drink, and baklava, a pastry filled with honey, nuts and raisins, for dessert. Ned was given a roasted shoulder of lamb and a bowl of water, to which he immediately gave his undivided attention. Eli raised a goblet of dark red wine to the boy and his dog.

"*L'chaim*,* Benjamin, to you, your dog and my Joshua. This wine is from our vineyards at Ascalon, where I live with my family and friends. Let me tell you about us.

"We have held that land safe for centuries, our tribe has defended it against many foes, and it prospers under our care. Our retainers are husbandmen, shepherds and farmers, but we of the House of Shimon are warrior merchants. We trade both on land and sea, though now I am retired. I spend my days giving counsel to my son Jacob and his wife Miriam, who manage all the business. Joshua is their only heir, I have devoted myself to his education."

Here Eli gave a dry chuckle. "Though not always with great success, as you saw by today's incident. He is headstrong and adventurous, as are you, Benjamin, I think. Tell me about yourself and Ned, how you came to be here, with your fair skin, light hair and northern eyes. You interest me greatly."

Ned looked up from the bone he was gnawing. "Watch you don't trip up over your tongue, matey, he'd never believe our true history."

L'chaim (long life).

Ben helped himself to orange juice as he replied to the dog. "Leave it to me, I'll give him the same story I told to Al Misurata, that I was the son of a ship's officer, whose vessel was wrecked in the Gulf of Gascony, of which I have very little memory. Then you and I travelled the coasts for some years, until we were captured and enslaved by Al Misurata. From therein I'll tell Eli the facts as they happened. Will that be alright with you, mate?"

Ned chewed on some roasted fat. "I suppose so, but I'll be listening, to help you in case you slip up."

Ben launched into his narrative. The old man listened intently, never speaking, but watching him avidly. The strange boy hurried through his fictional earlier life, but told the truth, chapter and verse, about events which had occurred since he and Ned were found drifting off the Libyan coast in their small boat. When he had finished, the patriarch shook his bearded head slowly.

"Al Misurata—who in these seas has not heard that hated name? You did well to escape him, Benjamin—he is a pirate, a slaver and lots worse things, I have heard. I know he is neither Jewish nor Arabic, a truly evil parasite. So, young fellow, what do you plan on doing to rescue your friends, the Rizzoli Troupe? How will you liberate them?"

Ben explained as best he could. "They are held captive aboard Misurata's ship, the *Sea Djinn*. She's bound for the port of Piran in Slovenija, sir. He promised to give them passage there, so that they could cross the border into Italy. But he plans on selling them as slaves. If I can reach Piran, I'll form a plan to help them. Al Misurata will not expect me to show up there, so it will make things less difficult. If Ned and I could get passage to Piran, I'd wait my chance. I'm sure the right opportunity would present itself sooner or later. When it does I'll know what to do."

Eli patted Ben's shoulder. "I'm certain you will, Benjamin, you are a strange and resourceful boy. I hope Joshua grows up just like you. So, I'll give orders for the *White Ram* to get under way to Slovenija as soon as possible."

Ben was taken aback by the old man's sudden announcement. "But sir, you would be putting yourself and Joshua at great risk, I could not permit it!"

Eli Bar Shimon raised his bushy eyebrows in amusement. "I am captain of this ship, Benjamin, I say what is permissible. You forget, I am deeply in your debt—I owe the life of my grandson to you. There is no ship faster in all these seas than my *White Ram*. I have decided she will take you to Piran!"

Ben appealed to the patriarch. "It is not right that you place yourself in peril for me, sir!"

Eli spread his arms wide. "Peril, from what? I have fought pirates and Corsairs all my life, we of the House of Shimon are merchant warriors. My crew are all seasoned swordsmen, musketeers and cannoneers, they are sworn in loyalty to my family. Believe me, Benjamin, it should not come to a fight. The first duty of a warrior leader is to get out of trouble, not into it!"

However, Ben was not happy with the situation; he was still not convinced. "But sir, Ned and I can slip into Valletta harbour at night and stow away aboard almost any ship. One of them is sure to be sailing for Sicily, Italy or even Slovenija. You cannot go so far out of your way for us."

Eli refilled his goblet and took a sip. "I like this wine. If I did not have my grandson to educate, this ship to sail on and my own wine to drink, what else would an old man do, Benjamin? I am not out here on business, merely a summer cruise. I can sail my ship wherever my fancy takes me. Slovenija is a nice place at this time of year, they say. From there I will complete my trip back home to Ascalon. So, what do you say?"

Ben clasped the old fellow's hand fervently. "I cannot stop you, sir, you have my undying gratitude. But Ned and I sail with the *White Ram* on one condition. That you leave us ashore at Piran and set your course for home. We can handle everything else. What would you tell your son if anything bad happened to Joshua?"

Eli Bar Shimon arose from the table. He opened a long, cedar chest which stood nearby. From it he took a splendid in-laid sword, a broad, curved dagger and a thick, cupid-like bow, with a quiver of arrows. He smiled ruefully.

"I accept your terms, Benjamin. Ah, but it would be fine to use these one last time. You see this bow, it was made from the horns of a mighty ram by my grandfather. One day I will pass it on to Joshua. I was never one for muskets or jezzails—this is a true hunter's weapon!"

Ben inspected the bow. "It's a fearsome thing, sir."

Eli sighed. "A good archer can fire it faster than a man can load a firearm. Its string has sung the deathsong of many who sought to bring harm to the House of Shimon. A few seasons' work aboard this ship will make my Joshua's arms strong enough to draw it." He placed the weapons back in the chest. "You must be tired, Benjamin. Come, I'll show you and Ned to your cabin."

Ben settled down on a comfortable bunk, with Ned sprawled across his feet. Unlike his experience on the *Sea Djinn,* he had no qualms about sailing aboard the *White Ram.* It had a calm and soothing effect on his mind, devoid of visions featuring Vanderdecken and his hellship, the *Flying Dutchman.*

Ned liked it also. He yawned cavernously. "Extremely restful and cosy here, eh mate?"

Ben closed his eyes. "Aye, though it would be better if my legs weren't being numbed by some great lump of a dog lying on them. I can't feel my feet!"

The black Labrador snorted. "Ungrateful youth, be careful I don't offer my valuable services to Eli as permanent ship's dog. He'd jump at the chance!"

Ben prodded Ned. "Not if he had dead legs he wouldn't."

In the dark serenity of the peaceful cabin, the two friends soon lapsed into slumber.

It was shortly before midnight when they were awakened by the sound of shouts from out on deck.

BURSTING OUT ONTO THE
deck with Ned at his heels, Ben collided
with Eli. The old man hustled him back inside.

"Benjamin, you and Ned must stay out of
sight. Ezekiel and Abram, the man who went with
him, are being pursued along the shore by armed
men. They might be the very ones who are hunting you. Go to my cabin and watch from the windows. Try not to let yourself be seen. Go!"

The patriarch began calling orders to his crew. "Lower
the lifeboat, bring Ezekiel and Abram back here with all
speed. Marksmen, prime your jezzails and wait on my command!"

A sleepy-eyed Joshua came stumbling out on deck.
"Grandfather, what's going on, can I help?"

The patriarch ruffled the lad's brown curls. "Everything is
under control, my young warrior. Go to my cabin and keep
watch with Ben and his dog."

Hurtling into the surf, both crewmen began making for the
lifeboat, which was still some distance off. Bomba and a dozen
guards stood panting in the shallows, watching the escaping

men. Two horsemen came galloping out of the night. Al Misurata held his mount on shore, whilst Ghigno spurred on into the sea. He was yelling at Bomba.

"Keep after them, blockhead, stop them!"

The big slave driver complained, "Our cloaks and robes would drag us down out there."

The scar-faced Corsair lashed at him with the horse's reins. "Fool! They're wearing cloaks and robes, too. Now get going, you brainless jellyfish!"

Bomba watched the escaping men for a moment, then smiled maliciously at Ghigno. "See, they've been picked up by a boat, it's too late to chase them now."

Ghigno called to the guards. "Use your guns, stop them!"

Al Misurata galloped his mount into the surf, his horse striking the first man to raise his jezzail. The weapon discharged skyward as the guard was knocked flat in the sea. "Hold your fire, all of you, back to the shore!"

They obeyed their leader hastily. The pirate halted his horse beyond the tideline, where he issued orders.

"Bomba, take the men and hide among the rocks. I want no shooting at all for the present. Keep a watch on that ship, see if you can spot the boy or the dog. Stay awake and keep your eyes open. I'm going back for reinforcements, I'll return in the morning. Ghigno, an hour after I leave, make your way back to the *Sea Djinn*. Do it in secret, I don't want you seen from that vessel."

Eli came into the cabin, where Ned and both boys were crouching by the windows. The old man went to the chest and began arming himself.

"Did you recognise them, Benjamin, are they the enemies who are hunting you?"

Ben nodded grimly. "Aye, sir. The one who rode off alone was Al Misurata himself."

A knock on the cabin door announced Ezekiel and Abram. They were clad in dry robes. Ezekiel made his report.

"Lord, we found the fisherman Francisco. He was heading a religious parade, carrying a big cross. He was greatly pleased with your gifts, and sends his sincere thanks. He enquired about the boy and his dog, but I denied all knowledge of them."

Eli adjusted the dagger in his waist sash. "You did well. What happened after that?"

Ezekiel explained. "We were on our way back, coming through the foothills below the cliffs. I saw a band of armed men—they were obviously tracking us. One of them called to us to halt. I didn't like the look of them, so we made a dash for it and they gave chase."

Abram laughed nervously. "It was heavy going, carrying our weapons, and with the water weighing our robes down. We speeded up when the man on horseback began shouting. Luckily we had a good lead, and we made it to the boat safely."

Joshua interrupted. "The man on the horse knocked one of them into the sea, his musket ball went astray. Why did he do that, Grandfather?"

Eli placed his bow and quiver on the table. "I don't know, but he must have had his reasons. Are they still there, Benjamin?"

Ben watched the shoreline, nodding. "Still there, sir. I can see the other horse, and a faint glow amid the rocks. They've lit a fire."

Ned joined Ben at the window. "It is a fire. The rascals aren't going anywhere, looks like they've camped there for the night!"

Eli Bar Shimon's eyes glittered as he strung his bow. "Hah! Assyrians, planning to descend like wolves upon the shepherd's fold, eh? They won't find many sheep here, let them come and meet this old ram. My bow has slain more than one mangy wolf in its day!"

Ben was about to protest, when he glimpsed the patriarch's face: the light of battle was upon it, the old man was enjoying himself.

Sheathing his sword, Eli shouldered the quiver of arrows. He made a formidable sight, like some avenging biblical prophet of old. "Benjamin, stay here with your good dog and take care of Joshua. Ezekiel, Abram, let us go and prepare a reception for this wolf who trades in human flesh!"

OTTO HAD BEEN PACING THE CABIN SINCE BEFORE dawn; the big German was becoming more agitated with what he considered to be unwarranted confinement.

Buffo knuckled his eyes and blinked wearily. "Can't you stop marching up and down like that? It isn't helping anybody. Lie back and rest yourself, Herr Kassel."

The strongman pounded a ham-like fist onto the tabletop where the clown was leaning. "It is wrong, I tell you, no man keeps me prisoner against my will. I am getting out of here!"

Signore Rizzoli placed himself in front of the cabin door. "Please, friend, stay here, there are armed men out there. Soon they will come, if only to deliver our food. Then I will try to reason with them."

La Lindi stretched langorously and yawned. "What makes you think they will listen to reason?"

Mummo sighed. "Lindi's right. I've never liked Misurata, or any of his gang—I think we should never have trusted him and made this trip. What about you, Rosa?"

Mamma Rizzoli played with the fringes on her shawl. "I have said little so far, but I've been watching carefully. I think we've been lured into a trap. This Al Misurata, he was too smooth, too glib. Now he's changed completely. It will be a lucky day if ever we see our homeland again."

Gently, but firmly, Otto lifted Augusto Rizzoli to one side. "All this talk gets us nowhere, I am going out. *Ja!*"

Serafina, who had not ventured an opinion so far, came to stand alongside the big German. "I'm going with you, Otto. I don't think they would harm a girl. We'll say we're going to visit Poppea."

The door was bolted, but one powerful thrust from the strongman's shoulder sent both lock and timber splinters flying. Otto bowed to his pretty companion. "After you, *Fräulein!*"

Caught napping in the early morning sunlight out on deck, the guard came running and pointed his rifle at Serafina, who was standing in front of Otto. The big man reached over her shoulder and grabbed the long barrel. As he wrenched the weapon from the man's grasp, it went off with a bang. The ball shot past Otto's cheek, into the bulkhead behind him. Scarcely had Otto knocked the guard aside and led Serafina out on deck, when they were surrounded. Armed men had come running from everywhere.

Al Misurata came pushing through the cordon; he was wearing a brace of fine Spanish pistols in his waistband. Drawing one, he menaced the German strongman. "You should not be out here. Get back to your cabin and stay there!"

The strongman glared at the pirate. "I am not afraid of you!"

Al Misurata hissed viciously, "Get back inside!"

Serafina placed herself in front of Otto. "We were only going to visit our mare, Poppea."

The pirate answered, without taking his eyes off Otto, "The horse is well taken care of, return to your cabin."

The strongman thrust his huge, shaven head forward. "We are not going until we find out what you have done with our friends, Ben and Ned!"

The hammer clicked as Al Misurata cocked the pistol. "I have not seen the boy, or his dog. They have not been harmed. You are a brave and foolish man, *mein Heer,* but I think you will obey me and go back now." Sighting the pistol, he pointed it at Serafina's face.

Otto was left with no option.

"Come, *Fräulein,* we go back inside now."

Signore Rizzoli breathed a sigh of relief as they walked back into the cabin. "You were close to death then, my friends, we heard all that went on out there."

Buffo winced as the carpenters began hammering an iron swing bar across the damaged door. "Well, at least we know Ben and Ned are still alive."

La Lindi looked up from petting Mwaga, her python. "I don't believe a word from that shark, he's a liar!"

Tears beaded in Serafina's beautiful eyes. "Oh, don't say that, please, he wouldn't lie about a thing like that. Ben and Ned must be alive!"

Mamma Rizzoli shook her head at the snake dancer, silencing her. She wrapped her shawl about the girl. "Of course they're alive, *bella mia,** don't upset yourself."

Ezekiel leaned over the midship rail, pointing to the band who were rounding the point. "See, Lord, he's coming back with a lot more men!"

Bella mia (my beauty).

Eli Bar Shimon beckoned to him. "I see him. Don't stand up at the rails like that, you make an easy target for those guns in the rocks. Caleb, drop the ports and show them our teeth."

In the stern cabin, Ben felt the deck rumble underfoot. Ned's thought flashed through his mind. "What's that, mate?"

Before he could enquire of Joshua, the lad looked up from his breakfast. "They're lowering the ports to run out cannon. Look down through the windows."

Ned sent Ben another thought. "Cannon, eh, that old man doesn't mess about, does he!"

As they stared down through the windows, two slim brass barrels emerged beneath them. Joshua explained. "They're not big, full-sized cannon, but there's eight of them, three each side and these two astern. I've seen them fired for practice, they're very powerful, and our crew are expert gunners."

Ned interrupted Joshua to mentally contact Ben. "Here comes old miseryguts with another bunch of villains!"

They watched as Al Misurata, mounted on a prancing steed, led a score of armed men along the beach. He met with Bomba and the others, joining his infantry to theirs. The pirate took charge, issuing orders to them all. Then he strung the men out below the tideline, in full view of the *White Ram.*

Ben spoke aloud, as much for the benefit of Ned as Joshua. "They've certainly got enough men. But what's the point? They can't reach us out here."

Eli stood in the open cabin doorway. "That's merely a show of force to impress us, Benjamin. Tell me, do you think that is all Al Misurata's command, or does he have more men?"

Ben answered readily. "Many more, sir. Besides them he has a big ship and an entire crew."

Joshua clapped his hands eagerly. "Will we fight them,

Grandfather? Our warriors could beat them easily, and we've got cannon!"

The old man stroked his beard as he watched the men on shore. "We'll fight them only if we have to, my young rooster. But I would rather outthink them, and save any bloodshed. Meanwhile, you boys and the dog stay low. I don't want you seen from those windows."

Joshua looked glum, he had wanted to see battle done. "Are they just going to stand there on shore all day? Where's the sense in that?"

As the morning went on, the situation did not alter. Though the crew of the *White Ram* were vigilant and ready for action, Al Misurata stood with his men on the shoreline, making no attempt to do anything.

The sun was at its zenith when Ben spied the boat. It was a small ship's boat from the *Sea Djinn,* containing two rowers and two armed guards, already around the point and heading toward the men on the beach. Ben poked his head out on deck, calling to Ezekiel, who was standing nearby.

"Off the port side, see, they're bringing a boat!"

The seaman winked at him. "We've already spotted it, mate. Back inside and stay out of the way."

The small boat pulled into shore. Al Misurata boarded it, ordering the oarsmen to head for the *White Ram.* Eli stood on the stern gallery, watching. When he judged it was within hailing distance, the old man held up his arm and called out abruptly.

"That is far enough, you will come no further. State your business!"

Al Misurata rose, bowing courteously, touching fingertips to his heart, lips and forehead. "I bid you good day, sir. Are you the commander of this wondrous vessel?"

The patriarch folded his arms. "I am the captain and owner. Who are you?"

The pirate smiled disarmingly. "An honest shipowner like yourself, sir. I sail out of Libya, trading in horses."

Eli raised his bushy brows. "But you have not come to sell me a horse."

Al Misurata laughed, as though he appreciated the joke. "Alas, no, sir. I am making enquiries about a boy, a thief and a liar, who deserted his position as my servant. He will have a black dog with him, which belongs to me."

Eli Bar Shimon cut him short. "There are no thieves, liars or dogs aboard my ship. I suggest you search elsewhere, now go!"

The pirate's face grew hard, his voice became harsh and imperious. "Then I will search your ship. The boy and the dog were seen boarding this vessel, it was reported to me!"

Eli calmly laid a shaft upon his bowstring. He pointed the lethal ram's-horn bow at Al Misurata. "Then whoever reported it is a liar. Begone, slaver, carrion such as you are not welcome aboard this ship!"

Al Misurata smiled thinly. "We will see about that." He dropped his right hand to his side. One of the armed guards in the boat brought up his rifle quickly. Not quickly enough, though—Eli's arrow pierced his shoulder and he fell back screaming. The pirate was taken aback by the speed of the old man, who already had another shaft laid on his bowstring. At the same moment a shot rang out from the shore. The ball tore a chunk from the rail close to Eli, who called up to the rigging.

"Zachary, mark him!"

At the topmast spar, a lithe young man shouted back, "Aye, Lord, he's marked!" Taking rapid aim with a long, silver-inlaid jezzail, he fired. As the crack of the gun split the air, a guard on shore dropped his weapon and crumpled to the sand.

Zachary lowered his weapon, bellowing, "Ship under sail, off port amidships!"

The *Sea Djinn,* with her foremast repaired, was in plain view, racing toward the *White Ram.*

Abram came hurrying to the old man's side. "She's either trying to cut us off or ram us!"

Eli put aside his bow as he scanned the big ship. "We can't fight off a monster like that. Set a course to starboard, slip the anchor cable, and lay on all sail, then await my orders!"

Ghigno put the spyglass to his eye, yelling out commands as he did. "Helmsman, take us out a point and come in on the curve. We'll catch her on the far side of the bay and ram her into the rocks on the coast. Stand by ready to board—look sharp now, I think she's slipped anchor!"

On board the *White Ram* the crew were working frantically. A brawny deckhand severed the thick anchor rope with half a dozen blows from a broad-headed axe. Men scrambled nimbly through the rigging loosing sail, whilst some on deck hoisted extra canvas. Abram leaned on the big brass-and-mahogany wheel, bringing the vessel onto a starboard tack. Eli stood at his side, judging their perilous situation.

"We need to catch the wind and clear the bay, before they get a chance to smash us against the rocks on the point. That big ship looks to me like she's set on a collision course!"

The *White Ram* began pulling away sluggishly; she was having difficulty catching the wind. Eli looked over the stern, to where they had moved about a cable length away from the small boat. He could see Al Misurata sitting with his arms folded, smiling triumphantly as he watched the huge *Sea Djinn* closing on the *White Ram.* The old man took the wheel from Abram, holding their course as he whispered instructions to him.

Ben heard the footsteps pounding by the cabin door. Swinging the door open, he saw Abram leaping down a flight of stairs. Joshua pushed past Ben into the alleyway, shouting, "Ben, Ned, come on!" All three dashed into the lower hold. Abram was crouched beside an older man, who was manning one of the brass cannons. Joshua joined them, shaking with excitement.

"What's going on, are we going to fight now?"

Abram called to Ben, "Keep him out of the way, all three of you stay back there by the stairs!"

As Ben pulled the younger boy back, he heard Abram talking to the older gunner. "Just sink it, Caleb, don't blow it to smithereens or kill anybody aboard. Can you do it?"

Caleb's weathered face creased into a broad grin. "Aye, if that's what our cap'n wants. Leave it to me!"

Al Misurata watched his ship arcing in toward the *White Ram.* He waved encouragement to Ghigno, who was standing in the prow signalling orders to his steersman. It was a foregone conclusion, the smaller vessel could not escape.

Baarrrrooooommmm.

There was a crash like thunder bursting overhead. The stern of the small craft that held Al Misurata vanished in a cascade of splinters and seaspray. He found himself suddenly floundering in the bay, shocked and gasping for breath as he spat out gouts of salt water. The remainder of the boat disappeared beneath him, and sudden terror had him screeching in panic.

"Eeeyaaah! Save me, Ghigno! Save meeeeeee!"

It is a known fact that some seamen cannot swim, despite having spent most of their lives sailing the main.

Al Misurata was one such seaman.

Ned lay flat, with both front paws covering his ears. "Ben, have we been hit, mate?" Luckily it was a thought, because no voice would have been heard in the echoing, smoke-filled space where the cannon had discharged its ball.

With stars flashing before his eyes and thunder echoing in his ears, Ben staggered through the gunpowder-fogged space. He joined Joshua, who was peering down the cannon barrel, yelling enthusiastically.

"Hahaha, good shot, Caleb! You did it, the big ship's having to halt and come about to rescue that rascal in the water. I wish there were some hungry sharks about, that'd teach him a lesson, eh, Ben!"

Ned pushed his head between the shoulders of both boys. "Hoho, does my doggy heart good to see a sight like that! I bet that was the old fellow's idea. You tell Joshua that his grandad's a genius, Ben!"

Al Misurata was scrabbling about like a madman, alternately sinking and clawing his way up. He was clutching frenziedly at the two guards and the rowers, who were struggling to get away from him as they fought to save themselves. Choking on seawater, the pirate screeched like a demented animal as the *Sea Djinn* hastened to his aid.

"Heeeelp! Ghignooooo! Heeeeeeeelp!"

The Corsair was urging a boat crew to hurry themselves, whilst other crewmen began flinging ropes and cane fenders from the decks. It was a scene of total chaos.

Ben shook Joshua's hand heartily. "Your grandfather is a hero, and a very wise old man!"

Leaving the *Sea Djinn* to her rescue mission, the *White Ram* drifted calmly off. After awhile she cleared the bay, heeling slightly as a lively breeze sent her scudding out under full sail into the open Mediterranean Sea. Accompanied by Caleb the master gunner, Ben, Ned and Joshua hurried out into the fresh air of the open deck. Ben and Ned joined Eli, who was acting as steersman, but Joshua and Caleb linked their arms about the shoulders of Ezekiel, Abram, Zachary and other crewmen, who had formed a circle. They danced slowly around, stamping their feet and singing.

"Yayla ho hah! Yayla ho hah!
The House of Shimon is mighty,
and fearless stands each son,
each daughter fair and comely,
like lilies of Sharon.

"Yayla ho hah! Yayla ho hah!
We wield the sword or sickle,

the chariot or the plough,
we breathe the air of freedom,
and to no tyrant bow.

"Yayla ho hah! Yayla ho hah!
My sheep graze in the pastures,
my grape bloom on the vine,
no cruel inquisition
will steal this land of mine."

Old Eli patted Ned and winked at Ben. "What white ram ever headed a flock like mine!"

CAPE PASSERO OFF THE SOUTHERN
TIP OF THE SICILIAN COAST.

THE MAN SHOOK A SMALL BOX OF CORN GRAINS,
watching the pigeons circling overhead. Whistling softly
to the birds, he spread a few grains on the sill of the loft.

 One by one they began landing, pecking at the
corn before entering through the light wire
grill.

He whistled and clucked patiently, biding his
time until his champion homing bird, a fine, big,
bronze-feathered pigeon, came to perch on the sill. Immediately it had entered the loft, the man went inside and retrieved
it. He stroked its head gently against his cheeks, making soft,
soothing clucks as he removed a tiny cylinder which was attached to its leg.

Having read the contents of the little scroll from the cylinder, he left the loft. Mounting a donkey, which was tethered
outside, he set off for the coast, urging the beast to a trot with
his bare heels.

• • •

Padre Marlanese read the letter three times, slowly, following the lines with a dirty fingernail and mouthing each word.

The pigeon man raised his brows. "Well, Padre, is good information worth its price?"

The fat little wrecker and coast robber rummaged in his voluminous waist wallet. He drew out four coins. "Three silver or one gold, my friend?"

The man did not hesitate. "One gold. Half your silver is tin, gold is always best."

Marlanese parted reluctantly with the worn golden coin. "You are lucky I am not a man who is easily insulted."

The pigeon owner took the gold and left immediately.

Padre Marlanese, the False Priest, lived on his boat, a long, flat-bottomed skiff. He commanded six such craft. Like a small gang of sharks, they preyed upon anything that moved through the waters from Passero up the Sicilian coastline to the Strait of Messina, and the Italian mainland on the other side above Taormina. Smaller craft he would attack; the larger ships, the padre could lure onto the rocks with his considerable skills as a wrecker.

Wheezing laboriously, he heaved himself from a battered armchair, which was nailed to the deck inside a little shack containing the tiller. His second in command, Bulgaro, a sombre-faced villain with a set of whalebone teeth which had once belonged to a Dutch merchant, smiled eagerly as his chief clambered ashore. Marlanese was clad in stained and greasy clerical garb, with a wide-brimmed hat. He resembled a fat, black beetle as he waddled along the strand.

Bulgaro joined him. "Is the news good, Padre?"

The little wrecker smirked, holding out the message. "Here, you long-faced heathen, read for yourself."

Bulgaro's countenance returned to its usual mournful look. "You know I can't read words, what does it say?"

The False padre chuckled. "Excellent news, for those who know how to deal with it. It comes from my cousin Ghigno. His master, Misurata, wants us to stop a ship which should be coming our way. He wants a fair-haired boy who sails with her, the rest is plunder for us. Good, eh?"

Bulgaro clacked his teeth, which were a few sizes too large. "A fair-haired boy, does he want him dead or alive?"

Marlanese shrugged. "Either way will do, what do you care? This ship is a swift vessel called *White Ram*. It was heading away from Malta, on a course which my cousin Ghigno thinks should take it right by here. If it follows the trade route, it will coast up past Siracusa and Catania, then head off to Melito at the toe of Italy. But it is my guess that the *White Ram* will never get that far."

Bulgaro cackled. "We'll wreck it on the rocks!"

The False Padre looked at Bulgaro scornfully. "Donkey! It is too fine a prize to wreck, we'll take the vessel unharmed. I'll make it my own."

Bulgaro removed his teeth and began carving at them with his dagger. "What d'you suggest we do, Padre?"

Marlanese shot him a disgusted glance. "I suggest you put those things back in your mouth, before your chin beats your nose black and blue. We'll lie in wait for the ship, myself and three boats off the coast at Siracusa, you and three other boats offshore. That way we'll trap her from both sides at night, and take out her crew silently with blades and strangling nooses, watch and deck crew first. It will be over quickly."

Bulgaro clacked his whalebone teeth together. "Aye, Padre, like that Slavian trader two years ago. They were dead before they had a chance to wake up."

Marlanese eyed his companion sourly. "As long as you can keep those teeth from clacking. If they heard them they'd think there were being attacked by a band of Spanish dancers with castanets!"

Bulgaro muttered indignantly, "I can keep them quiet when I want to!"

The False Padre ignored him, continuing with his plan. "It should go smoothly, providing we're not seen. I'll come in from landward with three boats to one side, you from the sea with our other three boats. Ten crew to each craft should get the job done well.

"Go to the villages of Pachino, Noto and Avola, get the men together. Tell them to come armed and bring them here to me. Say there is a rich payday to be had for any who know how to kill and keep their mouths shut. They know that there is better money to be had following me than chasing fish, or scratching a living from the earth. Go now!"

Marlanese waddled back to the armchair on his boat, where he sat honing his blade on the sole of a boot, dreaming of the riches to come.

From the small port in their cabin on the *Sea Djinn,* the Rizzoli Troupe had glimpsed the encounter between *White Ram* and the larger vessel. They had also witnessed Al Misurata's boat being sunk beneath him. Otto nodded his big, shaven head regretfully. "Ach, such a pity that man was not drowned or eaten by der sharks!"

Mamma nodded her agreement. "At least the ship got away unharmed, so we know Ben and Ned are safe."

Serafina questioned Mamma anxiously. "You think Ben and Ned are aboard that ship?"

Signore Rizzoli smiled reasurringly. "For sure, *ragazza,* why else would Misurata bother with it? The *capitano* of that ship is a very brave man, to face the slaver and his men down, and escape as he did."

Mummo chuckled. "I'd like to be a fly on the wall of that pirate's cabin right now. He didn't look in the least pleased when they hauled him aboard dripping wet!"

The clown was right in his assumption—Al Misurata was in a furious mood. Clad only in a silken wrap, he paced the cabin in a rage, venting his spleen on Bomba and Ghigno.

"Why did you not fire upon them before they had a chance to sink my boat? Must I forever be surrounded by fools and halfwits?"

Bomba kept silent, knowing it was the best course in the present situation. The pirate ignored him, staring fixedly at Ghigno, demanding an answer. "Why?"

The scar-faced Corsair tried to sound reasonable. "But Lord, we thought only of your safety. You were between them and us, we could not risk cannon fire!"

Al Misurata knew Ghigno spoke the truth, but he was not prepared to accept any explanation in his irate mood. "Hah, or you're not a good enough shot! Did you send word to my agent, the one who keeps messenger birds?"

Ghigno nodded vigorously. "With all speed, Lord, I sent my best man. Your message is on its way."

Al Misurata poured wine, but only for himself. The irony in his voice was not lost on Ghigno. "Oh good! Let's hope that cousin of yours, Padre Marlanese, can read. Right, set a course for Passero, there's too much time been wasted idling in these waters!"

It was Ghigno and Bomba's turn to take their wrath out on the crew, which they did with malicious pleasure. Shortly thereafter, the *Sea Djinn* was heeling around the point of Gozo Island, bow on for Cape Passero on the southern tip of Sicily.

When they were out in open water, the Rizzoli Troupe were allowed on deck to take the air and stretch their legs. La Lindi immediately set about charming one of the more gullible deckhands. With the information she had elicited from him, she joined the others on the fo'c'sle.

"We're sailing to Sicily, after the ship Ben's on."

Augusto Rizzoli was much cheered by the news. "Eh, *bella* Sicilia! It's only a short hop from there to Italy. If we dock there I think we should try to jump ship at the first opportunity, my friends."

Mamma shook her head. "All nine of us, including Mwaga and Poppea? What chance would we stand?"

Her husband shrugged. "Any chance would be a good chance, my love. We've got to start helping ourselves. We cannot rely on the boy and his dog forever."

Otto nodded. "*Ja,* you are right, *mein Heer.* I wonder where they have stowed our wagon?"

Buffo nodded toward the midship hold. "Down there, but it would be impossible to take it with us if we had to run for it."

The German strongman lowered his voice. "It is not the wagon I am thinking of, but the gun hidden underneath it.

If they have not already found it, that gun will come in handy."

Mummo objected. "Hah, that gun is an ancient wreck. It must be bunged up with sand and dust from travelling under the wagon. A gun like that would be more dangerous to the one using it than to anyone he was firing at!"

Serafina joined in the conversation. "But nobody knows that except us. I think Otto is right, the very threat of a gun gives us an advantage—it would come in handy during an escape."

Mamma held up her hands. "Keep your voices down, please. Maybe the gun is a good idea, but will they let us into the hold to get it? I don't think so."

La Lindi spoke up. "I have an idea. Otto, where exactly is the gun?"

"Just under the platform by the back door of the wagon. It hangs upon two hooks. There is also a little bag with it, containing powder, flint and musket balls. How do you plan on reaching it, Frau Lindi?"

The snake charmer looked to the large basket in which her python was coiled. "If Mwaga got loose and slithered down into the hold, I don't think any crewman would be willing to go after him. But I would."

Serafina was beginning to see the possibilities of her friend's scheme. "Of course! You are the only one who could handle Mwaga. Let's go down onto the hatch covers and pretend we're rehearsing our act. Everybody will be doing something, it will create a diversion."

Otto beamed at his beautiful young friend. "*Sehr gutt, Mädchen!** Let us get our equipment, *ja*!"

---

*Sehr gutt, Mädchen (very good, miss).

• • •

The vessel was riding easily under a steady breeze, sails thrumming tautly in the fine weather. Most of the crew were not busy, so they gathered to watch the free show put on by the troupe. Buffo and Mummo had mops and buckets; they played the part of two stupid sailors, mopping the deck. Amid hearty laughter from the onlookers, the two clowns slipped and slithered in an imaginary storm at sea, arguing and buffeting one another with the damp mops.

La Lindi opened the basket and took the giant python out, as Signore Rizzoli tuned his mandolin and Serafina began setting up a rhythm on her Kongo drum. La Lindi found a space in the hatch boards. She was getting ready to slip Mwaga between them when she heard Mamma's urgent whisper.

"Be careful, that Bomba fellow and the scar-faced one are watching us!"

The pair were leaning on the rear deck gallery rail, viewing the show.

Signore Rizzoli nodded to Serafina. "Come, *cara mia,* let's divert them with your voice. Sing!"

Together they strolled aft along the hatch tops, halting close to Bomba and Ghigno. Mounting the stairs to the rear deck, the beautiful black girl broke out into song.

"Sandalwood from Lebanon, fragrant and sweet,
ripe pomegranates delicious to eat,
and oh, the aroma of Rahat Lakoum,
roses which grow 'neath Anatolia's moon.
Silks from Cathay and the flow'rs of the East,

spread o'er the table of our wedding feast.
Bear them o'er deep seas and wild bounding main,
tell me, o tell me, you love me again.
And again . . . and again.

"Laden with spices and incense so rare,
ivory combs to grace long raven hair,
camels and caravans traverse the sands,
out of the dust of old Egypt's far lands.
Bright are the stars in the dark skies above,
yonder the ship comes which carries her love.
She sings as the waves softly break on the shore,
O tell me you'll care for me, love evermore.
Evermore . . . evermore."

Serafina's vibrant, husky voice clung to the final note, as Bomba and Ghigno stood caught in its spell. Signore Rizzoli cast a swift glance back to the hatch tops. Mummo nodded to him—both La Lindi and Mwaga were nowhere to be seen.

Fully dressed in black and white robes and turban, Al Misurata appeared behind both his henchmen. His mood had not improved greatly; he scowled sourly at them.

"Haven't you seen enough of these fools performing? Get to my cabin, we have things to discuss!"

Neither man argued. They went dutifully ahead of him into the captain's quarters.

Otto lay flat on the hatch cover with his back against the boards. He held a weighted barbell, with Buffo and Mummo sitting atop the iron balls at either end. The crew were counting aloud as he performed a number of press-ups with the formidable weight. "Seventeen! Eighteen! Nineteen!"

La Lindi's voice reached him from beneath the board below his head. "I've got it, bring me up, the gun is in the basket!"

The strongman carried on until he had done thirty presses with the barbell. He put it aside and allowed the two clowns to roll it away. Still lying flat out, Otto waved to acknowledge the crew's cheers, then he made as if to rise, but fell back, calling to them, "Enough, I've done enough. Oof! My back hurts, I'll lie here awhile. The show's over, thank you!"

The sailors drifted off gradually. When they had gone, Mamma tapped Otto's shoulder. "Now, quickly!"

He leaped up with a bound, which belied any injury to his back. Buffo and Mummo whipped back the section of hatch cover speedily, as Otto hauled La Lindi, her snake and the basket onto the deck with a single jerk. The clowns slid the hatch cover back into place, and the Rizzoli Troupe wandered casually back to their accommodations.

Signore Rizzoli examined the gun, which was an old blunderbuss his father had used for scaring birds from the crops on their land. He shook his head doubtfully.

"This gun will need a lot of attention. All the rust must be scraped off, and it will have to be cleaned and oiled, especially the mechanism."

Otto had been checking the pouch. "At least the powder's still dry, and the flint is in good order, the balls, too. So, once the gun is cleaned up we will have something to fight back with."

Mamma frowned. "Let's hope it doesn't come to that!"

Signore Rizzoli patted his wife's hand comfortingly. "Justice will prevail, *cara mia,* don't fret. We are all in the hands of the Almighty, He will help."

Otto looked up from inspecting the bore of the gun. "That is true, Mamma, though sometimes the Almighty does not mind us helping ourselves!"

IT WAS TWILIGHT OF THE FOLLOWING EVENING when the *White Ram*'s lookout spotted land. He bellowed out from the masthead, "Cape Passero, Sicily, sighted off the for'ard bow!"

Eli followed Joshua, Ben and Ned to the prow. He complained affably as Ned dropped behind to accompany him, "You young fellows are forever dashing places. Have a little respect for your elders and wait for me!"

Ned nuzzled the old man's hand, which pleased Eli. "Ah, here is the only one aboard with any manners. Thank you, my friend."

Ned sent him a thought, which he had no means of hearing. "Think nothing of it, sir, though you'd be surprised to know just how old I am!"

They stood gazing at the approaching coast as Ben questioned the patriarch. "So that's Sicily? I've not been there before—have you, sir?"

The old man nodded. "Oh yes, I know Sicily well, Ben. It is an ancient and beautiful island that has seen much hardship through conquest and oppression. The people are a hardy race, and do not trust strangers on sight. For the most part they are good and simple folk, though a few can be very dangerous."

Joshua tugged at his grandfather's sleeve. "Will we be going ashore? I want to see what it's like for myself!"

Eli stroked Ned's head absently. "Not in Sicily—we'll skirt the coast, past Siracusa and up to Catania, then we'll change course for Italy. There's a place called Melito, down at the southern tip of Calabria. Perhaps we'll call in there to stock up on supplies. We'll spend the better part of a day there. You'll like Melito, I have friends there."

Eli broke off to issue orders for the evening. "Abram, don't take the ship in too close to shore. Post a watch for reefs and shallows, we'll take her up the coast under half-sail for tonight."

The trusty Abram bowed, and strode off to do his captain's bidding.

Eli had noted Joshua's disappointment at not being able to go ashore. His eyes twinkled as he ruffled the boy's curls. "What would you say if I told you that we'll roast some lamb and fish, up here on deck? We'll sing a few songs, tell a few tales and you can stay up late, eh?"

The lad smiled happily. "Good old Grandad! I'll go and get charcoal and lemons and olive oil. Let me be cook, you know how you like my cooking!"

As he ran off, Eli called after him, "Don't forget my wine, it's the only thing that soothes my digestion after your burnt offerings!" The old fellow turned to Ben, winking. "I was only joking—my Joshua inherited his cooking skills from his mother. He's a very good cook."

In later years, Ben would remember it as a lovely evening, drifting up the Mediterranean Sea on the calm neap tide, with a few shorelights twinkling on one side and the air still warm from the day's heat. He and Ned sat with Eli and the crew, some of whom were playing flutes or strumming guitars. Ezekiel rigged a contrivance up over the midship rail—a grill with a charcoal fire burning beneath it, a sort of barbecue set up over the water to protect the deck from being burned. Ned pawed impatiently at Ben's hand; as usual he was ready for food.

"Mmmmm, smell that lamb, mate, Joshua's got it crackling well. I hope that shoulder's for me!"

Ben could not fail to inhale the aroma: roasting meat and fish, with the sweet scent of oregano, lemon rinds, rosemary and olive oil, all cooking over the coals. He tugged Ned's tail playfully. "Be quiet, you great walking stomach, I'm trying to listen to this song which the crew are singing."

Actually, it was only one of the crew, a young man with a deep, rich, bass voice, who sang the verse. The rest hummed along, joining in on the chorus.

> "There is a land beyond the stars,
> where I will be someday,
> but let me be all full of years,
> with beard so long and grey.
>
> "O Zion! O Jordan! O Israel! O come you angel band,
> and let me see beyond the stars that other promised land.

"I'll leave behind my trusty sword,
my sons will bear it well,
my flocks of sheep will follow still,
the ram that wears the bell.

"O Zion! O Jordan! O Israel! O come you angel band,
and let me see beyond the stars that other promised land.

"I'll leave behind grandchildren,
like grapes upon the vine,
and daughters fair to say in prayer,
This is our father's wine.

"O Zion! O Jordan! O Israel! O come you angel band,
and let me see beyond the stars that other promised land."

Joshua turned from the meal he was tending and called out, "Sing a song for us, Ben, do you know any good ones?"

The crew began cheering and encouraging Ben, but Eli called for silence.

"Let Benjamin be, perhaps he does not want to sing."

Ben thanked the old man, then stood up to speak. "I have a dreadful voice, and Ned's is no better. But I will show you some magic, performed by the Mysterious Benno and the Magnificent Neddo."

As he spoke, Ben caught an indignant thought from his dog. "Well, thank you very much for asking me did I want to be a magician again. Hmph! It would be good if I were allowed to make a few decisions for this team now and again. Pray tell, what'll you do if I don't feel like performing the act?"

Ben sent the black Labrador a ready reply. "Oh that's easy, I'll tell them you don't want any food, that you just want to go to our cabin and sleep, and that your real name is Bundi!"

Ned leaped upright smartly, trying to appear casual. "Oh well, just this once, but in future, would you please consult me first? And one other thing—don't ever dare to refer to me by that dreadful name again!"

Ben took Ned's head in both hands, staring into his eyes. "I'm sorry, mate, it was thoughtless of me not to ask you. I apologise. Of course I'd never mention that name to a living soul, ever!"

Ned treated him to a doggy grin. "Well, what are you waiting for, ask them for a blindfold and tell them to have their trinkets and objects ready!"

Eli, his grandson and the entire crew were astonished at Ben and Ned's act. Joshua immediately professed a desire to become a magician, just like his friend Ben.

Then the food was ready. They had a glorious late meal, sitting there on the deck, laughing and talking and congratulating the boy and his dog who had entertained them so well. The evening wore on, and whilst the men continued talking, Ben, Ned and Joshua curled up on some rope-matted fenders and dozed.

Surrounded by such safety and happiness, Ben was not expecting what happened next. Straight out of his dreams, the ghostly apparition of Captain Vanderdecken appeared, grinning evilly.

It was so sudden that Ben sat straight up, wide awake. Beside him, Joshua slumbered on, but Ned was up, teeth bared, and hackles rising. He shot Ben a thought. "Did you see that, too, mate? What's it all about?"

The boy glanced around. However, nothing had changed—
Eli and his crew were still gossiping idly, whilst two flutes
played a quiet duet in the background. He shook his head at
the dog.

"I don't know, but whenever the Dutchman shows up, it
usually means trouble, or danger nearby. You check for'ard,
Ned, I'll check aft!"

Ned was halfway to the fo'c'sle deck, when he peered off
amidships to port. He hurried back to Ben. "Come and have a
look at this, see what you think."

Before they had reached the midship rail, Ben glanced to
the other side. He alerted Ned. "Look, three big rowing boats
curving about to come astern of us. I don't like it, they're not
showing either sail or light. It looks like they're stalking us."

Ned answered mentally. "Aye, just like the three I spied on
our other side. Better tell Eli straightaway!"

The old man came to the stern, with Abram and Zachary on
either side of him. He watched the six boats moving stealthily
in their wake before murmuring quietly to Ben, "You were very
alert, Benjamin, thank you."

Remembering his dog's previous complaints, Ben answered, "Don't thank me, sir, it was Ned who saw them first."

Ned put his head against Ben's leg. "Thanks, mate, it's
nice to get credit where it's due." He cut short the thought as
Eli continued.

"There's no doubt that those men are wreckers. Skulking
along behind us without showing sails or lights, I see they have
muffled their oars, too, eh, Abram?"

The trusty crewman nodded. "They're dropping back a

bit, now that they know we've sighted them. Shall I go below and man the stern cannon?"

The patriarch stroked his beard, his keen gaze still riveted on the six boats. "I think not. Stay here with me, Abram. Wholesale slaughter is not the answer. I know those men are ruffians and villains, but they are only peasants with families to feed. I could not bring myself to kill them. So if needs be I will take the snake's head."

Ben understood the old man's meaning. "You mean that you will slay their leader, sir?"

Eli bowed his head at the boy. "Ah, you understand my plan, very good. However, I will only take a life as the last resort—the House of Shimon breeds warriors, not murderers. First I will talk with their chief. Abram, bring me a light."

Holding up the lantern with which Abram had provided him, Eli whispered an order to Zachary, who stole off to do his bidding. The old man then raised his voice, shouting to the small flotilla of boats, "Who is your chieftain, I would speak with him!"

The foremost of the boats was rowed forward until it stood about ten yards off the *White Ram*'s stern. The False Padre, Marlanese, ignited a torch of reeds and stood in the rowboat's bows.

Ned's assessment reached Ben. "Hah! There's a real villain if ever I saw one! How anyone could trust that rascal I'll never know. Look at that ragged cassock and his big greasy hat—he could be mistaken for a poison toad in disguise!"

Ben stroked his dog's ear. "A perfect description, mate. Hush now, let's hear what he has to say."

Eli spoke sternly to Marlanese. "Who are you, and why are you stalking us?"

The False Padre took off his hat, revealing a pale, bald dome, with lank strands of greying hair plastered across it. He smiled unctuously. "Sir, you mistake our intentions. We are not stalking your fine ship, merely following a custom of this coast. I am Padre Umberto, and these men are my parishioners. We wish to visit your ship, so that I can bestow on it a special blessing. We will come aboard with your permission."

Eli folded both arms across his chest. He looked for all the world like some biblical prophet straight from the pages of the Old Testament.

"Blasphemer! You are no holy man, you are a wrecker, with murder and plunder in your heart. Begone—I warn you!"

The fat, little scoundrel turned ugly then. He spat into the water, drawing back his threadbare cape to reveal a sword and musket thrust into his belt.

"No man talks to Marlanese like that! Listen, old fool, you are in my waters now, trespassing on my coast. Now let me aboard, or it will go badly for you!"

Eli stood firm, pointing at the wrecker. "Go quickly, before you stir my wrath!"

The False Padre drew his sword, quivering with rage. "Wrath? I'll show you wrath. I'll gut you and hang you from your own yardarm by the feet. Attack!"

As the boats pulled forward to charge the ship, Zachary came hurrying up. He was carrying Eli's big bow, the one made from ram's horn. With it was a single arrow, its heavy, barbed point wrapped with oil-soaked cloth, which he passed to the old man. Eli thrust the shaft into the lantern, drawing it forth spurting flame. In a few swift movements he set it upon the bowstring and hauled back mightily as he took aim and let fly.

The wrecker did not even have time to scream. The arrow

pierced his throat, the burning cloth falling loose to send his cassock and cloak up in flames. He fell back into the boat with his clothing aflame as his crew gasped at the rapidity of Eli Bar Shimon's action.

The patriarch held up his bow, calling out in a voice like thunder to the wrecking crews, "We are warriors, not fools like your leader. Look to my ship and see what awaits you if you stay here!"

Zachary had given orders to the crew below decks. They ran out the six cannon to port and starboard, firing off a broadside. The explosion deafened the wreckers, and lit up the night with its force.

Ben and Ned stood on either side of Eli, wreathed in smoke, watching the six boats splashing off like pond beetles pursued by pike. There was a hiss and a sizzle as the last boat crew tossed the burning body of Marlanese into the sea.

Joshua came dashing up from where Ezekiel had been restraining him on the for'ard deck. "Grandfather, Ben, what's going on?"

Ben threw an arm around the lad's shoulders. "Your grandfather has just been dispensing a bit of justice to some ruffians who wanted his ship."

The old man smiled at the two boys. "It worked well. Remember what I told you, Benjamin?"

Ben returned the smile. "Aye, sir, cut off the snake's head. Of course you forgot to say—and the rest of its body is useless."

Eli winked at Ben. "But you already knew that!"

Ned was wagging his tail furiously whilst sending out thoughts. "That old Eli's as good as a one-man army. I'm glad he's on our side, mate. Whew, that excitement has given me an appetite. I wonder if there's any of that good food left?"

Ben spoke aloud to the dog. "Don't you think you've had enough to eat for one evening, old hunger guts?"

Joshua stroked the black Labrador's back fondly. "I'll get you some food if you're still hungry, Ned. Come on, boy, there's plenty left."

They galloped off together. Eli looked curiously at Ben. "How did you know your dog was hungry?"

The strange boy shrugged. "Oh, Ned, he can say more with his tail and eyes than some people can with their tongues, sir."

The old man looked as if he only half-believed Ben. "Yes, I'm sure he could. I feel a bit peckish myself now, what about you, young fellow?"

Ben flicked a tawny-coloured lick of hair from his eyes. "Oh, I imagine I could manage a bite."

The patriarch chuckled. "You've got a good imagination. We'd best hurry before those two clean it all up!"

Next morning the wind had changed, though it was still a bright, blustery day. The *Sea Djinn* had to tack and veer to come off-shore of Cape Passero. Ghigno and Bomba took a ship's boat and rowed ashore, to where the six wrecking boats had been hauled up beyond the tideline. As he waded hurriedly through the surf, Ghigno was already sensing that something was amiss. Making his way to a collection of rickety hovels, the scar-faced Corsair strode into the first one. A stick-like old woman was tending a small fire, over which an iron cauldron was simmering.

With his eyes smarting from the smoky atmosphere, Ghigno crouched by the old woman and made enquiries. "Where is my cousin Marlanese?"

The crone uttered one word. *"Morte!"**

The Corsair's jaw tightened. Apart from that he showed no emotion, but continued his interrogation. "And the rest, where are they?"

The old woman nodded in the direction of the other shacks. "Some are in the big hut, others have gone back to their villages."

Ghigno thrust his face close to hers. "What happened?"

She shrugged. "I was not there, ask them."

Ghigno stood swiftly. "I will!"

There were about a score of men in the largest dwelling, lounging around a fire and passing jugs of red wine back and forth. They were holding a murmured conversation, which ceased the moment that Ghigno walked in. A sullen silence prevailed. Then one big, rough-looking villain stood up to face the intruder.

Ghigno spoke, almost casually. "I have just heard the padre is dead. Who killed him?"

The rough-looking man drew a long knife from his belt and ran it through his scruffy red beard, as if grooming it. His tone was bold and challenging. "Marlanese is dead, let that be an end to it!"

In the enclosed space, the musket report sounded like a small cannon. The redbeard collapsed beside the fire, with a hole between his eyes and a shocked look on his face. Ghigno coolly blew down the musket barrel as he drew another one, already cocked and loaded, from the back of his sash. His voice still casual, he spoke as he placed the gun against the forehead of the man sitting nearest to him. "How do they call you?"

Morte (dead).

The man's Adam's apple bobbed visibly as he answered. "Beppino of Montalto. I have a wife and four children, signore. . . ."

Ghigno cut him short. "If you wish to see them again then answer me truly, Beppino. How was my cousin slain?"

Beppino closed his eyes tight as the musket pressed hard against his brow. "It was the old one, the master of the *White Ram*. We were not told that it was heavily armed. They saw us coming up on the vessel, the old *capitano* ordered your cousin not to come further. Marlanese would not listen, so the old one shot him with a fire arrow. They fired cannon at us, that ship carries many cannon. We were forced to retreat, or they would have blasted us out of the sea, signore. We were not told they were fighters with a heavily armed ship."

Bomba had been holding the boat in the surf. He watched Ghigno climb in. "What happened, did you fire that shot?"

The scar made the Corsair's face wrinkle wickedly as he hissed at Bomba, "What business is it of yours? Get me back to the ship!"

Al Misurata listened to Ghigno's report. He sat in silence for a moment, then nodded, showing neither disappointment nor temper. He strode out on deck, followed by Ghigno, to whom he issued rapid orders. "Put on all sail, head into deeper water, but keep the coast in sight. Steer a course for the Italian mainland, and post lookouts. Let me know the moment that ship is sighted. Get those performers off the deck and back into their accommodation!"

As they were being herded back into their cabin, Serafina, who had caught Al Misurata's orders, confided to Mamma,

"We're not landing at all in Sicily, we're going to Italy. I heard Al Misurata saying so."

Mamma raised her eyes thankfully. "I'm grateful for it. This idea of making a break and escaping, I've never liked it. There's too many of them, some of us could be hurt, or even killed."

Her husband shook his head. "If we make a landfall in Italy, we must still try to escape. Right, Otto?"

The strongman had taken the blunderbuss from its hiding place. He continued working on it.

"*Ja,* right, *mein Heer.* I would sooner be dead than live as the slave of another. Escape is our only hope!"

La Lindi watched the big German oiling the trigger mechanism. "That goes for me also!"

Mummo nudged Buffo. "What would you sooner be, a slave or a dead man?"

Buffo scratched his head, as if thinking hard. "Well, I wouldn't mind being a slave, as long as I was sold to a young, pretty woman. But on the other hand, being dead might have some advantages. Dead men don't have to get up early, or work, or feel hungry. Yowch!"

Signore Rizzoli withdrew his foot from the clown's rump. "What are you saying, muddlehead? Dead men cannot breathe the air of freedom, they cannot laugh or move. Besides, what pretty young woman would buy a thick-headed buffoon like you, eh?"

Buffo put on a mournful face. Serafina laughed and hugged him.

"I would if I had the price, he'd make a lovely slave!"

Buffo fell on his knees in front of her. "Then I'll save all my money and give it to you, so you can buy me. But I've always

been your slave, O Beautiful One, from the moment I set eyes
on you!"

Mummo hung his head in mock despair. "You mean you'd
break up our act? Traitor!"

Serafina hugged him, too. "I'll buy you both. When I'm a
rich girl, I'll need two slaves!"

Otto drew the hammer back and clicked it. "There'll be no
slave trading done once I've got this gun fixed!"

MELITO, IN THE REGGIO DI CALABRIA. ON THE
SOUTHERN TIP OF THE ITALIAN MAINLAND.

AT MIDNOON, TWO DAYS OUT FROM SICILY, THE *WHITE
Ram* sailed in to harbour at Melito. Ben and Ned stood on the
fo'c'sle deck, with Eli and his grandson. There was quite a

crowd gathered on the dockside, everyone
seemed to be waving and cheering.

Joshua waved back—the boy was happy, but
perplexed. "Why are they cheering, is it for
us, Grandfather?"

Eli shrugged. "Who knows? They seem a happy bunch. It
must be some sort of celebration, or a saint's day. Ah! We'll
soon find out, there's my old friend Fra Salvatore." The old
man waved and shouted, "Salvatore, *amico,* is it really you?
Wait, we're coming ashore!"

Fra Salvatore was an old monk of
the Franciscan order. He wore a
worn, brown habit, girdled by a
simple white cord. His face was
nutbrown and heavily wrinkled by
the sun. Ned sent a thought to Ben.

"I like him, he looks like an old saint."

Fra Salvatore made way for them through the crowd, who all seemed to want to pat their backs or shake them by the hand. Eli and the old monk embraced.

Eli introduced Joshua, Ben and Ned, then looked in wonderment at the people surrounding them. "It's so good to see you again, but what have we done that pleases these good folk so much?" The old monk led them away, toward a quayside tavern. "First we'll eat and drink. Concepta makes the best seafood frittata in the world. Come!"

Fra Salvatore spoke truly. Concepta, the tavern owner, lived up to his words. She seated them by the window and placed fresh, crusty bread, wine and huge platters of her famous seafood omelettes before them. As they ate the monk explained.

"I keep messenger pigeons, Eli. Nothing goes on in these waters between here and Sicilia that I don't know about. You and your friends are the ones who rid the coasts of the evil Marlanese, the False Padre. That fiend has plundered and murdered our shores for years. He has struck here at Melito many times. We have lost husbands, wives and children to him and his wreckers. Goods, valuables, even animals. He was the servant of Satan himself—what he could not steal, he would kill, or burn. As soon as I got the word and description, I knew it was you, my Lion of Judah. Tell me, did your great ram-horn bow sing its song to him?"

Eli watched as Concepta poured more wine for him. "Though the death of a fellow creature gives me no joy, it was I who slew him. He got only his just deserts, and I doubt he will be greatly mourned. But enough of that, what other news do you have for me?"

Fra Salvatore gripped his friend's hand, looking concerned. "Nothing good, I fear, Eli. Your enemies pursue you swiftly. Sometime after midnight, another ship will berth here."

Ben interrupted. "Aye, Al Misurata and the *Sea Djinn*!"

Fra Salvatore crossed himself. "The Barbary Pirate, another one who sails under the banner of evil. Do you know of him, Ben?"

Ned looked up from under the table, where he was dealing with a mighty hambone. "Hoho, do we know of him? I could tell you a thing or ten about that rascal!"

Eli nodded to Ben. "Tell our friend your story."

The monk looked on intently as the strange boy with the clouded blue-grey eyes related the experiences of himself and his dog. When he had told all, Fra Salvatore spoke gravely. "Then you cannot stay here. You must go, as soon as you are able. But let me warn you, Eli, the seas are wide betwixt here and Piran. Misurata has many allies in his pay. I fear for you all!"

Joshua spoke out boldly. "My grandfather fears nothing, the Shimon are warriors!"

Eli allowed himself a smile at the lad's faith in him. "Joshua, what our friend says is true. There will be great danger ahead before we reach the shores of Slovenija."

"Unless!" All eyes turned to Ben at his outburst.

"Unless what, Benjamin?" Eli replied.

Ben outlined his plan. "Unless Ned and I can find another vessel sailing for Piran—we could board her secretly. Then, sir, you could provide a decoy with the *White Ram*. Lead Al Misurata off to where he has not planned to go. After awhile, you could sail to your homeland. That way things would be a lot safer for both of us."

Eli shook his head. "But I gave my word I would convey you to Piran. I am in your debt for saving Joshua's life. I would not leave you at the mercy of foes!"

The monk appealed to his old friend. "The boy is right, Eli, that is the solution. It makes good sense to me, and gives him more chance of helping his friends, the Rizzoli Troupe."

Eli leaned his elbows on the table, stroking his beard. "But where would he find a ship sailing for Piran soon? One whose captain could be trusted?"

Fra Salvatore had the answer. "You remember Kostas Krimboti the treasure hunter?"

Despite the urgency of the situation, Eli chuckled. "What? You mean Kostas Gold Jaw? Is that madman still scouring the seas for sunken treasure?"

The monk smiled. "No, he found a treasure ship, a Roman galley, right here off Cape Spartivento. Kostas became a rich man, but he could not give up the sea life. He gave up treasure seeking, though, and bought a ship, the *Blue Turtle*. I know for a fact that he is sailing before evening today."

Ben asked eagerly, "For Piran?"

Fra Salvatore patted the boy's hand. "No, Ben, he goes to Muggia, a little place right on the Italian border, very close to Piran. I know this because Kostas is taking some items to the nuns there, at the Convento di Santa Filomena. Habits, beads and a painting of the Madonna and Holy Child surrounded by many angels, which I painted myself."

Ben's eagerness was rekindled. "Would he take Ned and me?"

The old monk nodded. "For certain, he would not refuse me." Fra Salvatore stared enquiringly at Eli. "So?"

The patriarch hesitated momentarily, one hand stroking

Ned beneath the table as he reached out with the other and laid it on Ben's head.

"Do it, go now, Benjamin, whilst you still can. I will put to sea within the hour and set sail south into the Mediterranean for home. You will be heading the other way, up into the Ionian Sea. But tell me, Salvatore, how do you know Misurata will follow us?"

The old monk rubbed the tips of his thumb and index finger together. "Money, Eli. I will put it about, the course you are on. There are always those seeking to gain gold for information."

The time had come for Ben and Ned to take leave of their dear friends, right there in the tavern. Joshua hugged Ned, his tears wetting the black Labrador's coat. Ned was passing thoughts to Ben. "If we don't leave soon, I'm afraid I'll be howling. It's breaking my heart to leave these good people."

Ben replied mentally, "Mine, too, mate, but we've got to help the troupe. Look at Eli, he's almost weeping."

Eli Bar Shimon took Ben's hand. "We may never meet again, Benjamin. Now go, and take my heart with you. What a grandson you would have made!"

Ben blinked back unshed tears. "Thank you for everything, sir. If I had a grandfather I'd want him to be just like you. Joshua is your grandson, he will make you happy—and proud of him, too, someday. Come on, Ned, Fra Salvatore is waiting, we must go now."

Ned licked Eli's hand, and Ben shook Joshua's.

"Good-bye, mate, don't go swimming where there are sharks."

Without looking back they left the tavern, following the monk. Joshua buried his face in his grandfather's robe.

"I don't want them to go!"

Eli stroked the lad's curls. "Nor do I, Joshua, but one day you'll see it was the right thing to do. Come on now, let's go home."

Fra Salvatore led his two charges up a side alley, explaining, "The fewer people who see us travelling together, the better. Kostas has the *Blue Turtle* moored about a mile up the coast."

Ned sent Ben a random thought. "I hope this Kostas can cook lamb as good as young Joshua."

The boy tugged his dog's tail. "Still thinking of food? I think you should have been a wild hog."

Ned huffed. "I like thinking of food, it stops me grieving over absent friends."

Any further conversation was stalled as they were passing a mean-looking house. There were several painful yelps, and a scruffy-looking puppy bounded out. It was pursued by a small man with a cruel face. He was lashing at the little dog with a stick, shouting at it, "I'll teach you to steal bread from the table, I'll take the hide off your mangy back!" He cornered the puppy and began beating it. However, he did not have much time to administer the punishment.

Ned hit the man's back like a roaring lion. The fellow went down, screaming for his life. The puppy dashed off, and Ben called to his furious dog. "Ned, come away!"

However, such was Ned's fury that he was oblivious to all pleas or commands—he continued his attack upon the puppy beater. Ben was forced to haul the big, black Labrador off by main force, assisted by the old monk. The man's clothing was almost ripped from him; he was bruised, scratched and bleeding from several places. Immediately the dog was pulled from him, he hobbled off, screeching.

"Mad dog! Mad dog! I'll have that beast destroyed by the *guardia.** Help, I've been savaged by a rabid dog!"

Fra Salvatore alerted Ben speedily. "We'd best get out of here quickly, my son, or your Ned will be shot without question!"

As they hurried off, Ben was doing his best to reprimand Ned with stern thoughts. "Really, mate, what were you thinking of? I thought you were going to kill the fellow, the way you threw yourself upon him!"

Ned was unrepentant. "Aye, and I would have if you and the old man hadn't pulled me off. Did you see that cowardly little bully beating the poor pup?"

Ben was forced to agree, but he continued berating his dog. "I saw it, and I was about to run in and deal with that man, but you were too quick."

The black Labrador had recovered himself somewhat. He huffed, "I'm not sorry for teaching him a lesson, I'd do it again without a second thought. By the way, where's the puppy got to?"

As they ran through the side streets, Ben took a quick glance around. "There's no sign of him, I expect he's cut off and gone to hide somewhere."

They came out onto open coastland, dotted with rocks. Ahead of them at a small jetty, the blue-sailed masts of a ship could be seen.

Fra Salvatore slowed his pace to a walk. "There she is, the *Blue Turtle*." He clasped a hand to his heaving chest. "Take it slowly, friend, I'm too old to run any further."

Guardia (police).

Ben slowed, and took the old fellow's arm. "I'm sorry about the way Ned behaved back there, Brother."

The monk's wrinkled face relaxed into a smile. "Your dog did the right thing, boy. Only a few days ago I took a staff to a rascal who was flogging a little mule. Sometimes the wrath of the Lord against wrongdoers can manifest itself in strange ways."

Ned liked the old Franciscan. He grinned, in a smug, canine way, at Ben. "Hah, you see, I knew I was justified. Well said, sir!"

Ben was about to reply when the puppy trotted out from behind a rock and joined them, as though it was the most natural thing in the world to do. It looked to be no more than a few months old, and was of indiscriminate breed. The little dog was a dusty brown, with black patches. Its bristly hair stuck out at odd angles, it had virtually no tail, lollopy paws and would have been flop-eared except for its left ear, which stood up straight.

Though Ben felt sorry for it, he knew there were far more important things to occupy him. "It's the oddest little dog I've ever seen, eh, Ned? Go on, mate, back to town with you, we can't take you with us, I'm sorry."

The pup took no notice of the boy, and frisked around Ned, snapping at his tail.

Ben sent his companion a thought. "Tell it to go away, please."

Ned returned the thought. "What d'you think I'm doing? I can't get any sense out of the rascal. Listen to him yapping, d'you know what that bark means?"

"I don't even know what it means when you start barking. I never learned dog language. What's he saying?" Ben replied.

Ned whisked his tail away from the little dog's teeth. *Amico,* that's what he's saying—friend. I don't suppose the good Brother wants a dog?"

As if preempting Ben's enquiry, Fra Salvatore shook his head pityingly. "I can't take him, that cruel fellow will claim him as soon as he gets back to the town."

They were getting close to the ship now. Ben urged Ned, "Listen, mate, you'll have to have a serious word with that pup. Tell him we're sorry, but he can't come with us."

Ned sat down on the path, pinning the puppy with a paw and holding him still as he informed Ben, "It's no good, this wretch'll soon have my lovely tail chewed to the bone. I've tried to reason with him, but all I get from the villain is that one word. *Amico!*"

Kostas Krimboti was a jolly giant of a man. He welcomed them aboard with a smile which beamed out like the midday sun. His teeth were all pure gold. Ned pointed this out to Ben.

"Good grief, what a set of choppers! They're not very well-made, though, you can see they were once gold coins. Look, there's heads, writing and shields on some of them. He must have carved them himself. I like him, though, what d'you think, mate?"

Ben sized Kostas up as the Greek captain and the monk spoke together about taking them as passengers. Kostas Krimboti was a formidable-looking fellow. He was dressed in fisherman's garb—open shirt, baggy, knee-length pantaloons and a broad green sash into which many lethal pointed and curved knives were thrust. His huge head of curly red hair was complemented by a pair of thick, gold, hoop earrings. He laughed constantly as he conversed with the old monk, finally hugging him and declaring aloud, "For my sins, which are many, I will do what you ask, my friend! My father was a very holy man, it will rest his memory to know that his bandit of a son is doing some good in this miserable world, eh!"

Still laughing uproariously, he tweaked Ben's cheek. "Welcome aboard the *Blue Turtle,* Beniamino, and your wonderful Ned, whom Fra Salvatore has told me about." He swept the puppy up in one big, calloused hand, and kissed it resoundingly on the nose. "Hohohoho! I have many rats for you to catch aboard this ship, *bambino.* So, what is your name, eh? Are you a son of the noble Ned?"

The black Labrador gave an indignant bark. "I should sincerely hope not! That creature, a son of mine? But what do you suppose the pup's name is, Ben?"

"Amico!" The word slipped out as Ben said it aloud. "Aye, Cap'n, that's what his name is, Amico."

Kostas bent to kiss the puppy again—it bit his nose.

He went off into gales of laughter. "Hohohoho! What fangs! When he sees the rats he will be like Achilles among the Trojans, won't you, Amico!"

The little fellow yapped, renewing his assault on the big man's nose. Kostas was delighted.

"See, he understands me. Take your dogs to the cook, boy. Tell him to feed them the crackling off the pork we had last night. Here, Saint Salvatore, let me help you ashore. My *Blue Turtle* must sail the seas now!"

The old monk stood on the jetty, waving to Kostas and Ben as the blue-sailed ship turned bow on to the sea and put out into deep water. The big Greek captain sang aloud in a fine baritone.

"O take me away from the land,
ye four winds that blow mightily,
to the isles I've seen only in dreams,
far away o'er the deep rolling sea.
O ship. Carry me!

"Where waves like tall mountains abound,
with dolphin and many blue whale,
while gales through the rigging do sing,
wild songs to a vessel in sail.
O ship. Carry me!

"For my hand finds no rest on a plough,
and my heart knows no joy on the shore,
like the seabirds which soar in my wake,
I will follow the sea evermore.
O ship. Carry me!"

The wind stood fair in the cool late evening, as Kostas and
Ben sat sharing a basket of almonds and raisins on the foredeck. The Greek captain tossed a nut high; catching it in his
mouth, he winked at Ben. "So, my friend, where are your two
faithful hounds, still feeding their faces in the galley, I
wager, eh?"

The boy tried catching a nut, but it bounced off his lip.
"Aye, Cap'n, your cook, Nico, is very pleased with them. Little
Amico chased a big rat out from behind the stove. He couldn't
catch it, but Ned batted it over the side into the water. Nico
said it's just as well he did, because it was so large that it might

have eaten Amico. Nico's rewarding them, though if he doesn't stop feeding them pork rinds, they'll both be sick."

Kostas laughed heartily. "Sick as dogs, eh. Hohohoho!"

Ben questioned him about their destination. "Where's this convent, I've forgotten the name of the place. Is it far from Piran?"

Kostas picked his gold-coin teeth with a dagger tip. "Not far at all, less than a day's walk. It's the Convento di Santa Filomena at Muggia. You'll like it there, Ben, the good nuns are excellent cooks, and their Abbess is a very charitable lady. She thinks I'm a villainous pirate who has reformed. Hah, I ask you, do I look like a pirate?"

The boy regarded his friend's thick, red curls, jangling earrings, gold teeth and the daggers which bristled from his sash. He tried to stifle a smile. "Well, you don't exactly look like the Archbishop of Greece!"

Kostas put on what he thought was a soulful look. "Maybe not, but I'm piling up rewards in heaven for myself. Carrying cargo from Fra Salvatore to the nuns, and helping you to rescue your friends from a life of slavery. What could be more noble than that, eh?"

Ben also adopted a pious expression. "I hadn't thought of it that way, you're right, Cap'n. I wouldn't be surprised if you came to be known as Good Saint Kostas of the High Seas."

Starlight reflected off the gold teeth as the big Greek went into another fit of laughter. He cuffed Ben playfully. "Away, you mocking wretch, off to your bunk before I have you keel-hauled!"

Kostas had not seen Ned and Amico loping up behind him. The black Labrador knocked him flat and began jumping on him, sending messages to his master. "Grr, d'you want me to chew off both his legs, mate?"

Ben could not help chuckling as he replied, "You don't have to, Ned, Amico's doing the job for you!"

The puppy was joining in the fun, growling as he nipped at the fallen captain's ankles. Kostas was laughing again as he pleaded with Ben. "Help, I'm being attacked by wild dogs! Mercy!"

Not many hours had elapsed since the *Blue Turtle* sailed from Melito when the *Sea Djinn* made landfall there. Al Misurata stood on the main quay, warming his hands by a fire, where some fishermen were cooking their catch. He strode impatiently from the firelight toward four men approaching him. It was Ghigno and two of his aides, who were frog-marching one of the locals between them. Al Misurata glared fiercely at the Scar-face. "Are you going to keep me waiting all the night? What's going on, who's this gutter rat?"

Ghigno took hold of his captive's hair and shook him. "One who I'm told has information for us, Master."

The pirate took a glance at the fishermen, who were craning to hear the conversation. He nodded toward his ship. "Get him aboard quickly!"

Once on board the *Sea Djinn,* Al Misurata listened briefly to Ghigno's report.

"This one has news of the boy and his dog—they're not travelling on the old man's ship anymore."

The man, realising that Al Misurata was a rich and important person, adopted a cringing attitude. "Lord, the dog and the boy set upon me, I was attacked, bitten and injured. Your servants dragged me from my sickbed and forced me to come with them. But I know where that whelp and his cur went, is that not worth a reward from one as magnificent as you, sire?"

The pirate's tone did not warn the man of the danger he was in. "It might be worth some gold, if I had time to waste on wharf scrapings such as you. But I need information now. Bomba!"

The slaver whipped a noose around the man's neck, and tossed it over a rigging spar. He heaved on it until the unfortunate was gagging on tiptoe, both hands trying feebly to loosen the strangling rope. Bomba raised his cane and laid a stroke across his victim's back. At a nod from his master, Bomba let the fellow fall to the deck, where he lay gurgling with pain.

Al Misurata stood over him, speaking menacingly. "I'll wager that hurt. There are ninety-nine more strokes to come, if you decide to play the fool with me, my friend. Bomba, hoist him up again!"

Before the slave driver had a chance to obey the command, the man was pleading in hoarse terror. "I'll tell you! I'll tell you! Please, no more!"

When he had given his information, Al Misurata turned to Ghigno. "Well?"

The scar-faced Corsair nodded. "It must be the truth. Nobody saw the boy and dog return to the old one's ship, it sailed off, bound south. This other one, the *Blue Turtle,* it's captained by a Greek. He sailed just before sunset for a convent in Muggia. I spoke to a man who loaded cargo onto her. It looks like the boy is headed for Piran. If we cast off now we should be able to catch them—the Greek's ship is nought but an old tub, it does not have our speed."

The look on his master's face caused Ghigno to fall silent.

Al Misurata stirred the man lying on the deck with his boot. "Did you hear that?"

The fellow shook his head furiously, still in a panic. "No, sire, hear what? I heard nothing, I swear it!"

The pirate nodded noncommittally. "Go ashore, then, and speak no word to anybody." He glanced significantly at Bomba, who touched the hilt of his curved dagger and nodded.

Al Misurata watched the man scrabble over the side to the quay. Bomba waited a moment before following him.

Confronting Ghigno, Al Misurata hissed savagely, "Why didn't you shout our plans from the mast top, fool! Sometimes I think the older you get, the softer your brain becomes. What possessed you to gabble on like that?"

The scar-faced Corsair bowed his head. "It was stupid of me. I apologise, Master."

The pirate sighed. "I'll let it pass this time, but only because of our years together. Make ready to sail as soon as Bomba gets back."

La Lindi had her ear to the cabin door; she had heard all that transpired on deck.

Otto put aside the loaded blunderbuss, knowing that any chance of a sudden escape had been foiled. "We will be under way shortly, there is no time for us to make a break. But it is good to know that our friend Ben is still trying to help us, *ja!*"

Mamma Rizzoli covered the gun with her shawl. "I know the convent at Muggia, a girl from my village went there as a novice. If only we could reach it, I'm certain we would be safe there. It is only a short distance from Piran, eh, Augusto?"

Signore Rizzoli was in total agreement. "*Si,* the Convento

di Santa Filomena is a strongly built place. I think we should make our break when we come ashore at Piran, we'd stand a better chance there."

Otto nodded. "I am with you, *mein Heer.*"

Even Serafina brightened up considerably. "Ben will be there to help us, I know it!"

Buffo interrupted. "Ssshh! Somebody's coming."

Bomba entered the cabin. He looked around, checking that everything was in order. Testing the blade of his curved knife on his thumbtip, he leered at Serafina. "We're under way for the Adriatic Sea, it shouldn't be too long before we catch up with your boyfriend and his hound. I'm eager to meet them, aren't you, pretty one?"

Otto stepped forward, his eyes blazing with anger. "*Ja*, and I am eager to meet you, *Dummkopf,* your knife does not scare me!"

Bomba backed out of the cabin hastily, slamming the door behind him.

Otto smiled at Serafina. "Pay no attention to him, *Schatze*, he is only a big windbag who loves the sound of his own voice."

La Lindi put her arm around the girl. "Maybe he is, but the scar-faced one said that Ben is on a ship, which he called a leaky old tub. What chance does it stand against this *Sea Djinn*?"

THE IONIAN SEA. SOUTH
OF THE GULF OF TARANTO.

KOSTAS KRIMBOTI LEANED OVER THE STERN RAIL,
pointing at the water. "I can always tell when we are getting
into deep seas, Ben. This Ionian Sea gets even deeper. In my
treasure hunting days I was told of a Roman
galley which went down in this area many
centuries ago, carrying the gold of Egypt in
her hold."

Ben stared at the dark blue water. "And you
never tried to hunt for it?"

Kostas flashed him a gold-toothed smile. "No, but some-
day I will—the thought of all that treasure lying down there, it
is a challenge to me."

"But a very dangerous challenge," Ben replied.

The Greek captain shrugged. "Danger is the spice of life
to Krimboti. Hah, here come our rat seekers, maybe they have
rid my *Blue Turtle* of pests, eh?"

Ned looked appealingly to Ben. "I'm doing all I can, mate,
but this little villain must think my tail's a rat, he keeps attacking it. Gerroff, you young pestilence!"

Ned shook Amico off his tail. The puppy, thinking it was some sort of game, went straight back to the attack.

Ben's attention was distracted by the lookout, who called down to his captain, "Ship astern!"

Kostas avoided the two dogs as he ran for the mainmast. "Come on, boy, let's take a look!"

As they mounted the rigging, a glimpse of the *Flying Dutchman,* floundering in the icy waters off Cape Horn, flashed across the boy's mind, accompanied by a thought from his dog. "That can only mean one thing, mate!"

High on the mast head, Ben and Kostas clung to the ratlines as the lookout passed the spyglass over. Kostas gave it to Ben. "What do you make of it, my friend?"

A single glance through the lens at the five dark red sails—four triangular and one square—told Ben all he needed to know. He returned the glass to Kostas. "That's Al Misurata's ship, the *Sea Djinn.* I wonder how he knew to follow us? It was supposed to be a secret that we were on your ship."

The Greek squinted his eye to the glass. "Hah, who can keep a secret in a small port such as Melito? Coins change hands there at a single whisper!"

Ben had gained sufficient knowledge of ships and the sea to voice an unhappy opinion. "At the rate she's travelling we'll be run down within a day. The *Blue Turtle* couldn't make it in a sea chase with that vessel."

Kostas clacked his golden dentures noisily. "That's right, boy, but there's something you haven't realised yet. We are a small craft compared to her, we're only a third of the *Sea Djinn*'s size. We can see them, but I'll wager they haven't spotted us yet." Kostas descended to the deck, with Ben close behind.

"So, it's only a matter of time before they do. Have you got a plan, Cap'n?"

The Greek laughed. "I wouldn't be Kostas Krimboti if I hadn't. We'll pile on all sail and make for the isle of Kérkira, just off the mainland of my country. If we keep far enough ahead, we won't be sighted. Maybe my *Turtle* isn't the fastest ship, but once I'm in Greek waters I'll lose that *Sea Djinn*. Watch me!"

He took the wheel, roaring out orders. "Kristos, Babiko, put on every stitch of sail, quick now! Fotis, Herakles, haul in those fenders. We're bound for Kérkira with a good breeze behind us. Hohohoho!"

Ben and Ned helped the sailors to pull the heavy rope fenders aboard. Ned passed his master a thought. "Does that Kostas never do anything except laugh? Here we're in deadly peril, and he's guffawing again!"

Digging both hands into the saturated fenders, Ben hauled swiftly. "I'd sooner have him laughing than crying, mate, he can't help being a happy type."

The black Labrador growled. "Talking about happy types, there's one hauling on my tail instead of the fender. What d'you think, would it lighten our load if we slung him overboard?"

The boy cast a reproving glance at his dog. "Really, Ned, were you never young once?"

Ned sighed resignedly. "Aye, almost a hundred years ago!"

As evening approached, the lookout had good news to shout down to his captain. "No sight of the red sails, I think we've lost her!"

Kostas played the wheel skillfully to and fro. "Keep tacking like this and we may sight Kérkira by tomorrow night. Let's hope Al Misurata thinks we've kept to the Italian mainland side, up Brindisi and Bari!"

A thought from Ned reached Ben. "Huh, I'd steer clear of either coast with the weather we're due to have. We'd be smashed on the rocks!"

The boy answered his dog urgently. "What weather? Speak out if you know something we don't!"

Ned pointed with his muzzle. "Sorry, mate, I'd forgotten that humans don't have the same senses as dogs. For awhile I've felt it brewing out there to the southeast. I know it's going dark, but look at the cloud building up over there. I've heard thunder, too, bit of a distance away, but you'll be hearing it before too long."

The boy patted his dog's head. "Well spotted, mate, I'd best go and inform our cap'n."

Kostas Krimboti continued to steer the vessel as he listened to Ben's report.

"I think we're in for some heavy weather soon. I can tell by the way Ned keeps looking southeast and whining."

"Excuse me, young man, but when did you last hear me whine? I'm a barker, a growler, but a whiner, never!"

Ben ignored his dog's indignant complaint as he watched Kostas scanning the horizon on the port side.

"By all the powers that be, boy, that Ned of yours is a truly wonderful creature. Look, there it goes again!"

There was a dull, distant boom, followed by a faint flash of lightning. Kostas began taking the wheel around, sending his vessel head-on into the increasing breeze. "Hah, no wonder I had to tack to keep her on course. I should have known, Ben, the air was becoming warmer, being driven onward by the colder front. Well, boy, we're in for real trouble this night, we'll have to keep to the open sea and ride out the storm. My *Blue Turtle* is an old lady now, so pray to any saints you know that she's not overwhelmed by the storm. Get your dogs below decks, it's going to get pretty rough!"

Kostas bellowed orders to his crew. "Take her down to half sail, look lively! Kristos, batten everything down! Herakles, run out some lines across the decks for hand holds! Nico, secure your galley! Babiko, lend a hand with this wheel!"

Ben gave an involuntary smile as he saw Ned lift the puppy by its neck scruff. He read his dog's thoughts.

"Come on young 'un, you'll be safer in the galley with the cook. Be still, you little worm, I'm not hurting you. Oh, another thing, I wish you'd learn a few more words. Amico, Amico! Is that all you can say?"

Within half an hour of Ned's warning, the evening calm of the Ionian Sea was transformed into a roaring thunderstorm. Suddenly the waves became an endless panorama of foam-torn hills and valleys. Cold rain in blinding sheets whipped the vessel from stem to stern as howling gale-force winds battered the weathered old craft. Blinded by the salt spume, Ben joined Kostas and Babiko as they battled to keep the ship bow on into the storm. It was like being on some mad fairground ride, tossed high on the towering wave crests, then falling, with frightening speed, into the deep troughs below.

Memories of his time aboard the *Flying Dutchman* filled

Ben's thoughts. The accursed Captain Vanderdecken, yelling insults at the Lord as his vessel foundered in the meeting place of three mighty oceans, at the foot of the world, off Tierra del Fuego. Mutiny and murder, starvation and desolation, with one boy and his dog being swept overboard at the command of heaven's angel.

A splintering crash from up for'ard snapped Ben back into reality—he heard it clearly, even over the noise of the gale. Then Ned's voice was in his brain. "Quick, mate, help, the galley's been broached!"

Scuffing spray from his eyes, the boy left the two at the wheel. Grabbing a handline, he pulled himself across the heaving midship deck, toward the shed-like structure which formed the galley. A heavy mast spar had snapped off and fallen onto the galley roof, caving it in. The rough-hewn door was jammed shut. Ben banged upon it, sending out an urgent message. "Ned, are you alright, mate? Answer me, Ned!"

The Labrador's answer came straight through to him. "The place is on fire, Nico's been knocked out, I think his leg's hurt. Hurry, this pup's panicking, he's jumping all over the place!"

Ben replied as he dashed for the for'ard accommodation. "I'll be with you quickly, stay away from the door!"

A big axe was held to the bulkhead by a cord and a staple. Ben tugged it loose and lumbered back to the galley. He struck the door several hefty blows with the axe. It splintered and leaned crazily on one hinge. Kostas, who had delegated his turn at the wheel to Herakles, came staggering along to Ben's assistance. Smoke was pouring out of the galley. The rain and spray blew in, causing a pall of hissing steam as it hit the big iron stove. The Greek captain pulled Ben to one side, shouting, "Here, boy, leave this to Krimboti!"

Disregarding the splinters and burning wood, he grabbed the door with his bare hands and tore it off the remaining hinge with a powerful tug. Amico, with his coat aflame, came skrieking out. Hardly touching the deck, he flew through the rail into the sea. Before Ben could catch his breath, Ned followed, like a streak of black lightning, straight in after the puppy. Without thinking, Ben vaulted over the rail after the two dogs.

Still with the noise of the storm ringing in his ears, Ben shot beneath the surface. Something brushed his face; his hand reached out and grabbed it as he clawed his way to the surface. It was the pup—for the first time he heard its tiny, shrill voice echoing through his head. "Amico! Amico!"

"Be still, you pestilence! Ned, I've got him!"

He saw the black Labrador pawing the stormswept waters alongside him. Ben and Ned held the little dog between them. Ben saw the side of the ship thundering toward him, he could not avoid it. *Bump!* It struck the boy's forehead, stunning him.

Then the ghostly Vanderdecken had him, the black-edged fingers of his skeletal hands latching into his victim's hair as he laughed triumphantly. "Come with me, boy, sail into the seas of eternity. You and the dog were always part of my crew!"

For a second, Ben felt himself losing his grip on reality. He called out, "Ned, save me!"

Fiery needles of pain pierced the back of his hand, then Ned's voice intruded into his consciousness. "Get off, you little savage, or I'll chew your head off!"

Spluttering seawater, racked almost double with coughing, Ben woke. He was on the deck of the *Blue Turtle,* with Kostas leaning over him, chuckling.

"There, my friend, you'll live. Hah, it's amazing how a little dog's bite can bring you round. That Amico, he has teeth like small needles, eh!"

The puppy was flat on the deck, with both of Ned's front paws holding him there. "Be still, you confounded cannibal. Huh, talk about biting the hand that saved you!"

The gold teeth of Kostas shone in a flash of lightning. Kostas called to a crewman, "Yanni, get our friend out of the storm, into my cabin with Nico!"

Ben, Ned and little Amico were bundled into the captain's cabin, where the cook, Nico, lay fast asleep. He had his leg bandaged up in a splint, and an empty brandy bottle lay by his side.

Ned licked the patient's hand. "Good old Nico, hope he recovers speedily. He does the best pork crackling I've ever tasted, what d'you think, mate?"

The puppy growled as he tugged at the cook's bandaged leg. "Grrr, Amico, Amico!"

Ned cast a despairing glance at Ben as he cuffed the pup away from Nico with a sweep of his paw. "Hmph, not very good at the art of conversation, is he?"

Despite being buffeted about the cabin as it rolled about in the storm, Ben could not help smiling. "Good old Ned. Pass me some of that sheet, will you, mate?"

The Labrador used his teeth to tear off some of the bedsheet, which had been used to bind Nico's leg. "Sorry I can't help you, Ben, but paws aren't much good for bandaging up wounds. Besides, I've got this little nuisance to deal with. Gerroff my tail, Amico!"

The puppy, none the worse for his scorched coat and dip in the sea, was worrying at Ned's tail again. Ben bandaged his hand, laughing as Ned tangled Amico up tight in the remainder of the sheet. The boy winked at his dog. "You seem to be doing a fine job there!"

After awhile Kostas popped in to see Ben and check on Nico. "How are you doing my friend, eh?"

Ben nodded toward the sleeping cook, who every now and then let out a groan. "Better than him I think, Cap'n. Is the storm showing any signs of letting up out there?"

Kostas shrugged. "I'll give it until dawn, if it hasn't stopped by then we're sunk. Just look at that bulkhead."

The boy followed the captain's finger. The bulkhead, which was the wall protecting the side of the vessel from the sea, was leaking. Dribbles of seawater were seeping their way through into the cabin. Ben shook his head. "Is it very serious?"

Kostas scratched his mop of red curls. "Bad enough, boy. As I told you, she's an old lady, and past her best days now. It's worse in some parts than in others. The stern chain locker is almost rotted through. I've got all hands bailing out to keep her afloat. We'll last until dawn, but no longer."

Ben rose swiftly. "I'll come and lend a hand, Cap'n!"

Kostas pushed him back down. "No no, you've been through enough for a young fellow."

Ben pulled himself back up, declaring firmly, "Sorry to disobey orders, sir, but I'm going to help the bailing gang!"

The Greek captain allowed Ben to pass, patting his back. "You're a good boy, Ben. Ned can stay here and watch Nico. Oh, I see you've got the little Amico to lie still, eh?"

Ben took responsibility for the bundle. "Aye, Cap'n, he kept leaping about, I had to do it."

The puppy attempted to rise, but fell back whimpering.

Ned cast a stern eye at him. "Be still, rascal, or I'll put splints on your legs, just like poor Nico. D'you want me to come, too, Ben?"

The boy shook his head. "No, mate, you play nursemaid here."

WITH THE ADVENT OF THE STORM, THE *SEA DJINN* had put about, not venturing into open sea but taking refuge in the Gulf of Taranto, which forms the arch in the foot of the Ital-

ian mainland. Ghigno, an experienced seaman, ordered the anchor to be dropped where there were no reefs or hazards. This allowed the big ship to ride out the foul weather, partially shielded in the lee of the gulf.

Al Misurata instructed Ghigno to head the vessel bow on to the open sea. Lookouts were placed to scan the waters in case the *Blue Turtle* was sighted. The pirate knew there was little chance of this during the heavy, windswept rain and high-running seas. However, he hoped that when the weather turned for the better, they might spot their quarry floundering somewhere out there.

With such bad weather, even the *Sea Djinn* took a considerable pounding. In the cabin accommodation, the Rizzoli Troupe were a sorry sight. Only Otto and Signore Rizzoli somehow managed to avoid seasickness. Mama, La Lindi, Serafina and the two clowns were all pale and wan about the gills. They rocked back and forth with the constant heaving of the ship, with fumes from the oil lamps making the atmosphere warm and smoky.

Augusto Rizzoli made his way from one to the other, constantly wringing out a dampened cloth as he bathed their faces, comforting his friends. "There there, be brave, this storm will soon pass and the sea will go calm again."

His wife lifted her head miserably. "You've been saying that for three hours now. Oh, what I wouldn't give for just a whiff of fresh air!"

La Lindi agreed with her. "Even if we get drenched by cold rain, it would be good to stand in the open air."

Otto lifted Serafina's chin with a thick forefinger. "Is this what you want also, *Mädchen*?"

The beautiful, dusky-skinned girl nodded. "Yes, please."

The big German strongman spoke softly. "Then you shall have it, all of you."

The cabin door was locked, but that did not seem to bother Otto. One thrust of his mighty shoulders burst the lock. He beckoned them to follow him.

Finding a heaving line, he rigged it from the foot of the stern steps to the lower mid-deck rail. One by one they ventured out into the stormy night air, where they stood, faces up to the pouring rain, breathing gratefully. Otto kept his eyes on the backs of the lookouts, who were posted for'ard, thankful that the rest of the crew were in the mess below decks.

Signore Rizzoli was watching in the other direction, when he saw a shaft of light from the galley door. He whispered urgently, "Otto, someone is coming!"

It was Bomba. The slaver was staggering slightly, and looked as if he, too, was suffering the effects of seasickness. He carried a half-empty wine bottle in one hand, steadying himself against the rail with the other. The troupe began hurrying back to their cabin, but Otto stopped them.

"You must stay here awhile until you feel better. Leave this one to me."

Bomba spotted them immediately. Grabbing a belaying pin, he lurched up to confront them. "Who gave you permission to be out here?"

Otto stared levelly at him. "I did. These people are sick, they need to stand out in the air awhile."

Bomba brandished the belaying pin, snarling. "Back inside now, all of you!"

Signore Rizzoli appealed to Otto. "Do as the man says, Herr Kassel, we are not looking for trouble. Let's go inside."

Otto turned to Serafina. "Do you want to go back to the cabin, *Fräulein*?"

The girl caught the pleading look in Mamma's eyes. "Yes, I feel much better now, let's go inside."

The strongman shrugged. "As you say, *Fräulein.*"

Bomba stood with a smug look on his face as he watched them file past him. He nodded at Otto. "A wise decision, eh?" He chuckled drunkenly, then halted Serafina by placing the pin under her chin. "Not you, pretty girl, you can come to my cabin and sing for Bomba."

Otto moved as quick and silent as a big cat. Cupping one hand around the slaver's mouth, he grabbed him by the back of his neck and twisted.

Bomba went limp in his grasp, his neck broken. The bottle smashed as it fell to the deck.

Otto murmured, "Inside, quickly!"

From the cabin doorway, Serafina saw him heave the body of Bomba over the side. Swiftly loosing the heaving line, Otto hurried to the cabin. He murmured something to Buffo, who suddenly shouted, "Man overboard!"

Mummo fiddled momentarily with the lock, then closed the cabin door. He shook his head doubtfully. "It won't stand close inspection."

Mamma adjusted her shawl decisively. "Sit quietly, all of you, I'll deal with this!"

The sound of footsteps pounding the deck outside came to them, mingled with the shouts of the lookouts, who had come to see what was happening.

"Man overboard, who is it?"

"I don't know, did you shout out?"

"Not me. There's no sign of anything in this storm!"

"Get back to your posts, Ghigno's coming!"

The sound of Ghigno's voice came next. "Stand fast, all of you. What's going on here?"

The answer sounded rather lame. "Er, man overboard, I think—we saw nothing, sir."

The cabin door opened, and Mamma Rizzoli bustled out in an agitated state. She waved her hands in Ghigno's face. "It was that Bomba fellow, signore. He came to our cabin, drunk as a pig. Look!"

The scar-faced Corsair stared down at the broken wine bottle in the scuppers. "Drunk eh, well, that's nothing new for Bomba. But what did he want, did he say anything?"

Mamma's voice went shrill. "I'll tell you what the drunken beast wanted—he wanted to take young Serafina back to his cabin! Our menfolk tried to send him away, they locked the door on him, but he smashed the lock. I fixed him, though. Hah, I said I'd report him to you. He hurried off when he heard that. My husband saw him stumble and trip, didn't you, dear?"

Augusto Rizzoli backed his wife to the hilt stoutly. "Yes, signore, I saw it all, the man struck his head and went straight into the sea. It was me who called out the alarm. The rest of my troupe were too seasick to do anything. Look at them, *Capitano!*"

Ghigno hustled the Rizzolis back into the cabin. "Yes yes, now go inside, or you might be washed overboard. Stay in your quarters until the storm dies down. And you up there, get back to your watch, never mind what's going on down here. Huh, it's not enough that we're in the middle of a storm, but we have some drunken fool going over the side. It's his own fault!"

Al Misurata sat in his lavishly appointed cabin, watching the pale wine slopping back and forth in its goblet as he listened to Ghigno's report. He took a sip, glancing at his companion over the rim. "Why do you look so happy at our friend's untimely end—were you not fond of Bomba?"

The Corsair's scarred face twisted into a sinister grin. "Lord, I did not notice you shedding any tears at the news. Bomba was a pig and an oaf. I miss him like one who has rid himself of a rotten, aching tooth."

Al Misurata laughed. "And I do also. Tonight that fool will be in pig paradise. I pity the other pigs!"

Both men laughed then. Seeing his master in a good mood, Ghigno took advantage to press a point. "A great man like you does not have to worry about minor things. Why don't we just press on to our destination after the storm? The boy and his dog are probably drowned by now. Why let them bother you?"

Al Misurata put aside his wine. "Because he is no ordinary boy, and because he defied my will. He escaped and got the better of me. I cannot allow anybody, boy or man, to do that. You should know me well enough to understand that by now, my friend."

Ghigno traced his facial scar with a finger. "Aye, Lord, I know it well, but if anything goes further wrong on this ill-starred voyage, you may lose the slaves—and the respect of Count Dreskar, which I think you value highly. I am only trying to help, Lord."

The pirate gazed out of the stern windows at the wild night, stroking his sword hilt. "Maybe you are right. I thank you for your counsel. So be it then—if we do not find the Greek's ship or the boy by tomorrow, we will sail on to Piran."

Ghigno stood and bowed. "It is not my counsel that speaks, O Master, it is your wisdom!"

After the Corsair had departed to his own cabin, Al Misurata continued looking out at the storm, ruminating aloud. "Then I will find you tomorrow, boy, and your dog!"

Book Three

ISTRANI
WOLVES

BEN SPENT MOST OF THE NIGHT AS PART OF A HUMAN
chain, passing bowls, buckets, ewers and pans up from the
chain locker and stern cabins. It was heavy, remorseless labor,

 sometimes almost waist-deep in cold seawater,
passing brim-slopping containers from hand to
hand. Alternately sweating and shivering, the boy
toiled doggedly on, sometimes being hurled flat
in the wild motion of a storm-rocked ship. He
could hear the gale, still howling furiously. It was becoming
obvious that the *Blue Turtle* would be lost, but the bailing crew
battled on desperately against their inevitable fate, even joking
about it.

Herakles handed a bucket to Ben, remarking as he passed
it up to the next man, "One bucketful out, two bucketfuls in,
eh, Ben!"

The boy licked a skinned knuckle, commenting, "Aye, if
they find any fish down there let's hope somebody saves them
for supper!"

Babiko took the bucket from Ben, reaching back for another. "Huh, by the look of things it'll be the fish having us
for supper!"

Kostas Krimboti came clambering down the waterlogged
stairway. As usual, the big Greek was laughing. "Hohoho, if I

were a fish I'd let you go, old Babiko skinny bones. No, my friend, those fish will be looking for a fine, big, meaty fellow like me!" Shoving Ben aside, Kostas took his place on the line. "Go on, young 'un, up on deck, you've had enough for now."

The boy protested, "I can work, Cap'n, let me carry on."

The big Greek flashed his golden smile. "Yanni, tell this little fish what happened to the last fellow who dared to argue with Krimboti!"

Yanni answered cheerfully. "Was that before or after you broke both his arms and bit his ears off, *Capitano?*"

Ben saw it was useless continuing the discussion further. Pulling himself wearily up on deck, he went to see how Ned was faring with his duties as nursemaid.

As Ben entered the cabin, he took heed of his friend's warning. "Hush now, they're both fast asleep!"

Nico was still unconscious, and Amico, bundled up in the torn sheet, was in a deep slumber on the bunk.

Ned rose stiffly. "I managed to tie that villain up so tight he couldn't get free. After awhile he gave up the struggle and went to sleep. Let's go out on deck, mate, I need to stretch the old legs."

They slipped out quietly, climbing the stairs to the fo'c'sle deck, with the Labrador expressing his surprise. "Just look at the midships, they're almost underwater!"

Ben patted his dog's head. "You should see the stern quarters, the water's pouring in down there. What a time I've had, mate. Well, Ned, who'd have thought we'd live all these years, only to end up like this, eh?"

However, the dog was not listening. He had turned to face the prow, and was pointing like a setter.

Ben knelt by his side. "Ned, what is it?"

"A ship, it's a ship!" The dog's reply sent Ben peering off into the rainswept distance. Ned pushed the boy's face with his paw, giving directions. "Over there, far off on the starboard bow. It's a ship, I know it is!"

Ben was quivering with excitement, though he could not see anything as yet. "If you say so I believe you, mate!"

The black Labrador butted his head against Ben's ribs. "Then what're you hanging about here for, idle youth? Go and tell Cap'n Krimboti. Now!"

A moment later, the boy was yelling down the stairs, "Cap'n, I can see something off to starboard, I think it might be a ship!"

Kostas was at his side in a flash. Seizing Ben's arm, he dashed him for'ard, splashing through the midships. "A ship, you think? By the Archbishop of Athens, boy, you'd better be right. Show me!"

Ned was waiting on the foc'sle deck, sending thoughts to Ben. "It's a ship right enough, I can see her clearly now, prob'ly because that's the dawn coming up. Follow my nose, mate, show our cap'n!"

Looking in the direction of his dog's nose, Ben pointed the ship out. It looked like a big vessel, even from a far distance. He heaved a mental sigh of relief that it was not the *Sea Djinn*.

Kostas Krimboti kissed his open palm to the heavens. "Thank you, Father, thank you, Sir! Hohohohoho! Look at that beautiful ship, see it, Beniamino!"

It was, however, Ben's turn to see something. "And look at the weather, Cap'n, it's slacking off, the wind's died and the sea's becoming smoother. I'll wager it's not long before this rain stops!"

Ned licked his friend's hand. "Nicely observed, m'boy!"

As pale dawn separated the sky from night, the rain died to a drizzle. All hands gathered for'ard to see the ship, which was headed straight for them, but still some distance away. Herakles had the spyglass, which he was focusing on the oncoming vessel. He passed it to his captain.

"It's not your lucky day, my friend—that's the *Callisto*."

Kostas thrust the glass to his eye, squinting wildly. "The *Callisto*? No, surely not, it can't be. Boy, you speak our language well enough, see if you can read it, too. What's the name of that ship?"

Ben took the spyglass, through which he could easily discern the name on either side of the prow, which was fronted by a fine, carved figure of a huntress. "Herakles is correct, Cap'n, she's called the *Callisto*."

The big Greek bit at his thumbnail for a moment, then he nodded to Ben. "Go to my cabin, boy, I've got some thinking you can help me with. Yanni, you'd best come, too, Little Alexi knows you as well as me. All hands stay low and say nothing until we return!"

Thoroughly mystified by the odd turn of events and the Captain's behaviour, Ben went to the cabin, sharing his thoughts with Ned, who was following him.

"I thought the cap'n would be glad to be rescued, but he doesn't welcome the sight of that ship."

Ned pushed the cabin door open with his paw. "Aye, and I wonder who Little Alexi is, mate?"

Kostas paced the cabin, waving his arms dramatically as he complained aloud, "Why me? Chased by Barbary pirates, battered by the storm and now who comes sailing over the horizon? Little Alexi and the *Callisto*! And all this with my poor *Blue Turtle* almost sinking under me! Father, why have you placed this black raven on my shoulder?"

Yanni shrugged philosophically. "Maybe Little Alexi does not sail with the *Callisto* these days. Maybe he is master of another vessel."

Kostas exploded. "Aye, and maybe the Krimboti is a donkey with feathers! You talk foolish, Yanni, Alexi is attached to that ship like a banker to money!"

Ben took it upon himself to interrupt. "Cap'n, you won't solve anything by carrying on like this. Tell me, what is the problem?"

The big Greek scratched his curly mop distractedly. "It is a long story, my friend, it is. . . . Aaah, you tell him, Yanni!"

Both Ned and Ben listened intently as Yanni explained. "Kostas, Alexi and myself all came from the island of Naxos, we were the greatest of friends as boys. All three of us wanted to be sea captains one day. Alexi was small, and given to book learning—his father was wealthy, also. Kostas and I were both from poor families, our fathers were only fishermen. But Kostas was a tall boy, handsome and strong. He was very popular. Alexi secretly disliked him for this. Having said that, Kostas also disliked Alexi."

"Yanni, how can you say that? Little Alexi was as close to me as a brother." Kostas was off once more, waving his arms and gesticulating.

Ben shared a thought with Ned. "I wish he'd shut up and sit down, we're getting nowhere like this. I can't tell him to be quiet, though—he's a captain."

Ned acted as he replied. "Aye, but I can, mate. Sit down, sir, down I say!" The black Labrador stood on his hind legs, pushing Kostas down into a chair with his front paws.

Ben winked at the Greek captain. "Ned wants you to sit quietly while Yanni tells me the story, Cap'n."

Kostas stared at the dog oddly for a moment, then he waved at Yanni. "I'm sorry, friend, continue the tale."

Yanni patted the dog's head fondly. "Where was I—oh yes. Well, time went by, and we three boys grew up, but fate took us down different paths. Alexi's father paid for his son to go to naval college. He did well there, and soon was sailing with the Greek navy as a young officer. Huh, the Krimboti and I, we were still running about the coast barefoot, no naval school for us, my friend. So, we fell into the pirating business, which was common among adventurous lads such as we. Now I must take you forward some years. Kostas and I had risen in the ranks— now he was a first mate and I was a gunner, aboard a Corsican vessel. We weren't slavers or murderers, just good old-fashioned wave robbers, you understand."

Ben nodded briefly, remembering the time he had spent aboard a French pirate vessel, *La Petite Marie,* captained by the buccaneer Raphael Thuron.*

"Aye, I understand, Yanni, go on."

The seaman once more took up his narration. "It was just outside the harbour, at the isle of Kríti, where we had raided a garrison and borrowed some ammunition during the night. We sailed out, laughing, straight into a ship of our country's navy— we almost bumped right into it in the dawn light."

Kostas smote the table and burst out laughing. "Hoho-

*See *The Angel's Command.*

hoho! Can you guess who was standing on the forepeak, in his smart tasselled uniform? None other than our old friend. I shouted out to him, 'Good morning to you, Little Admiral Alexi!'"

Ned gave a sharp bark. Kostas covered his mouth. "Oops, carry on, Yanni—tell Ben what we did."

Yanni was smiling as he explained. "We were younger and quicker then. Kostas and I manned the cannon, and blasted the navy ship right under the bowline. Alexi was jolted off into the sea!"

The big Greek leaped to his feet, gold teeth flashing. "Let me tell it, Yanni! Hohoho, we left her with her stern in the air and her head going down. I tell you, it was a sight to see, Ben. All the navy crew had heard what I called that tiny peacock. They threw rescue lines to him, calling, 'We'll save you, Little Admiral Alexi!' His lovely new uniform was ruined, he was hauled aboard with the seat torn out of his breeches. He grabbed one of those hailing trumpets and yelled out after us, 'I know you, Kostas Krimboti, and you, too, Yanni Karopolis. Villains! Pirates! One day, when I'm a captain, I'll hunt you both down and hang you from my ship's yardarm. I swear on my life I will!'"

Ned heaved a doggy sigh, resting his head on Ben's foot as he communicated. "Oh dear, and it's that very same Little Alexi who's sailing to our rescue at the moment. Well well, our friends have got themselves into a right old pickle."

Ben questioned Kostas and Yanni. "Let me ask you two things. One, how do you know Alexi is captain of the *Callisto*? And two, does he know that you are aboard the *Blue Turtle*?"

Yanni allowed his captain to reply.

"The word that Little Alexi had been appointed as master

of the *Callisto* was all up and down the coast. As I said, his father was a wealthy man—he practically paid for *Callisto* to be built, then made a gift of it to the navy. So Alexi was the natural choice. We heard in every port and waterside taverna that he had been given a commission to root out piracy on the high seas. The little maggot made it no secret that he was going to stretch our necks at the first opportunity. So we decided to fool him. Yanni and I gave up the pirating life. We bought ourselves this old tub, the *Blue Turtle,* out of our ill-gotten gains, and set ourselves up as treasure hunters. Right, Yanni?"

Yanni grinned at Ben. "Right! We became reformed characters, and dropped out of sight. You see us as we are now, practically saints, carrying cargo for the good sisters of Santa Filomena. I don't think there's much chance Alexi knows that we're aboard. But that's where the problem arises. If he's going to help us, then he'll want to come on to the *Blue Turtle,* to assess the damage and speak with her captain. So you see, boy, the moment he spots the Krimboti, or me, we're dead men!"

Ned shared a thought with Ben as they sized up both men. "Huh, you couldn't miss those two rascals underwater on a dark night, and this Alexi fellow's known them both since they were boys. What d'you think, mate?"

Ben spoke his thoughts aloud. "Then we must stop him seeing you both, and boarding us."

Kostas spread his arms expressively. "But how are we going to do that, my friend?"

Yanni shook his head mournfully. "You can't stop the Greek navy boarding you in these waters."

There was a moment's glum silence, then the boy caught his dog's message. "Run up a yellow pennant?"

Ben patted Ned's back heartily. "That's the answer, well done, mate!"

The black Labrador arched his back casually. "Think nothing of it—just remind our cap'n that this is going to cost him more than a bone and a scrap of pork rind."

Ben explained rapidly to his friends, "Now listen carefully, there's not much time. Here's what you must do. . . ."

Captain Alexi Constantinou of the warship *Callisto* stood perched on a small powder keg, with a canvas awning erected over it to protect his splendidly ornate uniform from the fine drizzle. The squat vessel, with its tattered blue sails, sat low in the water, a little over a cable length from the *Callisto*. Ever eager to use his cannon, he murmured to the master gunner standing alongside him, "D'ye think she has the look of a corsair about her?"

The gunner discouraged the idea politely. "Nay, sir, more like some old cargo coaster who's lost her way. A good puff of wind'd send her to the bottom."

The diminutive captain scanned her needlessly through his telescope before conceding. "Hmm, looks to be held afloat by only prayers and peeling paintwork. Hold fast, what's that, a yellow ensign? See what she's doing out here flying a quarantine flag—hail her immediately!"

The gunner placed the hailing trumpet to his mouth. "Ahoy, *Blue Turtle*, send your master on deck. My captain would have words with him. D'ye hear me?"

There was no sign of life from the other vessel. Little Alexi stamped his double-heeled shoe on the keg. "Are they all dead or deaf? Hail them again, gunner!"

The man did as he was commanded. About half a minute went by, then three figures emerged on the fo'c'sle deck: a man, a boy and a dog.

The cook, Nico, had a blanket draped about him, and he was limping badly. Flour and stove soot had done a good job on him—dark rings circled the agonised eyes, peering from an ashen face. The boy looked to be in the same condition; he was bravely trying to support the limping man. Two large and disgusting sores could be seen on the dog's back. Little Captain Alexi recoiled at the unsavory sight, even at that distance. He drew forth a spotless silk kerchief and held it to his face.

Nico gave a strangled gurgle and grasped at his throat. Deputising for him, Ben called out in a reedy voice, "For pity's sake, send us some clean drinking water, sir!"

The gunner replied, "We'll send ye water, but first tell my captain how ye came to be here."

"Go on, mate, lay it on thick, you poor lad. This pork rind is itching my back, can't wait to pull it off and eat it!"

Ignoring Ned's thoughts, Ben told their story. "We were bound for Muggia, carrying goods for the convent there. Then the cholera struck us, it must have been through drinking contaminated water. I beg you, sirs, help us—our captain, mate, and four crew have all perished from the sickness. There's only me, the cook, and the dog who can still move about. The rest are below decks, it's awful down there. For mercy's sake, send us water, Cap'n!"

Little Alexi and his master gunner held a brief, whispered

conversation, then Alexi took the hailer. "Water will be arriving shortly, stay where you are. We will not be boarding your vessel, and you will certainly not be boarding my ship. Understood?" Nico gave a feeble wave of acknowledgment, allowing Alexi to continue. "With a dead captain, I don't think you'll have anyone capable of reading charts or setting courses. Last night's storm has blown your craft well up into the Adriatic Sea. You are about three leagues off the Dalmatian Islands. I propose to take you in tow. You are going to a small, uninhabited isle, not far from Losinj and the greater Dalmatians."

Ben seemed bewildered. "An uninhabited island, sir, but who will be there to minister to us?"

Little Alexi answered sternly. "Even if there were people there, who would come aboard a plague ship? No, boy, it is up to what's left of your crew to heal yourselves, and make your ship seaworthy again. If you ever make it to the convent at Muggia, I am sure the sisters there will care for you. Now, stand by to receive water and a towing rope!"

Kostas suddenly appeared on deck, carrying a huge painting. It was the one of the Virgin and Child surrounded by many angels, which Fra Salvatore himself had painted for the Mother Superior of the convent. Kostas Krimboti had removed his gold coin teeth and covered his mop of red curls with a turban made from a bedsheet. He had dotted his face with bits of pork rind, stuck on with grease. The effect was frightening. He laughed and cackled as though he had lost his mind from the fever. Dribbling from the side of his mouth, he winked at his old adversary.

"Your Honour, accept this lovely painting as a gift from our dead cap'n. I took it from his stiff hands for you!"

Little Alexi stumbled from his perch on the keg. He hurried off to his cabin, calling back to the gunner, "Tell them to keep that idiot below decks! Fire on the vessel if they try to pass the painting over!"

Ben caught the heaving line, to which the cask of fresh water and the towing hawser were attached. Nico, Kostas and Ned helped him to haul it in and attach the tow to their forepeak. Under the gaze of the gunner and several horrified navy crewmen, they shuffled off to the captain's cabin.

Yanni eyed Kostas fiercely. "Why did you do that? You promised to stay out of sight!"

The big Greek paused to insert his golden teeth. "Hohoho, where's your sense of humour, Yanniko? I just had to take a look at that pompous little oaf. He hasn't changed a bit. No, wait, I think he's grown even smaller. Hohohoho!"

Ben pointed an accusing finger at the captain. "Aye, but if he'd recognised you, your neck would have grown longer by now, and Yanni's, too!"

Kostas looked shamefaced, but only for a moment. "I'm sorry, boy, it was silly of me." Then he held up a cup of the fresh water they had taken from the *Callisto*. "Let's drink a toast to Little Admiral Alexi! Hohoooo!"

Everyone laughed. Kostas Krimboti was not a man you could stay mad at for long. He quaffed off the water. "This far up the Adriatic, eh, that storm must've driven us along like a wild eagle. That's the fastest my old *Blue Turtle* ever went. Well, let's settle down for a good rest. Little Alexi isn't going to hang us by his rope, he's going to tow us to safety! Here, Nico, let me help you back to your bunk. Easy now, don't wake the baby Amico, he's still snoring like a dog."

Ned huffed. "Snoring like a dog? I wonder if humans listen to themselves when they're asleep. Still, you can't help liking Kostas, the golden-mouthed rogue!"

Ben curled up alongside his dog, thinking, "I wonder how the Rizzolis went on in that storm?"

Ned opened one eye. "No, you mean you wonder how the beautiful Serafina went on, and does she still love you?"

Ben tweaked the Labrador's tail. "Silence, Bundi!"

The day brightened as it progressed. Ghigno even allowed his captives out on deck to take the air. Serafina stared out over the sunlit waters, pointing.

"Oh, look, Lindi, dolphins, aren't they beautiful!"

La Lindi joined her to watch the graceful mammals following the ship. The snake charmer lowered her voice. "They've stopped searching for Ben and Ned, I heard one of the guards chatting. We're headed straight to Piran, with no stops in between. At least that's good news for him, not being pursued anymore."

Serafina never took her eyes from the dolphins. "Not such good news for Otto, though—that leaves him only one chance to see that we escape."

La Lindi opened the basket lid to allow her python, Mwaga, a little warmth from the sun. "It's just as well, I have a bad feeling about this idea of escape. It's far too dangerous. Do you imagine Al Misurata would sit still and twiddle his thumbs if we were free?"

Mamma Rizzoli had been eavesdropping close by. "We've got to do something, or face a life of slavery. Leave Otto to his plans, we are all in the hands of the good Lord above and his angels."

• • •

Ghigno passed the wheel to a crewman as Al Misurata appeared on deck. The pirate looked about him before addressing the Corsair. "What course did you set this morning?"

Ghigno pointed. "Nor'east, out into the Adriatic. We'll drift by the Dalmatians, and follow the coast up to Piran. Unless you'd like me to change course and stay on the Italian side, Master?"

Al Misurata considered the alternative awhile. "No, you're right, my friend. Nor'east it is. Those Dalmatian Islands, there are lots of small coves there where a ship might lie low to avoid pursuit."

Ghigno fingered the scar on his face. "You are still searching for the boy, then?"

Al Misurata narrowed his eyes. "I have always succeeded— failure was never in my nature. If you are a fox seeking a rabbit, it does no harm to visit the places where that rabbit may be hiding."

Ghigno nodded. "We are bound for Kornat. From there we will follow the island coasts, past Dugi Otok and Losinj, then across to Pula and the Slovenijan mainland. Not far to Piran then, Lord."

Al Misurata dropped his tone to a murmur. "Not far, Ghigno. Send those entertainers back to their quarters. The snake lady has ears that hear too much."

THE ISLE OF LOSINJ. DALMATIA.

A CURVING INLET FORMED THE BAY WHERE THE
Blue Turtle lay beached. It was a bright, sunny noon as Ben
and Ned surveyed the beautiful island.

Captain Alexi Constantinou called out from
his ship, "You there, boy, cast off the tow rope.
Let it drop into the sea, there's nothing like
salt water for cleaning up a rope from infec-
tion."

The boy unlooped the haltered tow rope from the prow and
let it splash into the shallows, taking in Ned's thoughts.

"That's a wise move, I'd do the same thing if I were cutting
loose from an infected craft. He's no fool, that Little Alexi!"

Ben signalled the *Callisto*'s crew to haul
in the line. "Aye, that's why I'm keeping up the act of a stricken
cabin boy. I hope Nico has
the sense to do the same."

He had no need to be worried. The ship's
cook acted his role to the hilt. Hunching his body, he gave

vent to a bout of rasping coughs, calling plaintively to the naval captain.

"Don't go and leave us here alone, sir. Surely you can spare a little food, and more water for sick men!"

But the little captain had already ordered his ship to put about for sea. He replied impatiently, "I've given you all the help I can, fend for yourselves now. The island is sparsely populated, but I'll wager there are farmers, shepherds and streams for your needs. If you survive the cholera, you can repair your vessel and carry on to Muggia. Good luck to you!"

The *Callisto*'s master gunner whispered to the bosun, "Listen to that pompous little toad, wishing good luck to cholera victims. Still, better them than us, eh?"

The bosun nodded sadly. "Aye, it's like pouring water on a drowned man. Look at the state they're in, that plague will kill them all soon, rest their souls!"

Ben, Ned and Nico waited until the *Callisto* was out of hailing range, then hurried down to the cabin. Kostas was cleaning the mess from his face with a bowl of warm water. He replaced his gold teeth, whipped the turban from his red curls and danced a lively jig.

"Hohoho, your plan worked well, boy! Ah, what I wouldn't have given to fire a broadside at Little Alexi as a farewell. Oops! Get that puppy from under my feet!"

Amico had joined in with the dance, almost tripping Kostas. He licked away at Ben's face as the boy picked him up. "Amico! Amico!"

Ben placed him down alongside Ned. "Here, mate, see to him before he gets trampled flat."

Ned gave a snort of disgust. "Yurgh! Look what the little savage is up to now. He's eating the pork rind off my back! Oh well, carry on, you little horror, it'll save me a job. Here, what about this bit that's stuck to my tail? Yowch, go easy!"

The crew waded ashore in good spirits, with Kostas carrying Nico on his back. They gathered driftwood and lit a fire, with Herakles standing in as cook and preparing a fish stew. The carefree Kostas opened a jar of retsina wine for his men. Borrowing a bouzouki from Babiko, he tuned it and began singing.

"One day I met a pretty girl,
who fell in love with me,
I stole her father's fishing boat,
and off I went to sea!
Away oh hey ho, yes off I went to sea!

"I took her mother's speckled hen,
The one that lays so good,
and borrowed her brother's fine red coat,
I think he wants my blood!
Away oh hey ho, I think he wants my blood!

"Farewell to all who seek my hide,
fat mothers-in-law to be,
far o'er the bounding main I'll go,
where you can't follow me!
Away oh hey ho, where you can't follow me!

"There's pretty girls in foreign lands,
they've kissed me lovingly,
now I've a girl in every port,
but my true love's the sea!
Away oh hey ho, yes my true love's the sea!"

Warm noontide progressed into early evening. Ben sat with his back against a rock, watching Kostas. The big Greek was splashing in the shallows, wrestling playfully with Ned and Amico. He came bounding up the shore, roaring with laughter, toward Ben. The boy held up a hand as Kostas shook himself like a dog, then flopped down beside him. "It's a good life, my friend!"

Ben wiped seawater from his face. "Don't you ever worry about anything, Cap'n Krimboti?"

The big Greek picked up the wine jar and drank. "Of course I do, boy! I'm worrying now about how to get my *Blue Turtle* seaworthy again. I tell you, that old lady is going to need a good patching up. It will take some time to finish the repairs. Which brings me on to my next worry."

Ben refused a drink from the proffered wine jar. "You have another problem? What's that?"

Kostas tapped a thick forefinger against the boy's chest. "You, Ben! Oh, I may look carefree, but all the time this Krimboti is thinking. You are a good boy, and you have helped me, saved my life even. But you have things of your own to do. What about your friends aboard the slaver's ship? They are bound for Piran, you must save them. I have to think of a way to help you to do this!"

Ben was surprised at his friend's thoughtfulness. "But how can you help, Cap'n, we're on a lonely island with a broken ship—what can you do?"

The gold coin teeth glittered in the evening sunlight. "Come with me, I'll show you!"

Ned trailed along behind Ben as they went aboard the *Blue Turtle* with Kostas. "Where are we off to, mate?"

The boy helped his dog over the rail. "I'll let you know as soon as the cap'n tells me."

Kostas searched his cabin, muttering as he opened drawers and cupboards. "Who ever needs charts except when you can't find them? Ah, here it is!" From under the bunk mattress he pulled an untidy sheaf of parchment, riffling through until he found the one. Spreading it on the cabin table, Kostas pointed. "It's many a day since I've seen this old thing. It's the chart of the Adriatic Sea. This is where we are, Losinj, in the Dalmatian Isles. Now, this narrow strait is called the Kvarner, it's not that far from the Slovenijan mainland. This place here, the town of Pula. I can take our ship's boat, Yanni and me, we can row you there overnight. From Pula it's only a couple of days' travel by land to Piran. How will that do you, Beniamino, eh?"

Ben stared at the chart, with Ned at his elbow. "It would do fine, Cap'n. Ned and I can walk to Piran if you get us to Pula. Thank you very much!"

Kostas ruffled the boy's hair. "Walk? Who said anything about walking, boy! No, you will ride like the wind!"

Ned pawed his master's arm. "Ride! How am I expected to ride? Ask him."

Ben stroked the Labrador's head, asking, "What about Ned? I couldn't go anywhere without him."

Kostas chuckled. "I meant you will ride on wagons, with the Istrani Wolves!"

Ben's words echoed his dog's thoughts. "The Istrani Wolves, who are they?"

Kostas Krimboti winked at his two friends. "Good people, smugglers and bandits. They are led by my dear friend Janos Cabar, a rare and bold one, believe me!"

Ben scratched his tow-coloured mop. "Smugglers and bandits—you're putting us with outlaws?"

The big Greek looked indignant. "Aye, boy, the best smugglers and bandits you've ever travelled with. They run the coast between Pula and Trieste, over the border into Italy. The gang of Janos Cabar have never once been caught or imprisoned by the authorities on either side of the line!"

Al Misurata took the wheel of the *Sea Djinn,* steering her toward the other ship. It was not wise to ignore the warning shot of a Greek navy warship. When both vessels were close enough, he had his crewmen bring lanterns. He watched as Little Alexi and three of his officers were helped aboard from a small cutter. Handing the wheel over to a crewman, the pirate went to meet them. As ever, Al Misurata was courteous and considerate to his guests. He bowed low to the diminutive captain.

"I bid you a pleasant evening, and welcome aboard my humble vessel, friends. I trust you come in peace?"

Little Alexi adjusted the collar of his fine tunic. "I am Captain Alexi Constantinou of the Greek warship *Callisto.* Please identify yourself, your destination and your cargo."

Al Misurata handled the navy man tactfully. "Sir, I am Mehmet el Jama, sailing out of Tunis. My ship is bound for Piran, in Slovenija. Our cargo is comprised of blood stallions and four men who are taking passage with us. Normally we would travel by way of the Italian coastline, but unfortunately we were set off course by the storm a few nights back. This is not a route I would normally take, I am not familiar with these waters. I would be grateful for your advice, *Kapitano.*"

Little Alexi puffed out his chest, toying with the tassels on his sword hilt, as if he was weighing up an important decision. "Set your course to the mid channel. When you sight the city of Venezia* to your portside, change tack eastward. Piran is on the far side of the Gulf of Venice."

Al Misurata bowed low, touching his forehead respectfully. "I thank providence for the wisdom of a Greek navy commander. No doubt, vessels that could not take heed of your counsel would have perished in the storm. I sighted an old, blue-sailed merchant craft, directly before the tempest struck. Alas, it was probably sunk by the heavy weather."

Alexi took advantage of this statement to air his knowledge and expertise further. "I sincerely hope you did not board or have contact with that ship?"

Al Misurata spread his arms. "No, we did not. But why?"

The little captain strutted away like a bantam cockerel, then whirled to face the other man dramatically. "Because it was a plague ship, in the grip of cholera! Oh yes, my friend, count yourself fortunate that you stayed well away from the blue ship. When we encountered her, she was wallowing, leaking fit to sink. I saw only a few left alive, the captain and most of his crew had perished from the disease. I did what any right-thinking captain would—took the vessel in tow, gave them a cask of fresh water and left them quarantined on one of the Dalmatian Islands."

*Venezia (Venice).

Al Misurata cut in smoothly on the narrative. "And there were only two left alive, you say, sir?"

Alexi shook his head. "No, there were three in all, plus a dog. The ship's cook, a crazy deckhand, and the young cabin boy. They all looked to be on their last legs to me, staggering about, pleading for water—even the dog was infested with huge scabs. A piteous sight indeed. Those old merchant ships are teeming with rats, no doubt the cause of their predicament. Nothing could be done for those who were still alive. They are more than likely dead now, all of them. Cholera, or whatever plague it was that visited them, had swept through that craft like a fire, speedily devouring every living thing it laid its foul hand on." Little Alexi fell silent, staring at the deck, so that the other captain could see what a model of human kindness and compassion he was.

Al Misurata murmured, "Truly you did all you could for them, *Kapitano*. I will keep my course to mid channel and shun the islands, not having your courage and fortitude!"

The little captain nodded solemnly. "I must bid you a safe voyage, there is other business I must attend to."

Al Misurata bowed low again. "May heaven reward you, sir. I am pleased to have made your acquaintance!"

Once the *Callisto* was a safe distance from the *Sea Djinn*, Ghigno made an appearance. The pirate told him all that had transpired. His companion took the news pensively.

"So we are finally rid of the brat and his hound. I'm not sorry, Lord, though I would not wish a fate like the plague on anybody, man or beast."

Al Misurata gazed out at the broad expanse of the Adriatic.

"There was something about that boy, he intrigued me. Still, he brought it on himself—he should never have deserted me and escaped. Keep the course to mid channel, and await my orders."

Ghigno cast a glance to the midship hold. "Shall I release the women and let them rejoin the others?"

The pirate stroked his beard, pondering before he answered. "Maybe not. Keep them apart, it will ensure the good behaviour of the menfolk. Particularly that German strongman, he could be dangerous."

Ghigno tapped the musket he kept stowed in his sash. "Rest easy, Lord, I'm not afraid of that one!"

Al Misurata smiled thinly. "Neither was Bomba, and look what happened to him."

The scar-faced Corsair showed surprise. "You mean it was the German who did away with Bomba?"

Al Misurata tapped the side of his head with one finger. "I did not get to be Lord of the Barbary Coast by going about with my eyes closed and my brain in a slumber. The next question you are going to ask is, why did I not put the German to death?"

Ghigno stared at him in awed silence as he continued. "Bomba was worthless, a thief, a coward, one who would sell his mother for a crust. I would have had to kill him myself, sooner or later. However, the strongman will bring a good price, so I kept silent. Let him be someone else's problem, he will go to his new owner unharmed. Remember, Ghigno, there is no profit in a dead man."

In the lower hold, Mamma Rizzoli banged upon the door of the cabin where she had been confined with La Lindi and Serafina.

The guard, a lean, sombre Tunisian, refused to open the door. He tapped it sharply with the butt of his jezzail. "What do you want, woman, more food or water?"

Mamma banged harder upon the door. "I want to go back to my husband. We want to be sent back to our old cabin, where the men are!"

The guard's voice came back at her. "That is up to my master. I am only a guard who takes orders. It is no use asking me."

Mamma persisted. "Then let me speak with your master!"

The guard squatted down against the doorpost, resting his brow against the muzzle of his rifle. "You have no say in this, woman. My master will speak with you when he is ready. Shouting and banging will do you no good. Now be silent!"

Serafina put her arms around the older woman. "Do as he says, Mamma, come and sit down, you'll only get splinters in your hands if you keep banging the door."

Signora Rizzoli allowed herself to be seated on some bales of carpet. She shook her head despairingly. "Why are they doing this to us, what has Misurata got to gain by locking us down here?"

La Lindi took things more calmly, lying on the bales, with her head against the timbered wall. "We're probably hostages against the men's good behaviour. Maybe they've got wind that we might try to escape. I wonder if they've found Otto's old gun. Useless thing, we should have thrown it into the sea. . . ."

The snake charmer paused and sat up straight. "Serafina, listen, I think I heard a horse whinny, it sounded like our Poppea. Right here, in the cabin next to this one!"

Serafina climbed up alongside her friend. She smacked on

the bulkhead, calling softly, "Poppea, is it you, old girl? Poppea!"

A snort and neighing came through from the adjoining cabin. The pretty girl laughed happily.

"It is! That's our Poppea, I'd know her sound anywhere!"

Mamma climbed up to Serafina's side. She listened to the mare's whinnies. "Oh, you poor old lady, have they kept you down here all this time?"

La Lindi crawled along the top of the bales to the rear of the cabin. "Here, Mamma, pass me the lantern!"

Mamma unhooked the lantern from a ceiling beam.

La Lindi held the light up, dispersing the shadows at the back of the bales. "There's a door here, like a stable door. Wait!" Serafina heard a bolt being withdrawn. La Lindi sounded excited. "It's one of those half-doors, like we have on our cart. I can see Poppea, come and look. The door's jammed by these bales, but I can see her. Hello, my beauty, and how are you, eh?"

Poppea thrust her muzzle into the opening and Serafina planted a kiss on it.

"You've put on weight, lady. My, but you do look well, all brushed and groomed. They must have been taking good care of you!"

The presence of the troupe's mare cheered them up. Mamma began trying to move the bales. "Let's get the door open, then we can be all girls together!"

Between them, the three got to work. It took quite awhile, but they managed to roll the bales forward. There were three tiers of them, and it was not possible to clear a space large enough for a horse to come through. However, they did the next best thing. Clearing six bales from the rear, they dropped down and released the lock on the bottom half of the door. It opened enough so that the trio could go through.

Serafina was first into the stable cabin. She laid her cheek on the mare's arched neck, whispering, "You couldn't come into our cabin, so we've come to visit you!"

La Lindi sat down on a heap of dry straw. "This is better than the place they put us in. They must clean it regularly. We'll probably get into trouble for being in here."

Mamma folded her arms decisively. "Trouble, aren't we in enough trouble as it is? We never asked to come down here. I'll give them trouble if they want it, you'll see!"

It was Ghigno who finally came. They heard the guard opening the cabin on the other side, and heard him call out in astonishment.

"They're not here, sir, where can they have gone?"

Mamma smiled as she listened to Ghigno beating and kicking the guard soundly.

"Where do you think they've gone, misbegotten donkey? Can't you see the rear hatch door open back there!"

La Lindi chuckled. "We should have closed it behind us, that would have had them really puzzled!"

There was no time for further comment, as Ghigno booted the door to the stable cabin open and strode angrily in. His scarred face was livid with rage. He looked as though he was about to strike someone.

Mamma placed herself boldly in front of Serafina and La Lindi. "I demand that you send us back to the men's cabin!"

Ghigno took a step toward her, his fist upraised. "You de-

mand? Who are you to demand, you old she-goat! Get back
into your cabin while you can still walk!"

Fearing he was about to strike Mamma, La Lindi's shout
rang out, loud and abrupt. "Don't you dare harm her, get back!"

Poppea knew the term "back." It was always used by the
troupe members whenever they reversed her into the shafts of
the cart. The mare whinnied and backed up two paces, her
stamping left rear hoof pounding down onto Ghigno's
right foot.

The Corsair roared in agony. "Yaaarrgh! Get the horse off
my foot!"

Serafina clicked her tongue at the mare, who obliged by
taking a step forward, releasing the man.

The guard supported Ghigno as he hopped about on one
leg, uttering agonised sounds.

Mamma did nothing to disguise the satisfaction in her
tone. "There, let that be a lesson, you bullying coward! Well
done, Poppea, good horse!" She turned smiling to her two companions. "We girls have got to stick together, eh!"

All three broke into peals of laughter. The Corsair's face
was almost purple with pain and rage, his scar like a ragged,
white lightning flash. When he finally regained his voice, he
snarled viciously, "So, you think it's funny? Well, I'll give you
some news to wipe the smiles from your faces. Your young
friends, the boy and his dog, they're dead. Now laugh that
one off!"

Mamma Rizzoli folded her arms defiantly. "Liar, how could
you know that? Neither you or your master are clever or fast
enough to catch Ben and Ned. You are telling lies!"

Leaning heavily on the guard, Ghigno managed a malicious smile. "Then don't believe me, but take the word of one

I heard it from, a captain of the Greek navy. What reason would he have to lie, eh?"

Their tormentor knew by the shocked looks on the women's faces that his words had the desired effect. He carried on his report with relish. "Plague it was, the cholera! Your Ben and Ned were aboard a merchant vessel that was overrun by infected rats. The whole crew were killed by the disease. It can run through a ship like wildfire, a horrible death, I've been told. We crossed paths with the navy craft, that's why you were put down here, to keep your men from speaking out. Now do you believe me? The boy and his dog are both dead. What, no more laughter, ladies?"

He slammed the door. They heard him laughing as he was assisted up the stairs by the guard.

Mamma burst into tears. "Oh, my poor Ben, that wonderful boy, may the Good Lord rest his soul. And Ned, that lovely dog. Gone!"

La Lindi hugged Mamma as they wept for their two friends together. However, though Serafina stood stone-faced, she was completely dry-eyed. Mamma turned her tearstained face to the beautiful girl. "Did you not hear him, *cara mia*? It must be the truth—the Greek navy captain said so!"

Serafina put her arms around both her friends, her voice held an unwavering certainty. "No! Ben is not dead, neither is Ned. I don't care who said what. They are not dead, I feel it here in my heart, I am sure they are alive!"

La Lindi wiped her eyes on the hem of Mamma's shawl. She stared at Serafina, then nodded. "I believe you!"

THE TOWN OF PULA ON THE
SLOVENIJAN MAINLAND.

IT WAS TEN O'CLOCK AT NIGHT WHEN BEN AND NED
entered the Tavern of the Tipsy Hog, close to the harbour in
Pula. They had left the ship's boat tied up there. Kostas and
Yanni went in first. Ned stopped at the door, looking up at the swinging sign. It depicted a hog,
dressed in human attire, guzzling down a big pail
of beer.

Ben sent his dog a thought. "If you were land-
lord here they could have called it the Tipsy Dog!"

The black Labrador huffed. "Oh, very droll, and if you were
the owner I'd have named it the Boozy Boy. Now get in there,
insolent youth!"

The tavern was packed, a welter of noise and music. The
customers looked a rough lot, arguing and swigging at foaming
flagons, hacking at roasted meat with daggers, singing, fight-
ing and gambling. Kostas waved them to a table. "Sit here, I'll
order us some supper."

A waiter served them with plates of fried beef and a mixture of mashed turnip and potato, plus a flagon of dark beer

apiece. Kostas took a coin from his pouch and tossed it to the server.

Craaaack!

Before the man could catch the coin, it was whipped out of midair by a wild-looking woman wielding a long bullwhip. She caught the coin, and spun it back to the Greek. At the report of the whip, the place fell silent. The woman was only small and lightly built, but her voice was loud and commanding.

"No good friends of mine pay for supper here!" *Craaack!* The whip snaked out once more. Ben was surprised that it did not harm Kostas. It wrapped several times about his wrist. The wild-looking woman tugged Kostas toward her.

"Krimboti! When I saw that red mop of yours, I thought my tavern was on fire. Come here, you great Aegean shark!"

Roaring with laughter, Kostas ran at her, tossing her into the air and catching her before she hit the floor. "Hohohoho! Janos Cabar, how long is it since I last set eyes on your pretty face?"

Digging both hands into his mass of red curls, she tugged them in playful reproach. "Too long, Golden Jaw. So, who's hunting you, or who are you hunting? I'll help you—between us we'll slay all your foes, and help ourselves to their gold!"

Kostas carried her to the table and sat her on his knee. "Ben, this is my friend, Janos Cabar!"

The boy regretted his words as soon as they slipped out. "Janos, I thought we were coming to meet a man!"

The woman took a long pull at Ben's beer flagon. Wiping her lips on the back of her hand, she grinned. "Look at me, lad, what would you have called me, Caterina, Cecilia, or Collete Cabar? I named myself Janos—I like the name well!"

Ben heard Ned's mental chuckle. "You'd better apologise in case you've hurt her maidenly feelings, mate!"

The boy shook Janos Cabar's outstretched hand. "No offence, marm, I think the name suits you well."

The woman had a grip like a vise. She winked at Kostas. "Hey, Krimboti, I like this one. He's good-looking, and has far better manners than you. Hah, he owns a handsome dog, too. Hello, boy!"

Ben read Ned's thoughts as he proffered his paw, which was shaken heartily. "Handsome dog, eh? At least she got my name right. Good grief, she could strangle a tipsy hog with that grip!"

Ben introduced Ned to Janos, then applied himself to his supper as Kostas and the woman talked together.

"Well, wild one, how does being a taverna landlady suit you?"

Janos played with strands of her long black hair. "Oh, good enough, I suppose. It keeps long-nosed officials off my back, seeing I've got an honest trade."

The Greek dropped his voice. "But it's only a blind, to hide your real business. Do you still run a gang?"

Janos Cabar coiled the bullwhip and hung it over her shoulder. "Ah, you rogue, I knew you wanted something the moment you walked in here. Yanni, bring the food and follow us, we're going downstairs. Too many little pigs with big ears around waterfront taverns these days."

They reached the basement by a trapdoor, set into the floor of a back room. It was a spacious chamber, with bales, barrels and chests stacked against the walls. There were about twenty women sitting at various tables, eating, drinking and gossiping.

Every one of the women was garbed in men's riding clothes, well-armed, too, by the sight of blades and muskets tucked into their belts. They fell quiet as the visitors entered, but at a nod from Janos they carried on talking. Ned did the rounds of the tables, and was rewarded with choice morsels from many plates.

Kostas clacked his gold teeth happily. "Aye, I see you're still in the highway trade. That's what I wanted to talk with you about, my friend."

Janos draped an arm around Ben's shoulders. "Go on."

Kostas pointed at the boy. "He needs to get to Piran, and he wants to be there soon. That's why I've brought him to you. I require passage for Ben and his dog."

The woman turned to Ben. "You must have urgent business in Piran. Tell me, will it keep until just before dawn after tomorrow night?"

Ben nodded eagerly. "That would be marvellous, marm!"

Janos pulled him close, muttering with dark humour. "Just you marm me one more time, lad, and I'll break every rib that you possess!"

By the strength of the hold she had on him, Ben never doubted her word. He forced a smile. "Not one more marm, I promise, Mrs. Cabar."

She gave him a final squeeze as a reminder. "Call me Janos, that'll do."

Kostas interrupted, "What do I owe you, friend?"

The tough woman shook her head. "I don't take payment from friends, you should know that."

Ned nuzzled her hand until she stroked his ears. "This is a very wild and wonderful dangerous lady, Ben."

Ben turned his attention to Kostas Krimboti.

"How can I thank you for all that you've done for us, Cap'n?"

The gold teeth flashed in a wide grin. "Me, helped you? It's the other way around, Beniamino. You gave me the gift I have always longed for. Something my parents would not allow me to have—a puppy dog! Once I have the old *Blue Turtle* fixed up, I will be Kostas Krimboti, the man who got everything he always wished for. To be captain of his own ship, and to own a dog that will become the terror of all seagoing rats!"

Ben shook the big Greek's hand fondly. "I'm sure he'll be a fine dog for you, Cap'n."

Kostas stood up. "And now I must go, my friend. You'll need to rest up before tomorrow evening, and I must get back to my ship and heal her wounds. Janos, I'm taking the boy outside to have a final word with him."

Ben and Ned followed Kostas and Yanni back to the boat in the harbour. Out of sight from prying eyes, Kostas held out his hand. "Yanni, my pocket money."

From inside his billowing shirt, Yanni brought forth a heavy leather pouch.

Kostas instructed Ben, "Now listen to me, boy, if you refuse my gift I'll be very sad, and angry, too. Here's gold for you. Don't look so surprised, did you think I was a poor man? I was a treasure hunter, you know. I've got gold and jewels that I'll never be able to count. Janos Cabar must be paid, her business is risky. She won't take money from me, so you pay her. Keep some for yourself, you may need it before you and your friends are safe. Now don't argue!"

Ben accepted the pouch. "Thank you, Cap'n."

Kostas stared long and hard at the strange boy with the clouded eyes, regretting that he had no children. "Should you get to the Convent of Santa Filomena, tell the Mother Superior that you are my friend. Say that I will deliver her supplies as soon as I can."

Yanni was already in the boat, manning an oar. "Kostas Krimboti, are you coming? The tide's beginning to turn. Good-bye, boy, good luck to you and your fine dog!"

The big Greek captain scratched Ned's ear gently. "Ah yes, such a fine dog. I hope you don't get lonely without the little puppy, Ned. I think he will be as good a friend to me as you are to your master."

The black Labrador looked soulfully up at Kostas, knowing he could not read his thoughts. "I resent that remark, sir, no dog is more friendly or faithful than I am to this wayward youth. And as to the dreaded Amico—well, I may miss him now and again, but at least my tail won't be chewed to the bone!"

Ben held forth his hand. "You'd best be going, Captain, good-bye and may good fortune follow you."

Kostas pulled the boy to him and kissed the top of his head. "Good-bye, Beniamino, the son I never had. I hope you will re-member the Krimboti in the years that lie ahead of you. Go now, don't look back!" He leaped into the boat, sniffing audi-bly. Grabbing his oar, he pulled away with might and main. "Well, are you going to sit there complaining all night, Yanni? Come on, bend your back, man!"

Ben and Ned strolled back to the taverna, exchanging thoughts.

"Something in your eye, mate?"

Ben wiped his sleeve roughly across his face. "Oh, you know how it is, Ned, always hard to part with good friends."

The dog nodded. "Aye, it is indeed. D'you know, Ben, I've just had a thought. We've hardly seen the ghost of the Dutchman lately, nor have we heard from the angel. Who knows, maybe the spell of wandering for eternity might be wearing off?"

The boy stopped. He sat down on the front steps of the tavern, resting his head against Ned's neck and sighing wistfully. "If only it was! Imagine being able to live your life like others. Never having to keep on the move in case they see you staying young forever. I'm tired, Ned."

The faithful dog nuzzled his master's face. "Oh, come on, or you'll have me moping about soon. Who ever lived through the adventures and excitement that we've had together?"

The boy rose slowly and went inside, adding to his friend's thoughts. "Nobody, I suppose. Nor have they had the sorrow and hardships we've been through. Being chased through our dreams by an accursed captain. Hungry, thirsty, frozen by cold weather, roasted by tropical climes. Being enslaved, losing good friends, ordered to travel hither and thither by an angel. . . ."

Ned threw back his head and bayed sorrowfully. It caught the attention of all the taverna customers. Ben tugged at his dog's tail. "What are you doing?"

Keeping up the mournful din, Ned told him. "I'm yowling and moaning of course, just like you're doing, and I won't shut up until you do, mate, so there!"

Ben was forced to smile—his friend was right. He tugged hard on the drooping tail. "Oh, alright, I'll quit if you will. Come on, let's go and see if there's any of that nice fried beef left before we turn in for the night!"

Ned immediately ceased the noise he had been making. "Now you're talking, mate. One thing about being a creature of respectable age, you get to taste some pretty decent stuff. Lead me to it, comrade. Or on second thoughts, you follow and I'll lead you, us dogs have a finer developed sense of smell than mere humans!"

They were halfway through their second supper, accompanied by two portions of cherry pie which a friendly cook had found for them, when Janos Cabar appeared, accompanied by an older woman who looked very hard and capable. Janos whispered to her, "Round the rest of the pack up, we meet down below for the midday meal."

She turned her attention to Ben and Ned. "You two, clean your plates and get up to bed. Upstairs, second room to the left. You'll need all the rest you can get if you're to ride with the Istrani Wolves. Good night!"

Uncoiling her bullwhip, she cracked it several times above her head, shouting in a harsh voice, "Taverna's closed now, everyone out. Come on, haven't you got homes or ships to go to? Move!"

No man seemed prepared to argue with her; the customers left immediately. Ned picked up his piece of pie in his mouth and headed for the stairs. "Quick, mate, before she makes us scrub the place out!"

It was a quiet little room, rather sparsely furnished, but spotlessly clean. Ned settled down at the foot of the bed, dropping off into a slumber without further ado. Ben sat up, gazing out of the open window at the harbour and the sea beyond. A half-moon flecked the countless acres of water with silver radiance; the horizon betwixt sea and sky was barely visible. He had seen many such nights over the years, it usually was a calming influence on his mind. Yet Ned's former thoughts had made him restless. Suppose the visions and voices had left him? Maybe the angel's command had been brought to an end.

Then he saw it. A pale, cold patch of light, far off, illuminating the *Flying Dutchman.* The doomed vessel appeared in the apparently calm main, its tattered sails billowing and flapping. Still on an endless voyage, captained by the wraith of Vanderdecken, crewed by lost souls. Ned whimpered in his sleep, breaking the spell, and the boy knew what his dog's dream was. He was yearning after the puppy, Amico. All his disdain for the little dog had been only bravado. Ben smiled, smoothing his friend's back lightly. When he looked again, the phantom ship had disappeared. He lay back and sought sleep. However, it was a long time coming—a sight of the *Flying Dutchman,* no matter how far off, was always a precursor of ill fortune lurking ahead.

AL MISURATA BROUGHT A CHART OUT ONTO THE DECK.
Sheltered from the blustery breeze in the lee of the stairs leading to the afterdeck, he outlined the route to Ghigno.

"Soon the city of Venice will be visible on our
port side. That is our marker. Set a course eastward, for Piran, here!" He was marking the chart
with his finger when Augusto Rizzoli's voice rang
out from behind.

"Take us to the women, signore, or you are a
dead man!"

The pirate and his aide turned to see the male
members of the troupe confronting them. Otto
headed the group, holding the
blunderbuss levelled at both men.

Ghigno's face twisted into a
contemptuous sneer. "What do you propose to
do with that rusty old fossil?" He gave a sharp whistle.
Within moments the troupe were surrounded by guards, their
long jezzails primed and ready.

Otto stood his ground, drawing back the weapon's hammer. "*Mein Heer,* this gun is old and rusty, but it has a loud
bark, and a fatal bite. I can take you and your master out with
one blast!"

ISTRANI WOLVES ❖ 281

Al Misurata held up both hands, speaking reasonably. "Then we would all die. The moment you pull the trigger, my men will fire also. What would we all have gained by such a foolish act?"

Signore Rizzoli repeated his demand. "Take us to the women. We do not wish to see death and bloodshed, only to be reunited with my wife and our other two friends. But Otto will fire if he has to!"

Al Misurata did not seem unduly disturbed. "Then I concede to your wishes. Follow me, please."

The entire assembly moved awkwardly to the midship hold, the guards trying to keep the troupe hemmed in, and Otto still menacing both pirate and Corsair with his ancient firearm. On reaching the stable cabin, Al Misurata ordered the guard to open the door, which he did. Before anybody could even guess at his intent, Al Misurata strode inside, grabbed the closest woman—La Lindi—and held her in front of him. Ducking his head so that he was at shoulder level with the snake charmer, the pirate called out, "Ghigno, tell one of the guards to shoot her in the skull unless the German surrenders his gun!"

Otto was loathe to release the blunderbuss. Signore Rizzoli placed his hand on the big man's arm. "Please, my friend, give up your gun. These are wicked and godless men, they will kill La Lindi. Do as he says or she will die!"

The strongman relaxed his hold on the blunderbuss. Ghigno took it gingerly from him. Al Misurata let go of La Lindi and strode out of the cabin. "There are your women, now get in there with them, or I will order my men to fire on them!"

The troupe were left with no choice—they filed dejectedly into the cabin. Al Misurata smiled. "Pigeons should never try to defy hawks. Signore, you will all stay together until we reach our destination. It will not be long, I assure you." He signalled to the guard, who slammed the door and locked it. As they went back upstairs, a cry rang out from the lookout.

"Land ho off the port bow! Land ho!"

There was a gloomy silence in the cabin below decks. The awful finality of their plight had finally come home to the Rizzoli Troupe. Short of a miracle, their fate was sealed now. Their last slim chance had gone with the loss of the gun—ancient and rusty as it was, the weapon had come to symbolise their hope of freedom.

They sat quietly, each with his, or her, own thoughts. Mamma and her brothers-in-law, Buffo and Mummo, still looked to Augusto Rizzoli; the plump little showman had always been their source of inspiration, it was he who made most of the troupe's decisions. But even he was stuck for any solution, the glum expression on his normally cheerful face telling its own story. La Lindi attended to the python Mwaga, her face like an Egyptian carving in black jet, impassive and resigned.

Otto sat flexing his huge hands, making each knuckle pop loudly in turn. The big strongman's jaw tightened as he muttered, "Ach, that Misurata and the scar-faced one, they are the scum of the seas. I can do nothing against their guards, they are too well armed. We are lost, *mein* friends, there is nothing left for us to do!"

Only Serafina had not given up hope. Her hand looked small and delicate as she placed it upon the German's arm. "What we cannot do, Ben and Ned will do for us. They are alive, I know they are. They will help us!"

Mamma crossed herself, kissing her thumbnail. "I will pray to Heaven that they do, *cara!*"

Mummo spread himself out on a bale of straw. "It's hard to tell whether it's night or day, locked up down here in the belly of this great sea beast. We may as well rest and sleep while we can."

Buffo clambered up onto Poppea and lay flat out on the mare's broad back. "Aye, let's take a good, long nap, for who knows what may lie ahead."

The *Sea Djinn* rolled slightly as it changed course, bound across the gulf for Piran.

In the late afternoon of the following day, Ben and Ned watched the final preparations being made for their journey. Six low-sided wagons, all with their axles well-greased, stood laden and covered with tarpaulins in the back courtyard of the Tavern of the Tipsy Hog. A score of women, all dressed in men's clothing, were roping cargo onto the wagons and securing the horses in harness. Four horses to each wagon—matched pairs, mainly bays, with some greys and whites—tall, sturdy animals, eager to be on the road.

Alongside the boy and his dog, Janos Caran sat mounted on a magnificent black stallion, whom she called Hari. She nodded toward the women. "See my Istrani she-wolves, they are the finest smugglers on this, or any other coast. Nobody messes with them, let me tell you, eh, boy?"

Ben agreed willingly. "They certainly look capable enough, Janos. What do you carry on the wagons?"

Janos Caran coiled her bullwhip around the saddlehorn. "Whatever brings the best price. Silks, perfumes, Turkish coffee, velvet rugs, all manner of things that are highly taxed by the authorities. I do good business with the merchants of Trieste. We'll be dropping you off at Piran, not far from the Italian border. You and your dog can ride on the back wagon. Hah, you may get a chance to work for your passage on the road."

Ned reminded Ben, "What about the gold Kostas gave us?"

Ben took out the pouch. Extracting four gold coins, he offered them to Janos. "Please take this, I hope it is enough to pay for our passage."

Janos Cabar smiled."Krimboti must like you well to part with his gold. This is more than enough, look at these coins. The wealthy collectors of Trieste will pay highly for just one. They are in mint condition—solid gold, good, big, heavy coins. Two bear the heads of Egyptian pharaohs, and two have Roman Caesar's heads. They must have lain aboard some wreck on the seabed for many centuries. This trip has paid for itself four times over already. Thank you, boy!"

Ben and Ned mounted the rear wagon, which was driven by a wiry woman named Magda. She was heavily tattooed and smoked a pipe.

Ned shared a thought with his master. "I wouldn't like to get on the wrong side of her!"

Magda gave them a gap-toothed smile. "Sit at the back with Katya, my babies. She'll tell you when you'll need to borrow my pipe!"

Ned sniggered. "Imagine me smoking a pipe!"

Katya was a burly girl, with arm muscles that a man would not be ashamed to own. She smiled at Ben's puzzlement over why he would need a pipe. "Don't worry, friend, it'll become clear enough if we get into a chase. Hold on tight now, I think we're off!"

Janos Cabar reared her stallion onto his back hooves. She cracked the bullwhip back and forth over her head, giving vent to a wild howl, which her she—wolves took up: "Howooooo yaaaaa!"

Ned joined in lustily, urging Ben, "Sing out, mate, this looks like it's going to be fun!" They were both jolted backward as the wagons shot forward.

In an amazingly short time, the convoy had left the town of Pula behind. They thundered along the coast road, with the sea and shore on one side and the high rocky hills and woodlands on the other. The women drivers yipped and howled wildly, urging their horses ahead, whilst Janos rode alongside on Hari, cracking and popping her long bullwhip. Ben's towcoloured hair streamed out in the breeze, as did his dog's ears.

Ned lolled his tongue out happily. "Howooooh! This ride's well worth the price, mate!"

The boy caught his breath. "Just look at those horses run!"

The mood was infectious. Katya and the women sang:

"Down the road like the wind we go, Yahaaaah!
No man can stop us now,
like lightning swift or thunder crash,
'mid harness jingle, wagon clash,
the wolf pack passes in a flash,
to bella mi Italia!

"At the foe as we go we shout, Yahaaaah!
Don't dare to follow us,

ye jackals of the Revenue hark,
in sunlight bright or moonless dark,
we'll leave you at the Border mark,
at bella mi Italia!"

In the early evening they halted, in a grove just short of a town called Porec. Everyone got down to stretch their legs. The horses were given a rubdown, a light drink and a small measure of bran. Ben and Ned sat with the Istrani Wolves. They were given pieces of sausage, chunks of bread and wine heavily laced with water.

Janos Cabar cut off a bit of sausage with her long folding knife, nodding at the road ahead. "The Revenue have a garrison post at Porec, that's where we might run into a spot of bother. The main thing is to do as you're told and keep your head. Fear is the best weapon we have, so we use it. Those bumpkins at the garrison never learn, we've got by them every time so far. They're badly mounted—most of them are on foot—and they're used to dealing with fools like themselves. Watch me, and follow the lead of Katya and Magda, you'll be alright. Our horses run better on their second wind, we've not pushed them too hard so far. Give it a short while yet, then we'll take off again—but this time no shouting or singing. Understand?"

Ben saluted. "Right y'are, Cap'n!"

She flicked his earlobe gently with her bullwhip. "I thought you were going to call me marm just then."

Ned nudged Ben with his head.

"Bet you wouldn't have asked her what she'd do if you had?"

Ben gave the Labrador a wry smile. "Not likely. Why don't you ask her yourself?"

Ned scratched his ear with a back paw, casually. "I'm not afraid of her, you know."

When they set off again, the drivers kept their horses to a lively canter. Nobody spoke, sang or called out; all that could be heard was the creak of wagon wheels and the steady clop of hooves. It was a glorious evening, with the setting sun lighting the seaward horizon in scarlet, gold and a dusky blue-grey. Ben sat on the back of the rear wagon with Ned and Katya. The burly girl chewed on a straw, folding both hands behind her head.

"I like this part of the journey. Once all the jouncing about and shouting have stopped, it's peaceful."

Ned expressed a thought. "Like the calm before the storm."

Keeping his voice down, Ben murmured to the girl, "It's a bit too quiet for my liking, how far are we from Porec?"

Katya chuckled. "Soon be passing it now, that's when the fun usually starts."

Their driver, Magda, called back to them, "It's about to start right now, look up ahead!"

A roadblock had been set up about a quarter mile ahead. It was nothing sophisticated, merely the trimmed trunk of a pine tree set upon two small columns of rocks and rubble. Behind the barrier stood a group of townsmen and the mayor of Porec.

Katya explained, "They're not real Revenue officers, just volunteers. See, they're only wearing armbands, not uniforms. If they catch any smugglers, they usually help themselves to the best of the cargo. Then they hand the rest over to the Revenue captain."

Ben sized the distant men up, Katya was right, but the men were carrying pitchforks, staves and any implements they felt were handy in dealing with smugglers. "There's about thirty of them, and they look like they mean business. What are we supposed to do now?"

The girl spat out the straw she was chewing. "Obey whatever orders Janos gives, and leave the rest to her. She's good at this sort of thing."

In the short time following, both Ben and Ned realised that good was an understatement where Janos Cabar was concerned. The chief of the Istrani Wolves was a whirlwind of boldness and ferocity. She burst into action, setting the black stallion, Hari, full tilt at the barrier. Janos gave her wolf howl, cracking the bullwhip back and forth as she charged.

Crack! Crack! "Howoooooyaaaaah!" *Crack! Crack!*

The mayor of Porec lost his tricorn hat, flinging aside his warrant parchment as he dived for cover. The townsmen scattered to either side. Baying and flailing the long whip, Janos Cabar leaped her horse over the barrier. She lashed out, sending the whip curling round and round the pine trunk, and urging the stallion onward. The barrier was wrecked in an instant. She pulled it to one side, skillfully flicking her whip free.

"Howoooooyaaaaah!" Rearing the big, black horse onto its back hooves, she set about scattering the townsmen into further disarray.

Suddenly the wagons lurched forward. Ben and Ned joined the smuggling crew, howling like madbeasts straight for the opening. They shot through like cannonballs in a cloud of dust and reckless speed. The boy saw a man thrown high as he bounced off one of the horses' flanks. Teeth bared, wind streaming around him and both fists clenched as he roared out the Istrani Wolf call, Ben caught a glimpse of Janos Cabar as he sped by her.

She was caught up in the moment, and thoroughly enjoying herself. The bullwhip in her hands was like a vengeful snake, whipping pitchforks and hoes from the men's half-hearted grasp. The mayor was picking himself up from the dust, like a plump black beetle, when she caught him a parting shot across the seat of his tight britches. *Crack!* He screamed like a stuck pig, throwing himself into the roadside bushes, with both hands clutching his bottom.

Ned winced at the sight. "Ooh, I bet he has his supper standing up for a week or two, mate!"

Tears of mirth coursed through the dust on Ben's face. "Go on, tell me you're not afraid of her now!"

The teams of horses were thundering along the rough-hewn track. Wagons bounced and jumped over rut and rock. Everyone was shouting for joy, but holding on tight. If anyone fell from a wagon, they would be left at the mercy of the mayor of Porec and his townsmen. After galloping several miles, the horses were slowed to a steadier pace.

Janos Cabar caught up with the back wagon, hailing Ben. "Hola, boy! Are you and your dog having a good time?"

The boy's strange, clouded eyes were alight with excitement. "We certainly are. You were marvellous back there!"

She saluted him with the coiled bullwhip. "Aye, it beats washing a man's dirty shirts by the streambank. I'm going on ahead to see how the going is. Don't fall asleep in the dark now, keep your eyes open." She galloped off, leaving Ben to talk with Katya.

"Is Janos married? I can't imagine her washing and cooking for a husband!"

The girl shook her head. "No, she says she has enough to do, running this crew and managing her taverna. The rest of the women are. Magda is my mother, I have another sister at home, and two brothers. I'm the eldest. My father is a farm labourer. He works hard, when there's work about, but it's Mother and me who really butter the bread on our table."

Ned glanced up to the wiry, pipe-smoking driver. "I hope she washes her hands before she butters the bread!"

THE GOING WAS EASY BY NIGHT. BEN FOUND HIMSELF
blinking and wiping his eyes to ward off sleep. After an hour or
so, their leader came back, signalling the wagons to halt. Every-

one got down from the wagons to hear what she
had to say.

"There's a cottage further up the road, on
the outskirts of Buje. The old woman sells eggs
and vegetables. I've known her since I was a little
girl. She told me that a half-mile further on, the Revenue officers are lying in ambush. Somehow they must have got word
from Porec, maybe by way of a carrier bird. So now we leave the
road, take the wagons down onto the shore. Watch out for soft
sand, and rocks that might smash the axles. Go quietly, but
keep an eye on me for any signals. Remember, these are real
Revenue men, so be careful!"

The team drivers took their horses down
a side path onto the shore. Crossing the
sand, one of the wagons got stuck when
it strayed from the line. Ben and Ned
lent a hand and a paw, to dig it out.
Janos hitched her stallion to the team,
heaving it free of the soft sand. The
tide was coming in, so they rode through

the shallows, where the sand was wet, but firmer. The boy and his dog walked alongside the wagon, splashing along in the cool seawater.

Katya pointed out the town from the wagon. "See off to the right there, that's the lights of Buje."

They rolled on by in the peaceful night, with the surf sighing gently up onto the shore. Janos Cabar appeared at Ben's side, like a shadow out of the darkness on her black stallion. She spoke calmly to him.

"Get back up on the wagon, the dog, too. We've been seen. I should have known they'd post a lookout down here, to watch for any contraband coming in by boat. It's our bad luck he spotted us instead. I hope you've got sharp eyes, boy, I'm putting you to watch our backs."

Ned lay at the back of the wagon, with his chin on the tailboard as he scanned the shoreline to the rear. "This is my job, mate, I've got perfect vision at night."

Ben stroked the Labrador's ear fondly. "So you have, old faithful hawk-eyed hound."

Ned replied indignantly, "Old yourself, ancient youth!"

Katya liked Ben's dog. She patted his back. "Keeping watch, eh, good old Ned!"

Ben corrected her. "Better call him good young Ned, he doesn't take kindly to being called old, do you, my nice young puppy?"

The black Labrador shook his master's hand off. "Cease this foolish prattling, both of you. It's not apparent to you yet, but we're being followed!"

The boy signalled Janos Cabar, who steered her horse to the backboard. "What is it, can you see anything?"

Ned followed the direction of his dog's nose, pointing.

"Aye, back there, up on the road . . . wait!" He made as if to peer hard in the direction, relaying Ned's information to Janos. "They've moved up a bit . . . now they're leaving the road. There's eight of them, wearing helmets and dark uniforms. They're all mounted, too. They've crossed the shore now. They're into the tideline, coming through the shallows. Can you see them?"

Janos leaned forward in her saddle, narrowing both eyes. "Aye, they're Revenue officers alright, though they're not coming with any speed. Trying to sneak up and jump us from behind. We'll keep just ahead of them until we're ready to run. Watch for my signal. Magda, is that pipe of yours well lit?"

They caught the faint glow as their driver sent a fragrant cloud of Turkish-cut plug their way. "Aye, it's smoking smoothly, Janos, just give the word."

Ben caught Ned's thought. "Give what word, what do we need Magda's pipe for?"

Ben kept his eyes on the riders, whom he could see clearer now. "I don't know, mate, let's wait and see."

Janos Cabar had been studying the Revenue officers, too. The moment she saw them begin to increase their pace, out came the bullwhip. She gave it one sharp crack. "No noise yet, but ride! Ride!"

Within seconds spray was blossoming up from every wheel as the wagons took off.

Ned licked brine from his lips. "Never dreamed I'd be going to sea like this!"

A warning bugle blast rang out behind them. Magda cackled. "We're supposed to halt and surrender when they blow that silly thing. Have they put their pretty little flag out yet?"

Katya spotted the pennant on the lead rider's lance: some

sort of black design of a spread-eagled bird on a yellow-and-red background. She called to her mother, "Aye, but it'll take more than a bugle and a flag to stop the Istrani Wolves. Pass the pipe!" She caught the pipe which Magda tossed to her.

Janos galloped alongside. "Make ready, but wait for my signal. Now we'll see if they have trained cavalry horses like ours. Give them their head!"

The teams put on extra speed. Spray was flying everywhere as the horses pounded the surf with their racing hooves.

Ben shouted a warning to Janos. "They're moving faster, too, I think they're beginning to close on us!"

The smugglers' leader cracked her whip. "Back to the road, hurry!"

The wagons splashed out of the shallows, going breakneck across the shore, up an incline and back onto the road. The Revenue riders were in hot pursuit, gaining even more ground.

Katya shook her fist at them. "Maybe we can't go as fast as you with loaded wagons to pull, but all you'll eat tonight is our dust!" Pulling aside the tarpaulin cover, she lugged a box up onto the tailboard. Puffing on her mother's pipe to keep it going, she winked at Ben. "Yukk! How does she enjoy this foul thing? Here, Ben, help me to get this box open!"

The boy scrabbled with the cords that bound the box shut. His nimble fingers soon unfastened the knots. Looking up he could plainly see the riders, in black uniforms with brass buttons, each one carrying a sabre and musket. They were getting dangerously close when Janos Cabar gave the cry.

"Howoooooyaaaaah! Give them a good, hot meal!"

Katya removed the pipe from her mouth. "Pass me one of those and stand by with another!"

Ben took one of the packages from the box. It was a cylinder of tree bark and parchment, sealed with candle wax. A wick of some kind protruded from one end. Katya set the wick to the bowl of the pipe. It began to spew forth thick smoke and twinkling sparks. She dropped it over the tailboard onto the road, reaching out her hand to Ben.

"Give me another, and another, quick as you can!"

In swift succession another two cylinders bounced onto the road, just as the pursuers reached the spot where the first one had fallen.

Three almighty explosions followed, catching the front, centre and rear of the Revenue horsemen. Clouds of choking smoke enveloped the scene, horses were screaming and whinnying as they bucked in terror, unseating their riders. Ned passed a shocked thought to his master.

"They've blown them to bits, haven't they?"

Ben grabbed Katya's arm, shouting in her face, "They were bombs, you've killed them!"

The girl slammed the box shut, laughing. "Killed them? Rubbish! Hey, Janos, tell this poor boy about our bombs, he thinks we've killed them!"

Janos pulled alongside the tailboard. Looping her horse's reins over a cleat, she jumped aboard the wagon and punched the boy's arm playfully. "Hah, they're not dead. There's nothing in those bombs but a touch of powder and smoke, no metal of any sort, not even stones. The horses won't be fit to ride, if they ever catch them. As for the Revenue officers, there may be a broken bone or two from being thrown, and they'll all be deaf for a couple of days, but they'll recover alright. Better than being hanged, eh?"

Ben repeated the word incredulously. "Hanged?"

Janos Cabar nodded solemnly. "That's what I said, boy—

hanged. If we'd been caught, a week from now you'd be standing in chains before the high judges at Zagreb. Smugglers and pirates are treated alike by them. Doesn't matter whether you're young or old, male or female. It's the rope in the city square for criminals who cause the nation to lose valuable revenue. No excuses, or pleas for mercy taken!"

She smiled at the horrified look on the boy's face. "Relax, my Istrani Wolves have never been caught. Huh, those Revenue oafs don't even know whether we're men or women. In a day or two, these ladies will be back in their homes, looking after their families."

Ned's thoughts sounded rather scathing. "Oh, wonderful, I'm so pleased for them!"

Ben interrupted, "But why do you take such dreadful risks?"

The face of Janos Cabar hardened. "What would you do if you were a mother with a family and a husband who could not find work, or even a widow, with young children to care for? Men are watched by the authorities, women are not so noticeable. So boy, what would you do, sit at home and watch your young 'uns starve? I did, when I was a much younger woman, because I knew no better then. But not now!"

Ben heard his dog's thoughts. "So now we know, eh!"

He stared at the tailboard. "I'm sorry, it was a foolish question to ask."

Janos Cabar ruffled his hair. "We all ask foolish questions at some time, Ben. Cheer up, you'll be eating breakfast in Piran just after dawn."

Ned's ears waggled. "Did I hear the word breakfast?"

Ben shook the smuggler's hand gratefully. "Thank you, I can't wait to get there."

Janos Cabar cautioned him solemnly. "Hark to me boy, slow

down a little, or you may go rushing straight into unforeseen trouble. Tell me more about these friends of yours, and this slaver from the Barbary Coast who owns the big ship."

As the wagon cantered through the night, Ben related his tale to Janos Cabar. Ned gave him constant mental reminders of any points he missed. When he had finished his narrative, Janos looked from one to the other quizzically.

"Does that dog know what you are saying?"

The boy patted the black Labrador's back. "Of course he does. When nobody's watching us we talk together quite a lot, don't we, Ned?"

His dog remained impassive, mentally chiding him. "Y'know, one day somebody's going to believe you!"

As if to confirm Ned's thoughts, Janos chuckled. "I believe you, Ben, but whether he talks to you or not, that dog is a good and faithful friend to you."

Resting his head on Ben's knee, Ned closed his eyes. "What a splendid lady she is, recognises quality the moment she sees it. My thanks to you, marm!"

Janos Cabar continued, "When we get to Piran, I will make enquiries about the slave ship. I want you and the dog to stay out of sight, so I will get you a room a the Inn of the Grey Swan, which is owned by an old friend of mine. Tell me, are those big gold coins all the money you have?"

The boy nodded.

Janos handed him some small gold and silver currency from her pouch. "Take these. No, don't shake your head at me like that, take them! Piran is a dangerous place, a young 'un like yourself should not be seen spending large, valuable coins in that town. You must stay unnoticed. Sit tight at the Grey Swan and wait until I get back to you."

Ben accepted the small coins. "You are a true friend—thank you!"

Without further incident on the road, the wagons rolled into the port of Piran as dawn was wakening the birds. It was like a lot of other coastal towns Ben and Ned had seen. The convoy halted in a quiet back lane, outside the Inn of the Grey Swan, a modest establishment built in a quaint, old-fashioned style. Janos accompanied Ben and Ned inside. A thin, dignified old lady in traditional dress came from the kitchen to greet them. She and Janos embraced, kissing one another's cheeks. The smuggler was obviously very fond of the old lady.

"Annalisa, you never changed since I was a child. Still as beautiful as ever, such clear skin and bright eyes, you look marvelous!"

The old lady, Annalisa, smacked Janos's hand in mock reproof. "I see you haven't changed either, Nadia Valeska. Still the notorious smuggler Janos Cabar, running the Revenue blockades with your outlaws and carrying a bullwhip. A real lady, eh?"

Janos had obviously heard it all before from Annalisa. She beckoned the boy and his dog forward. "This is Ben, the dog's name is Ned. I hope you'll let them stay with you awhile."

The old lady sized her new guests up carefully. "A handsome boy, fair-haired, too, with strange eyes. Is your dog well-behaved?"

Ned urged Ben to sing his praises. "Go on, mate, tell her I'm totally adorable and trustworthy, good-looking and highly intelligent!"

Ben ignored his friend. "He's no trouble, marm!"

Ned was dumbfounded. "No trouble, is that the best you can do?"

Annalisa interrupted his train of thought. "Good, as long as he doesn't bother Pandora."

A huge, white, shaggy-haired Persian cat appeared around the kitchen doorway. It bounded onto a table, preening itself under the old lady's hand.

Ned chuckled. "Look, mate, a walking doormat!"

The cat stared balefully at Ned, who glared right back at it, sending out a thought. "Aye, and the same to you, fat-head fish whiskers!"

Ben tugged the Labrador's ear. "Ahoy, what's going on here, mate?"

Ned continued glaring at Pandora. "She called me a big black bonehead!"

Further argument between the animals was cut short as the old lady moved toward the kitchen. "Would you like breakfast, Ben? I'm just scrambling some eggs with peppers and ham. You and your crew will have to feed yourselves, Janos Cabar. I don't have enough to go around for my own guests and your ruffians."

The smugglers' leader shouldered her bullwhip. "I can't stay anyway, too much business to attend. Stay indoors until I get back, boy!"

Annalisa led Ben and Ned into her kitchen, seating them at a table by the fire. Ned kept turning in the cat's direction and hurling out insults. "Great hairy sausage! Do you ever get beaten up by mice, plinkypaws?"

The boy tugged his dog's tail sharply. "Now just stop that, I won't have it, d'you hear?"

Ned retreated sulkily under the table. "Well, that moving mattress started it. Ooh! Who are you calling twaddle tail, you overstuffed pillowcase!"

Ben watched Annalisa cracking eggs into a large skillet as he sent out a threatening message. "One more word out of you, mate, and I'll tell the old lady that you never eat breakfast, and you only like stale crusts and water!"

The Labrador rested his chin on both front paws, complaining, "That's right, take Miss Pandora Pussyface's side, I'm just a poor old dog without a friend in the whole wide world!"

Ben rubbed his foot soothingly down Ned's flank. "Try and ignore her, mate, I'm your friend."

Ned stared soulfully up at his master. "I knew you were all along. Right, I'll take your advice, friend. I'll totally ignore that fleabound fat-ridden feline. The smelly, tatty-furred relic. . . . Oh great stuff, here comes the food, hope she doesn't give that meowing moocher any!"

The morning passed on pleasantly enough at the Grey Swan. Ben made himself useful to Annalisa, fixing a loose door hinge and moving some furniture about for her. Every so often she would reward her helpful guest with a slice of her plum cake, or some bread and cheese. The old lady was of the opinion that boys were always hungry. Ben shared his titbits with Ned, who ate them with smug gusto, smirking at Pandora.

"Go on, idle paws, go and catch a mouse, you're not getting any of this. Mmm, tastes lovely, delicious!"

Just before midday, Janos Cabar arrived back with information for Ben. "The word is that this Misurata villain will dock in the harbour sometime tomorrow, maybe mid-noon. That's all I can tell you, my friend, so keep your head down until then. I've got to go to Trieste now—can't hang about here too long, or folk will start asking questions, and word might get out to the authorities. You're safe enough here, though."

Ben took out the pouch of gold coins, which still weighed heavily in his hands. "Janos, when your business is done in Trieste, will you be coming back this way?"

The smuggler nodded. "Aye, I always come back through Piran. Why do you ask?"

The big gold coins clinked dully as Ben shook the pouch. "Listen, I have no need for gold, so I'll make you an offer. If you meet me here when you come back, I may need your help to break my friends free. Would this money be enough to cover your services?"

The smuggler toyed with the leather plaiting on her whip handle. "You really don't realise the value of Krimboti's treasure, do you? What's in that pouch is a fortune. If you don't need it, I know lots of women with families who do. I'll do it, boy, you'll have the assistance of me and my Istrani Wolves. I won't bother with a return cargo, I'll meet you here tomorrow night. If we leave Trieste driving unloaded wagons, we'll be here around seven of the clock. That's a bargain, friend!"

Janos Cabar spat on her palm, holding it out. Ben did likewise and they shook hands.

Ned pawed at his master's leg. "See, I told you she'd go for it. Who's a clever dog, then?"

Ben grinned at him. "Yes, good dog, clever dog! Roll over and I'll scratch your tummy."

Ned stalked off with his tail in the air. "Hmmph! Not while that cat's watching!"

LA LINDI HAD TAKEN HER PYTHON, MWAGA, OUT OF his basket. The snake coiled around her waist and arm, swaying its blunt face in front of her and touching her cheek with  its long, forked tongue. Signore Rizzoli watched Mwaga and his charmer, noting the interaction between them with interest.

"Your snake seems restless today, Lindi, is something the matter with him?"

The enigmatic black lady caressed her pet's shifting coils. "I think it must be raining outside. Mwaga often acts like this when there's rainfall."

Buffo looked up from his task of brushing Poppea. "You could be right. I wonder what time it is. Down here you lose all sense of night or day."

Mummo yawned. "Early morning's my guess."

Mamma commented wryly, "How would you know, you're always asleep? Just before you close your eyes, you always say it's late night. Then when you wake up it's always early morning to you. Serafina, what time do you think it is?"

The youngest of the troupe replied promptly. "Almost midday—time moves like a snail when you're cooped up and you can't see daylight."

Otto left off his moustache trimming, rubbing his stomach. "*Ja,* the *Fräulein* is right, it is time for lunch!"

Signore Rizzoli heard the key in the lock outside their cabin. "That sounds like them bringing food now."

It was Ghigno and four armed guards. The scar-faced Corsair beckoned to them.

"Come on, all out, I'm taking you up on deck. One false move from any of you and someone will be feeding the fishes in the bay. Step out one at a time."

Lunch was forgotten as the Rizzoli Troupe made their way up to the midship deck. Serafina had guessed right, it was midday. The world around them looked grey and overcast. A soft, steady drizzle was smoothing the sea into a waveless swell. They were herded in front of Al Misurata, who stood sheltered beneath the afterdeck stairs. He addressed them in commanding tones.

"In a few hours we will be docking at Piran. You will be confined to your cart until such time as we part company."

Mamma Rizzoli spoke out. "What about our horse, Poppea? She must not be left aboard."

The pirate held up his hand, silencing her. "Do not worry, the horse will be brought up and put into the shafts of your cart when we land."

Mamma persisted. "And what are your plans for us?"

Al Misurata's voice held no emotion. "I am not prepared to say right now, but you will not be harmed as long as you obey me. Let that be sufficient."

Signore Rizzoli carried on where his wife had left off. "You are an evil man! We trusted you, and you repaid that trust by selling us into slavery. Deny it—I dare you!"

Ghigno rested his hand, meaningly, on the pistol that was thrust into his waist sash. "My master is the Lord of the Barbary Coast, he does not argue with poor fools such as you. Be silent!"

Despite the armed guards, Otto's vise-like grip seized the Corsair's arm, causing him to wince. The big German strongman was glaring at Al Misurata. "Otto Kassel always keeps his word, not like you. I make you a promise, *mein Heer,* you will pay for this!"

At a wave of the pirate's hand, more armed men emerged from the cabin behind him. He smiled at Otto. "On the contrary, it is I who will be receiving payment. You are merely the merchandise that is being traded." Al Misurata wandered fearlessly amid his captives. "The treatment you receive from your new master will depend on your own good behavior. Take the girl!"

With a quick movement he swung Serafina into the arms of the guards, then stepped back holding up both hands. "Do nothing foolish, the girl will not be harmed! I need her as a hostage. Behave yourselves, and I will return her to you in due course."

Turning on his heel he went into the cabin, followed by three of the guards and Serafina.

Shortly before mid-noon, the *Sea Djinn* tied up at the harbour in Piran. Nobody paid much attention to the cart which was trundled down a ramp by a dozen well-armed men. With Poppea in the shafts, it rattled off, still with the men surrounding it. Once the cart was clear of the ship, Al Misurata dismissed the guards from his cabin. Serafina huddled in a corner watching his every move, her dark eyes fearful.

The pirate smiled benignly at her. "Why so frightened, my little African songbird? I have no intention of harming you, relax." He gestured to a tray of food on the table. "Come, help yourself to this good food—eat, drink!" Serafina stayed where she was. He laughed, speaking to her as if she were a recalcitrant child. "There's nothing wrong with the food, look." Selecting a large, yellow pear, Al Misurata bit into it and ate with relish. He cast it aside half-eaten, wiping his lips on a silk kerchief. "Perhaps you don't like me watching you. Alright, I will go and leave you alone awhile. Later on I will take you to see the town of Piran. Would you like that?"

Serafina was still frightened; her voice barely rose above a whisper. "I would like to go back to my friends, sir. Where have you taken them?"

The pirate answered like a kindly uncle. "You will see them tonight, I promise. First I want you to do something for me. It is a simple thing, a short trip into town. Then I will deliver you back to your friends. Agreed?" He watched until she nodded. "Good! I'll leave you alone now. When you've finished eating, open that chest in the corner. You'll find lots of pretty things for a beautiful young lady to wear. I want you to look good for our trip to the town."

When he departed the cabin, Serafina heard him lock the door behind him. She ventured across to the food, picking up a few purple-bloomed grapes. However, before she had even tasted them, she broke down in tears. Overwhelmed by her loneliness and fear of the unknown, the beautiful black girl wept, thinking of the only family she knew, the Rizzoli Troupe, and the two friends she held dearest of all: Ben and Ned.

• • •

At the Inn of the Grey Swan, Annalisa was busy peeling and chopping vegetables for a lamb stew. She sat at the kitchen table, wiping her eyes as she peeled the outer layer from a second Spanish onion. The cat, Pandora, prowled around her feet, meowing for attention. The old lady spoke distractedly to her pet. "What? You don't like raw vegetables? What is it that you want?"

Pandora hopped up onto the table, still meowing.

Annalisa pointed her knife at Pandora. "Now listen, madame, I don't have time for all this yowling and mewing. Go on, be off with you!"

The cat leaped back down to the floor, trotted as far as the small scullery and continued its noise.

The old lady rose from the table impatiently. "In there, do you want to go in there?" She opened the door, still speaking to Pandora. "Is it a mouse? Show me, is there a mouse in there?"

The big Persian bounded up onto the window, which had been unlatched and was lying wide open.

Annalisa went to the window and shooed the cat off the sill. She shut the window and latched it. "I never left that open—ah, the boy and the dog!"

Pandora meowed even louder, setting her claws in the hem of the old lady's skirt.

Annalisa nodded. "So that's it, they've both gone out. After Janos Cabar telling them not to. Oh, wait until she hears about this, eh, Pandora!"

The cat arched its back, almost smugly. "Meoooowww!"

• • •

With an old turnip sack split and worn over his head and shoulders, Ben squatted behind a stack of sawn planking with Ned. They had been at the quayside for over an hour, watching the *Sea Djinn* being moored and a ramp being set up amidships.

Ned shook rainwater from his head, then stopped suddenly. "Look, mate, here comes the Rizzolis' cart!"

The boy nodded. "They've got it well-guarded, too. Poor Poppea, she looks a bit shaky, don't you think?"

Ned saw the mare being backed into the shafts. "Aye, after all that time on the rolling main, she's probably trying to sort out her sea legs from her land legs. I hope the troupe are alright."

Ben ducked his head below the timber stack. "I just caught sight of Al Misurata at the stern cabin window. He was eating something, an apple or a pear. I wonder why he never went with the cart?"

Ned chanced a peek around the edge of the stack. "Aye, and that scar-faced rascal, too, wotsisname. I've just seen him going into his cabin. Hmm, one or the other should've accompanied the cart."

Ben licked rainwater from his upper lip. "Good job there's two of us. Listen, you follow the cart to see where they're taking it. I'll stop here. If Misurata or the Scar-face come ashore, I'll trail them to see what they're planning. We'll meet up back at the Grey Swan. Be careful, Ned, don't let them catch sight of you!"

The Labrador shook himself resoundingly, wetting Ben further. "Hmph, careful yourself, my lad!" He slunk off, dodging between the cases and bales which were piled along the quayside.

A moment later, Ben saw Al Misurata leave the cabin and lock it. He moved further along the wood stack until he found a small gap in the planking. From there he could view the ship without taking the risk of being seen by anyone aboard.

The drizzle continued into the sombre afternoon. Ben rubbed his legs to keep them from cramping up. Then he saw Ghigno emerge on deck. The Corsair was dressed finely, carrying a scimitar at his side. He strode aft, sheltering beneath the stairs. Al Misurata appeared from his cabin, sporting his fine Toledo blade, with a red linen cloak covering his expensive outfit. The two men chatted a moment, then the pirate went to a cabin door and unlocked it. He tapped upon the door, calling out something which Ben could not hear. Two of the Arab steeds, which the *Sea Djinn* had been carrying as cargo, where led down the ramp by guards. Ben noted that both horses were saddled, then looked back to the ship.

Serafina came out of the cabin and took the hand which Al Misurata was offering. Ben's heart was racing. He crouched there, staring at his friend—she had never looked so beautiful. The boy bit his hand to stop himself jumping up and calling out her name. Serafina! Serafina! She was here!

Clad in a gown of cream-hued silk topped by a soft, blue woollen cloak and hood, she walked slowly down the ramp like a saint descending from heaven. Hot tears ran down Ben's cheeks, but they were tears of joy from seeing his Serafina once more. The guards held the horses; as Al Misurata mounted one, he leaned down and swung the girl up in front of him, sidesaddle. Ghigno got up on the other steed and they galloped off.

Ben dashed out from behind the timber stack, never once taking his eyes from the graceful form of the girl. He tripped and fell flat on his face in the rainy mud. Scrambling upright, he rushed in the wake of the horses, ignoring a cut on his leg. They cornered at the junction of two streets, momentarily lost to sight. Tearing around the corner, Ben ran smack into the cart of a salt vendor. With the wind knocked out of him, he rose, staggering, in pursuit of the horses, which he had lost sight of. He was forced to halt at the next corner. Standing ankle deep in a puddle, the boy looked wildly about. But they were gone.

Ben ran up to the first person he saw, a fussily overdressed woman, with a maid holding a parasol over her head. He gasped raggedly, "Quick! Have you seen two horses go by carrying two men and young girl? Tell me!"

The woman brought a lorgnette up to her eyes, gazing in disgust at the muddy-faced boy, his trouser leg torn out, blood gouting from one knee and his features smeared with the wet dirt of the streets.

Ben pushed the torn sacking back from his brow, shouting, "Well, have you? Two men and a girl on horseback!"

The fussy woman turned to the maid holding the parasol. "Go and get help, he's mad, he's going to attack me!"

Ben looked pleadingly at the maid. "Did you see them?"

She shook her head dumbly as the woman grabbed the parasol from her and began belabouring Ben with it. "Help! Help! I'm being attacked by a mad boy!"

He stumbled off through the mud-spattered drizzle, with the woman's shouts growing fainter behind him. The boy hurried through a maze of streets, each one looking like the last, staggering into objects blindly, lumbering onward, until he finally tripped and fell headlong for a second time. He lurched upright, swayed, then sat down heavily, dragging himself backward until he felt a wall against his shoulders.

Licking the blood from a parasol wound on his lip, Ben sat wondering what to do next. Should he carry on searching, go back to the ship until they returned or go to the Grey Swan and get cleaned up? Yes, that was it, Ned might be back at the inn by now. They would carry on the search together—between them they would find Serafina. Groaning, Ben pushed himself upright and wiped mud from his eyes as he stared about. Then he realised—he was lost!

Nowhere was familiar. He had run willy-nilly around a strange town until all his bearings were completely turned around. There looked to be nobody abroad on the miserable streets, owing to the quagmire of mud and rain. Nobody except a ragged beggar, shuffling in his direction. Ben approached him and asked the way.

"Do you know the Inn of the Grey Swan? I need to get there."

The man cast a withering glance at the boy, who appeared to possess as little as himself. Pushing Ben aside, he carried on along the street. Ben took out some of the small coins which Janos had given him and jingled them.

The beggar halted, turning to face him. "What did ye say the name of the place was?"

The boy showed him a silver coin, but held on to it. "The Inn of the Grey Swan."

Gazing avidly at the coin, the beggar nodded. "Follow me, young sir, I know the place."

He took Ben along a few back alleys and out onto a broader street. As they were passing a narrow passage to a courtyard, the boy glanced sideways. There was a covered section in the courtyard; the two Arab steeds were tethered there.

Ben grabbed the beggar's grimy hand, pressing the coin into it. "Here, this place will do me!"

The man protested, "But the Grey Swan is only around the next corner on the right, sir."

Ben patted his arm. "Thank you, I'll find it myself." He gave the beggar his coin and watched him shuffle off.

Ben's mind was racing with excitement when an idea occurred to him. Mentally he projected his thoughts as he walked around to the front entrance to the building. "Ned, are you there? Speak to me, mate!"

Some jumbled phrases entered his mind—it was Ned. "Rotten old furryface, it was you who locked that window, I know it was. If I get my teeth around your tail. . . . Eh, what . . . Ben, is that you, can't you get in here, either? Huh, that confounded Pandora!"

Ben interrupted his dog's prattle. "Ned, listen to me. I'm just on the next street to you, outside a hotel called The Crown of Slovenija. Serafina's in there, with Misurata and the Scarface. I need to know why they've brought her here, so stop arguing with that cat and get round here quick!"

The Crown of Slovenija appeared to be a high-class establishment. Its front hall was thickly carpeted, the walls were hung with gilt-framed paintings and chandeliers dangled from the ceiling. The Major Domo who stood between Ben and the dining salon was a portly, uniformed fellow. He gave the ragged, mud-besmirched boy a jaundiced stare, then beckoned him to be off with a fluttering gesture of his white-gloved hand. Knowing there was no way to get by him, Ben went back to wait outside the courtyard entrance.

He did not have long to wait. The faithful Labrador came bounding out of the drizzly curtain to his side. "Well, I know where the cart is, mate, just outside of town, by a stream in some woodland. Where's our girl, then, have you seen her?"

Ben crouched by his dog's side as he answered. "She's inside somewhere, but there's no chance of me getting in, I'd be ejected on sight."

Ned shook himself vigorously. "Right, you stay here, I'll sneak in the back way and see what's going on!"

Serafina sat at a corner table in the salon with Al Misurata. Ghigno had gone off somewhere to carry out his master's wishes. The beautiful black girl had allowed an attendant to take her cloak. Other diners stared openly at the man in costly Arab garb and the fascinating girl. Al Misurata ignored them, indicating a selection of small frosted tarts and an ornate pot of hot chocolate which had been served to them.

"Help yourself, girl. One as pretty as you should get accustomed to a life of luxury."

Serafina stared miserably at the woven damask table covering. "I'm not hungry, sir, all I want is to go back to the Rizzoli Troupe."

The pirate poured himself a dainty cup of the hot chocolate. "All in good time, miss. Ah, here comes Ghigno."

The Corsair was accompanied by a sallow-faced man whose attire suggested that he might be a country squire. Ghigno introduced him. "Lord, this is the head steward and aide to Count Dreskar. Ferenc Kuvan!"

Al Misurata viewed the aide with raised eyebrows. "I was told I would be dealing personally with your master?"

The aide bowed formally. "Sir, I am here to do business with you on Count Dreskar's behalf. He sends his apologies and regrets, but he has been called away on urgent matters of state."

Al Misurata appeared to digest this information for a time. Then he turned to Ghigno. "Take the girl and wait elsewhere for me."

Ghigno escorted Serafina away. Al Misurata beckoned the aide to sit in her place, noticing the way he had appraised the girl.

"A real beauty, that one—I think your master would agree?"

Ferenc Kuvan got straight down to business. "What about the others, did you not bring them?"

The pirate wagged a finger, smiling. "Piran has many eyes and ears, it would be foolish to bring them all. I am merely showing you the jewel of the collection. The others are safe enough, my friend."

The aide's face disguised the fact that he did not relish being called the friend of a Barbary pirate. He tapped a finger on the tabletop. "How many are they, and what about the fair-skinned boy your report mentioned?"

Al Misurata found lying as natural as drawing breath. "Alas, he was lost overboard in a storm. But the others are a worthy addition to the girl. There are six of them, including a German strongman, a prime specimen. Then there is a dancer and snake charmer, older than the girl, but very attractive, a real Nubian lady. There are two brothers, acrobats, clowns, Count Dreskar would find them immensely entertaining. Then there is an older couple, man and wife, they are very obedient and have many years service still in them."

Count Dreskar's head steward cut the pirate short. "I will

take the girl, the Nubian lady and the German. The others would not interest my master."

Al Misurata sat back. Making a tent of his fingers, he stared at Ferenc Kuvan over it, speaking levelly. "You will take them all, that is the deal I agreed with Dreskar. Or I can make you another offer—your master can forget any arrangements we made, and be satisfied to have you back, plus the gift of a dagger, which you will carry in your heart."

There followed a silence, in which the pirate watched the aide's Adam's apple bob up and down several times. When he had regained some composure, Ferenc Kuvan spoke.

"Let us discuss the price of your wares."

Al Misurata nodded casually. "I warn you, I drive a hard bargain, my friend."

Ben wandered up and down the mudwashed path outside, cold and hungry. It seemed an age since his dog had slunk inside from the courtyard entrance. Late afternoon was sinking toward evening when Ned emerged into the street. Ben hurried to him. "Well, did you see her?"

The dog grabbed Ben's torn trouser leg. "Come with me, hurry up. And don't stand gawping at her, or the Scar-face'll see you. Come on!"

He led Ben around to the front entrance. As they passed the hall doorway, the boy found himself staring straight into the eyes of Serafina. Ghigno was studying one of the paintings on the wall, but he had a firm grip on the girl's arm. Her almond eyes grew wide at the sight of Ben, who had only enough time to wink and nod reassuringly at her. Then the dog dragged him away, communicating urgently. "Don't stand there like a lovelorn duck. Move yourself!"

Serafina felt as though she was suddenly hovering on air at the sight of Ben. Ghigno turned and looked at her quizzically.

"What's the matter with you, girl, do you feel faint?"

She quickly turned her eyes to the carpeted floor. "Er, no! Well, a little bit. Please could I have something to eat? I feel a bit hungry."

On the way back to the Grey Swan, Ned explained what had taken place in the salon. "I managed to get into that room where old Miseryguts was sitting at a table with another fellow. I could see Serafina and the Scar-face waiting in the hallway. Anyhow, you know those long, padded seats that run along the walls? Well, I crawled under one end and bellied my way along. You're lucky to have such a clever and resourceful dog as me. I got to within less than a yard of Miseryguts and the other one. And here's what I learned . . ."

Nobody passing by would have guessed what was going on between the ragged, muddy boy and the saturated hound.

THE RIZZOLIS' CART STOOD
in a quiet woodland glade,
surrounded by armed men.

 But for the presence of the black-burnoosed guards with their jezzails and spears, it would have been an idyllic setting. Poppea, the troupe's mare, had been hobbled, so that she could crop the greenery or drink from a nearby stream. The only view which the passengers in the cart had of the outside was through a small, circular window in the upper half of the rear door. Augusto Rizzoli peered through it, trying to estimate the number of their captors.

"I can see six guards from here, but that's only about half of them."

Otto pointed a thumb over his shoulder. "*Ja*, the others are out there, I can hear them."

The normally happy Mummo was very down in the mouth. "Six or twenty-six, what can we do against armed men? This will probably be the last chance we have to escape!"

Mamma berated him sternly. "Shame on you, how can you even think of escaping without Serafina? We go nowhere without that girl!"

Buffo intervened on his brother's behalf. "We're all agreed on that, but Mummo was only expressing a fact. This time tomorrow we may all be whisked off to someplace unknown, sold off to some other villain."

La Lindi stood on tiptoe, looking over Signore Rizzoli's head at the two horses approaching the cart. "They're bringing our Serafina back, see, it's Misurata and Ghigno!"

Still dressed as she had been for Ferenc Kuvan's inspection, the girl was thrust into the cart.

Mamma kissed her cheek. *"Che bella,** what finery! Are you well, *cara mia*?"

Al Misurata interrupted from where he stood in the open doorway. "No harm has befallen her. Stay inside this cart, all of you. I don't want to leave any graves behind when you move out tomorrow. My guards have orders to shoot if you so much as poke a finger outside. You have the girl back now, so sleep."

Pink spots of anger showed on Signore Rizzoli's cheeks. "Where are you sending us, and who have you sold us to, flesh peddler?"

The pirate grasped his sword handle. "Old fool, I am running out of patience with you! I could have cast you and your wife overboard and saved myself some trouble. Instead I insisted that you were all sold together, even you and her, as useless as you are. So shut your mouth and be grateful!"

He slammed the door shut and bolted it, then began issuing orders to Ghigno. "Count Dreskar's aide will come for them before dawn. It is too late for us to travel back to the *Sea Djinn,* so we'll camp here for the night. See to it!"

Che bella (how lovely).

La Lindi, who had heard the pirate, scowled. "A pity the rain has stopped. I hope it starts again heavily and soaks the evil scum to the bone. Serafina, did you see the one who has bought us?"

The beautiful girl called them together and spoke in a whisper. "I saw a man, but I think he is in the service of someone more powerful. But listen, I saw Ben, too, and Ned, only for a moment. I think he means to help us, he smiled at me and winked, as if he had some kind of plan."

Signore Rizzoli felt hope for the first time in awhile. "Ah, Benno, I know that good boy will help us if he can!"

Shortly before that, Ben and Ned were having to endure a sound telling off from the proprietor of the Grey Swan. The finger of Annalisa was wagging back and forth under their noses like a metronome—the old lady was in full spate. "And where, may I ask, have you two been, eh? Just look at you both, have you been wrestling with one another in that mud? You deliberately disobeyed Janos Cabar, what did she tell you? Stay inside, and don't dare go out wandering. Now look at you, you . . ."

"Old one, give your jaw a rest before it seizes up!" The leader of the smugglers entered the room. She lifted the old lady off her feet and hugged her, frowning at the mud-coated boy and dog. "So, you've been out, eh?"

Ben explained, the words tumbling from him in a rush. "We saw the ship, it docked this afternoon. Misurata has sold my friends to the agent of some count. The cart is in the forest outside of town, Ned, I mean I, saw it, we can take you there, but we'll have to be quick, they might be gone before long—"

Janos silenced the boy's deluge of words with a wave. "Whoa, not so fast! Annalisa, run a bath, get some dry clothes for this muddy urchin and clean his knee up, he's dripping mud and blood everywhere."

Ben protested, "But there's no time, they may be taken away over the border someplace, we've got to—"

Snaaap! The bullwhip cracked an inch from his lips as Janos interrupted, "You two would frighten the horses, looking like that. Now go and get cleaned and changed, then I'll decide what to do. Don't argue with me. Go!"

As they went, Ned made sure he brushed his mud-plastered coat up against Pandora, commenting maliciously, "This is all the fashion. Here, try some, everyone's wearing it out there today!"

Spitting and yowling, the white Persian cat arched her muddied back.

Half an hour later, Ben, with a freshly bandaged knee, sat down beside the smuggler in the dining room. Annalisa had rigged him up from her slop chest, with some sailors' clothes and a pair of cut-down sea boots. Ned's fur was still glossy from the soap and water he had been rolling about in. They wolfed down cheese, bread and soup as they outlined the situation to Janos. She listened intently, then outlined a swift plan.

"Right, here's what we'll do! I'll take just two wagons, six horses to each wagon, and an extra six for the cart. No fancy schemes, we'll just hit them as hard and as fast as we can.

That's the best thing to do in a situation like this. Ben, you and your dog will be at the rear of the back wagon again, with Magda and Katya. It'll be your job to pelt them with the bombs, create as much confusion as you can. I'll get the six horses hitched up to the cart, it'll go like lightning."

Ned sent his master a thought. "What about Poppea?"

Ben explained about the troupe's mare. Janos had the answer immediately. "I'll cut her loose and tie her to the back of the cart, but she'll have to keep up. Once we're on the road, we'll head northeast, for the convent at Muggia. That place is like a fort, I'm sure you and your friends will get sanctuary there. Well, how does that sound to you, boy?"

Ben's clouded eyes began to gleam with the prospect of the daredevil idea. He handed over the pouch of gold coins to Janos. "It sounds great, friend, here's my part of the bargain!"

She opened the pouch, extracting four more coins, and handed the rest back to him. "This is quite enough, you may need more gold before you're all safe away. I'll be leaving you at Muggia. Once you go into the convent, I'm off. The idea of being cooped up with a pile of nuns doesn't sit too easy to me!"

Annalisa cleared away the dishes, chuckling drily. "On your way then, Sister Janos!"

The smuggler grinned. "I'll see you when I return for the rest of my wagons and stock, Grandma!"

Outside, the drizzle had ended; it was a quiet, clear night. The Istrani Wolves saw to the harnessing of the extra horses, then piled into the two carts. Katya patted Ned and winked at Ben. "Well, what's the orders?"

The strange boy laughed. "You'll be smoking your mother's pipe again, mate. We're planning on attacking some Barbary slavers and freeing my friends."

The big girl narrowed her eyes fiercely. "There should be more than just powder and smoke in those bombs, a load of musket balls and scrap iron, maybe. That'd put a stop to their slaving."

Ned agreed mentally. "What a savage young creature—splendid idea, though. Blow old Miseryguts to smithereens, wouldn't the world be a better place without him!"

There was no time for further discussion, as Janos Cabar leaped onto her black stallion and cracked the bullwhip. Reinforced by the extra horses, both wagons whirled off into the night.

OTTO TOOK THE TINY SCISSORS he used for clipping his moustache and began working on the flooring of the cart. Signore Rizzoli, wakened from a half-slumber, stared at the strongman. "Herr Kassel, what are you doing?"

The big German placed a finger to his lips. "Keep your voice down. If I can get one of these boards loose, we could escape through the floor."

La Lindi joined them. "But what about the guards outside? They're still awake, aren't they?"

Otto continued probing with the now-bent scissors. "Frau Lindi, it is two hours past midnight, and they are only men who have been awake all day. They must be half-asleep by now. It is a chance I am willing to take."

A small fire glowed beneath a canvas awning set up between the boughs of a tree. Al Misurata and Ghigno sat under the canopy, taking turns to nap. The pirate kicked the Corsair lightly, passing him a flask of wine.

"Here, drink some of this, but stay awake. Let me know when Dreskar's man shows up for his goods." Huddling down into his cloak, Al Misurata closed his eyes, listening to the sounds of the forest around him.

Ghigno drank from the flask, then sat staring into the fire. Immediately he began to blink. He drank again, deeper this time, looking away from the fire. Picking up a stick, he tossed it, catching a guard on the back. The man turned. Ghigno mouthed the words, "Stay awake!"

The guard nodded and stood to attention. After another drink of wine, the Corsair found his gaze turning back to the flames. Then his eyelids started to droop. He yawned silently, allowing his head to nod forward.

Ghigno was almost asleep when he heard the far-off rumble. The air was still and close. Again the rumble sounded, this time slightly closer. With his chin now on his chest, he sought an explanation for the dull, rumbling noise. Probably thunder, they might be due for heavy rain before dawn. Ghigno fell into a slumber.

Magda glimpsed the firelight through the trees. It was difficult keeping the teams to a canter. She tossed her lighted pipe back to Katya. "Here we go, girl!"

Janos Cabar kicked her stallion into a gallop, cracking her bullwhip as her Istrani Wolves bayed.

"Howoooooyaaaaah!"

They hit the camp like a sudden thunderbolt. Ned was howling like a wild beast as Ben passed the bombs to Katya. Touching off the fuses, she slung them, one at the fire, the other at the closest two men. "More, Ben, more, keep them coming!"

"Howoooooyaaaaah!"

Musket shots sounded out; a man's cloak took fire; explosions showered earth, pine needles, branches and foliage widespread. Two women leaped down from a cart. Grabbing the extra horses, they swiftly lashed two to either sides of the shafts and two in front. Jumping up onto the cart, they spurred the new team out of the camp.

Ben caught sight of the hobbled mare. "Poppea!"

Ned leaped from the wagon and ran to her. Luckily it was only a slipknot around Poppea's front legs. As Ned dragged at it, the thing came undone.

The black stallion, Hari, was up on his hind legs, kicking and flailing out at guards on both sides. They fled from the steel-shod hooves, the whip that was like a deadly snake, snapping and stinging everywhere. Poppea took off after the troupe's cart.

Katya hurled another bomb at the wreckage of the fire, and another which sent up a spray of water from the stream. Then they were off, rattling along the northeast trail. Ned made a spectacular leap, landing on top of Ben, and sending him sprawling in the back of the wagon.

"Howoooooyaaaaah!"

Even the Rizzoli Troupe took up the wild cry as the rescue convoy hurtled off into the night.

Behind them, the camp looked as though it had been struck by a tornado. Guards lay moaning, caked in sludge, many clutching injuries they had sustained in the whirlwind attack. Some threw themselves headlong into the stream to quench their burning cloaks.

Ghigno had been blown clear of the canvas awning. He sat up, spitting mud and wiping dirt from his eyes, staring about vacantly. Crawling over to the smouldering shelter, he pulled his master from it. Al Misurata was unconscious. His turban hung in rags from his brow, blood oozed from an ugly wound to his right ear. The Corsair dragged him to the stream, and splashed water on his face.

"Master, Master, can you hear me? Wake up!"

After a few moments, the pirate's eyes flickered. He stared at Ghigno, blinking to bring his face into focus as he croaked, "Whu . . . 'appened?"

The Corsair snatched a half-consumed flask of wine from a guard who was reeling about in a daze. He held his master's head, allowing him to sip slowly. "We were ambushed by a crew of women. At least I think they were women. I saw the boy and his dog!"

Al Misurata stared at him uncomprehendingly; all he could hear was a noise like a high-pitched siren. He grabbed Ghigno by the arm. "Say again?"

Realising that his master had been deafened by the blast of the bombs exploding, Ghigno mouthed words, trying to suit actions to them. "Ambush, we were attacked, I see boy, Ben, and dog!"

Al Misurata sat up straight. He winced, touched the wound on his ear and stared at the blood on his hand. "Boy, dog, how?"

Ghigno was at a loss to say or do anything. He held the wine flask to his master's mouth, but Al Misurata dashed it away, hauling himself to his feet. He stood swaying momentarily, then rasped out, "Find the horses!"

Ghigno dispatched two guards who looked reasonably fit to seek out their mounts. The pirate had taken off his waistband to bind up the wounded ear when the Corsair attracted his attention, mouthing, "What are your orders?"

The pirate cocked his good ear. "Say it aloud!"

Ghigno placed his mouth close and shouted, "Master, what are your orders?"

Al Misurata heard him faintly—his hearing was coming back slowly. He drew his sword. "They must die, all of them! Rally the guards, make sure their weapons are loaded and their blades are ready. We will hunt the boy and his friends down like dogs, but first we need horses, transport. Listen carefully, here is what we must do!"

In the hour preceding dawn, Count Dreskar's aide rode into the devastated camp. Both he and his servant were mounted on horses. Four more horses followed, harnessed to a forbidding-looking coach. It was plated with metal and iron bars for the transport of wild animals—or slaves. Two men sat on the front driving seat, another two sat on the back steps. They were dressed like footmen, but armed with swords and muskets.

Ferenc Kuvan stared about at the ruined camp and the two men who stood awaiting him, Al Misurata and Ghigno. Observing no courtesies and giving Al Misurata no formal title, the aide asked abruptly, "Where are the slaves, what happened?"

The pirate folded his arms, looking disdainfully away as Ghigno replied.

"We were ambushed, they escaped. My master will have them back with you before eventide. Wait here with your men, we will need your coach and horses to hunt them down."

Embolded by the sight of the pair in their sorry state, the aide forgot his fears of the previous day. His hand strayed toward the butt of the musket he had tucked into his belt as he addressed them scornfully. "You are in no position to demand anything from me. No one in the employ of Count Dreskar would permit common slaves to attack them and run off free!"

Ghigno nodded. "So you refuse the requests of Al Misurata, Lord of the Barbary Coast?"

The aide's confidence was growing. "I could pursue the slaves and take them myself. Your lord has lost them. Only a fool would agree to such outrageous terms!"

Al Misurata raised his arm and dropped it suddenly. The air resounded to the crash of rifle fire from the surrounding trees. When the last echo had died, Ghigno and the guards hurried forward and subdued the whinnying horses. Al Misurata slit open the shirt of the dead aide and retrieved the pouched money belt from about his waist. He hefted it in one hand, remarking to the corpse of Ferenc Kuvan, "Only fools defy the wishes of Al Misurata."

The bodies of the servants were thrown from the coach as the pirate's guards manned it. Mounting the two spare horses, Ghigno and Al Misurata raced off along the northeast road immediately.

OUTSIDE THE TOWN OF MUGGIA,
ON THE ITALIAN BORDER.

IT WAS AN HOUR AFTER DAWN ON A MISTY SUMMER
morn when the cart and the two wagons halted. Above them on
the brow of the hill stood a walled building. Ben and Ned
 jumped from their wagon, but before they could
reach the troupe's cart, Otto had broken the door-
lock with a single heave of his mighty shoulders.
The troupe tumbled forth, cheering and laughing
as they were reunited with the boy and his dog.
Serafina reached Ben first and embraced him, shedding tears
of joy upon his face and kissing them away. "Oh Ben, Ben, I
knew you'd save us!"

Augusto Rizzoli held the rest back. "Look at the young
ones, such a sight, eh?"

Buffo caught sight of Ben's face over Serafina's shoulder.
"*Magnifico!* His face is on fire!"

Mummo did a handspring on the path. "He'd make red
pepper look pale!"

Mamma cuffed both the clowns' ears. "Leave the children
alone, were you never young?"

Ned was sending out frantic messages. "Will someone kindly tell Otto to put me down!"

Janos Cabar shook hands with the rescued slaves. "My friends, I think you'll be safe in that place up there. I have heard the Sisters are kind folk!"

Mamma raised her hands to the building, as if in prayer. "The Convento di Santa Filomena, heaven be praised!"

"Vagabonds! Bandits! Be off, go away!"

A very old nun had the main gate slightly open. She was waving a broom at them, shouting, "I warn you, go away, or I'll set Sansone* on you!"

Janos approached, calling back to the ancient Sister, "Mind your manners, old lady, go and tell your Mother Superior that some friends of Kostas Krimboti wish to speak with her. Hurry now, we haven't got all day!"

The old Sister vanished, slamming the gate behind her.

Magda chewed on her pipestem, scanning the road behind them. "She'd better put a move on, those slavers could be right on our tail!"

There was a pause, then the main gate reopened. The Mother Superior came out to meet them. She was a small, well-built lady, not unlike Mamma Rizzoli, with lots of laughter wrinkles around her eyes. She pointed a finger at Janos. "Only you look wild enough to be a companion of the rascal Krimboti. I am Mother Carmella. What can I do for you, my child?"

The smugglers' leader was rather taken aback at being referred to as a child, so Ben answered for her.

"Marm, we are seeking sanctuary from a Barbary slave lord. Kostas Krimboti recommended your convent to me."

*Sansone (Italian—Samson).

Mother Carmella linked her arm in Ben's, smiling benignly. "Santa Filomena would never fail to open its doors to
the needy and oppressed. You are welcome here, signore."

The boy waved to the troupe. "Come on, everybody!"

Only Janos and her Istrani Wolves remained out on the
path. Ben went to her. "Won't you come inside for just a moment, friend? Who knows, they're probably serving breakfast
about now."

Janos watched her women hitching Poppea to the troupe
cart and sending her inside with the others. "No, no, Ben, I
must be on my way now. I will carry on to Trieste. There's a
cheese and olive oil merchant there, he'll load up my two wagons for the return trip. I'll pick my other wagons up at the Grey
Swan on the road back."

The boy endured the smuggler's vise-like grip as he shook
hands with her. "Janos Cabar, it has been a pleasure knowing
you. Thanks for all your good help, and a safe journey to you!"

The Istrani Wolves were ready and waiting. Janos sprang up
on her big black stallion, cracking the bullwhip.

As they pounded off down the trail, Ben could not resist
cupping both hands around his mouth and giving voice to the
wolf call. "Howooooooyaaaaah!"

Janos, Magda, Katya and the rest bayed back at him.
"Howooooooyaaaaah!" Then they were gone into the gold-
tinged mists of the summer morning.

The ancient Sister who locked the gate after she had
admitted Ben crossed herself, staring suspiciously at him.
"Howling like a wild beast, I still think you're some kind of
rogue or bandit!"

Inside, the convent building was beautiful in its simplicity.

Whitewashed walls, plain wood and woven rush matting bore witness to the nuns' modest way of life. Mother Carmella showed Ben to the refectory, where the troupe were seated for breakfast. She sat down beside him.

"First you must eat, we can talk later."

Ben looked around for his dog, sending out a message. "Ned, where are you? It's not like you to miss breakfast, mate!"

The black Labrador and another dog padded into the room. Both were carrying huge beef marrowbones. Ben was startled by the size of Ned's companion. He was absolutely huge, with a massive square head and a long, scraggly coat of black and grey.

Ned did a doggy chuckle. "Meet Sansone, the guardian of Santa Filomena. No need to worry about him, mate, he's soft as an old feather bed until the Sisters give him the order to attack. This fellow's living the life of a king here—imagine getting bones like this whenever you want 'em!"

They wandered over, and Ben patted Sansone's head. The big dog was definitely a softie.

Sliced ham, cheese, fresh bread, fruit and a variety of drinks soon appeared. Everybody bowed their heads in silence as Mother Carmella recited a Latin grace. Then they fell to. Mamma Rizzoli had far more to say than Ben; after the meal she talked animatedly with the Mother Superior about what had happened to them. Both ladies seemed to have hit it off so well together that Ben took the chance to steal off with Serafina.

Ned looked up from his bone, commenting to Sansone, "I've warned him, but he doesn't listen to me. Huh, humans, think they know better than us!"

• • •

There was an upstairs verandah at the rear of the convent, which had a wonderful view of the Adriatic Sea and the Gulf of Venice, now that the morning mist had cleared. Ben leaned on the verandah rail, looking out over the water. Serafina stood at his side, watching his face.

"You seem to know the sea well, Ben. I'd never set eyes on it before Lindi and I joined up with the troupe."

The boy turned to face her. "And do you like it?"

Serafina shrugged. "I don't know yet. It reminds me of something in your eyes, so cloudy and far off, mystic almost. What do you think?"

Ben turned back to the view. He wanted to tell her everything about his strange life. From that night in Copenhagen, over eighty years ago, when he fell in the harbour and was swept out to sea in the wake of the *Flying Dutchman,* clinging to a rope. Of the times he and Ned had shared on the world's great oceans. He wanted to tell of the curse the Lord had cast upon Captain Vanderdecken and his ship, condemned to wander the seas for eternity. Both he and his dog were the only ones spared, by an angel, from sharing that voyage.* Thoughts and yearnings flooded his mind, yearnings he dared not contemplate. Would she believe it? No sensible person would, it was all too fantastic.

Serafina tugged at his sleeve. "Have you gone to sleep, or are you going to answer me? What do you think of the sea, Ben?"

He spoke slowly, choosing his words as he avoided her lu-

*See *Castaways of the Flying Dutchman.*

minous dark eyes. "I am bound to the sea, in one way or another. Sometimes I love it, yet other times I hate it." He heaved
a sigh. "Serafina, there is something I must tell you. Something that might hurt you."

Alarm showed on the girl's beautiful face. "You could never
hurt me, Ben. What is it, what's wrong?"

He lowered his head to the rail, letting his forehead rest
there. "I cannot stay with you. Ned and I have to move on. It
might happen today, or even tomorrow, but it is my fate—I will
have to leave you!"

Tears sprang unbidden to the girl's eyes. "But why?"

Ben felt a leaden ache in his chest. "I cannot tell you that.
Just believe what I say. Go on with your life, you have friends
who love you. Go with the troupe, try to forget you ever
met me."

Serafina clutched his hand. "How can you say that? I will
never forget you. If you go I will stay here forever!"

At that moment, something echoed through Ben's mind. It
was not his dog trying to communicate with him. It was a distant sound of laughter, chillingly evil, filled with malicious satisfaction. He brought his head up sharply and saw the accursed
ship out in the bay—every detail of its barnacle-crusted hull,
tattered sails and ice-stiffened rigging. There was Vanderdecken, lashed to the wheel, beckoning him and laughing
like a maniac. The spell was suddenly broken by Serafina's
scream. Unwittingly, the vision of the phantom ship had caused
Ben to clench his hand so tightly that he had crushed the girl's
with his furious pressure.

As soon as he realised what had happened, Ben released his
grip. Serafina hurried off sobbing, clutching her hand close to
her. He shouted after her, "Serafina!" Ben was about to dash

after the girl, when Ned appeared in the doorway, blocking his path.

"Let her go, mate, it's better this way. I couldn't help but hear your thoughts, that's why I came up here. I felt the Dutchman somewhere out there, too. I know you feel terrible, Ben, but you did the right thing, even though it hurt you both so much."

The boy knelt, sobbing into Ned's fur, as the faithful dog attempted to reason with him.

"Serafina was right, Ben, she won't ever forget you, nor will you ever forget her. But take my word, she won't stay here to become a nun, she'll go with the troupe. Eventually she'll find some happiness in her life. I hate to say this, but time is a great healer." He nuzzled the boy's shoulder gently. "Let's stay up here awhile, you and I. Don't want everybody to see you like this, do we? Come on, we'll sit by the wall where the sun is nice and warm, you just relax until you feel better." Ned licked the tears from Ben's face. "Huh, left my marrowbone to come up here. That Sansone will be making short work of it by now, great hungry beasty, a big beef marrowbone is only a snack to him!"

Ben took his dog's face in both hands. "Ned, Ned, what human ever had a friend as true and faithful as you!"

The dog stared into his master's eyes, then blinked. "Hmm, I'll have to think about that one. Don't know really, I wonder if Mother Carmella has books on the subject. Maybe she has—*Loving Labradors*, Volume One, or *Devoted Dogs*, Volume Two. I'll ask Sansone, trouble is he's probably only read the illustrated edition of *Magnificent Marrowbones!*"

Despite himself, Ben smiled. "What about *The Amazing Adventures of Amico*?"

Ned stretched out, closing his eyes appreciatively in the sunlit warmth. "Don't talk such piffle. That little maggot hasn't lived long enough to have amazing adventures. Can't you think of a better one?"

Ben made a suggestion. *"Black Bundi the Bumptious Bounder?"*

Ned opened one eye. "What did I say about you mentioning that name ever again?"

Ben replied innocently, "What, you mean Bundi?"

Ned closed the eye again. "No, I meant Bumptious!"

Boy and dog lay there together until the sun worked its magic, leaving them both slumbering.

AT MIDDAY AL MISURATA SIGHTED THE WALLED
building that was the convent through a gap in the roadside
trees. He signalled the coach to halt. Ghigno rode to his side.

"Lord, why have you stopped the coach?"

The pirate pointed. "That place up on the
hill. Give me your glass."

The Corsair passed his master a small folding telescope.

Al Misurata spoke as he scanned through the glass. "Take
two guards you can trust, go and see what that place is. Make
sure you are not seen." He touched the bandage on his wound
gingerly. "I'll stay here and bathe this injury. My head's
throbbing so I can hardly think, and the bandage has
become stuck to it. Take your time, go carefully and see how the building is secured."

Ghigno dismounted from his
horse. "I'll find them, if that's where
they're hiding."

The pirate cautioned him, "Stay out of
sight. If you see them, don't do anything,
just report back to me!"

When Ghigno had selected his men and
departed, Al Misurata sat on the back step of

the coach, ministering to his wound and reflecting on the odd and unlucky turns his life had taken since he had met the strange boy and his dog. He had lost valuable slaves, been wounded and outwitted. Moreover, he had been forced to kill the emissary and servants of Count Dreskar. This last fact meant that he could no longer trade along these shores. Dreskar was no fool, he would find out what had happened. Men as powerful and influential as the Count could not be seen to let such incidents go unpunished.

Nor could Al Misurata. He had lost slaves, but more significantly, he had lost face. Ghigno and his own men had seen him hoodwinked and beaten. Now there would be no more lusting after gold until his honour, such as it was, stood restored. As Lord of the Barbary Coast, he had to uphold his standards.

Noontide shadows were beginning to lengthen when Ghigno and his men returned. The Corsican's scarred face showed that it had been a successful survey. He gave his master the good news. "Lord, it is a convent, a house of women. We could not go around the back of it, because there is a sheer drop down to the sea. Inside the wall which surrounds the main building there is a courtyard and gardens, the wall is high and well built."

Al Misurata drummed his fingers on the coach step, his tone denoting that he was running out of patience. "Forget courtyards and gardens—get to the point!"

Ghigno bowed deferentially. "The main gate, Lord, it is old, and not too tightly secured. It would be no problem for me to open it. A flat metal bar is all that holds it shut. I tried it by putting my sword blade through the doorjamb—it could be opened with one swift flick. There was also a big, rusty old lock with a wide keyhole. I took a peep through, no key has been used on it for years.

"Looking through the keyhole, I could see the performers' cart in the courtyard. They must be in there, though there was no sign of the two wagons, or the two teams that pulled them."

Al Misurata had heard enough. "You did well, my friend. The wagons and horses do not concern me. It will make things easier without having to deal with the crew that ran them. So, our birds have flown to roost in a convent, eh? Well, they'll soon find out that holy sanctuary means nought to me! You and the men rest until dark. No, wait, send one of them back to my ship, lend him your horse. Give him orders that the *Sea Djinn* must be brought up here. We will need to be away from this area by dawn."

That evening, Mother Carmella permitted all her nuns to attend dinner. The Convento di Santa Filomena rarely had such a number of colourful guests staying there. The Sisters were naturally curious. Intrigued by the presence of their visitors, they were delighted when the entertainers put on a little show for them. Buffo and Mummo were going through their act in full clown makeup, causing great hilarity among the nuns with their comical antics, when Mamma took her husband aside for a quiet word.

"Augusto, look at poor Serafina, the girl's eyes are all puffy from weeping. She doesn't want to sing tonight."

Signore Rizzoli tuned up his mandolin. "What do you suppose is the matter, *cara mia*?"

His wife raised her eyes upward, toward the high verandah. "It looks like she and Ben have quarreled. I went upstairs to have a word with him, but he is sleeping out on that balcony with Ned. What are we to do?"

The showman shook his head. "Stay out of it, we have no business interfering in a lovers' quarrel. Serafina and Ben are young, they'll soon get over it. You worry too much. Well, if the girl isn't singing tonight, I'd better fill in for her."

As the applause for the clowns died down, Augusto strolled into the centre of the floor. Picking out a melodic introduction, he began singing in his fine tenor voice.

"An old woman leaned out of her window one day,
as a handsome young fellow strolled by,
he was singing a song as he rambled along
'neath the soft blue Italian sky.
La la la la lala lala la

"O *bella ragazza,* the one that I wed,
must have two eyes as blue as the sky overhead,
her teeth will be white as the pale moon at night,
she'll be young and I'll love her completely.
La la la la lala lala la

"Her hair will be dark as a black raven's wing,
and her lips sweet and red as the cherry,
her manner so meek, and the bloom of her cheek,
like a blush made of peach and strawberry.
La la la la lala lala la

"The old one cried after the handsome young man,
I can't match your description alas,
my teeth are like stars, for they come out at night,
and the bloom on my cheek is long past.
La la la la lala lala la

"But I have some blue glasses as blue as the sky,
and I'm sure I can paint my lips red,
from the fortune in gold that my husband left me,
I could buy a black wig for my head.
La la la la lala lala la

"The young man turned round, he came walking back,
crying out I have travelled too far,
that fortune should cause me to pass by your door,
La la la la lala lala la!"

Evening faded to night as the entertainment continued. Mother Carmella was enjoying herself so much, she let the troupe carry on with their show. La Lindi performed her snake-dancing act with Mwaga, even though Serafina did not play the Kongo drum for accompaniment. The good Sisters stared at the python in horrified fascination, some of them crossing themselves. Never had they seen a reptile of such size and sinister grace within the walls of Santa Filomena. Then it was Otto's turn to elicit gasps of awe from the audience. He bent iron bars, lifted huge weights and performed a clever balancing act with the two clowns seated on a heavy bench.

Whilst all this was going on, Serafina sat in the corner silently. Though she was heartbroken and distressed, she cast frequent glances in the direction of the stairs, hoping to see

Ben and Ned coming down from the verandah. La Lindi came to sit by her. She, too, looked at the stairs.

"It looks like Ben is going to spend the night up there. He's probably cold and hungry."

"What can I do about that?" Serafina murmured sadly.

The snake charmer put forward her suggestion. "Take my cloak, and Otto's cloak, too, he won't mind. There's plenty of food left on the table, get some for Ben and Ned. I'm sure they'll be grateful to you. While you're there you can patch up your quarrel." Serafina sniffed, wiping her eyes. La Lindi stroked her friend's cheek. "Go on, do as I say, sometimes you have to make the first move to reach a solution."

Up on the verandah, it was dark, and a breeze was drifting in from the sea. Ben could not help a slight shiver. He huddled closer to his dog for warmth. Ned passed him a thought. "Why don't we go down, mate, there might be some food still lying about. It's getting a bit draughty up here, and I'm hungry."

Ben did not attempt his usual humourous comments about the Labrador's incorrigible appetite. "I'm not bothered about eating—you go down if you want to, Ned. Now that I've told Serafina that we must move on without her, I'm better off staying out of her sight. I don't want to cause her or myself any more pain."

Ned rested his head against the boy's shoulder. "I'm not going anywhere on my own, I'll stay here with you, mate. But how d'you know we'll be moving on soon? The angel usually sends us a message, like the sound of a bell, or something of that nature. I can't remember when it was that we last heard from our angel, can you, Ben?"

The boy let out an unhappy sigh. "No, I can't, but I've got this feeling that it's about to happen. We haven't heard from the angel, yet I know that if I look out over the sea I'll sight the *Flying Dutchman* out there. I'm worried, and frightened, too. We've rescued Serafina and our friends from slavery, I don't want anything happening to them now."

Ned grunted. "Neither do I. Maybe you're right, we'll just stay put up here for the night. Look out, what's that, mate, somebody's coming!"

It was Serafina. She came to them and draped the cloaks over Ben and Ned. "I brought you both some food, you haven't eaten since breakfast."

Ben sat up, wrapping Otto's cloak about him. "Thank you, Serafina, it was kind of you to think of us. I'm sorry about what I said to you earlier, but I *will* have to leave. Ned, too. I don't expect you to understand. I feel terrible about it."

The beautiful young girl shook her head. "I don't understand, Ben, but I know you'd never lie to me about something like that. If you feel you must go, then there's nothing I can do to stop you."

Ned's interruption hit Ben's mind like a thunderbolt. "Tell her! Go on, tell her the truth, Serafina doesn't deserve to be left like this. Tell her, Ben!"

The boy bit his lip, almost drawing blood as he replied, "I can't, don't you see, Ned, she'd never believe it!"

As if sensing his anguish, Serafina took Ben's hands in hers. "Please, Ben, tell me why you must go. I couldn't bear not knowing. Tell me, I don't care what the reason is, I promise you I'll accept it!"

The clouded blue eyes met hers. The strange boy held her hands tighter, then he began to speak. "Serafina, you will not believe this, unless you believe there is a God, and angels, and a heaven above."

Ben got no further. There was the bang of a door being slammed open forcibly down below, coupled with the shouting of men, the cries of the Sisters, the yells of the Rizzoli Troupe and the fierce barking of Sansone. Al Misurata and his slavers had arrived inside the convent.

PANDEMONIUM REIGNED AS THE GUARDS, WITH AL
Misurata and Ghigno at their head, charged into the refectory.
Otto and the big convent dog hurled themselves into the midst
of the guards. Nuns were screaming, running
about willy-nilly.

Buffo and Mummo grabbed the two iron bars
which the strongman had been using in his act.
They met the foremost two guards, striking the
long jezzails from their grasp. La Lindi had Mwaga wrapped in
both arms, menacing the attackers as she called to Mother
Carmella, "Get your Sisters out of here!"

Al Misurata and Ghigno stayed out of the fray, looking for
Ben and Serafina. The pirate caught an anxious
glance, toward the stairs, from
Mamma Rizzoli. He nodded to
the scar-faced Corsair. "Come
on, they're up there!"

Ben halted at the verandah door when he saw
both his enemies, swords drawn, coming up the
stairs. Slamming the door shut, he tried to lock

it, but the bolt was rusted stiff from exposure to years of the sea air. Both men hit the door at once, knocking it wide open.

The boy reeled, cracking his head against the wall. He staggered forward, half-stunned. Ghigno and Al Misurata had hold of Serafina's arms—she was struggling, trying to get loose of their grasp. Nightmare merged with reality for Ben: Vanderdecken was there, snarling in his face through frostbitten lips, his mad eyes red with fury.

The boy rushed forward, smashing blindly at the apparition with his fists. Ghigno's sword pierced his shoulder, searing like red-hot steel. Ned hurled himself upon the Corsair, his teeth seeking the man's throat as he blundered backward. Ben went down, his legs tangling with Al Misurata's feet. It happened with mind-stunning speed.

Four bodies—the two men, the girl and the dog—crashed through the verandah rail. Ben lay flat on the floor, his mouth wide in a screech that was lodged in his throat. He heard the rail shatter, and saw the four of them vanish into the night. Down, down to the sea far below. The boy lay with his head over the broken verandah, seeing the four figures grow smaller in the darkness which engulfed his senses. Then he lost consciousness.

Like a massive pale flame, the sight of the angel filled his mind. The vision's voice echoed out, encompassing Ben. It sounded as though it were the strings of a thousand harps, driven by hurricanes across all the seas of the world.

"Fate decreed that the Dark Angel would fall.
Ye who are left on earth must travel on!"

Downstairs in the refectory the Rizzoli Troupe were putting up a valiant fight. Headed by Otto and the big dog, Sansone, they drove the guards of Al Misurata back, out of the building and into the courtyard. Leading a final charge, the German strongman vanquished the attackers, sending them scurrying through the main gate, out onto the road.

No sooner had Buffo and Mummo barred the gate, than a fusillade of musket shots tore into the woodwork. This was followed by men shouting, and the butts of jezzails pounding the gate. Otto called Sansone to his side, cautioning the clowns, "It sounds as if there are more of them outside. Be careful, stay away from the gate!"

More musket balls hit the gate, making the wood quiver and crack under their impact. Buffo acted promptly. "I'll soon find out!" He leapt nimbly into a nearby tree, scaling it swiftly until he could see over the wall. Shots rang out, and the clown ducked, shouting, "Alle hoop!"

Both Otto and Mummo knew what he meant—they sprang forward with their arms outstretched. Buffo dived gracefully from his perch straight into their arms. "The *Sea Djinn* is here, in the bay! That's the rest of her scurvy crew trying to break in!"

Another salvo struck the gate. This time some balls found their way through, whipping waspishly through the courtyard. Otto took charge. "Get Poppea out of the way, find some rocks or logs!" Seizing the shafts of the troupe's cart, he pushed it single-handedly to the gate, shoring it up. Buffo and Mummo returned with a wooden gatepost and some rocks. They wedged the cart wheels as Otto set his shoulders against the back of the cart. The strongman felt a musket ball whiz by his cheek as it tore through the canvas covering. The clowns added their weight to his as the assault outside continued. Otto shook his big, shaven head. "We will hold this gate. *Ja!*"

Mummo gritted his teeth as the gate shuddered under fresh gunfire. "Aye, but for how long?"

Mother Carmella was the first to find Ben. She called down the stairs for help. "Come quickly, the boy has been hurt!"

The stairway was blocked by nuns as Augusto Rizzoli pushed his way through onto the verandah. "Mamma, Lindi, what is it, what's happened?" He had to shout to make himself heard, for La Lindi was wailing at the top of her voice as two Sisters dragged her away from the broken verandah rail.

"Serafina! Serafinaaaaaaa!"

Mamma's face was ashen with shock. "It's Serafina and Ned—they're gone!"

Mother Carmella was staunching the blood from Ben's shoulder with her habit. "We must get this boy downstairs before he bleeds to death. Signore Rizzoli, help us!"

Between them they carried Ben down to the Mother Superior's chamber. As they laid him on the bed, Mother Carmella was issuing orders for hot water, dressings and her medicine chest. Augusto Rizzoli kissed his distracted wife's cheek.

"*Cara mia,* stay here and help with Benno, I'm going to look for Serafina and Ned."

He raced downstairs into the courtyard, falling flat as jezzail bullets spanged off the stonework.

Otto shouted to him, "Over here, *mein Heer,* help us to hold the gate!"

Augusto scrambled across on all fours. As he put his shoulders to the back of the cart, there was a dull boom from outside which sent them lurching forward.

Buffo exclaimed as they pushed the cart back into place, "They're using something as a battering ram!"

Of the four who had fallen from the verandah, Ned was the only one who was conscious. The black Labrador floundered about in the sea below the cliff, fending off the rocks as he was washed up against them. The entire length of his hind leg on the left side was throbbing with a dull, sickening pain. Mentally he tried to contact Ben, but without success. As he was washed up against the rocks again, Ned saw both his enemies, Al Misurata and Ghigno. From the odd angles of the two bodies, the manner in which their limbs stuck out as their necks lolled loosely, Ned knew they were both dead from the fall. With agonising slowness, he paddled along the rockface, finding a spot to wedge himself in.

Then Serafina floated by. She was facedown, limp and motionless. The dog set his teeth into the waistband of her dress, hauling her in beside him. He licked her still face, calling out her name mentally until the truth finally dawned upon him. Then he threw back his head, howling like a stricken wolf.

At that moment, Kostas Krimboti was entering the bay, sailing his freshly seaworthy *Blue Turtle*. Yanni had the telescope focussed on the *Sea Djinn*, which was anchored not far from the cliffs where the convent stood. He took the wheel, handing the glass to Kostas.

"That's the slave ship which is carrying the boy's friends."

The Greek captain viewed it momentarily, then swung the

eyepiece over toward the cliffs. "Can you hear that noise? It's a dog howling." He moved the telescope along the rocks slowly. "Over there, I'm sure of it—see, there's something white, like a piece of sail. That poor animal's howling like it's in agony. We can't leave it there!"

Yanni steadied the wheel. "But what about the big ship? We've got to get past it."

Kostas slammed the telescope shut. "Arm all hands to the teeth, I've been wanting to meet this black-hearted scum. Stand by to board her!"

With the crew of the *Sea Djinn* attacking the convent, there were only two watchmen left aboard. As soon as they spied Kostas and his tough-looking crew ploughing through the night toward them, they jumped overboard, abandoning ship. Scratching his thick red curls, Kostas looked around in disappointment.

"So the rats have deserted their vessel, eh, where are they?"

Babiko came running from the fo'c'sle deck. "They're on the cliff top, attacking the convent!"

Kostas whirled about distractedly as Ned's howls rent the air. He issued orders rapidly. "Yanni, you and Kristos man the cannon—anyone who tries to board this ship, blow them out of the water! Herakles, take the small boat and get that dog off the rocks. The rest of you, back aboard the *Blue Turtle*!" The big Greek's golden teeth were bared in an angry snarl. "Barbary slavers, attacking a convent of nuns? Father, forgive me for what I am about to do!"

As dawn's first pale strands streaked the sky, the defenders holding the gate were shot backward forcibly. Otto scrambled upright, ignoring the raking scratches across his broad shoulders. He threw himself at the wagon, shunting it forward. Buffo gaped in dismay at the gate.

"That battering ram has broken through!"

Sure enough, the blunt end of a pine trunk had smashed through the door. There was a shout from outside, then the trunk was withdrawn for a second charge. This time it shot through the gap, hitting the wagon, and knocking it off the rocks and timber that were jamming the wheels in place.

The German strongman ripped a board from the side of the wagon. He brandished it, shouting above the cheers from the attacking guards, "You come now, Otto Kassel will meet you, *ja*!"

Then a crackle of musket fire rent the air, and the guards' jubilation was cut short as Kostas and his crew rushed them from behind.

"Hohoho! Rejoice, my good Sisters, Saint Krimboti is here!"

Steel rang upon steel as Otto pulled the wagon aside and unbarred the shattered gate. He and Sansone were first into the fray, followed by Buffo and Mummo. Arming themselves with the weapons of fallen guards, they hurled themselves at the foe. Without Al Misurata or Ghigno to lead them, the crew of the *Sea Djinn* broke into a disorderly retreat. However, there was no place for them to run but the clifftop, and there was no question of quarter or surrender for the slavers.

Having ministered to Ben, Mother Carmella left him in the care of two Sisters. Followed by a group of nuns, she hastened out into the courtyard toward the sounds of combat. They crowded in the open gateway, staring at the survivors of the battle. There was only Kostas and his crew, the dog Sansone and her three guests, Otto, Buffo and Mummo. Somewhere nearby a small bird chirruped its first song of the day as sunlight crept over the bay. The Mother Superior extended her hands to Kostas. "Now I know the Lord moves in strange ways, he sent you to us in our hour of need. Pray enter."

ONE WEEK LATER. SAILING SOUTH SOU'EAST,
THROUGH THE STRAIT OF OTRANTO TO THE
IONIAN SEA.

COOLING BREEZES SOOTHED THE MIDDAY HEAT,
bringing relief to the crew of the *Blue Turtle*. Kostas Krimboti
fussed like a mother hen around the four bearers who were

carrying Ben and Ned on a stretcher.

"Babiko, Yanni, hold your end up a bit. We
don't want them sliding off into the sea. Herakles,
Fotis, slow down, it's not a race. Mind those
stairs, steady now!"

Under their captain's directions, they deposited the
stretcher carefully on the fo'c'sle deck. Kostas waved his arms
at them.

"Well, don't stand there gawping, go and get fresh water.
Bring honey and grapes, too. Yanni, fetch me some of Mother
Carmella's special medicine, they might need to sleep some
more yet. Jump to it!"

Kostas sat down beside his two charges, shielding Ben's
eyes from the sun and murmuring, "This fresh air will do you
good, boy, sleep on if you want to. Ah, Ned, old friend, I see

you're back with us at last. Amico, get away from him, you little rogue, leave the poor fellow's tail alone!"

Ned opened his eyes, whining softly. "Ooh, this confounded leg, it feels like a floorboard. Ouch, that hurts!"

Kostas stroked the black Labrador's head gently. "Try not to move your back leg, that splint will stick into you, be still. Good boy!"

The dog's thoughts reached Ben. The boy's eyelids fluttered, then he stared dazedly up at Kostas. "Thirsty. . . . Can't move my arm. . . . Ned?"

The Greek's gold-coin teeth flashed in the sunlight. "Thank you, Father! Thank you, Sisters of Santa Filomena, for your prayers, and thank heaven for listening to the prayers of a wayward sinner like me. Mother Carmella, thank you for your wonderful magic medicine which kept this poor boy alive!" Ben's strange, clouded eyes came fully open. "Kostas Krimboti, what are you doing here? Where am I?"

The puppy, Amico, jumped on Ben licking his face. "Leave him alone, you savage. Hohoho!" Kostas perched the little dog on his shoulder like a parrot. He cradled Ben's head against his elbow. "Babiko, hurry up with that water, he's awake!"

Holding a goblet up to Ben's lips, Kostas allowed him to drink sparingly, "Relax, my friend, all you have to do is rest, you'll soon get well. Where else would you be, but aboard my lovely old *Blue Turtle,* bound for my homeland, Greece!"

Ben stared down at his bandaged chest, and the sling which held his right arm. He felt confused. "The convent. . . . What happened?"

The Greek captain laid him back down, placing the water bowl close to Ned's face. "Questions, questions. Be grateful you're alive, boy."

Ned's thoughts flashed urgently into Ben's mind. "Don't ask, it's all in the past, Ben. Kostas is right, just be grateful you're alive!"

The boy ignored his dog's pleas. Levering himself up on his good arm, he gritted his teeth. "What happened? Tell me, I must know!"

Amico was worrying at his master's curly red hair. Kostas lifted the puppy down to the deck and sent him off to play elsewhere.

"Alright, my friend, I'll tell you as much as I know. When we arrived in the bay below Santa Filomena, I sighted the *Sea Djinn* anchored there. Well, we boarded the vessel, and captured her. The slavers were attacking the convent, so I found a path up the cliff, and led my crew up there. We charged them from the rear, with the help of your friends—the German giant, the two clowns and Sansone the big hound. What a battle it was, no slavers were left to tell the tale, take my word. Those who didn't fall to our guns and blades fell from the cliff.

"You were found on the upstairs verandah, stabbed by a sword. Mother Carmella tended you—at first she thought you would die, you had lost so much blood, Ben. But the Mother Superior is a wise and clever doctor. She nursed you through it, keeping you asleep with her own special medicine. Your dog was found by Herakles, hanging on to the rocks amid the water. Ned's leg was broken, but my friend Mother Carmella treated him, too. I went back aboard the *Sea Djinn*. Yanni and I turned her own cannons into the hold. We blew out the keel and sunk her. You look tired, Ben, try and rest."

The boy's good hand shot out. He gripped the Greek's arm, yelling, "Serafina! Where's Serafina!"

Kostas seized Ben's hand, nodding to Yanni. Though he tried to struggle, the boy could not resist. Babiko and Herakles held his head as Yanni poured the Mother Superior's medicine into his mouth. Kostas Krimboti nodded. "That's enough, Yanni, he'll be asleep soon. Leave him now, I'll speak with him again tomorrow. Sleep, Ben, sleep. . . ."

With his eyes blinking groggily, Ben heard Ned's words filtering into his mind. "You'll remember sooner or later, mate, so I'll tell you. We fell through the verandah rail, Misurata, the Scar-face, Serafina and me. I was the only one who lived through it all. Both the slavers were killed as they hit the rocks, and it's hard for me to say, but we lost Serafina, too. I pulled her from the sea, and held on to her through the night. Herakles found us both as dawn was breaking. You were unconscious, there was no way I could let you know. Our poor beautiful girl is gone, but I hung on to her, the Dutchman did not take her. Can you hear me, Ben?"

From the realms of merciful slumber, the boy replied, "My faithful Ned, I can hear you. Where is she now?"

Crawling to Ben's side, Ned placed his cheek against the boy's arm. "She rests in the grounds of Santa Filomena, in the shade of an almond tree. The troupe and the Sisters laid her there in peace. It was a simple ceremony. The Rizzolis wanted to take us both with them to Vicenza, in Italy. Kostas gave them gold to buy a dairy farm there. I think our friends will be happy with their new life. But Mother Carmella and Kostas both agreed that you and I should not go along with the troupe, too many painful memories for us there. I lay at Serafina's graveside, watching them go off in their old battered cart, with Poppea pulling it. I knew that we would be going with Kostas, because that night I heard the angel's message. 'Now the Dark Angel has fallen, you must go from here.' So, here we are, back at sea once more."

The dog's thoughts faded from Ben's mind as his thoughts drifted back. He recalled Serafina as she spoke to him that last afternoon they were together.

"I will never forget you. If you go I will stay here forever!"

Did she know what was going to happen?

Through the enveloping darkness, a soft light began to shine. It grew until it filled the boy's whole being. There was the angel, tall and imposing. The celestial vision had placed both hands upon the shoulders of a girl. It was Serafina! Ben spoke her name loud.

"Serafina."

The soft, gentle eyes smiled at him. "I will always be with you. Do not grieve, I will wait until you join me one day. Be at peace."

A calmness descended upon Ben, a tranquility of spirit he had never known before.

From cloudless azure vaults the great, golden eye of the sun shone down on the sea below. It saw the ship, a small, blue-sailed, weather-beaten craft. On the fo'c'sle deck, a boy and his dog lay sleeping, side by side. Orphans of the seas, bound through the years to only the Lord knows where. Waiting for the angel's command. Always waiting.